Join the army of fans who LOVE Scott Mariani's Ben Hope series . . .

'Deadly conspiracies, bone-crunching action and a tormented hero with a heart . . . Scott Mariani packs a real punch'
Andy McDermott, bestselling author of *The Revelation Code*

'Slick, serpentine, sharp, and very very entertaining. If you've got a pulse, you'll love Scott Mariani; if you haven't, then maybe you crossed Ben Hope'
Simon Toyne, bestselling author of the *Sanctus* series

'Scott Mariani's latest page-turning rollercoaster of a thriller takes the sort of conspiracy theory that made Dan Brown's *The Da Vinci Code* an international hit, and gives it an injection of steroids . . . [Mariani] is a master of edge-of-the-seat suspense. A genuinely gripping thriller that holds the attention of its readers from the first page to the last'
Shots Magazine

'You know you are rooting for the guy when he does something so cool you do a mental fist punch in the air and have to bite the inside of your mouth not to shout out "YES!" in case you get arrested on the train. Awesome thrilling stuff'
My Favourite Books

'If you like Dan Brown you will like all of Scott Mariani's work – but you will like it better. This guy knows exactly how to bait his hook, cast his line and reel you in, nice and slow. The heart-stopping pace and clever, cunning, joyfully serpentine tale will have you frantic to reach the end, but reluctant to finish such a blindingly good read'
The Bookbag

'[*The Cassandra Sanction*] is a wonderful action-loaded thriller with a witty and lovely lead in Ben Hope . . . I am well and truly hooked!'

Northern Crime Reviews

'Mariani is tipped for the top'

The Bookseller

'Authentic settings, non-stop action, backstabbing villains and rough justice – this book delivers. It's a romp of a read, each page like a tasty treat. Enjoy!'

Steve Berry, *New York Times* bestselling author

'I love the adrenalin rush that you get when reading a Ben Hope story . . . *The Martyr's Curse* is an action-packed read, relentless in its pace. Scott Mariani goes from strength to strength!'

Book Addict Shaun

'Scott Mariani seems to be like a fine red wine that gets better with maturity!'

Bestselling Crime Thrillers.com

'Mariani's novels have consistently delivered on fast-paced action and *The Armada Legacy* is no different. Short chapters and never-ending twists mean that you can't put the book down, and the high stakes of the plot make it as brilliant to read as all the previous novels in the series'

Female First

'Scott Mariani is an awesome writer'

Chris Kuzneski, bestselling author of *The Hunters*

THE REBEL'S REVENGE

Scott Mariani is the author of the worldwide-acclaimed action-adventure thriller series featuring ex-SAS hero Ben Hope, which has sold millions of copies in Scott's native UK alone and is also translated into over 20 languages. His books have been described as 'James Bond meets Jason Bourne, with a historical twist'. The first Ben Hope book, *The Alchemist's Secret*, spent six straight weeks at #1 on Amazon's Kindle chart, and all the others have been *Sunday Times* bestsellers.

Scott was born in Scotland, studied in Oxford and now lives and writes in a remote setting in rural west Wales. When not writing, he can be found bouncing about the country lanes in an ancient Land Rover, wild camping in the Brecon Beacons or engrossed in his hobbies of astronomy, photography and target shooting (no dead animals involved!).

You can find out more about Scott and his work, and sign up to his exclusive newsletter, on his official website:

www.scottmariani.com

By the same author:

Ben Hope series
The Alchemist's Secret
The Mozart Conspiracy
The Doomsday Prophecy
The Heretic's Treasure
The Shadow Project
The Lost Relic
The Sacred Sword
The Armada Legacy
The Nemesis Program
The Forgotten Holocaust
The Martyr's Curse
The Cassandra Sanction
Star of Africa
The Devil's Kingdom
The Babylon Idol
The Bach Manuscript
The Moscow Cipher

To find out more visit **www.scottmariani.com**

SCOTT MARIANI

The Rebel's Revenge

avon.

Published by AVON
A Division of HarperCollins*Publishers* Ltd
1 London Bridge Street
London SE1 9GF

www.harpercollins.co.uk

A Paperback Original 2018

4

A catalogue record for this book is
available from the British Library

ISBN 978-0-00-823592-5

Set in Minion by Palimpsest Book Production Ltd, Falkirk, Stirlingshire

Printed and bound in Great Britain by
CPI Group (UK) Ltd, Croydon CR0 4YY

MIX
Paper from
responsible sources
FSC™ C007454

This book is produced from independently certified FSC™ paper
to ensure responsible forest management.

For more information visit: www.harpercollins.co.uk/green

PROLOGUE

Louisiana, May 1864

Built in the Greek Revival style, encircled by twenty-four noble Doric columns and standing proud amid a vast acreage of plantation estate, the mansion was one of the grandest and most aristocratic homes in all of the South. Its dozens of reception rooms, not to mention the splendid ballroom, had hosted some of Clovis Parish's most celebrated social events of the forty years since its construction, positioning Athenian Oaks, as the property was named, at the very centre of the region's high society.

On this day, however, the stately house was silent and virtually empty. Deep within its labyrinthine corridors, a very secret and important meeting was taking place. A meeting that its attendees knew very well could help to swing in their favour the outcome of the civil war that had been tearing the states of both North and South apart for three long, bloody years.

Of the four men seated around the table in the richly appointed dining room, only one was not wearing military uniform: for the good reason that he wasn't an officer of the Confederate States Army but, rather, the civilian owner of Athenian Oaks.

His name was Leonidas Wilbanks Garrett. A Texan by birth, he had risen to become one of the wealthiest land-owners in Louisiana by the time he was forty. Now, fifteen years on, the size of his fortune and spread of his cotton plantation were second to none. As was the workforce of slaves he owned, who occupied an entire village of filthy and squalid huts far out of sight of the mansion's windows.

But it was by virtue of L.W. Garrett's renown as a physi-cian and scientist, rather than his acumen for commerce, that the three high-ranking Confederate officers had made the journey to Clovis Parish to consult him. For this special occasion they were majestically decked out in full dress uniform, gleaming with gold braid. The most senior man present wore the insignia of a general of the C.S.A. He had lost an eye at the Second Battle of Bull Run and wore a patch over his scarred socket. He had also lost all three of his sons during the course of the conflict, and feared that he would have lost them for nothing if the Yankees prevailed.

A bitter outcome which, at this point in time, it seemed nothing could prevent. Since the crushing defeat at Chattanooga late the previous year and the subsequent appointment of Ulysses S. Grant as General-in-Chief of the Union forces, the turning point seemed to have come. Rout after rout; the tattered and depleted army of the South was in danger of being completely overrun.

'Gentlemen, we stand to lose this damn war,' the general said in between puffs of his cigar. 'And lose it we will, unless saved by a miracle.'

'Desperate times call for desperate measures,' said the second officer, who was knocking back the wine as fast as it could be served. He was a younger man, a senior colonel known for his fiery temperament both on and off the battle-field. The last cavalry charge he had personally led had

2

resulted in him having his right arm blown off by a cannon-ball. It had been found two hundred yards away, his dead hand still clutching his sabre. He now wore the empty sleeve of his grey tunic pinned across his chest, after the fashion of Lord Nelson.

'Indeed they do,' the general agreed. 'And if that yellow-belly Jeff Davis and his lapdog Lee don't have the guts to do what's necessary to win this war, then by God someone else must step in and do it for them.'

This provoked a certain ripple of consternation around the table, as it was somewhat shocking to refer to the President of the Confederate States of America, not to mention the revered General Robert E. Lee, hero of the South, in such harsh language. But nobody protested. The facts of the matter were plain. The dreadful prospect of a Union victory was looming large on the horizon. Leonidas Garrett, whose business empire stood to be devastated if a victorious Abraham Lincoln acted on his promise to liberate all slaves in North America, dreaded it as much as anyone.

After another toke on his cigar and a quaff of wine, the general leaned towards Garrett and fixed him with his one steely eye. 'Mr Garrett, how certain are you that this bold scheme of yours can work?'

'If it can be pulled off, which I believe it can, then my certainty is absolute,' Garrett replied coolly.

The third senior officer was the only conspirator present at the top-secret gathering who was yet to be fully convinced of Garrett's plan. 'Gentlemen, I must confess to having great misgivings about the enormity of what we are contemplating. Satan himself could scarcely have devised such wickedness.'

The general shot him a ferocious glare. 'At a time like

this, if it took Beelzebub himself to lead the South to victory, I would gladly give him the job.'

The objector made no reply. The general stared at him a while longer, then asked, 'Are you with us or not?'

'You know I am.' No *sir*, no display of deference to a man of far superior rank. Because rank was not an issue at a meeting so clandestine, so illicit, that any and all of them could have been court-martialled and executed by their own side for taking part. What they were envisaging was in flagrant contravention of the rules of war and gentlemanly conduct.

Silence around the table for a few moments. The dissenter said, 'Still, a damned ugly piece of work.'

'I'm more interested in knowing if we can *make* it work,' said the one-armed colonel.

'It isn't a new idea, by any measure,' Garrett said. 'Such tactics, though brutal, have been used in warfare throughout history. Trust me, gentlemen. We have the means to make it work, and if successful its effect on the enemy will be catastrophic. It will bring the North to its knees, cripple their infrastructure and force those Yankee scumbellies to surrender within a month. But I must reiterate,' he added, casting a solemn warning look around the table, 'that not a single word of this discussion can ever be repeated to anyone outside of this room. Not *anyone*, is that perfectly clear?'

Throughout the meeting, a young female negro servant dressed in a maid's outfit had been silently hovering in the background, watching the levels in their wine glasses and meekly stepping up to the table now and then to top them up from a Venetian crystal decanter. Nobody acknowledged her presence in the room, least of all her legal owner, Garrett. As far as he was concerned she might simply have been a well-trained dog, rather than a human being. A dog, more-over, that could be whipped, chained up to starve, or used as target practice without compunction or accountability at any time, just for the hell of it.

Like Garrett, none of the three Southern-born officers gave an instant's thought to the possibility that this young slave girl could be absorbing every single word of their discussion. And that she could remember it perfectly, so perfectly that it could later be repeated verbatim. Nor did any man present have any notion as to who the negro servant woman really was. Her role in the downfall of their plan was a part yet to be played. Just how devastating a part, none of them could yet know either.

'So, gentlemen, we're agreed,' the general said after they'd spent some more time discussing the particulars of Garrett's radical scheme. 'Let's set this thing in motion and reclaim the South's fortunes in this war.' He raised his glass. 'To victory!'

'To victory!' The toast echoed around the table. They clinked glasses and drank.

Her duty done, the slave humbly asked for permission to excuse herself and was dismissed with a cursory wave, whereupon she slipped from the room to attend to the rest of her daily chores. Though if any of them had paid her the least bit of heed, they might have wondered at the enigmatic little smile that curled her lips as she walked away.

Chapter 1

Ben Hope had often had the feeling that trouble had a knack of following him around. No matter what, where or how, it dogged his steps and stuck to him like a shadow. If trouble were a person, he'd have felt justified in thinking that individual was stalking him. If he'd been of a superstitious bent he could have thought he was haunted by it, as by a ghost. Whatever the case, it seemed as if at every juncture of his life, wherever he went and however he tried to steer out of its path, there it was waiting for him.

And it was here, pushing midnight on one sultry and thus-far uneventful September evening in the unlikely setting of a tiny backstreet liquor store in Clovis Parish, Louisiana, that he was about to make trouble's acquaintance yet one more time.

If the most recent round of airport security regulations hadn't made it more bother than it was worth to carry his old faithful hip flask across the Atlantic among his hand luggage, and if the bar and grill where he'd spent most of that evening had stocked the right kind of whisky to satisfy one of those late-night hankerings for a dram or three of the good stuff that occasionally come over a man, then two things wouldn't have happened that night. First, there would have been nobody else around to prevent an innocent man from getting badly hurt, most probably shot to death.

Which was a good thing. And second, Ben wouldn't have been plunged into a whole new kind of mess, even for him.

Which was less of a good thing. But that's what happens when you have a talent for trouble. He should have been used to it by now.

It was nine minutes to midnight when Ben walked into the liquor store. It was as warm and humid inside as it was outside, with a lazy ceiling fan doing little more than stir the thick air around. An unseen radio was blaring country music, a stomping up-tempo bluegrass instrumental that was alive with fiddles and banjos and loud enough to hear from half a block away.

The sign on the door said they were open till 2 a.m. Ben soon saw he was the only customer in the place, which didn't surprise him given the lateness of the hour and the emptiness of the street. Maybe they got a rush of business just before closing time.

The entire store could have fitted inside Ben's farmhouse kitchen back home in Normandy, but was crammed from floor to ceiling across four aisles with enough booze to float a battleship. A glance up and down the heaving displays revealed a bewildering proliferation of beer and bourbon varieties, lots of rum, a smattering of local Muscadine wines and possibly not much else. He was resigned to not finding what he was looking for, but it had to be worth a shot.

Alone behind the counter sat an old guy in a frayed check shirt and a John Deere cap, with crêpey skin and lank grey hair, who was so absorbed in the pages of the fishing magazine he was reading that he didn't seem to have noticed Ben come in.

'How're they biting?' Ben said with a smile over the blare

of the music, pointing at the magazine. The friendly traveller making conversation with the locals.

The old timer suddenly registered his customer's presence and gazed up with watery, pale eyes. 'Say what, sonny?' He didn't appear to possess a single tooth in his mouth.

It had to be thirty years since the last time anyone had called Ben 'sonny'. Abandoning the fishing talk, which wasn't his best conversation topic anyway, he asked the old timer what kinds of proper scotch he had for sale. Whisky with a 'y' and not an 'ey'. Ben had never quite managed to develop a taste for bourbon, though in truth he'd drink pretty much anything if pushed. He had to repeat himself twice, as it was now becoming clear that the storekeeper was stone deaf as well as toothless, which probably accounted for the volume of the music.

Finally the old timer got it and directed him to a section of an aisle on the far end of the store. 'Third aisle right there, walk on down to the bottom. Hope you find what you're lookin' for.' The Cajun accent was more noticeable on him, sounding less Americanised than the younger locals. A sign of the times, no doubt, as the traditional ways and cultures eroded as gradually and surely as Louisiana's coastal wetlands.

Ben said thanks. The old man frowned and peered at him with the utmost curiosity, as though this blond-haired foreigner were the strangest creature who'd ever stepped inside his store. 'Say, where you from, podnuh? Ain't from aroun' here, that's for damn sure.' Ben couldn't remember the last time he'd been called 'partner', either.

'Long way from home,' Ben replied.

The old timer cupped a hand behind his ear and craned his wrinkly neck. 'Whassat?' They could still be having this conversation come closing time. Hearing aids obviously hadn't found their way this far south yet. Or maybe the oldster was afraid they'd cramp his style with the girls. Ben just smiled and walked off in search of the section he wanted. The storekeeper gazed after him for a moment and then shrugged and fell back into squinting at his magazine.

Following the directions, Ben soon found the range of scotches at the bottom of the last aisle, tucked away in what seemed a forgotten, seldom-frequented corner of the store judging by the layers of dust on the shelf. He began browsing along the rows of bottles, recognising with pleasure the names of some old friends among them. Knockando, Johnny Walker, Cutty Sark, Glenmorangie and a dozen others – it wasn't a bad selection, all things considered. Then he spotted the solitary bottle of Laphroaig Quarter Cask single malt, one of his personal favourites for its dark, peaty, smokey flavour.

It had been sitting there so long that the bottle label was flecked with mildew. He took it down from the shelf, wiped off the dust and weighed his discovery appreciatively in his hand, savouring the prospect of taking it back to his hotel room for a couple of hours' enjoyment before bed. The precious liquid had come a long way from its birthplace on rugged, windswept Islay in Scotland's Inner Hebrides, for him to stumble across here in Southern Louisiana of all places. Maybe this was something more profound and meaningful than mere serendipity. Enough to make a man of lapsed religious faith start believing again, or almost.

Ben was carrying the bottle back up the aisle as though it were holy water when, over the blare of the music, he heard raised voices coming from the direction of the counter. As he reached the top of the aisle he saw a pair of guys who had just walked in.

One was big and ox-like in a studded motorcycle jacket with a patch on the back showing a gothic-helmeted grinning skull and the legend\ IRON SPARTANS MC, LOUISIANA. He was slow-moving and wore a calm smile. The other was a foot shorter, wiry and wasted in a denim vest cut-off that bared long, skinny arms with faded blue ink. He was agitated and angry, eyes darting as if he'd snorted a tugrope-sized line of cocaine.

The pair might have been regular customers, but Ben guessed not. Because he was fairly sure that, even in the Deep South, regular customers didn't generally come storming into a place toting sawn-off pump shotguns and magnum revolvers.

Great.

The armed robbers were too intent on threatening the storekeeper to have noticed that the three of them weren't alone. Ben retreated quickly out of sight behind the corner of the aisle and peeked through a gap between stacks of Dixie beer cans.

The hefty ox-like guy had the old timer by the throat with one large hand and the muzzle of the sawn-off jammed against his chest in the other. The storekeeper was pale and terrified and looked about to drop dead from heart failure. Meanwhile the small ratty guy tucked his loaded and cocked .357 Smith & Wesson down the front of his jeans, perhaps not the wisest gunhandling move Ben had ever seen, and vaulted over the counter to start rifling through the cash register. He was yelling furiously, 'Is this all ya got, y'old fuckin' coot? Where's the rest of it?'

The old man's eyes boggled and he seemed unable to speak. The disconcertingly calm guy with the shotgun looked as if he couldn't wait to blow his victim's internal organs all over the shop wall. It was hard to tell who was more dangerous, the little angry psycho or the big laid-back one.

Ben puffed his cheeks, thought *fuck it*, counted to three. Then he sprang into action.

Six minutes to midnight, but the evening was only just getting started.

Chapter 2

Fourteen hours earlier

It had been Ben's first visit to Chicago. Now he was sitting in the departure lounge at O'Hare International, counting down the minutes to his flight while gazing through the window at the planes coming and going, and sipping coffee from a paper cup. As machine coffee went, not too terrible. It almost quelled his urge to light up a cigarette from the pack of Gauloises in his leather jacket pocket.

It was a rare thing for Ben to leave his base in rural northern France for anything other than work-related travel, whether to do with running the Le Val Tactical Training Centre that he co-owned with his business partner Jeff Dekker or for the other, more risky kinds of business that sometimes called him away. But when the chance had come to snatch a few free days out of Le Val's hectic schedule and with no other pressing matters or life-threatening emergencies to attend to, Ben had seized the opportunity to jump on a plane and cross the Atlantic. His mission: to pay a visit to his son, plus one more objective he was yet to meet.

They hadn't seen each other in a few months, since Jude's somewhat rootless and meandering life path had led him to relocate from England to the US to be with his new girlfriend,

Rae Lee. Ben knew all about rootless and meandering from past personal experience, and while he accepted that it was fairly normal for a young guy in his early twenties to take a few years before finding his feet in life, he worried that Jude had too much of his father's restless ways about him.

It was Ben's greatest wish that Jude could instead have taken more after the saintly, patient and selflessly loving man who raised him as his own son all those years when the kid's real dad was off merrily raising hell in some or other war-ravaged corner of the globe.

Every time Ben reflected on that complicated history, he felt the same pangs of heartache. Years after the event, the deaths of Jude's mother and stepfather, Michaela and Simeon Arundel, were a wound that would always remain raw. The subject was never discussed between them, but Ben knew the young man felt the pain just as keenly as he did.

Rae was a couple of years older than Jude, the only daughter of a wealthy Taiwanese-American family, and occupied a nice apartment in Chicago's Far North Side overlooking Sheridan Park, where Ben had stayed with them for only one day before feeling it was time to move on. The brevity of his visit might have seemed unusual to more family-orientated folks, but Ben's and Jude's was not a normal father–son relationship and Ben was anxious not to overstay his welcome.

Ben got on cordially with Rae and liked her well enough, but wasn't completely sure that she was right for Jude. Jeff Dekker, never one to mince words, regarded her as a busy-body and a do-gooder – and there was some truth in that. She was a freelance investigative journalist with multiple axes to grind over anything she considered worth protesting about, and seemed to be pulling Jude deeper into her world of political activism despite the fact that he'd never hitherto expressed the slightest interest in politics or causes of any kind. They'd met during one of her trips to Africa to expose the human rights abuses of the coltan mining industry. A trip that had achieved nothing except very nearly lead her to a gruesome end, and Jude with her.

Having had to come to the rescue on that memorable occasion, Ben worried that the next idealistic crusade might turn out to be one from which nobody, not even a crew of ex-Special Forces and regular army veterans ready to do whatever it took, could save them.

Still, if Jude was happy, which he seemed to be, Ben could wish for no more; and even if Jude weren't happy it was none of Ben's business to interfere in his grown-up son's personal affairs. He had said his goodbyes and left with mixed emotions, sorry that he wouldn't see Jude again for a while, yet quietly relieved to get away. Now here he sat, waiting for another plane – but he wasn't planning on heading home to France just yet.

At last, Ben's flight was called, and a couple of hours later they were touching down at Louis Armstrong International Airport in New Orleans. Which struck Ben as tying in very well with his other reason for being in the States.

As a dedicated jazz enthusiast, albeit one who was incapable of producing a single note on any instrument yet invented, Ben had for many years been a fan of the venerable tenor saxophonist Woody McCoy. Now pushing eighty-seven, McCoy was one of the last of the greats. He'd never achieved the stardom he deserved in his own right, but had played with some of the most iconic names in the business: Bird, Monk, 'Trane, Miles, and Art Blakey's Jazz Messengers, to list but a few.

Now at long last, after a career spanning six decades, the man, the legend, was hanging up his spurs. But doing it in fine style, taking his Woody McCoy Quintet on a farewell tour all up and down the country. A few weeks earlier, Ben had seen the announcement that Woody was due to perform his last-ever gig in his home town of Villeneuve, deep in the rural heart of South Louisiana, in mid-September.

When the opportunity had arisen to free up the date in his work schedule, and with Jeff's insistent 'Go on, mate, you know you want to' in his ear, Ben had decided that this last-ever chance to hear Woody McCoy play live was not to be missed. He almost never allowed himself such indulgences. But he'd allow himself this one, as a special treat.

Now that he'd cut his stay in Chicago a little shorter than planned, it meant he had a couple of days to explore Woody McCoy's birthplace, sample the local culture, relax and take it easy.

Ben stepped off the plane in New Orleans and found himself in a different world. Welcome to Planet Louisiana. Though over the years he'd visited more places than he could easily count, his past travels around the US had been limited. He'd been to New York City, toured the coastline of Martha's Vineyard, spent some time in the rugged hills of Montana, and had a brief sojourn in the wide open spaces of Oklahoma. But he'd never ventured this far south, and had only a vague idea of what to expect.

The first thing that hit him was the humidity. It was so thick and cloying that for a moment he thought he must have fallen down a wormhole in the space-time continuum and found himself back in the tropical furnace of Brunei redoing his SAS jungle training.

He cleared security, strolled through the hellish heat over to the nearest car rental place with his new green canvas haversack on his shoulder and was happy to find that the near-blanket blacklist that bugged him in many other countries didn't seem to apply here. For some reason, the likes of Europcar, Hertz and Avis objected to his custom on the grounds that their vehicles never came back in one piece, occasionally in several, and other times not at all. But the pleasant young lady at Enterprise breezed through the paperwork and handed him the keys to a gleaming new Chevy Tahoe SUV with a smile like warm honey and a 'Y'all have a good day, now' that was Ben's first introduction to a real-life Southern accent.

The airport lay eleven miles west of downtown New Orleans, amid one of the flattest and most panoramic landscapes Ben had seen outside of the Sahara. He opened all the windows, lit a long-awaited Gauloise with his trusty Zippo lighter, which the airport security guys had scrutinised as though it were an M67 fragmentation grenade, and headed north-west for the South Central Plains with the wind blasting around him and a four-hour drive ahead. He intended to enjoy every minute of his freedom.

Ben Hope was an unusually skilled and capable man who claimed little credit for his many gifts. One he lacked, however, in common with most people, was the gift of prophecy. If by some strange intuition he'd been able to foretell what lay in store for him at the end of the long, hot road, he would have pulled a U-turn right across the highway and jumped straight onto the next plane bound for France.

Instead, he just kept on going.

But that's what happens when you have a talent for trouble.

Chapter 3

For the next few hours, Ben drove beneath a sky burned pale by the sun. Trying to dial up a jazz station on the radio, he found only country music of the croony, schmaltzy variety with pedal steel guitars that sounded like cats yowling. It was either that, or the radio evangelists fulminating against the state of the modern world, or silence.

He chose silence, and eased back in his seat, steering the big comfortable Tahoe with two fingers as he worked his way through a pack of Gauloises and drank in his surroundings. The highway carved relentlessly onwards through the flat landscape, passing cane fields and sugar processing plants and oil refineries. It didn't take much travelling through Louisiana to tell what the big industries were around here.

Deeper into country, the terrain was crisscrossed with bayous, waterways so sluggish and rimed with green slime that they appeared stagnant. He passed various settlements, a lot of them nothing but rag-tag clusters of dilapidated shacks along the edges of the bayous, where river folks dwelled and scraped their living off the water and raggedy little kids helped their fathers man flat-bottomed boats heavy with nets and lobster traps.

Third World poverty in the richest country on the planet. Maybe Rae Lee should come down here and check it out.

To a visitor from overcrowded Europe, the most vivid impression this landscape conveyed was of the sheer scale of its hugeness. Not even Montana and Oklahoma had seemed so spread-out and vast. The city of Shreveport lay a hundred miles to the north of his destination. Highway 84 connected Villeneuve to faraway Natchez, Mississippi to the east and Lufkin, Texas to the west. A whole different America to the one he'd experienced before. Especially as nobody was trying to kill him this time around.

Ben had done a little reading ahead of his journey to try and get a sense of Woody McCoy's birthplace, its geography, its history and culture. Where most other North American states had counties, Louisiana divided itself instead into sixty-seven parishes, of which Clovis Parish was one of the smallest with a population of just over nine thousand spread over six hundred square miles of land that comprised mostly lake and bayou, swamp and forest. Woody's home town of Villeneuve was the parish seat, historically best known for having been burned to the ground by Union troops during the 1864 Red River campaign of the American Civil War.

Long before the fledgling nation had decided to start ripping itself apart, this area had passed through the hands of various European colonists. First the French had come, back in the 1500s, and laid claim to the territory of *Louisiane* as part of what they dubbed 'New France', a vast tract of land that stretched from the Mississippi to the Rocky Mountains and encompassed bits of Canada and fifteen modern-day US states. After a couple of centuries of imposing their language, repressing the 'heathen savages' from whom they had wrested the land and shipping in countless thousands of African slaves to work on their plantations in the South, the French rulers had suffered a drubbing in the bloody and brutal French and Indian War

19

and, in 1763, King Louis XV had been forced to cede his prize to the Spanish and British, who promptly set about forcing their own ways on their newly acquired colonial subjects. Napoleon Bonaparte had snatched back Spain's land possessions in 1800 with a beady eye on re-establishing a lucrative French North American Empire, only to sell it all off again to the recently established United States in 1803, who had just a few years earlier kicked their British masters back into the sea and had their own ideas about developing their young nation.

The so-called 'Louisiana Purchase', a deal worth an eye-popping $15 million at the time, had formally ended France's colonial presence and, at a stroke, radically expanded US territory by almost a million square miles to make it the third largest country in the world. Whereupon, less than sixty years later, the brave and bright new nation descended into a tragic civil war that turned neighbour against neighbour, brother against brother, ravaged the land from coast to coast and top to bottom, left as many as 750,000 of its citizens lying dead on its scorched battlefields and among the ruins of its levelled cities, and scarred the identity of the United States more profoundly than any other conflict before or since.

Such was, and always would be, the nature of human civilisation.

As for modern-day Louisiana, the result of so many centuries of ever-changing colonial ownership was a colourful blend of French, Spanish, African, Creole and Indian influences. Acadian settlers who had landed here from France by way of Canada added to the mixture, their descendants later to become known as 'Cajuns', forming a core part of this rich, multi-faceted culture rooted in so much dramatic history. Predictably enough, a glance at the map showed

French names popping up everywhere. Villeneuve being just one of them, within a parish named after an ancient Frankish king. Many older Cajun folks still spoke their own form of French as a first language, although that tradition was slowly dying out.

The more Ben had read up on the background, the more he could see that he was going to have to abandon whatever preconceptions he might have previously had about this part of the Deep South. Here was a fascinating and unique place, and he was looking forward to learning more about it – almost as much as the bittersweet prospect of attending the Woody McCoy Quintet's farewell performance two days from now.

The highway thinned out to an arrow-straight blacktop that carried him between fields and tracts of swampland and forest, past rambling farmsteads and abandoned gas stations and along the banks of a bayou with a waterside shanty restaurant signposted *Mickey's Crawfish Cabin – come inside!* Ben hadn't eaten a bite since his early breakfast with Jude and Rae in Chicago. However hungry he might be feeling, the delights of Mickey's Crawfish Cabin were something he could live without. The roadside banner advertising FRESH COON MEAT, ½ MILE didn't do much for him, either.

At last, a sign flashed by: ENTER CLOVIS PARISH, as though it were a command. A few miles later, the Villeneuve town limits appeared ahead, and Ben had reached his destination.

The afternoon had turned even sultrier, a threat of rain from the darker clouds drifting on the hot breeze. Ben had a room booked at the only Villeneuve hotel he'd been able to find online, called the Bayou Inn, which happened to be just a short stroll from the Civic Center where the Woody McCoy Quintet would walk on stage the night after next.

The directions he'd been given took him on a tour of the town. Villeneuve's more affluent neighbourhoods were gathered on the south side, with ancient oak trees laden with Spanish moss, and old white wood colonial homes with all-around verandas. A mile north was the town square, featuring a pretty little parish courthouse with Georgian columns and a clock tower. The street was lined with a hardware store, a grocery market, a gun shop called Stonewall's that had a Confederate flag displayed in the window, a pharmacy, a gas station and a bar and grill with a sign that said CAJUN STEAKHOUSE and seemed a lot more appetising than fresh coon meat or Mickey's crawfish.

Off the square were narrower residential streets shaded by elm trees and lined with small clapboard shotgun houses, some well tended, others rundown with beaten-up old cars and rust-streaked propane tanks in their front yards, along with the obligatory chicken netting and tethered dogs prostrated by the heat. Every house had a mesh screen door to ward off insects, and sat up off the ground on brick pillars to protect against flood waters, with several steps up to the front entrance.

Ben found the Bayou Inn after a bit of searching, and checked in. The small hotel was owned and run by an older couple called Jerry and Mary-Lou Mouton. They greeted him with welcoming smiles and a 'How y'all doin'? Travellin' kinda light, aintcha?'

Which was true enough, out of long-established habit. His green canvas army haversack was a recent acquisition, to replace its predecessor which had been blown up inside a car in Russia. Another had been lost in a tsunami in Indonesia. He went through bags a lot. This one contained his usual light travelling kit – black jeans, a spare denim shirt and underwear, and a few assorted odds like his mini-Maglite and compass. When he got to his first-floor room he flung the bag carelessly on the bed.

The room was small and simple and basic, which was how he liked things to be. A tall window opened out onto a tiny balcony, where he pensively smoked a cigarette while gazing down at the quiet street below.

After a shower, Ben dug out his expensive smartphone with the intention of sending a couple of text messages to people back home, only to find that the damn thing had died on him. Terminal. Kaput. He'd had it a week. The joys of technology. He trotted downstairs and asked Mary-Lou where he might be able to buy another one, and she told him about a little store down the street that she thought might be able to help.

As it turned out, the only phones the store had were of the cheap, prepaid 'burner' variety. No names, no contracts, no frills. That suited Ben fine, and the untraceable anonymity of such a device appealed to the rebellious streak in him that objected to government surveillance agencies prying into the personal affairs of innocent citizens. The burner even had decent web access. He shelled out two ten-dollar bills for the phone itself, two more for credits, and was back in business.

By now it was early evening and Ben's hunger was sharpened to the point where he couldn't ignore it any longer. Remembering the Cajun Steakhouse he'd passed earlier, he set off at a leisurely pace in the direction of Villeneuve town square. The Moutons had given him a front door key to let himself in with, so he was free to take all the time he wanted and return as late as he pleased.

It felt strange to be so relaxed and at a loose end. He could get used to it, maybe, with a little practice.

The Cajun Steakhouse offered a baffling range of local

fare like filé gumbo, eggs with shrimp and grits, Creole jambalaya and something called Louisiana-style crawfish boil. Ben decided to play it safe and ordered a T-bone with fries and a Dixie beer.

'You jes' sit tight, handsome, and I'll bring you the best steak you ever tasted in your life,' promised his teased-blond hostess called Destiny, who kept flashing eyes at him. But she probably treated every tall, fair-haired stranger who walked into the bar and grill just the same way.

Destiny's promise was no empty claim. The T-bone was the biggest and most delicious he'd ever had, thick and succulent. After two more Dixie beers, Ben was definitely feeling at home. So much so, that he suddenly had a hankering for a glass of good malt scotch, the kind he'd occasionally – or more than occasionally – enjoy during quiet evenings at Le Val, sometimes over a game of chess with Jeff, or in front of the fire with his German shepherd dog, Storm, curled at his feet. At the bar, he asked Destiny what she had, and with an alluring smile she produced a bottle.

'What is it?' he asked. It was the colour of stewed tea.

'This here is Louisiana Whiskey, hon. Or else, we got Riz.'

'Riz?'

'Uh-huh. Made from rice.'

Ben shook his head. 'Not exactly what I had in mind.'

'How about rum?' Destiny suggested. 'Folks round here drink a lot of rum. But you ain't from around here, are you, sugah?'

'Is it really that obvious?'

Ben settled for a tot of local rum, which was probably made at one of the cane distilleries he'd passed on the drive up from New Orleans. It wasn't single malt scotch, but he was in a forgiving mood, and the Cajun Steakhouse was

24

definitely growing on him. He spent the whole evening there, watching the place fill up with local colour and listening to the diet of rock and country music that streamed constantly from the jukebox. He might even get used to that, too.

Two more tots of rum, and he sat thinking about Jude, about life, about a lot of stuff. Such as his hesitant, awkward relationship with a woman called Sandrine Lacombe, who was a doctor at the hospital in Cherbourg a few kilometres from Le Val. Ben was drawn to her, and she to him, but it was as though neither of them could bring themselves to take the plunge. Like one of the stalemates that so many of his chess matches with Jeff ended in.

The truth was that, however much they liked each other, Ben was never going to be the love of Sandrine's life, nor she of his. No, he'd already had that, and lost it, and there was seldom a day when he didn't reflect on it with regret and guilt.

It was late when Ben finally left the bar and grill. He went walking through the warmth of the night, a little cooler and less sultry and far more pleasant. The stars were twinkling in an ink-black sky and the scent of magnolia trees was in the air. The streets of Villeneuve were quiet and peaceful. He didn't feel like returning to the hotel just yet.

And that, as he strolled around exploring the small town, was when Ben spotted the lit-up store front with the sign above the door that said ELMO'S LIQUOR LOCKER, and decided to take a look inside. Just in case. You never knew what you might find.

Nine minutes to midnight.

Chapter 4

Of all the late-night liquor stores in all the sleepy little towns of rural Louisiana, he'd had to walk into the one where a couple of morons were intent on sticking the place up. And on all the nights the pair of armed robbers could have chosen to do the deed, they had to pick the very moment when someone like Ben Hope was lurking just around the corner, fifteen feet away out of sight in the far aisle behind a stack of Dixie beer.

It had to be fate.

On the count of three, Ben stepped out where they could see him, and said, 'Hello, boys.'

Ben was still clutching the bottle of Laphroaig Quarter Cask that he'd been about to carry over to the counter to buy. But at this moment, in his mind it ceased to be a vessel for seventy-five centilitres of one of the most venerable liquids ever crafted by human artistry, and became a usefully hefty club-shaped weapon weighing in at just under three pounds, perfectly balanced to inflict all kinds of damage to the human body. Ben's mind often worked that way, especially at times like these. In the instant it took for the two robbers to lock eyes on the unexpected newcomer, before they could even begin to react, his brain was already calculating factors of distance, velocity, spin and drop.

Most important of all, though, was picking the right target to aim for. The big guy might have been just a trigger pull of a sawn-off shotgun away from blowing the storekeeper's heart and lungs out his back, but Ben made him for the slower mover. If the big guy was a bear, then his partner in crime was a fox, nervier, whippier and more twitchy, hence more potentially volatile. Though he stood a couple of steps further away on the other side of the counter where he'd been rifling through the cash register, and thus presented a more distant target, Ben knew the foxy guy posed the greater immediate threat and needed taking down as a matter of priority.

True to Ben's prediction, the foxy guy moved first. His lean right hand, marked by a faded blue star tattoo on the web between forefinger and thumb, let go of the bunch of mixed-denomination dollar bills he'd yanked from the cash register. The money fell like confetti as his hand dived down to close on the butt of the cocked revolver protruding from the front of his jeans.

By then, the whisky bottle was already in the air. It completed a full 360-degree spin from leaving Ben's hand to flying past the storekeeper's nose, over the counter and impacting the foxy guy smack in the middle of the forehead with its heavy glass bottom.

Being no kind of a physicist, Ben was dimly aware that the force of a thrown object was based on some complex formula involving vectors of mass and velocity, acceleration and momentum. Newton's Second Law, if he remembered rightly. But however it measured up in scientific terms, it was plenty forceful enough to have a significant effect on its target.

And yet, it wasn't so much the high-speed collision between a full bottle of whisky and his cranial frontal bone that would forever change the foxy guy's life. It was the reflex nerve contraction that ran through his whole body at the moment of impact and caused his index finger to jerk against the trigger of his .357 Magnum while still tucked pointing vertically downwards inside the front of his jeans.

With the hammer cocked, the average Smith & Wesson revolver carries a very light trigger pull. A mere three or four pounds, requiring just a flick of a finger to release the hammer and drop the firing pin against the primer of a waiting cartridge. Which was exactly what happened within the confines of the foxy guy's trousers at the exact moment the bottle whacked him in the forehead and knocked him sprawling backwards off his feet.

The blast of the gunshot, even somewhat dampened by a layer of denim, was grenade-loud inside the store. Almost as ear-piercing was the shriek of agony that followed as the foxy guy realised that he'd inflicted some terrible damage to himself down there.

To the sound of his buddy's ululating wail, the big guy finally moved. He shoved the old storekeeper away hard and swivelled the shotgun one-handed towards Ben. The calm smile on his big moon face had creased up into a bared-teeth sneer of fury and hate. The twin muzzles of the shotgun pointed Ben's way.

But just as suddenly, they were pointing straight up towards the ceiling as Ben closed in on him and diverted the weapon with a flying high kick to the big guy's right forearm that dislocated his wrist tendon and sent the gun tumbling out of his grip. It fell to the linoleum floor with a thud, unfired. By the time it had landed, Ben had got the big guy's dislocated wrist trapped in a merciless Aikido joint lock. One that was so painful and debilitating, it didn't matter how big or strong you were; you were going down.

The big guy was on his knees in moments, helpless, head bowed, gasping. Keeping hold of the arm and wrist, Ben kicked him in the throat. Hard enough to knock the rest of the wind out of him without doing any permanent damage. The big guy toppled to the floor with a crash that made the cans and bottles on the store shelves wobble and clink.

The other moron was lying on his back a few feet away behind the counter, squealing like a pig and clutching his injured groin, far too preoccupied to think about reaching for the revolver that had spilled out of the waistband of his blood-soaked trousers. The barrel and cylinder of the gun were spattered bright red, and there was a lot more of it pooling on the floor. There was a perfectly circular weal the size of a bottle base imprinted on his forehead.

Ben let go of the big fellow and stepped around the counter to slide the fallen revolver away with his foot. Looking down at all the mess and blood, he saw the shattered remains of the Laphroaig Quarter Cask and shook his head in sorrow. What a waste. Why couldn't he have lobbed a six-pack of Dixie beer at the guy instead?

But there was no use crying over it. It was the idiot on the floor who had much more to cry about. Ben eyed the gory spectacle of his crotch and said, 'Looks like you emasculated yourself, pal. You'll be singing mezzo soprano in the parish choir from now on. Maybe that'll teach you. Then again, I doubt it.'

He turned to look at the storekeeper. The old guy was cowering against the counter, boggling from under a protectively raised arm as though he thought Ben was going to hit him next. So much for gratitude.

There was a phone with a curly plastic cord attached to the wall behind the counter. Ben pointed at it. 'I'm guessing the Sheriff's Office is only open nine till five, but there must be a number for the local dispatch centre. Call it. You'd best get them to send a couple of ambulances, too.'

The old man relaxed a little as he realised he wasn't about to become Ben's next victim after all. He lowered his arm and gaped down at the prostrated form of the big guy on the floor, then peered over the counter at the other one still yowling and thrashing in a slick of his own blood.

'Holy shit, mister. I never seen nuthin' like it. You went through those two boys like a goddamn hurricane.' Motioning at the big guy, he added, 'That there's Billy Bob Lafleur. He's one evil sumbitch, not right in the head if you get what I'm sayin'. Knowed his mother, way back. She was crazy too. This other fella, he must be from outta town. Jumpin' Jesus, look what he done. Plain shot off his own balls.'

You could hardly hear yourself think in the place for all the racket. Ben stepped back over to the castrated would-be robber and knocked him out with a quick kick to the temple. Silence at last. He pointed again at the phone. 'Make the call and let's get it over and done with. Then I'd like a replacement bottle of whisky to take back to my hotel.'

'I ain't got no more of those, sonny. You just broke the last one.'

'Then I suppose I'll have to settle for a Glenmorangie instead,' Ben replied.

'It's on the house,' the old man said. 'Least I can do for a feller who just saved my life.' He stuck out a wizened hand. 'Name's Elmo. Elmo Gillis. Owned this store since 'seventy-two and never had no trouble until these two dipshits showed up.'

Ben took his hand with a smile. 'I'm Ben. I appreciate the kindness, Elmo. But I'm happy to pay for it, and the broken one too.'

Elmo made the phone call. Ben rested against the counter and lit up a Gauloise, savouring the peace while it lasted, and not much relishing the prospect of having to deal with the cops. For some reason, he and law enforcement officials seldom seemed to gel.

It wasn't very long before they heard the whoop of sirens, and the street outside became painted with whirling blue light as a pair of identical Crown Victoria police patrol cruisers with CLOVIS PARISH SHERIFF'S DEPARTMENT emblazoned on their doors came screeching up at the kerbside.

'That's Sheriff Roque,' Elmo said, pointing through the store window at the car in front. 'Meaner'n a wet panther, that one.'

'Bad cop?' Ben asked him.

'Hell, no. Ol' Waylon is the best sheriff we ever had.'

From the lead car emerged a large, raw-boned officer in a tan uniform and a broad campaign hat jammed at an angle onto his greying head. His face looked about as soft and good-humoured as a mountain crag in winter. Joined by a pair of deputies from the cruiser behind, he pushed inside the liquor store and halted near the doorway, surveying the scene with gnarled fists balled on his hips.

And now Ben's evening was about to get started in earnest.

Chapter 5

The sheriff glanced around him. His eyes were pale and hooded, and threw out a flat cop stare that landed first on the prone shape of Billy Bob Lafleur, then on his unconscious partner in crime, and finally on Ben, scrutinising him carefully.

Ben noticed that in place of his regular service gunbelt and sidearm, Roque wore a fancy buscadero cowboy rig with an old-style Colt revolver nestling snugly in its holster. The floral pattern tooled leather went well with his boots, which were definitely non-issue as well. Deviations from the standard uniform evidently didn't matter too much down here.

Without taking the stare off Ben the sheriff asked, 'What the hell happened here, Elmo?' He spoke loud and slow, as if measuring every word. Which might have been partly to make himself heard by Elmo, knowing the old guy was hard of hearing. Ben guessed that in a small community like this one, everyone knew everyone else, their secrets, their problems, their history.

Elmo answered, 'These boys tried to hold up the store. And this fella here, he stopped it. Took 'em down in one second flat. You shoulda seen it, Waylon. Ol' Billy Bob had a gun right in his face. I never saw anyone move so fast.'

'They dead?'

'They're alive,' Ben said. 'Just sleeping. But they're going to need those ambulances PDQ. That one has a badly dislocated wrist. The other's got probable concussion, and he's losing a lot of blood from a gunshot wound.'

'Meatwagons are on their way,' the sheriff replied. Still in the same loud, slow drawl, strong and authoritative. He aimed a thick, gnarly finger towards Ben. 'Who shot'm, you?'

Elmo answered for Ben. 'He shot himself, Waylon. Damn fool blew off his own pecker.'

Apparently quite unmoved, the sheriff gestured to his deputies. One drew a pistol and kept it trained on the two robbers, as though they were in any state to resist arrest, while the other slapped on cuffs. A few late-night passersby had gathered in the street, drawn by the police sirens and rubbernecking through the store window at what was going on.

Keeping his back to the window the sheriff said, 'Elijah, would you move those folks on?' The deputy called Elijah hastened outside to carry out the command. The sheriff said to the other, 'Mason, get on the radio and find out where those meatwagons are at, before this asshole goes and bleeds to death right here in front of us.'

Mason was the deputy with the drawn pistol. He was hatless, with brown hair spiky on top and shaved up the sides like a Marine. His face was fleshy and pasty and burned by the sun and his eyes were somewhat dull. He glanced nervously at Roque. 'What about these boys?'

The sheriff replied calmly, 'They're unconscious, Mason. I think I can handle it. Now scoot and get on that darn radio.'

Mason holstered his weapon and ran out to the car. The sheriff watched him go, and shook his head with a sigh. ''Bout as sharp as a bowlin' ball, that one.' Then he turned his flinty eyes back on Ben. 'I'm Waylon Roque, Sheriff of Clovis Parish. I don't believe I know you, Mister—?'

'Hope. Ben Hope.'

'You ain't from around heah.'

'So everyone keeps telling me,' Ben said. 'I'm just a tourist, that's all. Arrived here in Villeneuve this afternoon and I'm staying at the Bayou Inn. I'm only in town for the Woody McCoy gig the night after next, then I'll be heading back home.' He slipped his passport from his pocket and held it out.

The sheriff took the passport and gave it a quick once-over, then seemed satisfied and tossed it back. 'A Brit.'

'Half Irish, for what it's worth. But I live in France.'

Roque pulled a face, as if he thought even less of the Irish than the Brits. 'Jazz fan too, huh? I'm more of a Jimmie Davis man, myself.'

Ben smiled. 'You are my sunshine.'

But Roque wasn't one for chitchat. 'What's your occupation, Mister Hope from France?'

'I work in education,' Ben replied. Technically correct although economical with the truth. He didn't think it necessary to reveal to Roque what kind of education the training facility at Le Val offered, or to whom. Information like that tended to invite too many questions.

'Teacher, huh?' If Ben had said he was a smack dealer, Roque wouldn't have looked any less impressed.

'Near enough,' Ben said.

Roque reflected for a moment, eyeing him suspiciously. 'Well, Teach, seems to me you must either be the luckiest sumbitch alive, or you're some kinda trained ninja assassin in your spare time.' He jerked his chin in the direction of Billy Bob Lafleur. 'Sleepin' beauty here is a local white-trash scumbag well known to Clovis Parish PD for his violent and

34

intemperate ways. Put many a man in the hospital, and keeps all manner of unsavoury company out there on Garrett Island. His buddy looks kinda rough, too. I'm just wonderin' how in hell an ordinary tourist, a schoolteacher, could manage to take these bad boys both down in one second flat like Elmo said, bust 'em up real good and walk away without taking so much as a scratch hisself.'

'I never said I was a schoolteacher,' Ben replied. 'And actually it was more like two seconds. Maybe even longer. I must be getting slow in my old age. And they're not as good as they think they are.'

The sheriff eyed him for the longest moment. 'Just who exactly are you, boah?'

Ben didn't like being called 'boy'. In fact there was little he was liking much about Sheriff Waylon Roque in general. Which came as no great surprise to him. 'Would you care to rephrase that question, Officer?'

A knowing kind of look crinkled the sheriff's pale eyes. He nodded to himself, as though savouring an idea. 'I have a pretty good notion who you are. Tell me. What's your unit?'

Ben said nothing.

The corners of Roque's lips stretched into a humourless smile. 'I knew right off you weren't no teacher. You got the soldier look, for sure. Maybe you think you can hide it, but I can see it as sure as if you was still wearin' the uniform. I can see it in your eyes, and from the way you're standin' there lookin' back at me. I saw it before I even walked in here.'

Roque paused. Enjoying the moment. 'Am I right, Mister Hope? You a military man?'

'I'm not a soldier,' Ben said. Which was another technically truthful answer, as he had quit that life a long time ago. 'But even if I were, Sheriff, I can't see how it would be any business of yours.'

The deputy called Mason had got off the radio and now returned from the car to say the ambulances were en route and would be with them 'momentarily'. Ben always wondered at the way Americans used that particular word. In the Queen's English it meant the ambulances would appear one instant, and then vanish again the next like a disappearing mirage.

In the event, when they did turn up a couple of minutes later and parked behind the police cars, the paramedic units hung around long enough to strap the wounded robbers onto a pair of gurneys and prepare to ship them to hospital, from where they'd be going straight to jail.

Billy Bob Lafleur had woken up by then and had to be sedated to prevent him from trying to escape. He had his Miranda rights read to him before he fell back unconscious. The sheriff directed the police deputy called Elijah to ride with him in the back of the ambulance. Meanwhile, Billy Bob's friend was still passed out and looking very pale. The medics wheeled him hurriedly aboard and took off with the lights and siren going full pelt.

'Now what?' Ben said to Sheriff Roque.

'Say you're gonna be in town until the night after tomorrow?'

Ben shrugged. 'Or the morning after that. I'm not in a rush.'

'Good. I'll need you to come down to the station to make a formal statement and fill in a few blanks for me.'

'What kind of blanks?' Ben asked.

'Call it satisfyin' my curiosity. I like to keep tabs on what's happenin' in my parish, just like I like to know who comes and goes. See you around, Mister Hope. Don't you leave without payin' me a visit, now, you heah?'

'Something for me to look forward to,' Ben said.

The sheriff pulled another half-smile. He tipped his hat to Elmo. 'Y'all have a peaceful rest of the night.'

After the police were gone, the liquor store and the street fell back into tranquil silence. Only the mess and the blood remained to bear witness to what had happened there that night. Ben felt bad about leaving the old man to clear it all up himself, and spent an hour helping him. When Elmo asked 'Say, you really a soldier?' Ben replied, 'Your sheriff has a heck of an imagination.'

Finally, well after 1.30 a.m., Ben returned to the Bayou Inn with an intact bottle of twelve-year-old Glenmorangie tucked under his arm. He encountered no more armed robbers on the way back. The night was fresh and fragrant, and all seemed well with the world.

And that was the end of all the trouble.

Or, it should have been.

Because trouble would waste little time in finding him again. Sooner than he might have thought.

Chapter 6

By the time Ben got back to his room at the Bayou Inn, the urge to spend a couple of the wee small hours enjoying the Glenmorangie had left him and all he wanted to do was go to bed. He rose early the next morning, as the dawn was breaking over the town and painting the white houses vermilion and gold.

Feeling that last night's meal had been a little overindulgent, he spent longer than usual on his morning exercise routine, clicking off set after set of press-ups and sit-ups on the floor. He showered and dressed, then used his new burner phone to fire off that text message to Jeff asking how things were going at Le Val, and one to Sandrine to say nothing much in particular except that he'd arrived safe and sound in Louisiana.

Nobody needed to know about last night's spot of bother. It was already a fading memory, soon to be forgotten altogether.

Standing on his balcony afterwards he smoked a Gauloise and watched the sun climb and the streets come to life, as much as they seemed to do in Villeneuve. Most people around here appeared to drive pickup trucks. A skinny African-American kid on a bicycle with a bulging mailbag swinging from his shoulder worked his way down the street lobbing rolled-up morning newspapers into front yards.

Clovis Parish was obviously the last place on Earth where folks hadn't yet gone all digital. Ben liked that.

Ben was a coffee addict and could pick up its scent from any distance the way a German shepherd smells raw steak. His nose began to twitch just after seven, by which time he was dying for his first caffeine fix of the day, and he followed the enticing aroma downstairs to the kitchen where Mary-Lou Mouton was preparing breakfast.

The morning meal at Le Val tended to be a rushed, hectic, on-the-hoof affair that involved slurping down four or five coffees in between cigarettes while organising trainees, feeding guard dogs and prepping a variety of weaponry for the day's busy class schedule. That wasn't how things were done here at the Bayou Inn. Mary-Lou directed him to a white pine table covered with an embroidered cloth and set for one, since he was the only guest, and he sat quietly sipping a cup of excellent black coffee as she bustled about the kitchen.

Mary-Lou was a devout believer in the old saying that breakfast is the most important meal of the day. The plate she shoved under Ben's nose was piled high with eggs, bacon and sausage patties, home fries, grits and toast, and she stood over him like a prison guard to make sure he finished every bite. He'd have to triple his exercise regime to work it off. Maybe go for a twenty-mile run, too.

Mary-Lou finally left him alone to wash down his break-fast with a second cup of coffee. The copy of the *Clovis Parish Times* that the bicycle kid had delivered lay unread on the kitchen table. Out of curiosity he picked it up and unfolded it in front of him. Then nearly sprayed a mouthful of coffee all down his shirt as he saw the front-page headline.

BRITISH ARMY VETERAN FOILS
LIQUOR STORE HOLDUP

'What the—?'

He had to blink several times before he could bring himself to believe it. Reading on, he almost choked all over again at the reference to the 'intrepid stranger', believed to be an English military veteran, who had 'heroically intervened' during an armed robbery at Elmo's Liquor Locker on West Rue Evangeline Street late Thursday night.

Clovis Parish Sheriff's Dept. sources had released the names of the two men taken into custody: Billy Bob Lafleur, 34, and Kyle Fillios, 32. Lafleur and Fillios had entered the store 'brandishing' (that favourite word of the media) lethal firearms (was there any other kind, Ben wondered) and demanded its proprietor, Mr E. Gillis, hand over the contents of the cash register, threatening his life. Whereupon the two thugs had been tackled and disarmed and the police called to the scene.

Fillios had been rushed to the nearby Clovis Parish Medical Center requiring surgery for 'a self-inflicted injury' while Lafleur was now locked up in the Clovis Parish jail awaiting a trial date. A quote from Mr Gillis proclaimed, 'I thought I was dead, for sure' and praised the unnamed hero for his actions. The Sheriff's Department was unavailable for further comment.

Ben re-scanned the article three times, more perplexed with every reading. The *Times* had moved pretty damn fast to get the story out for the next morning's edition. Some intrepid reporter must have dragged poor old Elmo Gillis out of bed before daybreak to get the quote.

Ben couldn't blame the local press for being eager to jump on such a sensational story, considering how news-starved their sleepy little town likely was the rest of the time. He also had to be thankful that his name wasn't mentioned. But the 'British army veteran' reference bothered him a lot.

40

He doubted the reporter had got that from Elmo, as the old guy had no reason for spreading such rumours. No. Ben was certain that information had leaked from the mouth of Sheriff Waylon Roque himself. Ben had the impression that once Roque got an idea into his head, he'd let go of it as easily as a starving dog gives up a meaty bone.

Not to mention the fact that Roque's instinct about Ben was perfectly accurate. An ordinary tourist, a teacher no less, wouldn't have stood a chance against two desperate trigger-happy imbeciles like Lafleur and Fillios.

If Sheriff Roque had divulged that much to the *Times* reporter, what else had he told them? That the hero of the liquor store holdup was in town for the Woody McCoy gig tomorrow night? Or that he was staying at the Bayou Inn?

Ben valued privacy above most things, and he disliked being talked about or, worse, written about. It was his nature to be that way, a character trait that had fitted very well with his covert, secretive life in Special Forces. Anonymity was an obsession with SF operatives. While his own SAS background and Jeff Dekker's history with its sister outfit the Special Boat Service were part of the attraction that drew hundreds of delegates from all over the world to train at Le Val, outside of his work Ben never voluntarily shared that side of his past with anyone. Sandrine knew virtually nothing of it. Even Brooke Marcel, to whom Ben had been engaged for a while before it all went south, had been kept in the dark about a lot of things.

And now he'd allowed himself to become the subject of gossip in a small town where nothing ever happened. Bad move. The word would spread faster than pneumonic plague. He was irritated with himself; and yet what else could he have done but intervene in the robbery? What was he supposed to do, stand by and let an innocent old man get killed just to satisfy his sense of discretion? How could he have predicted that some hick sheriff would turn out to be so wily and perceptive?

As these worrisome thoughts swirled around in Ben's mind, Mary-Lou reappeared, looking somewhat bemused, to say there were two men at the door looking for a Mr Bob Hope. 'I think it's you they want. Said they were reporters for the *Villeneuve Courier*.'

Bob Hope.

Ben heaved a weary sigh. Someone had been gabbing, all right. Now the press had found him, he couldn't hide behind the sofa and wait for them to go away. He followed Mary-Lou along the sweet-smelling passage to the door, where a reedy individual wearing a cheap suit hovered on the front step accompanied by an acne-spangled photographer in ripped jeans and an LSU Tigers T-shirt, who aimed his long lens at Ben like a gun.

'Mister Hope? It's you, right?'

'That depends. Who the hell are you and what do you want?'

'Dickie Thibodeaux, from the *Courier*. I wondered if I could have a minute of your time?'

As politely as possible, Ben explained to them that he wasn't interested in giving interviews and had nothing to say. 'I'm on vacation. Now please leave me alone.'

'Come on, man, you gotta give us somethin'. This is a hot story. You're the star of the liquor store holdup! Some kinda superhero, like the British Jack Bauer.'

'I have no idea what you're talking about. Who told you that?'

Dickie Thibodeaux smirked. 'Sorry, I never reveal my sources.'

'Tell your sources to get stuffed.' Ben turned to glare at

the photographer, who was clicking away. 'And you, get that camera out of my face before I ram it down your bloody throat.' Amazing how fast politeness could melt away. Reporters had that effect on people, and especially on Ben.

The pair stalked to their car, shooting resentful glances back at him. Dickie Thibodeaux was already getting on the phone, probably drumming up reinforcements.

Ben watched them go. He'd successfully repelled the first wave. But there would be more, and the scrutiny on him would intensify fast as the story gained traction. By lunchtime there might be TV crews for CNN, WNBC and *Good Morning America* blocking the street and swarming all over the Moutons' front lawn. Ben was about to become the world's most reluctant celebrity. And that could mean only one thing.

He muttered aloud, 'I need to get out of here, right this minute.'

Chapter 7

In fact it was a whole twenty before Ben had packed his things, checked out of the Bayou Inn and was speeding out of Villeneuve, cursing whichever wagging tongue had put him in this predicament. His plan was now to find a discreet new place to stay in a quiet location not too far away, where he was less likely to be recognised.

He had only to lie low for another thirty-six hours or less before sneaking back undetected into Villeneuve in time for the Woody McCoy gig. How hard could that be?

Then, the moment the Great Man's final performance was over, Ben would hustle back to New Orleans. Before Sheriff Roque or the local press were any the wiser, he'd be flying home to the sanctuary of rural Normandy.

On his map the nearby small town of Chitimacha, forty-five minutes' drive to the west, looked like a promising place to hole up. He spurred the Tahoe along a meandering two-lane that cut through the cane and sweet potato fields and flat marshlands striped with industrial waterways and oil pipelines. As he got closer to Chitimacha he started looking around for a motel, but passed only a tattered billboard for Dixie beer. Was that the only kind of beer anyone drank around here? Minutes later, he entered the town itself.

If Chitimacha could be called a town, then Villeneuve

was a city by comparison. The small settlement had grown up piecemeal along the east bank of a broad, glass-smooth waterway called Bayou Sainte-Marie. Access from the western side meant crossing a wooden bridge that straddled the bayou's narrowest point and looked as though it had been there since Civil War days.

It was only mid-morning and already the air was as hot and thick as caramel sauce. Clouds of insects drifted over the water like smoke. It made Ben think of the Amazon. The smell of the bayou hung heavy, fishy and stagnant like an aquarium left standing uncleaned. Beneath the bridge, the bank's edge was a buzzing hive of industry, crowded with small jetties where stacks of lobster traps stood piled man-high, and moored flat-bottomed river boats bobbed gently on the almost imperceptible swell of the mud-brown water. Back from the jetties were store huts and bait and tackle shops advertising live worms and boat hire.

Traffic entering and leaving Chitimacha was thin and sporadic. Like everywhere else in the region, two out of every three vehicles were pickup trucks. Once over the wooden bridge Ben passed a couple of roadside fish shacks selling wares such as gaspergou and gar balls, and other arcane specialities of Planet Louisiana at whose nature he could only guess. He slowed the Tahoe to gaze from his window at a huge fish that hung tail-up from a hook outside one of the shacks.

Once, in the Cayman Islands, Ben had seen a man torn apart by tiger sharks. This thing was even more fearsome. Part giant pike, part alligator, its massive jaws bristling with fangs. He couldn't imagine anyone wanting to eat it, but it was easy to imagine the creature taking a bite out of any unlucky fisherman who fell in the bayou.

Ben drove on into the centre of Chitimacha, which made

the Villeneuve town square look like New Orleans in the middle of Mardi Gras. If Ben had wanted quiet, he'd certainly found it here. Seemingly, if you wanted action in Chitimacha you needed to be on the bayou itself. Here in town the sidewalks were almost completely deserted. A solitary pickup truck rumbled past, heading the way Ben had come. A few parked vehicles, many of them older than he was, sat gathering dust in the sun. There was a hardware store displaying racks of everything from chainsaw oil to crawfish boilers, and a grocery store with sun-faded ad placards in the windows saying '*Drink Coca-Cola in bottles*' and '*If it ain't Jerry Lee's, it ain't boudin*'. Next door was an empty barber's shop, and next door to that an equally empty café with chairs and tables spilling out into the deserted street for nobody to sit at.

Possibly the liveliest spot in town was an ancient relic of a filling station that consisted of a weedy patch of blacktop, two pre-war gas pumps and an old man in oily dungarees outside on a dilapidated bench with a corncob pipe in his mouth, sunning himself in the burning heat like a reptile on a rock.

Ben pulled up by the pumps and got the old man to fill up the Tahoe, which he set about doing without uttering a word, the pipe still stuck between his teeth. It was lit, but if the old man didn't worry about going up in flames, Ben wasn't going to worry about it either.

'I'll bet this place really comes alive in the high season, doesn't it?' Ben said by way of initiating a conversation. The old man just looked at him and muttered a response in what sounded like a weird version of French. Ben realised he was speaking the Cajun dialect handed down from the Acadian settlers way back. The historic language had been heavily altered by isolation and the passing of the centuries, but (or so Ben had read) was still basically intelligible to a modern French speaker. Which Ben was, and so he switched from English in the hope that they could communicate.

'Don't suppose you have anything resembling a hotel here in Chitimacha?'

The old man plucked the pipe from his mouth with a moist sucking sound, and waved the wet end of its stem to point down the street while jabbering more of his dialect. Maybe it wasn't that intelligible after all, at least not to anyone but a Cajun. Ben was stumped for a second or two, then understood he was being directed to a local *pension*, which was French for a guesthouse. Ben got the rest of the directions, paid up for the gas, said, 'Merci, monsieur' and drove on.

The directions led him to a street quarter of a mile away on the edge of Chitimacha, which could have been lifted straight out of Villeneuve's most down-at-heel neighbourhoods. Signs of neglect and poverty were all too obvious in most directions he looked.

Except for one. The guesthouse stood out from the adjoining properties, spick and span and resplendent from a fresh coat of white paint that was almost blinding in the bright sunshine. The tiny green GMC hatchback outside the front gate looked new and clean and well maintained, unlike most of the beaters parked up and down the street. A flowery hand-crafted bilingual sign on the gate said, *'Bienvenue à la pension de Lottie'* and underneath *'Welcome to Lottie's Guesthouse'*.

Ben parked up behind the miniature GMC, which could probably have fitted in the Tahoe's rear cargo space. He climbed out into the hot sun and opened the gate and walked up a neat little path to the door to ring the bell. A minute later he heard movement inside.

The inner door opened, then the screen door, and a large African-American lady with a smile that made the house's dazzling pearl-white paintwork seem dull and faded greeted him with a vivacious 'Well, hello there, sugah. I'm Lottie Landreneau, and how are you today?'

Chapter 8

Ben knew from the start that he'd struck lucky with Lottie. The warmth of her hospitality was as endearing as her smile and from the moment he walked into her house he felt right at home. The place was filled with flowers, light and Southern charm, like her personality. 'Where y'all from, sugah? You sound English without soundin' English, if you know what I mean.'

'I've moved around.'

'Oh, I know all about that,' she said mysteriously, and seemed to enjoy keeping him in suspense for now. 'Come, let me show you your room.'

He followed her from the richly carpeted entrance hall and up a switchback staircase with a thick gleaming mahogany banister rail that she clutched as she hauled her weight up the stairs. 'That's me,' she said, motioning towards a glossy white door at the end of the galleried first-floor landing.

Spaced out along the passage were two more doors, each adorned with a little brass number plaque. 'Y'all are the only guest I got right now, so you get your pick of the rooms.' She pointed at the door nearest to hers. 'How 'bout this one?'

'What's up there?' he asked, nodding towards a drop-down wooden staircase that led from the opposite end of the landing to an open hatch in the ceiling.

'Rooms three and four. It's an attic conversion. Ceilings are kinda low.'

'I love attics.'

'Okay, well then let me show you.'

The attic conversion was a work of genius, executed with style and taste. The drop-down wooden staircase was a fine piece of carpentry that could be retracted from above by means of a rope pulley to create a cosy, isolated sanctuary at the top of the house. As for the bedrooms themselves, room three was nice, but room four was perfect. The inverted V of the sloped ceiling was all decked out in gleaming white tongue-and-groove panelling, and the floor was sanded and varnished bare boards with a furry rug. The single bed ran along the middle, where the ceiling was at its highest point. It had a simple iron frame and a patchwork quilt, and a small table with a reading lamp. The single dormer window looked out beyond the slope of the nearest neighbour's roof to offer a view of Chitimacha as far as the winding brown snake of the bayou in the distance. The room reminded Ben a lot of his quarters in the old farmhouse back home in France.

'This is the one I'd like.'

'No problem at all. It's yours, sugah.'

Lottie led the way back down to a little salon on the ground floor, where she made a fuss of serving home-made iced tea with lemon in tall, slender glasses. Not too sweet, not too lemony, perfect and refreshing after the wilting heat. Then, wedging her not inconsiderable bulk into an armchair, she began to talk. Which was something she loved to do, as Ben now discovered. But she did it so beautifully, mesmerising him with her accent and laughter, that he could have sat listening all day.

He got the whole life story. Born and bred right here in

Chitimacha, she'd moved to Villeneuve in her teens and ended up living there for twenty-plus years until a bad marriage had grown worse and she'd eventually escaped with the intention of *doing something* with her life. A goal that Lottie had taken extremely seriously, celebrating her fortieth birthday with the vow to waste not another single minute of whatever time God had provided for her. The last three years had been spent travelling and studying in Europe, from where she'd returned to Louisiana only a few months ago.

'Studying how to run a guesthouse?' Ben asked, to which she giggled and replied, 'No, dearie, studying cookery. The guesthouse thing, that's only temporary. What I'm gonna do, my real plan, is to set up my own restaurant, the best eatin' house for a hundred miles around. It's gonna put this little ol' town back on the map and bring folks from all over.'

Lottie's travels had taken her to London, Paris and Rome, where she'd scrubbed pots and waitressed in all the top restaurants, while using her divorce settlement money to take classes in some of the most famous cookery schools in Europe. Now armed with the requisite skills and a clutch of diplomas, she had proudly returned to her roots in order to realise her grand ambition of bringing together the finer points of classical cuisine with the best of traditional Cajun cooking. 'Because there ain't nothin' like it in the world,' she assured him.

'Everywhere I go around here, it's all about food, food and more food,' Ben observed with a smile. 'Everything from Mickey's crawfish to fresh coon meat to Creole jambalaya to boudin to gumbo to gar balls. I've done nothing but eat since I got here. Does anyone in Louisiana ever think about anything else?'

She laughed. 'We do worship our bellies, that's a fact. Fattest state in America, and we's only just gettin' started.'

'Whatever the heck gar balls are.'

'Those are a kind of patty, made from alligator gar. That's this ugly big ol' fish the river folks catch. Might look like a livin' nightmare, but sure tastes like heaven.'

Ben remembered the fanged monster he'd seen displayed outside the fish shack on the way into town. He still didn't fancy eating it. 'And what on earth is gumbo? Where do you get these names?'

Lottie's big brown eyes opened wide. 'Heavens, honey child, you mean to tell me you ain't never eaten no Louisiana gumbo before?'

'I can't say I've had that pleasure yet.'

'Then you sure came to the right place, sweetie. And I know just what to put on the menu for dinner tonight.' Lowering her voice and turning on the accent even more strongly, she said, 'Mm-hmm, you is in fo' a treat!'

But before the treat could happen, some preparations needed to be made, and so did a confession. Because she was still getting on her feet with her new guesthouse business, and because Ben was her only customer and had turned up out of the blue the way he had, Lottie had to admit the shocking truth that her larder was all but empty. Which to her was a major embarrassment, but to Ben was completely unimportant. All he wanted was a room for the night.

'Don't worry about it. You don't have to feed me. I saw a café in town. I can eat there.'

'You don' want to eat there, trust me.'

'How bad can it be?' He could have offered plenty of examples to illustrate how used he was to roughing it, but there were already enough citizens of Clovis Parish with more insights into his past than they really needed to have.

Despite his protests Lottie was resolute, her eyes already beginning to glaze as she visualised the feast she was going to cook up to mark the occasion of her first-ever customer.

Hence, a serious shopping expedition was called for – and hence, as Ben had nothing else to do for the next few hours, nor for the rest of that day for that matter, he happily allowed himself to get roped in as a general aide and grocery carrier. And, as it turned out, he soon became the chauffeur for the occasion too, after pointing out that Lottie's matchbox-sized bright green GMC, as cute as it was, couldn't hold more than a couple of bags of shopping whereas his Tahoe could haul enough goods to stock a restaurant kitchen for a month.

He gallantly escorted Lottie to the passenger side and opened her door for her. An elderly man painting his fence across the street paused to wave, and she smiled and waved back with a cheery 'Afternoon, Mr Clapp'. Then Ben tossed a pile of empty shopping bags in the back, and they were off.

Lottie eschewed the local grocery store and instead directed Ben a few miles further west of Chitimacha, to a tiny rural town called Pointe Blanche where, she explained to him with a conspiratorial wink, there existed a sensational food market that was destined to be the secret weapon in her quest to establish the best restaurant in Clovis Parish. 'They got all the good stuff, real Cajun specialties you won't find anywhere else.'

Ben was happy to take her word for it, though privately he was thinking back to the weird and wonderful local dishes he'd seen on offer at the Cajun steakhouse and beginning to wonder what he was letting himself in for.

Pointe Blanche was maybe half the size of Chitimacha, but a good deal busier. 'Why not set up your restaurant here?' he asked her as they searched for a parking space. 'Closer to your suppliers, bigger clientele.'

She shook her head. 'I grew up in Chitimacha. That's where I'll die.' Stubborn.

Ben finally managed to park the Tahoe just three minutes' walk from the food market, so they wouldn't have too far to haul their goodies. They locked up the car and strolled down the street, her talking, him listening and enjoying the moment as he took in the local sights.

On the same street as the food market was an auto repair yard called DUMPY'S RODS, with nobody in sight and a variety of custom cars in various stages of dismantlement behind a locked chain-link gate. Next door to Dumpy's was the compulsory town gun shop, and finally the food market itself, a kind of Aladdin's cave of esoteric gastronomy purveying such delights as bayou gator burger, blackened catfish and roast beef with 'debris'. What kind of debris, Ben didn't even want to know.

Lottie invaded the place like a nine-year-old let loose in a toy store, and instantly began spending far more cash than Ben was paying her for a night's board.

'You don't have to do this,' he protested. 'Not on my account.' To which she replied, 'Shush, now,' and silenced him with one of her retina-searing smiles.

Lugging multiple bags of Cajun delicacies back to the Tahoe half an hour later, they passed by the auto repair yard again. This time the chain-link gate was open and a cluster of young guys were gathered in the forecourt, five of them all drooling over a flame-painted lowrider with suspension so close to the ground that it wouldn't have made it halfway up the track to Le Val without bottoming out. To Ben the car looked like a big chrome polishing headache, but the young guys all seemed entranced by it.

One of them, a lean hairy individual with close-set eyes full of nastiness and a roll-up dangling from his mouth, managed to peel his gaze away from the absurd car long enough to cast a lurid glance Lottie's way and crack a grin that showed off his rotten teeth. He yelled, 'Yo, Mama!' Then nudged the guy standing next to him and added loudly, shaking his head in mirth, 'Damn, that's the porkiest nigger bitch I seen all week.'

The other one laughed and cupped his hands to his mouth to call to Ben, 'Hey buddy! Don't feed the gorilla!'

Which was more than enough to make Ben want to set down his shopping bags, walk into the yard and lay the five out flat, in such a way that they wouldn't be getting up again too quickly. But only after he'd made them watch him reduce the lowrider to a smoking pile of scrap metal.

Lottie just stiffened a little and hastened her step past the open chain-link gateway, motioning for him to do the same. 'Another reason for not livin' in Pointe Blanche. Lot of trash round these parts.'

'Maybe someone should clean it up,' Ben said.

'Forget it. That there's Dwayne Skinner.' She seemed too afraid to point out which one she meant, but Ben guessed it was the lean hairy one.

'You know him?'

'We was in middle school together. This is a small community. Ever'body knows ever'body around here.'

'So what?'

'So, you don' go gettin' into fights with Dwayne Skinner.'

'I don't like his language.'

She looked at him. 'Ben, if you're fixin' to go pickin' quarrels with every redneck who says the N-word, y'all gonna have your hands full, believe me.'

Ben thought, *fuck it*. He went ahead and set down the bags. Stood staring at the group and felt that familiar coldness coming over him as his body went into fight mode.

Now all five were staring back and beginning to bristle like the real tough guys they were.

The lean hairy one who might be Dwayne Skinner yelled, 'You got a problem, asshole?'

Ben didn't have a problem, beyond the fact that he was mildly irritated by their behaviour. But they did, if he walked into that yard. Five against one. They probably thought they were in with a pretty good chance. Which constituted a serious error of judgement. Because in reality, the fight would be over before it even started.

Lottie halted and turned, giving him an imploring look. 'Come on, sugah. Let's go.'

'This won't take long,' Ben said.

Now the five were moving away from the car and slowly walking towards him. They were putting on the whole display of menace. Fists thumping into cupped palms. Brows furrowing, jawlines tightening, eyes narrowing. Radiating total self-confidence, as though they'd done this a hundred times before. And maybe they had, too. Experience had taught them they had nothing to fear. But that just meant they'd been lucky, until today.

Ben smiled to himself.

'You ain't gonna be smilin' when they're scrapin' your ass off of the sidewalk,' Dwayne Skinner said.

Ben said to him, 'Ever used a wheelchair? It's harder than it looks. But you'll get plenty of practice in the weeks and months to come.'

Lottie said, 'Ben.' Her voice sounded tight with apprehension.

Ben fished the Tahoe key from his pocket and tossed it to her. 'You walk on. I'll meet you back at the car in one minute.'

Ben had decided he'd go for Dwayne first. Then his buddy

beside him, the one who'd made the gorilla remark, in that order. They were the two doing all the talking, which meant they were psychologically the leaders of this little peer group, the lean hairy one being number one and the other his second-in-command. Like in a dog pack, where the animals naturally arrange themselves into a hierarchy with the alpha and beta dogs at the top and everyone else in order of ranking below.

In war, Ben had learned long ago, you always take the officers down first if you can. With the alpha and beta broken and helpless and pissing their pants on the concrete, the rest would probably try to bolt. *Try* being the operative word. None would get further than a few steps before they received a dose of the same medicine as their pals.

Lottie said, 'Ben, please.'

Chapter 9

Ben was half a heartbeat away from walking into the yard. All he had to do was let events play out exactly as he could already see them happening on the mental screen inside his head. After last night's heavy dinner and the excessive breakfast he'd eaten back in Villeneuve that morning, a little bit of exercise was the exact thing he needed.

But then he hesitated. Actions had consequences, and while he wasn't the least bit concerned how those consequences would affect the five guys in front of him, it occurred to him that certain repercussions were best avoided in his own interest. It was a busy street. Not Piccadilly at rush hour, but a lot busier than the sidewalks outside Elmo's Liquor Locker at midnight. If Ben stepped through the gate into the forecourt of Dumpy's Rods and things followed their inevitable course, someone was bound to call the cops. The aftermath of the fight was as predictable as its outcome. If Ben remained with the five unconscious bodies until the police turned up, he'd face all kinds of questioning. Even if he left before they arrived, there would be enough witness descriptions for the cops to identify him. Either way, it pointed to the likely reappearance of Sheriff Waylon Roque into Ben's life soon afterwards.

All of that, combined with the fact that he'd have compromised his anonymity once again, when the whole damn point of leaving Villeneuve was to lie low.

Stupid.

Lottie said, 'Do what you like, I ain't waitin'.' She started walking off, shaking her head.

The gang were just a few steps away. Ben watched them approach, still undecided. Then the decision was made for him when one of the five who hadn't yet spoken a word pointed at Ben and said, 'Hey, I seen this guy before. He's on the news.'

Dwayne Skinner shot his buddy a sneer. 'Yeah, right. How's this asshole on the news?'

'Straight up, man. It's him for sure. He's the dude who busted up Billy Bob Lafleur.'

Dwayne and the others were now eyeing Ben more hesitantly. 'Is that a fact?' Dwayne said, with as much bravado as he could sum up. 'Don't mean shit if he did. Lafleur's a fuckin' pussy faggot. Hell, my grandmother could whip his ass.'

But now their curiosity was stronger than their fighting spirit. 'You the guy, mister?'

'Forget it,' Ben said. He picked up his bags, turned and kept walking. Dwayne Skinner and his pals instantly started up a chorus of chicken sounds, strutting and flapping bent arms like wings. They would never, ever know how lucky they were.

'Changed your mind, huh?' Lottie said as he caught up with her, handing him back the Tahoe key with a look of immense relief.

He shrugged and replied, 'Five against one. It wouldn't have been a fair fight.'

They walked in silence back to the vehicle. Ben's arms

and legs were tingling and trembly from the pent-up adrenalin that would now slowly start to reabsorb into his system. It was a familiar feeling. All combat soldiers were used to it. Nine times out of ten, whenever his old SAS unit had been all kitted out and psyched up for battle, they'd been stood down and had to return to their quarters to shake off all the tension. But what wasn't such a familiar feeling, and one he disliked intensely, was being recognised everywhere he went. Damn and blast Dickie Thibodeaux from the *Courier*, or whatever his rag was called. Ben should have smashed the photographer's camera when he'd had the chance.

They reached the parked Tahoe, and Ben blipped the central locking and opened the rear hatch and loaded in the mass of groceries, which filled only a fraction of the cargo space. Only when they climbed aboard and Ben started the engine did Lottie reach across to touch his arm and break into a dazzling smile. 'Wow. There was me thinkin' there were no gentlemen left in this world. Thank you.'

'For what? Nothing happened.'

'You kiddin' me? A lot happened. You stood up for a lady. Even though you hardly know me and we only just met. And that's somethin'.'

Ben replied, 'We're shopping for groceries together and you're going to cook me dinner. In some countries that's the same as being married.'

She laughed. 'Maybe. But trash like Dwayne Skinner ain't worth gettin' beat up over, not for my sake.'

'Who said anything about getting beaten up?'

By the time they reached Chitimacha, Ben had relaxed and mostly forgotten about it. He helped Lottie unload the groceries and bring everything inside. With her larder replenished and all her ingredients for the cooking session laid out systematically on her gleaming kitchen surfaces, Lottie said, 'Oh joy.' She rolled up her sleeves, donned a well-used and appropriately-stained apron that said LEITHS SCHOOL OF FOOD AND WINE, and got to work with a fiercely concentrated gusto that was awesome to behold.

It soon became obvious that Ben's presence in the kitchen was getting in her way, and so he left her to it and wandered out to the garden for a cigarette. As he smoked, out of a kind of morbid curiosity he googled up 'Clovis Parish Louisiana local news' on his burner phone and found the *Courier*'s website. Sure enough, there next to D. Thibodeaux's trashy and sensationalistic article on the attempted liquor store holdup was the photo of Ben taken outside the Bayou Inn.

Which, needless to say, was how Dwayne Skinner's buddy had recognised him.

Damn it, once again.

The rest of the afternoon passed languorously. It still felt odd to Ben to have so little to do except mooch about the guesthouse and wait for evening to come. When it finally did, he was in for an eye-opener. Whatever reservations he might have been holding on to about Cajun cooking were soon to be blown away as Lottie seated him at her immaculately set, candlelit table and began lifting lids off steaming dishes of the most beguiling food he'd ever encountered.

'So this is gumbo,' he said, gazing at the vast helping she'd put on his plate.

'No, this is *Lottie's* gumbo,' she corrected him with a gleeful laugh. 'I'm spoilin' you for anyone else. Now, please. Don't talk. Eat.'

Ben willingly obeyed the command. The gumbo was a rich, sumptuous meat stew made from chicken and andouille sausage cooked with celery and bell peppers and onion, all melted together on a glutinous and indecently flavoursome bed of what Lottie called dirty rice. If this was dirt, he was happy to gobble it down, three or four heaped forkfuls to Lottie's every one.

'What's that seasoning?' he tried to ask, but his mouth was too crammed full to speak. He chewed, swallowed and repeated the question more coherently, and Lottie explained that it was something called filé, which was a classic Cajun spice that came from dried leaves of the sassafras tree and was used for flavour and thickening. She said, 'My opinion, some Louisiana cooks, like those Creole folks along the Cane River, lay on the filé till you can't taste nothin' else. I like to mix it up with okra for a more subtle effect.'

The delicious concoction was accompanied by a bottle of Sauvignon Blanc so chilled that it numbed the tongue. Ben was generally more of a red wine person, but the pairing was perfect. He ate and drank, but especially ate. Lottie seemed delighted with his enthusiasm for her cooking. After two platefuls he wanted to stop, though somehow the fork just wouldn't leave his hand. Or stop shovelling food up to his mouth.

It was just as well he didn't live here. Too much of this stuff, and his daily runs would start to become a waddling stagger.

'So, you like it, huh?' Lottie said. Fishing for compliments, naturally.

Ben managed to pause between mouthfuls and looked her in the eye across the table. 'When I get home, you know the first thing I'm going to do? I'm going to call up whoever compiles the Oxford English Dictionary.'

'Oh really, and why's that?' she said, showing every one of her white teeth in a beaming smile, knowing a compliment was coming and loving the anticipation.

'Because if they're not specifically mentioning your cooking, they're seriously misdefining the word "tasty".'

For dessert Lottie had whipped up a Southern-style chocolate gravy sauce, which she poured over beignets so rich in eggs and butter that Ben was amazed he didn't drop dead right there of heart failure. What a way to die, though, if he had. When the last crumb was gone he leaned back in his chair, clutched his belly and said, 'That's it. That's all I can take.'

Chapter 10

Lottie said, 'How 'bout we retreat to the salon for a lil' drink?'

She put on an Aretha Franklin CD and they sat in her soft, comfortable armchairs either side of a coffee table. When she proposed an after-dinner tot of rum, Ben had a better idea. He'd eaten so much that he wasn't sure he could haul himself out of the armchair, but with a manful effort managed to lurch to his feet and run up to the top floor to unbuckle his bag and fetch out the bottle of twelve-year-old Glenmorangie he'd bought from Elmo Gillis. It was still unopened. Tonight seemed like the ideal occasion. He carried the bottle back downstairs. Lottie grabbed a pair of crystal tumblers from a sideboard and they happily attacked the Scottish nectar as Aretha sang about r-e-s-p-e-c-t.

In between refills of whisky, of which there were many, Lottie filled in the gaps in her life story. Her first ten years had been spent growing up as an only child on a tiny chicken farm just outside Chitimacha. It was right on the site of a Civil War battlefield, where a bloody little skirmish had taken place between rebel holdouts and a superior force of invading Union troops in the final days before Lee's surrender. She remembered how the chickens were always scratching old musket bullets up out of the ground.

'Poppy could've made more money from sellin' the lead for fishin' weights than he ever done from raisin' poultry,' she reflected.

Her father's lack of talent as a farmer had eventually led them to sell up and move into town, where he ended up wandering miserably from one menial job to another. Life hadn't been easy for the family, which she speculated might have been why the seventeen-year-old Charlotte Landreneau had run away to the 'big city' to rashly marry Neville Dupré. Neville was sixteen years older and well-to-do, and had the distinction of being the first and only African-American dentist ever to set up a practice in Villeneuve. He was also, it later turned out, a violent control freak who somehow contrived to keep no fewer than four mistresses scattered about Clovis Parish, who between them had borne him six children. For Lottie, never having been able to have any of her own, it had been the cruellest kind of betrayal.

'I guess we all have our secrets,' she said. 'Just took me a long time to find out what that sumbitch was up to all them years.'

'I'm sorry.'

She looked at him. 'Do you keep secrets, Ben?'

'Not that kind,' he said, struck by the directness of her question.

'I have a secret,' she said. 'One that goes back a long, long time. Momma told me when I was a lil' girl. She said never to pass it on to another livin' soul, 'cause folks would hate us for it.'

'Why would they hate you?'

'History,' she said with a shrug. 'History matters a lot here in the South. Like the song, you know? *I wish I was in the land of cotton; old times there are not forgotten.*'

'Dixie,' Ben said. 'So are you going to tell me?'

'Tell you what?'

'Your secret. I'm intrigued.'

She smiled. 'You're a livin' soul, ain't you?'

'Managed to stay that way until now.'

'Then I can't. Don't take it personal.'

'Fair enough,' he said.

'Let's change the subject,' she said. 'You never told me much about yo'self, Ben. What do you do for a livin'?'

'I'm a restaurant inspector for the US Health Department.'

'Oh, come on now.'

'I'm a teacher.'

'Maths? English? Geography?'

'No, I teach people to do some of the things I used to do. Like how to protect folks who need protection, or help people who're in danger. Stuff like that.'

'Now I'm the one who's intrigued,' she said. She watched him curiously for a moment, then added, 'You don't like to talk about yo'self much, do you, sugah?'

'It's kind of a habit with me,' he admitted.

'So I ain't the only one who keeps secrets. Well, I guess that makes me feel better. You married?'

'Once upon a time.'

'Kids?'

'Just the one. He's grown up now.'

'Family?'

'My parents died a long time ago. I have a sister. Haven't talked to her in a while.'

'You should. Even though my folks are both passed now, there ain't a day I don't think about them and pray to my Lord to keep a special eye out for the both of them. God and family, that's all there is. That's my strength.'

'I haven't talked to Him in a while either,' Ben said.

66

'He ain't forgotten you,' Lottie said. 'He watches over all of us, ever' moment of ever' day.'

'I used to think that way, too.'

'So what changed?'

Now it was Ben's turn to want to change the subject. That was a part of his life he definitely didn't wish to discuss and he regretted having raised it.

'Let's have another drink.' He held up the bottle. There was surprisingly little left. He was a fairly hardened whisky drinker and it took a lot to make his head spin. He'd have been lying if he'd said it wasn't spinning now. Lottie seemed more or less unaffected, apart from maybe a very slight thickening of her tongue and the very fact that she'd brought up the subject of her mysterious secret. He suspected that she was itching to tell, but wasn't yet drunk enough. Maybe he should have bought two bottles from Elmo instead of just the one.

'Don't take this the wrong way, but I've never known a woman who could knock back the scotch the way you can,' he said as he emptied the last of the Glenmorangie into their glasses.

'Fulla surprises, ain't I?'

'I'll drink to that.'

When at last the whisky was finished, Ben was ready for bed. He thanked her for a wonderful dinner and a pleasant evening. She said, 'Why don't you stay a week or two longer?' and they both laughed.

He gave her a hug and then trudged up to his room. He thought about retracting the pull-down staircase behind him, then decided against it. The combination of the white wine and the scotch was kicking in harder now, everything whirling a little. There seemed to be two beds in the room, both of them gently swirling around in circles in front of his eyes, and for a moment it was hard to decide which one to crash into fully clothed, jeans, boots and all.

'I'm getting too old for this kind of nonsense,' he muttered to himself. Then his head hit the pillow and he closed his eyes and was instantly asleep.

He dreamed fitfully, the kind of ethereal reverie that seems vivid at the time but is burst like a bubble in the morning, forever lost to memory. It was through his dreaming that he heard the strange sounds that some more focused part of his mind told him weren't imaginary. His eyes snapped open and he sat upright.

He definitely hadn't dreamed it. A *thump* that had seemed to resonate through the floor beneath him. Followed by the crash and tinkle of breaking glass. Some kind of commotion. And it had come not from outside, but from somewhere in the house. From downstairs.

And then he heard another sound that blew away the last fog of sleep and whisky, and had him jackknifing out of bed in alarm.

The sound of a woman's scream of terror.

Followed a moment later by another cry. A much worse sound, of a very different nature, the kind of wailing shriek that can only be caused by the most unspeakable kind of agony.

Ben ran for the bedroom door.

Chapter 11

He crossed the pitch blackness of the attic bedroom in two long strides and tore open the door. The little landing outside his room was every bit as dark. The world of the blind. And the deaf, too, because now all he could hear from below was dead silence.

He called out, 'Lottie?' Heard the tension in his own voice. Trying to understand where the screams had come from. It was a big house. They could have come from anywhere on the two floors below him.

No reply.

He hurried down the drop-down stairs to the first-floor landing, which was dimly illuminated by a narrow chink of light escaping from Lottie's part-open bedroom door. He hesitated, then ran along the landing to the door and peered inside. The room was large and cosy, and empty. The light was coming from a little wall lamp above the double bed. The covers were rumpled aside, as though she must have got out of bed in a rush. Ben's pulse was quickening as he ran back along the landing. The luminous green skeleton hands of his watch told him it was 4.13 a.m. He stopped again at the head of the stairs, listening hard.

Still total silence from below. Too quiet, even for the middle of the night. The kind of silence that hangs heavy, like a dumbstruck witness in the immediate aftermath of something bad, really bad. Another light was on in the downstairs hallway, its glow reaching around the twist in the winding staircase.

He was trying to compute what could have happened. Had she gone downstairs for some reason, maybe to get a drink of water or visit the ground floor bathroom, and fallen and hurt herself? Was the tinkle of breaking glass the smashing of something like a glass or a lamp? He was about to call her name again, but instinct made him stay quiet. There were other ways to interpret the sounds he'd heard. Ways that were beginning to paint a worse picture in his mind.

He rushed down the first few steps as far as the twist in the staircase, to meet the glow of light that shone up from the hallway below.

The hallway wasn't empty. A shape lay on the floor. The shape of a large body. A woman's body.

Lottie's body.

She was wearing a fluffy pink towel bathrobe hastily pulled on over a long satin nightdress and tied around her middle with a cord belt. She was lying on her back with her arms outflung to her sides and her face turned away from him. She wasn't moving. Blood showed shocking red on the pink of her bathrobe and the creamy material of her nightdress. A lot of blood. It glistened on the brown skin of her legs where the nightdress had ridden up to her knees as she fell. It was soaking into the carpet under her, steadily spreading outwards in a dark stain.

But Ben wasn't looking at the blood. He was staring in bewildered horror at the curved, glinting length of steel blade that was protruding from her sternum, right below the ribs, sticking straight up in the air like a flag that had been planted on her.

Not a knife blade. A sword, long and wicked and stuck deep through her body to pin her to the floorboards.

Ben leaped down the last few steps to the hall, calling her name again, hearing his voice in his ears as though it were someone else's, knowing that nothing could save her from this terrible injury, his mind whirling to comprehend what he was seeing, and why.

At the end of the hall the front door was hanging ajar a few inches, and beyond that the screen door was wide open and letting in the night air and insects. The inner door had a window consisting of four little dappled opaque square panels. Lottie hadn't dropped a glass, or knocked over a lamp, or anything else. The window panel nearest the lock was smashed and lying in fragments on the entrance mat, as if someone had punched it through to pass their arm inside and unfasten the lock and security chain from inside and let themselves into the hall.

Which, Ben realised, was exactly what had happened. Lottie, a floor closer to the hall than Ben up in the attic, must have heard the sound of breaking glass. She must have got out of bed to investigate, wrapping the gown around herself as she trod downstairs, clicking on the hall light from the switch at the foot of the staircase. That must have been when she came upon the intruder, or intruders. Hence, the first scream Ben had heard.

And that must also have been when the intruder, or intruders, had attacked her with the sword, knocked her to the floor, stood over her and stabbed her brutally through the body. Hence, the terrible wail of agony that had followed soon after the first scream.

Everything had happened in the space of a few moments. And it had ended only moments ago. Which had to mean that whoever had done this couldn't be far away.

71

Even as he stood there thinking it, Ben heard a revving car engine from outside in the street. Someone in a hurry. Someone in the process of fleeing from the scene.

Choices. He needed to stay with Lottie and do whatever he could to help her. At the same time, if he didn't act instantly to go after her assailant, *right now*, that chance would be gone.

In a perfect world, you wouldn't have to choose. Back when he was heading up his SAS troop, he'd have been able to deploy one guy to stay with her and more to go after the enemy. But he was on his own now, and this wasn't a perfect world. It was a world in which armed attackers burst into the homes of innocent and defenceless people and hurt them. And you had to do something about that.

Ben made his choice. He jumped over Lottie's body and raced for the half-open front door. Burst outside, leaped down the steps and onto the path.

Chapter 12

There were no lights on in any of the neighbouring homes, but the street was full of the hard white glare that blazed from the headlamps of a black car in the middle of the road, double-parked beside his Tahoe with the driver's door facing Lottie's entrance gate. It was too dark to see what kind of car it was. Some kind of long, wide, old-style American saloon. Its engine note was the deep, rumbling clatter of a V8. A big, powerful, thirsty engine, harking back to the distant days when gasoline was as cheap as water. The tang of exhaust fumes cut through the sweetness of the night air. The unseen driver was impatiently gunning the throttle, as though urgently waiting before he could take off.

As Ben ran down the path towards the gate, he realised why. The running figure of the person the driver was waiting for had just cleared Lottie's entrance gate and was sprinting towards the waiting car. The driver's accomplice. Lottie's attacker. A classic two-man team, perp and getaway driver. Ben heard the clap of the guy's running footsteps on the sidewalk, echoed by his own as he gave chase. He saw the dark figure flit across the white glare of the headlights, crossing the front of the car to make it to the passenger side.

Ben ran faster. He reached the gate and vaulted over it and raced towards the car. The escaping figure wrenched open the passenger door, and for a brief moment the car's interior was lit by the flare of its courtesy light, and as he ran Ben caught a glimpse of its two occupants. Both male, both white, both around the same age, older than their twenties and younger than their forties. The driver had long reddish hair tied back, the passenger had short reddish hair and wore a dark jacket over a white T-shirt.

That was all Ben was able to take in before the door closed and the car's interior went dark again. By then, the driver was already slamming the transmission into drive and booting the gas. The V8 roared and smoke poured from the rear wheels as the tyres spun and screeched on the road.

Ben reached the edge of the sidewalk and ran out in front of the car, dazzled by its headlights which were suddenly veering right towards him and forcing him to dance back out of its path. The car roared by him, almost running over his toes. Because he'd gone to bed wearing his jeans, the Tahoe key was still in his pocket.

More choices. And it still wasn't a perfect world. By the time he'd run to the Tahoe, got it fired up and into drive and away, the attackers would be gone. Chasing after the escaping car on foot seemed crazy, but he couldn't afford a moment's hesitation.

He sprinted after the car for all he was worth. It was still accelerating, the driver's foot right down on the floor. Giving it so much gas that the power delivery of the big V8, designed for pure brute muscle back in the days long before US automotive engineers conceived of anything as sanitised and wimpy as traction control, was losing its grip on the road and fishtailing all over the place and spinning the tyres so hard that Ben could taste the molecules of burning rubber mixed up with its exhaust smoke. In seconds, it would get away from him. But for a few precious instants he could still catch it.

What he thought he could do once he caught it, he had no idea. He just knew he had to try.

He ran faster than he'd ever run before. Legs pumping, heart pounding. If he ran any harder he risked tripping over his own feet. But it was working. He was catching up, thanks to the driver's own haste. Ben was within just a few strides of the back of the car's swaying, screeching, gyrating rear end when he saw it had some kind of raised wing perched a few inches above its tail-lights, like a racing car. Something to hang on to, if he could make it. He didn't hesitate. He hurled himself at the rear wing.

Pain lanced through him as his body slammed against the back of the car, but it would have been a lot worse if they hadn't both been travelling in the same direction. His fingers latched on to the horizontal blade of the wing and held on with an iron grip. He was being dragged now, the toes of his boots scraping the road, clinging on for all he was worth with his chest pressed hard against the rear panel of its boot lid. Chrome lettering wide-spaced across the rear bodywork that spelled out the word M-U-S-T-A-N-G digging into his flesh through his shirt. Burning red tail-lights either side of him. Hot exhaust from its twin pipes searing his legs like dragon's breath.

He held on. The car gained more speed. They were already a long way down the street. On the outside it felt like eighty miles an hour. In reality the car was probably just hitting forty. But soon it would be fifty, then sixty.

If he could somehow drag himself up onto the big, wide boot lid, maybe he could kick through the back window and scramble inside. It wasn't much of a plan, but he was angry and upset and didn't have time to think. All he knew right now was that he couldn't let these two men get away.

But Ben also knew that all tactical plans had a way of

going to hell the moment bullets start to fly. That was what was about to happen to his, as Lottie's attacker suddenly leaned out from the passenger window. They must have spotted Ben in the rear-view mirror, or sensed from the car's handling that someone was clinging wildly to the back. The guy hung out as far as possible, clutching tightly on to the roof sill with one hand while pointing something back at Ben with the other. Something small and black that glinted in the peripheral glare of the headlights. The guy's aim wavered, swaying this way and that with the gyrating motion of the car. Not great conditions for target shooting. But Ben was just a few feet away. A sitting duck. He tried to shrink away behind the bodywork but there wasn't anywhere to take cover.

Two gunshots snapped out, muted by the roar of the engine and the rush of wind in Ben's ears. But no less deadly for it. One round punched through the metal of the rear wing a couple of inches from his hand. The other passed over his right shoulder with just a hair's breadth to spare.

Yet more choices. He had only two, and little time to decide between them.

Hold on, get shot.

Let go, take your chances with the road.

He let go.

Chapter 13

The car was gaining more speed every instant, its wheels no longer spinning and the back end under control. It was accelerating down the street under full power.

Parachute training couldn't teach you how to land on a fast-moving road surface. Jumping from a moving vehicle was more like parachuting onto a whirling belt sander. Ben knew that it was going to hurt. And it did.

The impact knocked the air from his lungs. All at once he was slithering and sliding down the road on his back. Like coming off a motorcycle, without the benefit of helmet, leathers or gloves. He tried to keep his head and hands raised off the ground and his arms and legs spread-eagled to mini-mise the chance of rolling. That would do the worst damage, his own momentum breaking bones and flailing him to pieces against the road surface.

He slid for maybe twenty feet, but it felt like a mile before he came to a stop, dazed and bleeding in the middle of the road. The taillights of the car were a long way off now, shrinking to angry red pinpoints in the darkness. He craned his neck to watch as it rounded a corner at the top of the street; then it was out of sight and the roar of its engine was dying away to nothing.

Ben sprang to his feet. His elbows were torn up pretty

badly and his back would be a mess of abrasions. It was still better than getting shot. Either way he had no time to take inventory of his injuries. The pain could wait. He shelved it to the rear of his mind and started sprinting back towards the guesthouse. Some lights were coming on in neighbouring upstairs windows as residents, alerted by the commotion and the sound of gunshots, rushed from their cosy beds to see what was going on. Ben ignored them and ran on. The car had dragged him halfway up the street and it was half a minute before he reached the guesthouse. It was definitely too late to give chase in the Tahoe. That chance had been and gone.

Now all that mattered was Lottie.

She hadn't moved. The dark stain around her had spread almost wall to wall. Ben knelt beside her. The pressure of his knees on the carpet squeezed blood up out of its saturated pile like wringing out a sponge. It was everywhere. He felt its warm wetness soaking through the denim of his torn, abraded jeans.

Ben felt for her pulse and detected only a weak flutter. At his touch she lolled her head to try to focus on him. Her eyes were glassing over. Her mouth opened and she tried to speak, but all that came out was a low rasping moan and a bubble of blood that swelled and then burst, flecking her lips. Now he could see the terrible slash that the sword had cut across her face and neck before her attacker had knocked her over and thrust the long curved blade right through her body to pin her to the floorboards.

Ben stared at the weapon. If he'd been interested in semantics right now he'd have called it a sabre and not a sword. The kind of implement issued to cavalry troops right up until the early decades of the twentieth century, when military minds finally began to realise that mounted charges were little match for heavy machine gunnery. This sabre was older still. The length of blade that wasn't buried deep inside Lottie's body was speckled with over a century's worth of black rust. Its handle was wrapped with sharkskin and bound with gold wire, and encased within a fancy brass basket hilt designed to protect the hand during combat. The brass was tarnished and dulled with age, and bore all the nicks and scars of a weapon that had seen use in anger, a very long time ago. Basically, an antique. Probably worth money.

The question was, what kind of murderer would break into a house to attack someone with a valuable antique sword, when common implements like kitchen knives and hammers could be obtained easily and cheaply and were just as lethal? It made even less sense for the killer to leave the weapon behind.

Lottie began to cough and retch blood. More of it welled from the gaping wound where the blade was stuck through her. Her robe and nightdress were black with it. Out of desperation Ben reached up and grasped the hilt, then on second thoughts took his hand away. Pulling out the blade, whether a knife's or anything else's, could kill a stab victim just as fast as pushing it in. Blood vessels that were constricted or blocked off by the pressure of the blade could suddenly start gushing so fast that their life would ebb away in moments. But he had to do something. He looked around him and spotted the little stand across the hallway where the landline phone rested on its base unit.

'I'm going to get help, Lottie. Hold on.'

He started to get to his feet to reach for the phone. Before he could stand up, Lottie raised a bloody hand off the floor and, with what must have cost her last reserves of energy, gripped his sleeve.

At first he thought she was attempting to struggle upright.

But she was too far gone for that. These were her last moments, and she knew it as well as he did. He realised she was trying to pull him down closer, so that she could whisper something in his ear before she died.

Ben put his hand on hers and leaned down and said, 'What is it, Lottie?'

'I . . . I always . . .' It took a monumental effort for her to speak. She coughed, and the act of coughing made her abdominal muscles clench around the sabre blade, and she let out a terrible shuddering gasp of pain and closed her eyes. For an instant she seemed to fade away and he thought she was gone. Then her eyes reopened, bloodshot and full of agony and focused on his own with all the urgency of a person frantically holding on to consciousness, slipping away and fighting it every inch and losing.

She whispered, 'I knowed it was comin', Ben. I *knowed* it.'

Ben understood that she was talking about the secret she'd alluded to earlier that evening. Whatever it was, she'd held on to it for most of her life out of fear. Now that death was so close, she seemed to want to let it out like making a confession.

'What did you know? Lottie, talk to me. What did you know?'

She was sinking fast. Her breath was coming in fluttering gasps. Her eyes were glazed. The grasp of her bloody fingers on his shirt sleeve tightened in a last moment of panic before the darkness swallowed her, then became slack. Barely audibly, she murmured, 'They was . . . they was bound to get me in the end. Like they done . . . to . . . Peggy Iron Bar.'

Ben laid his hand on hers and squeezed it. 'Who did it, Lottie? If you know who hurt you, you have to tell me. I'll find them. I swear. Who did it?'

But Lottie had given all she had to give. A last sigh hissed from her lips and her eyes closed, her body relaxed and Ben held her as he felt the life leave her.

He remained kneeling on the blood-soaked carpet next to her for some time, still clasping her hand in his, his head bowed with sadness for this woman he'd only just met and knew so little about. Wishing he could remove the sabre pinning her to the floor and let her lie there with a little dignity, if it wouldn't have been messing with a murder scene.

And wondering, *who in God's name was Peggy Iron Bar?*

Chapter 14

Ben was so lost in that moment that he barely registered the sound of the approaching siren until the police cruiser screeched to a halt outside the guesthouse and the open doorway behind him was lit up with flashing blue. It was no big surprise that one of the local residents must have called the cops. If they hadn't, he'd have had to call them himself.

He laid Lottie's limp hand down to rest on her chest and stood up. He glanced down at himself and saw that he was a mess. The parts of his clothing that weren't torn and tattered from sliding down the road were covered in blood-stains. Anyone who saw him would think he'd been attacked by something wild. It was how he felt, too. The abrasions on his back were hurting. But he had more important things to deal with.

He turned towards the doorway to see the solitary cop from the cruiser running up the path towards the guest-house's front entrance. The cop was hatless, in a tan deputy's uniform shirt and black trousers, a drawn pistol in his hand. It struck Ben as a little odd to send just one officer to attend to the scene of a violent crime, but he supposed that the fact that they'd managed to send anyone at all so quickly was fairly impressive, given that this was the rural

Deep South. The UK was no better, at the best of times. There were enough accounts of residents in the middle of London waiting twelve hours for a response to a 999 call.

As the cop approached the house Ben recognised his face. Fleshy, pasty features burned red by the sun. Brown hair, spiky on top and shaved up the sides like a Marine. It was the deputy called Mason, one of the pair who'd accompanied Sheriff Waylon Roque to the scene of the liquor store holdup in Villeneuve. The one Roque had said was as sharp as a bowling ball. Better than nothing, Ben thought, and ran through in his mind what he needed to tell the guy.

But Ben never got the chance to say much at all. As Mason hurried up the steps and entered the hallway, he saw Ben standing there and raised his drawn weapon to aim at him. The cop's finger was on the trigger, which definitely wasn't correct protocol for dealing with a nonthreatening civilian. Ben noticed that the gun wasn't Mason's issue sidearm, either. His Glock was still tucked and clipped into his duty holster, next to his cuff pouch, baton holder, Taser and CS canister. What he was aiming in Ben's face, with a little more aggression than Ben felt was warranted, was a big black revolver. Probably a forty-four, going by the size of the bore and the chamber holes in the cylinder.

Ben put his hands up at shoulder height, palms facing the cop to show they were empty. 'Easy, Officer. I'm a witness to a murder. If you wanted to shoot someone, you should've been here when the bad guys were still around.'

The deputy made no move to lower the weapon. He came closer. Ben retreated a couple of paces, carefully stepping back around Lottie's body, slow and easy, no sudden moves, keeping his hands raised and in plain view. Mason came on another step, still keeping the big revolver pointed squarely at Ben's face.

He was standing on the bloodstained area of the floor. His weight was pressing blood up from the carpet pile, so that it welled and bubbled up around the soles of his large, black police issue shoes. Lottie's body was between him and Ben, right there in the middle of the hall, a large mound of dead flesh with an antique sabre sticking up grotesquely from its highest point, like a banner raised on some conquered hilltop. It wasn't a sight that was easily missed. And yet Mason hadn't given Lottie's body even a single glance from the moment he'd entered the house. His focus was fixed totally and intently on Ben.

Hands still raised, Ben wagged a finger towards the floor and said, 'Watch you don't trip, Officer. There's a body on the floor.' Sharp as a bowling ball. Maybe it was true.

The deputy gave a grunt and shook his head, still holding the gun steady. 'Boy, y'all sure know where to go lookin' for trouble. Reckon you found more'n you bargained for, this time.'

Which struck Ben as a curious thing to say, under the circumstances. Very calmly he replied, 'Maybe you should lower the weapon so we can have a conversation about what happened here.'

Mason didn't lower the weapon. Ben could see his fingertip whitening against the blade of the trigger. Properly speaking a .44-calibre handgun was really a .43, firing a bullet of .429 of an inch diameter. But it was still plenty big enough to blow a fist-sized hole right through the middle of a man's chest. Hunters used them for killing grizzly bears. And the way Mason was pointing it at Ben, he seemed pretty serious about killing him with it too.

Ben considered his appearance, and it flashed through his mind that someone all covered in blood the way he was might, in a cop's way of seeing things, look exactly like the kind of person who'd just smashed their way into an inno-cent woman's house wielding a sabre and turned her entrance hall into a slaughterhouse. From that point of view it was fairly understandable that Mason was wary of him.

But none of that explained what happened next.

Mason fired. The BOOM of the big revolver in the confines of the hallway was stunningly loud and its muzzle flash was a tongue of white flame that spouted a foot from its muzzle.

If Ben hadn't seen it coming, there would have been two corpses on the hallway floor and a lot more blood. Even as Mason's finger tightened all the way on the trigger and the hammer was released and the firing pin began its short arc of travel, Ben was in motion. Superfast, he crossed the space between himself and the gun and deflected the barrel side-ways and upwards from its point of aim, hard and brutal, so that the gunshot discharged into the ceiling.

The blast and shockwave from the revolver were tremen-dous. He would have tinnitus for days, but a little ringing in the ears is preferable to fifteen grams of hardcast lead alloy entering your skull at over a thousand miles an hour.

Ben's training, and the way he taught his students, was to first take control of the weapon and then neutralise the assailant. In the same single continuous fluid movement that had been rehearsed a zillion times and saved his life for a percentage of that number, he twisted the revolver out of Mason's hand and kept hold of his wrist as he sidestepped in towards him and used his own body as a fulcrum to yank Mason off his feet and dump him hard on the floor.

Ben could have finished his disarming move with a stamp to the neck or an arm-breaking twist, or beaten the guy's brains out with his own ASP expandable baton. Instead, not wanting to hurt him any more than was strictly necessary, he just reached down to where Mason lay half-stunned on the floor and snatched his badge wallet, then removed his duty belt and tossed it away across the room.

In retrospect, Ben could come to see that as his first mistake.

Relieved of Glock, cuffs, tear gas and baton, Mason wriggled away across the floor like a beaten dog. His uniform was all bloodied from the mess on the carpet, his face mottled with anger. Ben quickly examined the revolver, then shoved it into his own belt behind the right hip. Pointing at Lottie's body he said to Mason, 'That there is a murder victim. I'm a witness to said murder. You're a cop. Remember how this goes? Are you going to behave now?'

'You're in deep shit, Hope,' Mason rasped. 'You just assaulted a police officer.'

Ben flipped open the badge wallet. It had the deputy's six-pointed Clovis Parish gold star on one side and a police ID card on the other, giving his full name as Mason F. Redbone. Ben tossed the wallet away and shook his head.

'Wrong, Deputy Redbone. You're guilty of discharging a firearm without provocation at an innocent member of the public. All I did was protect myself in such a way that avoided using undue force. There isn't a mark on you. Which any police misconduct investigation panel in the country would agree puts me right in the clear. They might have a few questions for you, though. Such as what you're doing in possession of a non-issue weapon that's had its serial number filed off. And why you attempted to kill me with it just now. I'd kind of like answers to all those questions myself, so you'd better start talking.'

Mason muttered something that Ben didn't catch. He leaned closer. 'Speak up, Mason. Thanks to you I've got ringing in my ears.'

Leaning closer was Ben's second mistake.

Mason was lying on the bloodstained carpet, his head and shoulders propped against the skirting board, his feet drawn up under him, knees bent, his body quite still except for the deep rise and fall of his chest as he breathed. His eyes were full of fear and hatred. Then his right hand suddenly darted down the length of his right leg, whipped something hidden from inside his right boot and flashed towards Ben.

Ben twisted away to avoid the knife, but he'd been leaning too close and he reacted half a second too late. He felt the razor-sharp steel puncture his flesh, below the ribs on his right side. The pain shot through him.

Mason lunged up at Ben, to stab him again. Ben was ready for him this time. He palmed the incoming knife aside and rammed a savage upward blow with the heel of his hand into Mason's philtrum.

The space between the nose and upper lip is one of the most vital points of the human body. Done hard enough, the strike would drive a man's nose bone backwards into his brain and kill him instantly. Ben knew that, because he'd inflicted the same technique on plenty of enemies, with lethal results. He didn't want Mason dead. Just totally incapacitated.

Mason dropped without a sound, unconscious before he hit the floor. He lay on his back side by side with Lottie, arms and legs splayed out like a starfish.

Ben reeled backwards a couple of steps. He pressed both hands to his belly and saw the blood leaking out between his fingers.

And that was when two more police cruisers screeched up outside and a bunch more cops came running into the guesthouse.

Chapter 15

There were four of them, clad in blue uniforms with gold piping and dimpled campaign hats with gold badges and silver cords and acorns. The insignia on their arms said LOUISIANA STATE POLICE. A sergeant and three troopers, two with pump shotguns and two with Glocks. The sight that greeted them as they swarmed inside the hallway was what they took to be a dead fellow officer lying prone beside the body of a female murder victim, along with one man still on his feet who had a gun in his belt, blood all over his clothes, and could more or less be assumed to be the perpetrator of both assaults.

If Ben had been inclined to think about it, he couldn't have blamed them for jumping to conclusions. They had much better reason than Mason had for supposing that he was the threat here.

The hallway filled with the sound of hoarse urgent yelling as the troopers fixed him in their sights and all began screaming and bellowing at him at once. DROP THE WEAPON DROP THE WEAPON DROP THE WEAPON!

As he stood there reeling from the stab wound his options flew through his mind at lightning speed. If he didn't respond one way or another in the next two seconds, the chances were they would all open fire at once and take him down. He could try to calmly explain the situation to them, which he wasn't too sure he could do with blood pouring out of him. Or he could whip the revolver from his belt and start shooting before they did. Five rounds, four targets. Maybe just shoot them in the legs, to avoid causing unnecessary harm.

Alternatively, he could throw down his gun and surrender. But he didn't fancy his chances of receiving fair treatment. Not after he'd already taken down one of their own. By the time the ambulance arrived the five state troopers would have beaten Ben to a pulp.

So Ben took the only realistic option open to him. He ran. Ignoring the agony in his belly and the tremors of shock jangling every nerve in his body.

Shots rang out and bullets cracked into the wall and splintered the banister rail as he charged up the stairs three at a time. He made it halfway up the staircase to the switchback, then flew up the second half heading towards the first floor landing. Three troopers thundered after him while the fourth stayed below, yelling into a radio that they had an officer down and needed assistance.

Ben raced past the open door of Lottie's bedroom and reached the drop-down staircase just as the police sergeant appeared on the landing behind him. The sergeant racked his shotgun and repeated his command to stop and throw down the weapon.

Ben pounded up the drop-down staircase, up through the hatch to the attic floor, turned and crouched at the edge of the hatch and grabbed the rope loop that worked the pulley mechanism and tugged it hard. The staircase folded in half, and the whole assembly slid upwards on smooth runners to retract through the hatch. Ben hauled up the length of rope that dangled down to enable it to be opened from below, then closed off the hatch with the stair panel that acted like a trapdoor. Definitely a fine piece of carpentry, and just the job when you were being pursued through the house by multiple armed opponents.

He'd bought himself a little time, but it wouldn't be long before they figured out a way to reach him. Nor would it be long before the whole street and surrounding area was swarming with every state trooper they could muster, along with SWAT teams and K9 units. He could hear the sound of frantic voices and crackling radios from beneath his feet as he ran into his bedroom. His legs were feeling like jelly. He had to grit his teeth and close his mind resolutely to the knowledge that he was badly hurt. He had to keep going.

He snatched up his bag from where it lay at the foot of the bed, crammed in the few items that he'd unpacked earlier, then pulled on his leather jacket and looped the bag over his shoulder. He went over to the dormer window and yanked it open. With an effort that felt like a halberd tearing out his guts he gripped the window frame and hauled himself up and through, scrambling out onto the slope of the roof.

The night sky was ink-black and starry. The air was warm, but felt like ice on his skin as the sweat poured from his brow. He felt woozy for an instant and almost lost his footing and went tumbling into space, then managed to regain his balance.

Got to keep going.

Careful not to slip and fall, he made his way over the sloping tiles. He peered over the gable end of the guesthouse and could see Mason's Sheriff's Department Crown Victoria and the two white state police cruisers in the street below, their engines still running and the big light bars on their roofs bathing the whole area in swirling blue. More windows of neighbouring homes were lit up now, as residents awoke to the drama and peeped out to see what was happening. Old Mr Clapp across the street had ventured into his front yard to spectate.

Ben kept low and stayed in the shadows as he padded along the slope of the roof to the point where the gap between Lottie's house and that of her neighbour was at its narrowest. He could see no lights in the next-door windows. Either the neighbours were sleeping through all the excitement, or the house was empty. He eased himself down as close as possible to the edge and readied himself to jump, visualising it in his mind's eye before he committed himself, and knowing it was going to hurt like hell. It was a long way to fall if he fluffed it. He took a couple of deep breaths, counted to three and then launched himself into space.

He cleared the gap easily, but his landing on the neighbour's roof almost made him cry out in pain. He knew he must be leaving a fine trail of blood spots as he moved on, keeping low so that the roof's ridge hid him from the street side. He ran with light fast steps along its length towards where he could see a big old hickory tree standing in the garden close to the far end wall.

This was going to hurt even more. And it did. Ben reached the edge and leaped into space. He dropped ten feet and then the foliage was ripping and clawing and scraping at his face and body as he went crashing downward through the branches. His fingers locked on to a thicker limb and he managed to arrest his fall. He scrambled down the tree as far as the lower branches, until his legs dangled free. It was maybe an eight-foot drop to the patchy grass of the back garden. He steeled himself and let go. The agony as he hit the ground went through him like a spear, but he didn't make a sound.

The neighbour's garden was all in shadow. Ben remained in a still crouch at the foot of the tree for a few moments, catching his breath and listening hard until he was sure his escape from the guesthouse hadn't been observed. Then he picked himself up and ran for the back fence and scrambled over it into the next garden, hoping he wouldn't drop down the other side into the waiting jaws of someone's pit bull. He landed in the bushes and kept running.

A tumult of sirens was growing steadily louder. It sounded as if every cop in Louisiana was racing to the scene. Probably a couple of ambulances, too, one for Lottie and one for Sheriff's Deputy Mason F. Redbone, who would soon be enjoying a little holiday in hospital. It was less than he deserved.

Ben crossed that garden, and the next, and then pushed through a hedge over a low wall and found himself in an adjacent street, maybe a couple of hundred yards from the guesthouse as the crow flew. The homes at this end of the neighbourhood were all in darkness, as if the residents here didn't care what kinds of major emergency situations took place up the road. That suited Ben just fine.

He kept going. A blind man could follow the trail of glistening spots and spatters that marked his route, but there was nothing he could do about that. The best he could achieve was to get away from here before he passed out from pain and shock and blood loss and collapsed in the street for the cops to find.

Quarter of a mile away, in a quiet little avenue on the edge of Chitimacha far away from the hubbub and excitement, he came across an old Ford pickup truck parked under the shadow of a spreading oak tree.

The SAS had taught him how to steal cars to make him an efficient operator behind enemy lines, when you sometimes had to improvise modes of transportation. He'd had a lot of practice at it since those days. Old vehicles were the best to steal. The older the better, as long as they were driveable. No alarms, no immobilisers, no on-board GPS trackers. Thirty-nine seconds later he was inside the Ford's cab, bleeding all over the cheap vinyl seats as he got to work hotwiring the ignition. Another half minute after that, he was gone and disappearing into the night.

Chapter 16

Ben drove fast away from Chitimacha, knowing that he couldn't stay on the road long. The state troopers would already be cordoning off the whole area, roadblocking every exit and stopping and searching any car within a perimeter that would rapidly expand state-wide as the manhunt intensified. Every hotel, motel and hospital would be flushed looking for him.

By dawn the horror story of the sabre murder would be airing on local TV, in all its gruesome detail for citizens to relish over breakfast. By midday the whole parish would be so jumpy about the desperate killer on the loose that they'd be loading up their guns and watching out of their windows for any sign of a suspicious-looking stranger lurking about the vicinity. By mid-afternoon he wouldn't be able to walk down the street without getting his head blown off by some trigger-happy Louisianan doing their civic duty.

That was, if he could walk at all. He could feel himself getting weaker with every passing mile. The blood was pooling under him on the car seat and leaking down to the floor, flooding the rubber matting and making his boot soles slippery on the gas and brake pedals. The pain was keeping him alert. He focused closely on it to keep from flaking out at the wheel.

He found a forestry track leading off-road and headed up it. He was grateful for the fact that when it came to stealing cars in rural Louisiana, virtually every vehicle you were likely to get hold of was a go-anywhere four-wheel-drive with rugged tyres and suspension. He bounced and lurched along for miles, bogging down here and there in deep ruts left by the last rains. Eventually he left the track to carve his way for another quarter of a mile into thick forest.

Unable to go any further, he stopped the truck, killed the lights and engine, clambered down from the blood-smeared seat and stood listening for a whole ten minutes, leaning against the side of the truck for support. Only the sounds of nature could be heard, along with the tick of cooling metal.

Wincing and clutching his wound through his bloody shirt, he hauled himself up onto the pickup flatbed and started rooting around in the dirty old crates loaded aboard. The truck belonged to someone with a handy set of skills and the tools to match. An outdoorsman or a hunter; at any rate the kind of guy who carried around a saw, a small sharp hatchet, a couple of green canvas tarpaulins, and a coil of light but strong rope. Among the assorted trash in the glove box Ben found an autographed photo of Dolly Parton, a roll of gaffer tape and an unlabelled quarter-sized liquor bottle whose clear liquid contents smelled like some kind of illicit home-brewed moonshine. He had no use for Dolly but took the tape and the moonshine.

Ben badly needed to rest but he had work to do first. The truck had been resprayed more than once in its life. In its current paint job it was bright orange, and couldn't be left as it was without standing out like a beacon to any police helicopter overflying the woods. He couldn't burn it, for the same reason.

He unfolded the larger of the two tarps and dragged it across the roof of the truck to cover it, then lashed the cover down at the corners with lengths of the rope. Next he spent thirty painful minutes sawing branches from trees and laying them over the tarp, until the shape of the truck was so well camouflaged that a passing deer would be unlikely to notice it, let alone a police chopper. Then he put the hatchet and saw in his bag with the remainder of the rope, strapped the rolled-up smaller tarp on top of it like a soldier's bedding roll, and set off on foot.

It was a weary march. Nothing he hadn't done before, but a knife hole in his side didn't make it any easier. A mile deeper into the woods, ready to drop, he stopped at a great fallen oak tree whose uprooted base had left a large hollow in the ground, an earthy cave deep enough for a man to crawl into and remain hidden. He could lie up and rest here for a while.

Using the small tarp as a groundsheet he wedged himself among the roots, as far from the mouth of his little cave as he could fit. The hollow was damp and smelled of leaf mould and the small animals that had burrowed into it before him. He'd spent time in much worse places.

Risking a little torchlight, he peeled off his jacket and unbuttoned his bloody shirt to inspect his injury. It was still bleeding profusely. Not as deep as he'd first feared, but still pretty damn deep, an ugly gash stretching seven inches diagonally from ribcage to navel.

Open wounds were always an infection risk, especially roughing it outdoors, but Ben had an excellent immune system. With a fastidious doctor for a lady friend he couldn't avoid being all up to date with his tetanus immunisations, too. Right now, though, what concerned him most was the continuous bleeding. If it had been his arm or leg, he might have been able to stem the flow with a tourniquet. Injuries to the torso were harder to deal with. He'd seen men bleed to death from abdominal traumas, and knew enough about the physiology of such injuries to worry him. Half a litre's worth of blood loss causes mild faintness, increasing in severity after a litre or so, when the heart rate begins to increase and breathing quickens. That was where Ben was at now. Another half litre drained out of his body, and he would be in danger of losing consciousness. Anything over 2.2 litres or four pints gone, death wasn't far off.

Setting down the Maglite he took off his shirt and tore a strip of material from the cleanest part of it to use as a swab. Then uncapped the little moonshine bottle, soaked some of the clear alcohol into the cloth, gritted his teeth against the sharp sting and started dabbing the wound. The more he swabbed away the blood, the more kept flowing. It wouldn't stop. Not good.

There was only one thing for it. He was going to have to cauterise the wound to seal the ends of the severed blood vessels. To do that properly he would need a strong heat source and something smooth and metallic, like a knife. He could hold his hatchet blade over a lighter flame for hours on end, until the fuel burned out or he bled to death, whichever happened first, and it still wouldn't warm the metal anywhere close to hot enough. Building a proper camp fire with wood was an option, though it was a tactical no-no for the same reason as leaving a bright orange truck sitting parked in the forest to be spotted a mile away.

But there were other ways to generate the kind of heat necessary to sear and seal damaged flesh.

He pulled the revolver from his belt and flipped open the cylinder. One round gone, five remaining. He tipped the muzzle upwards and the unfired cartridges slid out of their chambers and fell into his lap. Big, long magnum brass cases with heavy flatnosed bullets, each containing enough latent chemical force to stop a charging grizzly dead in its tracks.

Ben examined the saw. Its blade was made for cutting wood, not metal. But brass was softer than steel, and as a lifelong abuser of tools Ben felt confident that it was up to the job he had in mind. Next he took out the hatchet and set it down next to him with the flat of its blade level on the ground. Then picked up an unfired cartridge and laid it against the side of his boot to make an improvised cutting bench. He laid the teeth of the saw blade against the shiny cylinder of the brass case, about halfway between the cartridge base and where the bullet was crimped into place.

Cutting was hard at first, as the blade skipped and slid about the smooth surface. But then he started wearing a groove in the metal, and from there it got easier. Tiny bits of brass swarf collected on his boot as he cut deeper. When he'd sawed three-quarters of the way through, he was able to twist the cartridge between his fingers to open up the cut, then gently and carefully tipped out the powder granules to make a little pile on the flat of the hatchet blade.

The propellant in the cartridges was a fine, dark grey nitrocellulose powder. Very unlike old-fashioned gunpowder, which was a crude explosive formula made from sulphur, charcoal and saltpetre. The old stuff would flash up with a sudden and short-lived whoof of flame and a puff of white smoke when ignited, smelling of rotten eggs and leaving a mass of corrosive black fouling guaranteed to gunk up any gun mechanism in short order. Uncontained as loose powder, the sophisticated modern stuff would burn extremely hot, clean and steady for two or three seconds producing very little smoke or residue. There could have been no automatic weapons or machine guns invented without it. Few people were aware of the fact, but the transition from the old gunpowder to the smokeless innovations of the late nineteenth and early twentieth centuries had been the single most important technological step in facilitating the firepower and carnage of modern warfare.

Progress was a wonderful thing.

After twenty minutes of cutting, bent over his work and straining to see by the flickering lighter flame, Ben had sawed through all five cartridges and built a mound of about five grams of powder on the flat of the hatchet. Now, as he began to worry about the lighter running out of fuel, he had to decide on the best procedure for the next step. If he packed the dry powder into the lips of his still-bleeding wound, it would be ruined by the blood before he could light it, and he'd risk getting all kinds of chemical toxins into his veins. The alternative way would hurt like hell, but it would be a lot more effective.

Cruel to be kind.

Here goes, he thought. He took a couple of deep breaths. Then picked up the hatchet, careful not to spill powder everywhere, took out his Zippo and lit it and touched its fire to the little dark grey mound.

The dull orange flame of the Zippo was suddenly eclipsed by the white flash of the igniting powder. It flared up bright and fierce, roaring like a miniature inferno three or four inches high, hot as a furnace. Just as it reached its peak intensity he slapped the searing metal to his wound.

It hurt.

Chapter 17

It hurt so much, there was no word to describe the pain. There was a sharp sizzling like drips of meat fat spattering onto white-hot barbecue coals. The stink of burning flesh filled Ben's nose. A familiar enough smell to anyone who'd seen the combat horrors he had. But a little different when it was your own flesh cooking. He pressed the hot steel hard against his skin for as long as he could stand it, then dropped the hatchet and fell back onto the damp earth of his cave, stifling the scream of pain that wanted to burst out of his lungs.

It was some time before Ben opened his eyes and realised that he'd passed out. He raised his head off the earth floor and propped himself up on one elbow in the darkness, sick and dizzy and still hurting badly. The hatchet blade was now perfectly cool, one side coated in a blackened and dried crust of cooked blood and skin. The unpleasant battlefield smell of burnt flesh and gunsmoke still lingered in the air.

Ben hardly dared to look at his wound, frightened of what he'd see, and it took a moment to pluck up the resolve. As expected, the whole area was a scorched and ugly mess. But to his relief, the bleeding had finally stopped. He doused himself with more of the moonshine, then swallowed a gulp or two to help take the edge off the pain. The stuff was three times stronger than whisky, but thankfully didn't taste of much.

Funny, how the mind works. The nasty scar left behind when the wound eventually healed would be an impressive addition to the collection Ben had accumulated over the years. When he looked at them he could remember exactly how and when he'd acquired each one, yet the memory of the pain they'd caused him had faded away to zero. This one would ultimately go the exact same route as its predecessors. It was like people said about the female brain being hardwired to forget the pain of childbirth, as the mind–body connection's way of preventing women from being put off from repeating the experience. Ben's only experience of childbirth was his own. Not a subject he knew much about, but if the saying was true, then he could empathise with those women.

To finish the job he could have done with a suture kit to stitch himself up. Lacking needle and thread he tore another clean strip from his shirt, doused it with moonshine and laid it across the wound, then tore off a strip of gaffer tape to hold it in place. It didn't make a bad field dressing and would help hold things together and keep out dirt until he could seek proper medical attention.

He wrapped his leather jacket around his bare shoulders, turned off his torch and settled back against the wall of the cave, shivering a little, mostly from shock and blood loss. He took a few more sips of moonshine to relax. He craved a cigarette but his training warned him against it. The telltale scent of burning tobacco could carry an amazingly long distance in the wilderness, and was a fine way to betray your presence and position to the enemy. Overcautious, perhaps, but over was better than under.

Now, in the stillness of the pre-dawn, he was finally able

to turn his mind to the thoughts and questions that haunted him.

First and most obvious was the fact that he was in a great deal of trouble. The authorities had plenty of evidence to believe Ben was Lottie Landreneau's killer. Several police officers could confirm his presence at the scene of the crime. His prints were on the hilt of the murder weapon. There might be witnesses who could testify to seeing him entering the guesthouse earlier in the day. At least one neighbour, old Mr Clapp, had seen him go off shopping with Lottie, which would be easily confirmed when the forensic examiners found her DNA in his car. The woman who ran the food market in Pointe Blanche would describe the tall blond-haired white man who'd accompanied the victim shopping, while the gang who hung out at Dumpy's Rods could confirm he was the same British guy they'd seen on the local news.

Once they had his name, the authorities would seize on Ben's military past, or as much of it was on open record. Criminal profilers would have a field day creating all kinds of fictions about how a crazed ex-soldier had snapped and gone psychotic with a sword. Where they'd suppose he'd got it from was another matter, but no doubt they'd come up with something.

In short, Ben was in a serious mess. Might he have made things worse for himself by running? The answer was yes, for sure. Guilty men run. Then again, so do men who don't think they're going to get fair treatment at the hands of the law. He had done what he needed to do. There was no doubt in his mind that Deputy Sheriff Mason Redbone had fully intended to kill him.

But why? Ben had no answer to that. Only more questions, such as, why hadn't Mason used his issued weapon to confront him?

Ben examined the revolver again, looking at the scratchy marks on the frame where someone had crudely filed off the serial number. Typically, that someone would be a criminal, who'd later come to some sticky end and had his gun confiscated by the police. Since every bullet discharged from an issue service weapon had to be logged and accounted for, it wasn't unknown for dirty cops to use such illicit trophy weapons to carry out shootings they didn't want to be connected to.

What had been Mason's plan? To make it look as though the revolver had belonged to Lottie's killer, who had for reasons best known to himself murdered his victim using a sabre but then used a gun against the police? Stranger things happened in the world of crime, and who would have disbelieved the word of a sworn officer?

Once Ben was dead, all Mason would have had to do was blast a couple of rounds into the wall by the front door to make it seem as though he was being fired on as he entered the property. Next, he might have wanted to draw his issue Glock and shoot off a few judicious rounds, providing some 9mm holes to support his side of the story. Then he could have smeared the dead man's prints all over the grip, frame and trigger of the revolver. Mason's own prints would have been on it too, but that didn't matter. His story would have been simple and plausible: on entering the property in response to a 911 call and discovering Ms Landreneau's body in the hallway, he came under fire from the suspect. Whereupon the valiant lawman had attempted to disarm the assailant, who was shot by his own weapon during the struggle.

That wouldn't have accounted for the stab wound in the perp's body, because that hadn't been part of Mason's initial plan. In retrospect he'd have had to come up with something to convince his peers, such as 'sumbitch pulled a knife on me, too, but stabbed himself in the fight. It all happened so fast.'

All of which was pure conjecture on Ben's part. He might be getting it completely wrong. But nothing else seemed to explain why Mason had turned up at the guesthouse *already* brandishing the tainted revolver, even as he ran from his patrol car, even before he'd seen Ben in the hallway. Plus, how many cops went about with concealed stiletto daggers in their boots?

Again, pure conjecture. But if Ben was right about this, even halfway right, it all pointed to a premeditated frame-up job, one in which the deputy sheriff was heavily complicit. Mason had tooled up with the illicit gun because he'd known in advance that Ben would be there.

Boy, y'all sure know where to go lookin' for trouble. Reckon you found more'n you bargained for this time.

Next question: what was a Louisiana deputy sheriff, sworn to uphold the law, doing mixed up in something so dirty? There could be only two reasons for such actions: to protect yourself, because maybe you're being threatened or black-mailed into helping the bad guys; or to protect the bad guys themselves, because you're one of them. Whichever it was in Mason's case, one thing was for sure. He was in with some very bad people.

But if there was a frame-up, why was Ben its target? Could it be down to coincidence, a random roll of the dice that just happened to bring up his lucky number? He found that hard to believe. What were the chances that the same guy who just happened to draw the police's attention by walking in on a liquor store robbery in progress would also just happen to be picked out of the blue as a patsy for another crime the very next day? The odds against it were astronomical.

And so, logic dictated that if it wasn't just some dreadful coincidence, it had to mean that Ben had been deliberately chosen, in advance, to be set up as the killer. For some reason that he didn't yet understand, the spotlight was on him.

Then there was the issue of how Mason Redbone had been able to respond so fast to an emergency callout in Chitimacha, forty-five minutes' drive away from the Sheriff's Office in Villeneuve. Maybe he lived closer, or just happened to be in the area. Or maybe the speed of his arrival could be explained in other ways. Such as, maybe he hadn't been responding to the police call at all, but rather to another, earlier, call. Such as one made by Lottie's real killers to their accomplice as they carried out their attack. Or even beforehand. Which better fitted the timeframe, giving longer for Mason to come racing heroically to the scene in order to apprehend the villain. The last thing they'd have wanted was for their patsy to escape before the cops arrived.

If that were so, then Mason was just as guilty of Lottie's murder as the man who'd run her through with the sabre.

As Ben reflected on that dark thought, a fresh possibility made his mind swirl and his flesh crawl with horror. Had they killed her simply as a way to get to him? Why? Who were these people? What had he done to them?

He closed his eyes and pictured the two men who'd fled the murder scene. Both white, both around the same age, somewhere between thirty and forty, both with reddish hair. The one at the wheel of the Mustang wore his long and tied back. His passenger, the one who'd done the killing, was more nondescript-looking in a dark jacket and white T.

Even though he'd caught barely a glimpse of their faces Ben was certain he'd never seen either man before. Was it possible that this was connected to the altercation at Dumpy's Rods? The pair hadn't been among the gang, but perhaps they were friends of Dwayne Skinner, and this was their vicious reprisal. It was a small community. Everybody knew everyone else. If Dwayne remembered Lottie from school-days, he might know about her guesthouse in Chitimacha.

But a reprisal for what? Nothing had happened. Ben had walked away without a fight. In their eyes, the gang were the victors. Besides which, a redneck nobody like Dwayne wouldn't have had the brains to come up with a plan to frame Ben for Lottie's killing, let alone the weight of influence to make an obedient henchman of a deputy sheriff. Forget Dwayne. He was no more a part of this than old Elmo Gillis.

Then Ben remembered Lottie's cryptic last words. As he replayed them in his mind he felt an icy prickle down his back.

I knowed it was comin', Ben. They was bound to get me in the end.

She'd been carrying a secret for most of her life. A secret dating back to some point in history, according to her mother. One that involved the death of an unknown woman called Peggy Iron Bar, at the hands of unknown killers, a long time ago. Somehow, Lottie was tied up with it.

And somehow now Ben was tied up with it too.

He lay there for a long time, watching the red dawn light slowly creep across the floor of his little tree root cavern. And thinking. And when he'd thought about it long enough, he knew that the only way he was going to clear his name and get out of this mess was to find out the truth about her secret.

The truth would lead him to the men who had murdered her. Justice would be done. One way or another.

The law's way, or Ben's way.

106

Chapter 18

It was another couple of hours before Ben finally emerged from his hiding place. The forest was thick and wild and seemed to go on for ever. To most ordinary folks it would have seemed like the most hostile territory imaginable, filled with countless dangers real and imagined, a trap from which few might emerge alive. To a man like Ben Hope, trained to go to ground like an animal, to eat raw things that he'd hunted and fished with his bare hands, to slip through the harshest wilderness without leaving a trace of his passing, it was as familiar and homely an element as his own back yard.

But that was under normal circumstances, when he was healthy and alert and equipped to deal with the conditions. Alone, unarmed and hurt, with the whole of the Louisiana police probably after him by now, he was in a poor state to survive long on the run and he knew it.

Just survive, he kept telling himself. He picked his way through the forest a hundred yards at a time, fixing his eyes on a tree or a clump of ferns and not letting himself pause for breath until he'd reached it. Then a hundred dwindled down to fifty, and fifty shrank to twenty, and he was becoming so weak he could barely walk any more. He needed water and food and would soon collapse if he didn't find them.

Gradually, the terrain began to slope downwards making his progress a little easier. As he paused to rest against a mossy fallen trunk, he could hear the trickle of running water from further down the hillside, a wonderfully welcome sound that fired up his spirits and spurred him on. Getting closer, he caught sight of the sparkling water through the trees. Not some stagnant pond of a bayou but an actual flowing river, wide and clear and clean and beautiful.

The vegetation was thick almost all the way to the bank. Ben was heading for the water when he suddenly stopped and froze.

The boy was perhaps thirteen or fourteen. He was fishing twenty yards upriver, positioned among the rushes by the water's edge against a verdant backdrop from overarching cypress trees. Most people wouldn't have noticed him at all until they were right on top of him, because his outline was broken up by the military camouflage jacket and trousers he was wearing. Ben recognised them as an old pattern of US Army woodland battledress uniform, a couple of sizes too big and rumpled and baggy on his skinny frame but still effective at disguising him against the foliage. He was facing the water with his back to Ben, gazing into the fast-moving current and oblivious of the fact that he was being watched. He'd rolled up the bottoms of his trouser legs so he could wade out into the water without getting them wet. The line of the fishing rod that he clenched tightly in both hands was taut as he struggled to land whatever it was that he'd snagged. Obviously something large and determined, judging by the fight it was putting up.

Dressed like a young soldier he might have been, but he was a lot easier to sneak up on, even by an injured man close to collapse. Ben slipped through the bushes parallel to the bank, then stepped out into the open and approached silently from the rear. His head was spinning as though he had dengue fever, and he had to keep blinking to fight back the faintness. The boy's backpack lay on the ground a few yards from the water's edge. It was unzipped, and Ben could see a two-litre Pepsi bottle and a big bar of chocolate nestling inside with its silver wrapper already torn open and a few squares missing.

The other equipment the boy had brought with him, other than rod and line, was a hunting bow. It was a modern compound weapon, all aluminium and cables and eccentric pulleys, mounted with a quiver full of razor-tipped arrows. Maybe the boy was thinking of bringing home a wild turkey or a jackrabbit for the dinner table if the fishing didn't go so well. Or perhaps the bow was intended for self-defence against roving black bears. Either way it was a fine weapon for a youthful apprentice hunter, who should have known better than to leave it lying unguarded in the dirt. You never knew what kind of unwholesome characters might be lurking in the woods with malicious intent.

The boy had no idea that he had company, and was too preoccupied with his catch to turn around. Without a sound Ben set down his own bag and then slipped the Pepsi bottle from the boy's pack. He gulped some down, then broke a row of squares off the end of the chocolate bar and ate them. The sugar rush was instant.

The boy still had his back to him. It looked as though he was going to lose his fish, making him lose his temper and yell, 'Come on, you bitch! Come on!'

He was a good-looking kid, with strong features and an unruly mop of blond hair that he had to keep flicking out of his eyes. He reminded Ben of photos of Jude when he'd been younger. That brought a pang of regret, thinking of all the years they'd missed.

It was then that Ben spotted the second boy. This one was no more than a child, perhaps five or six. Ben was no judge of children's ages. While the older boy was fair-haired and white, this one was clearly of mixed race, with afro hair and skin the colour of dark caramel. He had been playing on his own among some rocks by the water's edge and now came over to join in the fun and yell encouragement as his companion struggled to land his fish. The age difference between the pair made them seem unlikely friends. Ben wondered why they weren't in school.

As he munched another chunk of chocolate he felt bad about stealing their supplies. Hurt or not, it was wrong to rob kids. He ought to trade them something in return, the obvious being money. His wallet was still full of all the US currency he'd got at the airport. He pulled out twenty bucks and slipped the cash into the backpack.

The two kids might spot him at any moment and he was afraid that they might freak out at his appearance and run off to report him. He decided to slip away unnoticed and return to the river once they were gone, so he could drink his fill and clean himself up better.

He was reaching for his bag and getting ready to make his silent retreat into the bushes when the movement among the riverbank rushes caught his eye. Something greyish brown and black, long and sinuous and as thick as a child's arm was winding its way through the grass towards the older boy's left leg. It had a triangular head and faint striations across its back. Some kind of pit viper.

Ben instantly knew the kid was in trouble. He was hopping about so much in his battle to land his catch that he must have disturbed the snake and now was too distracted to notice it slithering purposefully towards him.

Without thinking twice, Ben snatched up the bow. Like

lightning he plucked one of the carbon fibre hunting shafts from the on-board quiver and fitted it on the arrow rest and nocked its end onto the bowstring and raised it to fire. The weapon felt as heavy as a tree in his weakened state, and it took all his strength to draw. His aim was wavering badly. The tip of the arrow was tracing a circle in the air the size of a doughnut. He blinked and clenched his teeth and willed himself to hold it steady.

The snake was curling closer to the boy's leg. As it came within striking distance it suddenly whipped itself into a coil and reared its head off the ground, a forked black tongue flicking in and out of its mouth.

At that moment, the younger child turned and spotted Ben and let out a shrill cry of alarm. The older boy whirled round. He dropped his fishing rod with a splash into the water and stared boggle-eyed at the strange man who'd seemed to appear out of nowhere and was standing there swaying on his feet with filthy jeans and no shirt and a leather jacket over his bare shoulders and a taped field dressing covering half his torso. And the loaded, drawn compound bow in his hands.

And then the snake gathered its momentum and lashed out with jaws distended, so fast it moved in a blur.

Chapter 19

But Ben's arrow moved even faster. As he released the shot it hissed through the air towards its mark. The younger boy screamed like a piglet. Thinking he was about to get skewered by his own arrow the older boy stumbled backwards in a panic, tripped in the long grass and fell.

The arrow pierced the snake just behind its head and dashed it violently to the ground where it thrashed and convulsed for a moment and then lay as limp as a rope. The younger boy was still yowling in a total panic as Ben lowered the bow and hurried towards his fallen companion.

The teenager was lying motionless in the long grass. Ben dropped the bow and crouched beside him. Where the hem of his left trouser leg was rolled up to expose a couple of inches of pale flesh, Ben saw the two little puncture marks from the snake's fangs and his heart fell. He'd fired just a fraction too late. If his aim hadn't been so damn wobbly and his arms so pathetically feeble he couldn't even hold a bow straight, he might have saved the kid from being bitten.

The boy wasn't moving. For a couple of moments, Ben thought he was dead. But nobody died instantly from a snakebite. Ben realised he'd knocked himself out when he fell. There was blood on his temple where his head had hit a rock in the grass.

The little boy was bawling. He shied away in fear as Ben reached for his arm. 'I'm not going to hurt you,' Ben said. 'What's your name?'

The little boy blinked through his tears and managed to control his voice enough to reply, 'Noah Hebert.'

'Noah, your friend here is in a bad way. He needs to get to a hospital.'

The little boy blinked again. His panic was settling down to raw terror, still ready to bolt but too brave to abandon his companion. 'Caleb ain't my friend, he's my brother.' He wiped his eyes and swivelled towards the rise of the forest, pointing. 'We live right up there. Momma, she knows what to do. She can fix anythin'.' He looked quizzically at Ben, eyes round and full of anxiety. 'Who are you, mister?'

'Never mind who I am,' Ben said. 'Is your momma home right now?' The kid nodded gravely and replied 'Yes, sir.' Ben said, 'Okay, Noah, then you run on and show me the way. Let's get Caleb home as fast as we can.'

Little Noah hesitated, then took off and went bounding through the long grass like a gazelle. Ben felt so faint he thought he was going to collapse. He scooped up Caleb's limp body, struggled to his feet and followed.

A dirt path half-hidden among the tangled grasses and bushes led a twisting route up the slope and through the trees. Caleb couldn't weigh more than a hundred pounds but Ben's legs were buckling under him. The pain in his belly was excruciating. He was certain he must have ripped open his wound and got it bleeding again. He had to keep calling to Noah to slow down, scared that he'd lose sight of the little shape darting through the forest ahead. More than anything, he was afraid that the rising blackness that kept threatening to cloud his vision would make him pass out and he'd fall and hurt the kid, or that they'd go tumbling back down the slope to where more snakes might be crawling near the river's edge, or that the kid would die because he hadn't got him home to his mother fast enough.

Momma knows what to do. Ben could only pray that was the case. She must have an antivenom kit, which made sense living out here in the back of beyond where doctors could be hours away and many roads were probably impassable by ambulance.

The dirt track wound up and up through the woods for at least half a mile. By the time the little homestead came into sight, Ben was beginning to doubt he'd get there. The Hebert family home occupied a natural clearing almost completely encircled by trees. There was a tiny wooden house with a wraparound porch under a rusty tin roof, and a dilapidated barn, and various coops and sheds and lean-tos, all clustered around a beaten earth yard into which little Noah, sprinting for all he was worth, ran screaming at the top of his voice, 'Momma! Momma! Poppa! Caleb's bit! Caleb's bit!'

As Ben stumbled closer to the house with the weight of the boy sagging in his weary arms, a petite African-American woman in a bright yellow dress burst out of the screen door and onto the porch. It was unlikely that she was Caleb's mother, but she was certainly Noah's.

'Momma! Caleb's real bad!'

The woman stared at Ben, but all she could see was the limp form of her stepson. She let out a shriek and came bounding down the porch steps and across the yard to meet them. At the same time, hearing the commotion, a big white man with a grizzled beard appeared from the barn. He was wearing a greasy overall and still grasping the wrench that he must have been using to fix something when he'd heard all the yelling. 'What's happenin'? What's happenin'?'

The woman reached Ben first. She burst into tears and gripped the boy's hand in both of hers so tightly that the tendons stood out on her delicate wrists. 'Oh, my Lord!' Then, seeing Ben apparently for the first time, she recoiled from him, still clutching her son's hand. 'Who in the hell are you?'

'Matt Cole,' Ben managed to gasp. Fighting for breath wasn't a normal thing for a man who habitually ran ten miles and ticked off a thousand press-ups most days, but the trek from the river had almost killed him. 'They were fishing. Your boy disturbed a snake.'

'The creek's crawlin' with cottonmouths,' said the big white guy with the grizzled beard, whom Ben took to be the boys' father. 'I'm always tellin' them to be careful down there.'

'He kilt the snake, Momma,' little Noah said, tugging at her sleeve and pointing at Ben. 'Kilt it with Caleb's bow.'

'That right, mister?' the boys' father asked.

'Too late. He's bitten on the left calf.'

Ben laid the boy down on the porch as they all gathered anxiously around. Caleb was regaining consciousness after his knock to the head, and kept woozily muttering that he was okay. 'You hold still, baby,' the woman told him. Her tears were gone and she exuded an air of calm and control that made Ben think she must do this kind of thing for a living.

Her husband said, 'I'll get the medicine, Keisha.' He disappeared into the house. While he was gone, his wife closely examined Caleb's leg. She asked Ben, 'How long ago was he bitten?'

'Fifteen, twenty minutes,' Ben said.

She felt the boy's pulse and asked him a lot of questions about how he was feeling, to which he kept repeating, 'I'm okay. I'm really okay.' His father returned then, clutching a vial and a syringe.

'I don't wanna give the antivenom unless he needs it,' she said. 'There's a risk of anaphylaxis.'

'You sayin' he doesn't need it?' her husband asked anxiously.

'Shoulda been all swelled up by now. Look at these marks. Hardly broke the skin. His pulse is fine. Looks to me like a dry bite.'

Ben had done all his snakebite training with the SAS in jungles on the far side of the world when Keisha Hebert probably hadn't been much older than her stepson, but he still remembered. A dry bite was when the reptile had failed to inject its venom load into its would-be victim. Which was the luckiest day of that would-be victim's life, whether human or animal. In Caleb's case, the snake's fangs had only just grazed the surface before Ben's arrow had done its work.

'Thank God,' Keisha said, clutching her boy and kissing him. 'And thanks to you, Mister . . . Cole, was it? You hadn't done what you done, he'd have got poisoned for sure.' Her eyes narrowed and she peered more closely at Ben. 'Do I know you? Sure I seen you before someplace.'

'I don't think so,' Ben said. Maybe time to get out of here, he thought.

Her narrowed eyes lingered a moment longer on his face, then she lowered her gaze and frowned as she saw the improvised dressing through the open front of his jacket. 'Looks like you're hurt pretty bad yourself there.'

'I was in a car accident, back down the road,' he said, trying to sound all casual about it. 'It's nothing too serious.'

She shook her head. 'Did you patch yourself up? You ought to see a doctor.'

Now her husband was eyeing Ben too. He came a step closer. 'Where you from, Mister, ah—?'

'Cole,' Ben repeated.

116

'You sure do talk funny.'

'I get that a lot.' Ben didn't much like the way the guy was staring at him. Definitely time to get out of here.

'Be right back,' the guy said, and stepped into the house.

'I should be on my way,' Ben told Keisha. 'I'm glad the boy's all right.'

'I could check out that injury for you, if you want. You don't look well.'

'It's nothing,' Ben said. 'I'll be fine.'

Except that he wouldn't be fine. Not by a long shot. The wooziness was worsening. A curtain of darkness seemed to be rising up from the bottom of his vision. His legs no longer felt as if they belonged to him. He reached out to steady himself against the porch railing.

The boys' father re-emerged from the house. This time, what he'd fetched from inside wasn't medicine. It was a pump-action shotgun and he was pointing it at Ben. He racked the pump. *Crunch-crunch.* The most intimidating mechanical sound known to man. Especially when looking down the wrong end of the barrel.

The man said, 'One more chance, podnuh. And no more bullshit. Your name ain't Cole and I want to hear it from your own lips.'

Ben said nothing.

'Reckon that's all the answer I need,' the man said.

Alarmed by the sight of the gun, Keisha asked, 'What is it, Ty?'

Her husband said, 'This here fella's got every cop in the state lookin' for him. They say he murdered a woman.'

Keisha covered her mouth with her hand and stared at Ben in sudden recognition. 'That's where I know you from. You're *him*. Your face is all over the TV.'

Little Noah pressed himself to his mother's side. Caleb

was looking at Ben open-mouthed. Keisha backed away a step.

But Ty stayed right where he was.

The muzzle of the shotgun was just a couple of feet away from Ben's face. Under normal circumstances he could have snatched it out of the guy's hands and turned his own weapon on him before he even knew it was happening. But these weren't normal circumstances. Their voices sounded echoey and faraway in his ears. His vision was darkening. He was battling hard to remain conscious and on his feet. But losing. Losing badly.

He stumbled back a step and raised his arms to show he was no threat. Which he truly wasn't, and couldn't have been to anyone at that moment. He mumbled, 'I didn't do it.'

That was when the nausea finally overwhelmed him and the inky veil closed over him. He felt himself sinking to his knees.

Then the wood slats of the porch came up to meet him and—

THWACK

Chapter 20

Ben woke up with a start. He was confused and disorientated for a moment as he became aware of his surroundings.

He was lying on his back in a warm, comfortable bed. Diffused sunlight was shining in through the net curtain draped across the window of the tiny bedroom. The walls were wood panelling painted a cheery yellow. The sheets on the bed smelled pleasantly of lavender and the pillow was soft and plumped up beneath his head.

The nausea and dizziness had left him. The pain below his ribs was just a dull ache, which became acutely sharper as he tried to sit up in bed. The covers fell away from his chest and he saw he'd been stripped down to his boxer shorts and all bandaged up with clean white dressings neatly wrapped around his middle. On a wooden chair nearby lay a small pile of freshly-laundered clothing, folded and stacked. There was a bowl of fruit and a glass of water on the bedside cabinet.

All of which seemed to him very strange, because the last thing he could remember before he'd blacked out was a gun pointing in his face and two very scared and hostile people staring at him. Something was definitely different.

As Ben was contemplating the mysterious change in his circumstances, the bedroom door opened and the father of

Caleb and Noah Hebert walked in. He'd changed out of his greasy work overalls and was no longer clutching a shotgun, which Ben took as a further sign of progress although he was baffled as to why.

'Welcome back to the land of the livin', friend,' Ty said with a smile as he perched himself on the edge of the bed. The springs creaked and groaned under his weight.

'How long have I been lying here?' Ben asked him.

'Just over twenty-two hours.'

Ben realised that meant he'd missed the Woody McCoy gig. Not that he could easily have attended, under the circumstances. But it was a dark thought nonetheless. He sighed.

'How you feelin'?' the kids' father asked him.

'Better, apparently thanks to you. These bandages look pretty professional.'

'That'd be my wife's work, not mine. I couldn't put a Band-Aid on a cut finger. She cleaned and stitched you up, pumped you full of antibiotics and painkillers, vitamins and a bunch of other stuff. You'll live, I reckon.'

'Keisha, your wife – is she a doctor?'

'A nurse. Of the veterinary variety, but I guess there ain't much difference between stitchin' up a mutt or stitchin' up a man.'

'I'd like to thank her.'

'You'll get your chance. She drove into town this mornin' to buy shoes for Noah. Be home in a little while.' He stuck out a thick, coarse hand. 'In the meantime, how 'bout you and I start over and introduce ourselves? I'm Tyler Hebert. And you're that Ben Hope fella everyone's talkin' about. Right?'

Ben reached out, a little stiffly, and shook hands. 'Seems little point in denying it any more, doesn't there?'

'Damn right. And ain't you lucky it was us that found you. Lotta folks around here would just blow your damn head off and call the cops, in that order. Clovis Parish is kinda jumpy right now, after what happened to that poor woman. I mean, murder's nothin' new in these parts. This state's got the highest rate of it in America. But holy shit, a *sabre*? That's screwed up, even by our lousy standards. Right now you got every lawman in Louisiana huntin' your ass, headed up by our very own beloved Sheriff Roque. I'll bet there's even a nice reward on offer for anyone turns you in, too. Lot of folks round here sure could use the money. Me included.'

'I told you,' Ben said, 'I didn't do it. You have to believe me.'

Tyler pursed his lips. 'And believe me, neither Keisha nor I would never knowingly take a killer into our home, still less offer him comfort. We had ourselves a long talk while you were sleepin'. The two of us came to the same conclusion, for three reasons. So if you're here it's because we trust you. If it turns out we're wrong about that, then God help us, and God help you too. 'Cause whoever murdered that poor woman is goin' straight to hell, law or no law.'

'I appreciate the trust,' Ben said. 'And I'm grateful for your hospitality. I wouldn't mind knowing the three reasons, as well.'

'I don't mind tellin' you. Firstly, it seems to both of us a mite strange how a man plain wicked enough to do what the TV says you done to that poor soul would go out of his way to help a fellow human in danger, the way you saved my boy from that ol' cottonmouth and damn near killed yourself bringin' him home to us.'

'I did what anyone would have done,' Ben said.

'Not just anyone,' Tyler said. 'That was truly a Christian

act, for which I gotta thank you from the bottom of my heart. By the way, where in hell did y'all learn to shoot like that? Those critters move like a scalded haint when they strike. I never knew no one could hit one with an arrow. And I'm bettin' they don't teach bowhuntin' in the British Army.'

'Sounds like you've been following the local media, all right.'

'Me, plus every other trigger-happy hound dog who'd be fixin' to blow your Limey brains out soon as look at you. Gettin' yourself plastered all over the news is the kind of attention that's gonna get you killed.'

'How reassuring. What's the second reason?'

'Keisha. She has the gift.'

'The gift?'

'Meanin', she knows things about people. Second sight, extra-sensory perception, clairvoyance, call it what you like. She can see through folks like they were made of glass. I can't explain it, and neither can she. She's had that ability since she was a child. If she says there's no evil in you, then I have to believe her. It's that simple.'

Ben had to smile. 'What's the third reason?'

'That one's personal to me,' Tyler said. 'You might've noticed that Caleb ain't Keisha's natural born son, even though she loves him like her own.'

'As it happens, I did notice.'

'I'm real proud of my elder boy,' Tyler said. 'Lord knows, he didn't get his finer qualities from me. He takes after his mother, Grace. My first wife.' He heaved a sigh and clasped his hands in front of him. 'May God rest her in peace.'

'I'm sorry to hear she passed away.'

'Passed away one way of puttin' it,' Tyler said, a glint of anger coming into his eye. 'Another way of puttin' it might be that she got shot to death by Sheriff Roque and two of his punk deputies. Happened seven years ago, on Caleb's seventh birthday. I will never forgive that man for takin' my dear wife away from me. Which is my third reason for not turnin' you in to that sumbitch. If you was guilty, I'd sooner shoot you myself than let him take the credit.'

Ben stared at him. 'They shot your wife?'

Tyler gave another sorrowful sigh, and told the story.

'She wasn't the first or the only innocent soul to die that day. Roque's goons started the show by blowin' away an unarmed man on the streets of Villeneuve. That's where we lived back then. This fella named Gage McGary, worked at the sawmill over in Clermont, happened to bear a passin' resemblance to this other fella named Ethan Brister who was wanted for armed robbery. So on this particular day, eighth of August 2011, McGary's comin' out of the grocery store where's he been spendin' his hard-earned pay on food for his family, when up come Roque and his deputies and start a'yellin' and a'hollerin' at him, *"Ethan Brister, put your damn hands in the air and get down on your knees or we're gonna shoot."* Naturally the poor guy has no idea what's happenin'. Goes to take out his ID to show them he's Gage McGary instead of this Brister character they think he is. All three of 'em opened fire and gunned him down like a rabid dog right there on the sidewalk in front of the grocery store. Which would've been one thing, but that mother Roque was in such a rush to draw out that forty-five of his that his first shot went wide of McGary by about a country mile and straight through the store window. My darlin' Gracie was inside gettin' ingredients for a cake she was fixin' to bake for Caleb's birthday. Slug got her right here in the neck.'

Tyler poked a gnarled finger into the bush of his beard, below the jaw line.

'I was a lawyer back in them days. Bet that surprises you, huh? Anyhow, I was workin' in my office right up the street at the time and heard the shots. Someone comes runnin' to say Grace's hurt. I got there before the ambulance did. She died in my arms.'

Ben could think of nothing to say, except to repeat, 'I'm sorry.'

'Yup, me too. But that's more than I ever got from that piece of trash Roque. Weren't nobody's fault, is all the Sheriff's Office ever offered me in return for what happened. Collateral damage. Wrong place, wrong time. Just one of them things. Shit happens.'

Tyler paused and lowered his head, eyes closed, and Ben could see moisture on his lashes. After a moment Tyler collected himself and went on, 'Then it was just me and Caleb. You ever had to explain to a seven-year-old kid how his momma ain't comin' home, ever again?'

'No,' Ben said. 'I can't even imagine what I'd have said to him.'

'So, long story short, I got better reason than most folks not to trust Waylon Roque, and to know that what passes for justice in these parts don't amount to a hill of beans.'

'I get the message,' Ben said.

'So tell me somethin', podnuh. If you didn't do this terrible, heinous thing, then who the hell did?'

'That's what I'd very much like to find out,' Ben said.

Tyler had told his story; now it was Ben's turn to tell his. He laid the whole thing out: the reason he was in Louisiana in the first place, the liquor store episode and how he'd come to stay at Lottie's guesthouse; the drive out to Pointe Blanche, the dinner, the attack, the two men who'd escaped in the black Mustang, and what had happened afterwards.

By the time he'd finished his account Tyler's mouth was

hanging open and a deep frown was contorting his bushy eyebrows.

'That beats it all. Mason Redbone is one of the sorriest sons of bitches who ever disgraced a lawman's uniform in the state of Louisiana. That's a given. But to try to rub out an innocent witness, in cold blood? Why the hell would he do such a thing?'

'Another good question,' Ben said. 'For now, I have no idea what this is about. Except that I'm caught up in the middle of it, and my only way out of this situation is to discover the answers for myself.'

Tyler reflected for a moment. 'I'm thinkin' about the fellas in the Mustang. Like I said, I was a lawyer, once upon a time. Criminal defence attorney, in point of fact. Not a bad one, either, until my life got turned upside down and I finally learned some sense. For my sins, I must've represented every worthless sack of shit redneck delinquent for five hundred miles. I know 'em all. You mentioned Billy Bob Lafleur? What a beauty, that one. Anyhow, if you could describe these two assholes, maybe we could put names to the faces.'

'I didn't get a good enough look to offer much of a description, beyond the basics,' Ben said. 'Clothing, haircuts, nothing definitive. But I'd know them if I saw them again. Which I will, soon enough. And they'll know me.'

Tyler looked at him. 'Hold on a minute. It's one thing to try and figure out who done this and clear your name. It's a whole other thing to actually go huntin' for these dangerous sumbitches, if that's what you're sayin' you plan on.'

'I was in Special Forces for a long time,' Ben said. 'Hunting dangerous sons of bitches was what we did. They soon learned.'

'Learned what?'

'That there's always someone out there who's more dangerous, more skilled and more determined than you. Someone else is about to find out the same lesson. The hard way.'

Chapter 21

A short while later Ben smelled food and decided that twenty-two hours in bed was long enough, stab wound or no stab wound. He was still a little stiff as he got up, but thanks to whatever variety of canine or equine painkillers Keisha had been dosing him with he could move around and dress himself without too much difficulty. Sifting through the neat pile of clothing on the chair next to his bed he found that the spare jeans and socks he'd been carrying in his bag had been freshly laundered for him, in addition to which he'd been left a lightweight check shirt that must once have belonged to a much thinner and younger Tyler. It fitted almost perfectly.

Ben made his way from the little bedroom to an even tinier kitchen down the hall, where Tyler was banging pots and pans about and warming something delicious-smelling for lunch on a battered old stove. He turned as Ben walked inside the kitchen. 'Hungry? I'll bet you are. Come and sit yourself down, get some of this stew down your gizzard.'

Keisha and Noah hadn't yet returned from their morning shoe-buying expedition. Caleb was sitting at the kitchen table, buried in books and jotters, scribbling busily. He had a big wadded dressing on the side of his head where he'd hit himself, but seemed otherwise healthy enough. He paused to look up at Ben with a smile. 'I never thanked you, mister, for what you did.'

'Call me Ben. And I'm the one who should be thanking this family for taking me in.' He peered at the jotter Caleb was writing in. 'Yuk. Algebra?'

'Caleb's homeschooled,' Tyler explained from the stove as he ladled some stew into a bowl. 'That's kind of my job, apart from tendin' to this place, while Keisha's out earnin' the money. He's way ahead of his age for maths and English. Gonna be a scientist when he grows up. Ain't you, son?'

Caleb shrugged. 'Sure, maybe.'

Ben said, 'Good for you.' He sat beside Caleb at the table and gazed out of the window. The sun was bright outside. An array of solar panels attached to the barn roof glittered under its rays. Beyond the barn, he could see pigs milling about a fenced paddock. The kitchen walls, floor and ceiling were bare plywood.

He asked Tyler, 'Did you build this house yourself?'

'Hell, I built the whole place myself,' Tyler said proudly. 'Off grid, off the beaten track, deep in country where folks leave us alone and we leave them alone. That's the way we like to live, though it ain't for everyone. It's the best place to prepare for what's comin'.'

'What is coming?' Ben asked.

Tyler stuck a fork and spoon into the bowl of steaming hot stew and carried it to the table. 'Oh, you know, the second US civil war,' he said nonchalantly. 'Been brewin' for a long while and ready to kick off pretty soon, I reckon. Not to mention a thousand other ways the shit could hit the fan at any time. You gotta be ready for all eventualities.'

He set the bowl down in front of Ben. 'There you go, English. Our own chicken, with our own peppers, celery and chillies. Seein' as I do most of the cookin' around here, I call it "Gumbo à la Hebert". Bon appétit.'

Tyler's stew wasn't quite on a par with Lottie Landreneau's fare, but Ben could have eaten a hog with the hooves and tusks still attached.

'Well now, that's better, ain't it?' Tyler said as he watched his guest dig in.

As Ben was finishing up, there was the sound of a car outside. 'That'll be Keisha back from town,' Tyler said. 'Want to say hello?'

'More than hello,' Ben said.

He got up from the table and followed Tyler out of the kitchen and down a plywood passage to the main living area, where the front entrance was. He'd been unconscious last time he'd been through here. Seeing it for the first time, he was struck by the sight of the large Confederate battle flag on the wall. Two diagonally-crossed blue stripes over a red background, with an arrangement of thirteen white stars forming an X in the middle. The symbol of Dixieland. The classic emblem of Southern rebellion, whose significance in modern times went beyond its historical importance.

Tyler noticed him looking at it, and seemed about to say something when the front door opened and Keisha came in, carrying shopping bags and accompanied by young Noah, beaming as he showed off his shiny new sandals, and a little girl who was just a toddler.

Keisha smiled. 'This is Trinity. Trinity, say hello to our visitor. This is the gentleman who saved your brother.'

Trinity gave Ben a shy wave.

'Kids, you go on and play now. Momma will be with you in a minute.' Keisha ushered them from the room, then turned back to Ben. 'Well, it's good to see you back on your feet.'

Ben shook her hand and thanked her for her kindness. She brushed it off as though it were nothing.

'Please believe me, I didn't hurt anyone,' Ben said. 'I wouldn't have harmed Lottie Landreneau in a thousand years.'

'I know that,' Keisha said.

'You can't know that. I need to make you understand.'

'No,' she said firmly. 'I do know. You're welcome in our home, Mister Hope.'

'I'll be moving on as soon as I can.'

'If you must. But you're safe here for the moment.'

The kitchen was too small to seat six people for lunch, so they gathered at the living room table. Ben gladly accepted a second bowl of chicken stew, but before they could begin the family all linked hands around the table, inviting their guest to join in. Keisha turned to her daughter with a warm smile and said, 'Trinity, it's your turn to say Grace.'

The little girl screwed her eyes tight shut, and prayed out loud,

> *Thank you for the food we eat*
> *Thank you for the world so sweet*
> *Thank you for the birds that sing*
> *Thank you God for everything*

'Amen to that,' Tyler said.

Her mother touched her arm. 'That was beautiful, Trinity.'

Ben couldn't believe the kindness of the Heberts in accepting him into their home under such circumstances. Nor could he remember the last time he'd felt so moved by a prayer.

'You must be Church of England, right, Ben?' Keisha asked him as they began to eat.

'Was,' Ben said. 'Long time ago, in another life. One that I left behind for a lot of wrong reasons.'

'He ain't forgotten you,' Keisha said softly.

Startled by her words, Ben paused with his heaped fork in mid-air and looked at her. 'That's amazing. Lottie Landreneau said the exact same thing to me.'

Keisha just smiled in reply. Ben went back to eating, feeling quite shaken up. How could Keisha have known?

'I noticed you starin' at the flag earlier,' Tyler said, pointing up at the wall on which it hung. 'You got a problem with the Stainless Banner?'

'No problem,' Ben said, caught off-balance by his question. 'I was just thinking—'

'That it's strange how a white guy married to a woman of colour has a Dixie flag pinned to his wall? I'm proud of my Southern roots, Ben. That don't make me no racist redneck.'

'We shouldn't talk about such things at mealtime,' Keisha said.

'Why can't we talk about it?' Tyler replied.

'I didn't think you were a racist redneck,' Ben protested, glancing around the table at the three obvious examples to support his point of view.

'Hell, son, I wouldn't blame you if you did. The way liberals go on these days, fixin' to ban it as a hate symbol, you'd think it was a goddamn Nazi swastika and we Southerners was all runnin' around in freakin' Ku Klux Klan robes, burnin' crosses and lynchin' folks.'

'No cussin',' Keisha sharply scolded her husband. Noah and Trinity both cupped their hands over their mouths and giggled. Caleb just went on eating as though he'd heard it all a thousand times before.

'You really think there'll be another civil war in America?' Ben asked him, genuinely curious.

Tyler nodded gravely. 'I do, that.'

'Why?'

'Why? Same reasons as the breakaway states seceded from the Union first time round. A tyrannical government that's hell-bent on takin' away our liberty and steppin' on our rights.'

'I thought the North and South went to war over slavery,' Ben said. 'The South wanted to hold on to it while the North wanted to stop it. That's what the history books say, isn't it?'

'Sure they do,' Tyler agreed. 'Just like all the other packs of lies that're printed in half the history books.' He set down his fork and pointed again at the flag. 'Look. Let's get this one thing straight. The Confederacy never stood for any kind of racist ideology, and that there flag never symbolised white supremacy or any such thing, except maybe in the dumbass minds of a few morons.'

'I said, no cussin'!' Keisha repeated irritably. The younger kids were loving this conversation.

'Sorry, darlin'. It don't matter how these liberal historians nowadays might like to twist it. To claim that the war was fought over slavery is about the same as sayin' that we sent the troops into Iraq over weapons of mass destruction. In other words, a big damn lie. You were a soldier. You understand how it works, right?'

'I've been involved in enough conflicts around the world to know that we often fight wars for reasons that are never openly revealed to the public,' Ben conceded.

'Were you really a soldier?' Caleb asked, lighting up with excitement. 'Did you kill folks?'

'Shush, now,' Keisha told him, in her firm but warm manner.

Tyler stuffed a heap of stew into his mouth and chewed

loudly as he went on, 'My point exactly. In fact, a lot of folks in the South don't even call it "the Civil War". They call it what it really was, "the War of Northern Aggression". A conflict of old agrarian ways that were the tradition of the South, and the ruthless machine of industrialisation that was risin' up in the North. The creation of an empire that was all about subjugatin' its neighbours purely for control and gain. Just like it is today.'

Ben could see that his host was deeply passionate about his subject. 'Hold on, though, Tyler. You can't deny that the agrarian economy of the South was heavily based on slavery. Lincoln ended that with the Emancipation Proclamation.'

The moment he'd said it, he realised he'd touched a raw nerve by daring to mention Abraham Lincoln's name to a proud rebel patriot.

Tyler threw back his head and roared a scornful laugh. 'Now you're talkin' about the biggest PR scam in American history. Lincoln the liberator. Lincoln the friend of the oppressed blacks.' He snorted. 'Give me a break, okay? Abe Lincoln was no more of an abolitionist than his opposite number Jefferson Davis. Did he ever object to the slave states of Kentucky, Missouri, Delaware and Maryland fightin' on the side of the Union? No, sir, he did not. This is the cynical opportunist who said, "If I could save the Union without freein' any slave I would do it, and if I could save it by freein' all the slaves I would do it; and if I could save it by freein' some and leavin' others alone I would also do that."'

'I didn't know Lincoln said that,' Caleb said with his mouth full.

'Sure did. He also said black folks shouldn't have the same rights as us. Just like he was dead against blacks marryin' whites, and didn't want to let 'em vote either, unless they served in the Union army in which case, oh sure, step right aboard, welcome to the human race. That hypocritical sumbitch didn't even want the negroes in his own country. Believed white and black could not and must not live together on the same soil. Even as he was draftin' the so-called Emancipation Proclamation in 1862 he was pushin' for his own version of apartheid. Wanted to ship 'em all back to Africa, and when he realised that wasn't possible, talked about transportin' the whole bunch down to South America, just to get shot of 'em.'

Tyler shook his head in mock disbelief. 'Then to cap it all, what does the Emancipation Proclamation actually say? It doesn't free the slaves of the North, of which there were nearly half a million accordin' to the 1860 census. No sir, it specifically frees only the ones in what was rebel territory at that time. Effectively another nation, with its own government and president. Lincoln had no jurisdiction there. It was empty words, and he knew it. He only said it hopin' it'd encourage slaves in the South to run off to join up with the Union army. The whole thing was nothin' more than a sham.'

It was the first time Ben had ever heard any of this. He looked to Keisha, who just nodded and silently mouthed, 'It's true.'

Warming to his theme, Tyler went on, 'Anyhow, for an Englishman to look down his nose at the slavery tradition of the South is kinda rich, don't you think? What do you suppose the British Empire was built on? Who do you suppose was shippin' the poor suckers in by the million from Africa, and then shippin' 'em out from English ports to work in their colonies? Over two hundred ships in 1792 alone. That's way worse than even the damn French, who were tradin' human flesh into Louisiana for most of the eighteenth century. While native white Americans of the South, the ones who come in for all the crap, never brought in a single slave. Not one. They were already here when this land became ours. What were we supposed to do? It was like havin' a tiger by the tail, but we'd have gotten shot of slavery soon enough, left to our own devices. It was already in decline a decade before the war started. So put *that* in your mother truckin' history book.'

Keisha snapped, 'Enough of that, now. The past is the past. We ain't gonna change it with lectures. And Tyler Hebert, you speak one more cuss word in front of these innocent children and I'll beat you round the head with that saucepan, you hear me? Not to mention how rude you're bein' to our guest.'

The innocent children were having a hard time stifling fits of giggles. Noah choked so hard that some chicken stew came out through his nose. As for the guest, Ben had listened quietly to Tyler's diatribe and now sat back in his chair, frowning to himself in thoughtful silence.

Tyler flushed scarlet, suitably remorseful. 'I'm sorry. I tend to get a mite carried away with myself at times. Kids, I don't want you repeatin' any of the bad words I said. And Ben, if I offended you I apologise.'

Ben said nothing for a few moments longer. Then he replied, 'No, you didn't offend me. You made me think about history. Especially the kind of history that stays hidden, gets forgotten. Like secrets that go back into the past, and nobody ever talks about.'

'Brother, you're losin' me there.'

'Lottie Landreneau had a secret,' Ben explained. 'She told me so the night she died. It had to do with things that happened a long time ago, right here in Clovis Parish.'

'What secret?' Keisha asked, shaking her head.

'She faded away before she could share it with me, but I

think she wanted to. It was as if she needed to tell someone, while she still could. As if it was a weight she'd been carrying around ever since she was a girl, when she was made to promise never to tell a living soul about it. Her mother told her that folks would hate them if they knew the truth. That people down here in the South don't forget history.'

'That's true enough,' Tyler said.

'Whatever it is, it goes way back. Perhaps to long before she was born. I don't know. But I think it's connected with . . . with what happened to her.' He chose his words carefully, not wanting to dwell over any of the gruesome details in front of the kids.

With perfect timing Caleb piped up: 'This is the lady that got all hacked up with the sabre, right? Pretty gross.'

Keisha silenced the teenager with a look that would have frightened away the cottonmouth. To Ben she said, 'If it's important, we should try to find out.'

Ben smiled. 'You mean, *I* should. This is my problem. You've done enough for me already without getting involved deeper.'

'You just try and stop us,' Keisha said. 'You involved us when you saved Caleb. That's how it's gonna be.' She turned to the kids. 'Caleb, Trinity, Noah, it's time for you to go and rest now. Off with you.'

The three of them left the table and ran from the room, laughing and shoving one another.

Now Tyler was the one with the thoughtful frown. 'The thing with the sabre, I mean, that's kind of a weird choice of murder weapon.'

'Especially when the killers have guns,' Ben said. 'And aren't afraid to use them.'

'What kind of sabre was it?'

'I'm not an expert. It was long and curved, and old. The

blade was slim, the hilt was bound with fish skin and gold wire, and the handguard was brass, with two curved bars one side, flat on the other.'

Tyler jumped up from his seat, went over to a bookcase and drew out a tatty large-format hardback that he carried back to the table, flipping pages as he went. It was an illustrated history book on the Civil War. Finding the picture he was looking for he laid it open in front of Ben. 'Did it look like this?'

They were looking at an old picture of a Confederate trooper, posing in a fancy photographer's studio of the early 1860s. The period black-and-white image had been somewhat garishly recoloured as had been the fashionable practice in those times. He was a young man with a droopy moustache, doing all he could to look mean and tough in his grey uniform. He had a percussion revolver thrust through his waist sash and was holding a sabre as if he couldn't wait to get out there and take a swing at some Yankees with it.

'That's exactly the kind it was,' Ben said, recognising it instantly.

'1860 light cavalry sabre,' Tyler said. 'It was a replacement for the heavy 1840 model they called "Ol' Wristbreaker". Armourers hammered 'em out by the tens of thousands and they were carried by both sides in the war. Got to be a pricey collector's item now, the ones that didn't end up gettin' used to scythe wheat.'

Keisha leaned over to look at the picture, then drew away with a shudder. 'I can't imagine how horrible it'd be to have a sword stuck through you.'

'It's gotta mean somethin', though,' Tyler said. 'Why would they use one of these and not, say, a machete or a knife?'

'Lottie didn't say much,' Ben said. 'But she did come out with one thing. Her secret somehow involves a woman named Peggy Iron Bar. And I get the impression that she died the same way, a long time ago.'

'Killed with a sabre like this one?'

'She didn't exactly have time to describe it to me. But that was the impression I got.'

Keisha hugged herself as though she was cold. 'Sounds like bad, bad medicine to me.'

'Peggy Iron Bar. That's a mighty strange name,' Tyler said. 'You sure you heard right?'

'That's what she called her. Any idea who she could have been?'

Keisha shook her head. 'None, but I know someone who might have.' Turning to her husband she said, 'You thinkin' what I'm thinkin'?'

Tyler frowned. 'Sallie Mambo?'

'There ain't much old Sallie don't know about the history of Clovis Parish. I mean, she's been there for most of it. I reckon she might know who this Peggy was.'

'Is that old woman even still alive?' Tyler wondered.

'I hear she is,' Keisha said. 'Got to be close to a hundred years old, though. She seemed ancient when I met her, and that was more'n twenty-five years ago. Question is whether we'd get in to see her. Her people protect her like she's a queen.'

Ben said, 'Who are you talking about?'

Tyler replied, 'How'd you like to be taken to meet a real-life Louisiana witch?'

Chapter 22

The Heberts' nearest neighbours, half a mile away, were a kindly retired couple called Vernon and Ivy Tanner who adored Caleb, Noah and Trinity and were ever-willing to look after them for an afternoon or as long as needed. Once the kids were taken care of, Tyler and Keisha set off with Ben in Tyler's ancient Jeep Cherokee, which was falling apart but better suited to the trip than Keisha's runaround Mazda.

They were heading east, through near-empty tracts of sprawling country, in the direction of the Red River. Ben sat in the back while Keisha spent most of the long, hot, dusty drive turned around to face him and talking about Sallie Mambo.

As a girl, Keisha had been brought up with the old traditions of Louisiana folk magic and spiritualism, which she assured Ben were still very much alive today. When Keisha was eleven, her mother had taken her to a secretive late-night gathering deep in the heart of the forest. There, some forty or fifty devotees of the ancient practice had gathered to dance and perform sacred rituals and learn from the great wisdom of the old woman they revered as a Spirit Mother.

For the young Keisha it had been an enthralling and magical experience that she still remembered clearly. Its high point had been when Sallie Mambo, 'Mama' to her followers, had laid her hands on her and confirmed that the eleven-year-old did indeed possess 'the gift'. Keisha talked about Mama Mambo with heartfelt respect, almost awe.

'I thought Tyler said we were going to see a witch,' Ben said.

'Tyler was just kiddin'. Weren't you, Ty?' she added, with a menacing flash in her eye.

'Oh sure,' Tyler said, eyes front. 'Just kiddin'.'

'Sallie ain't no witch,' Keisha told Ben. 'In Vodou tradition "Mambo" means a Priestess. They're members of an ordained clergy, just the same as other religions.'

'*Vodou*,' Ben repeated. 'You mean Voodoo, as in goat blood sacrifice and conjuring up dark spirits.'

Keisha smiled. 'Forget what you think you know. Folks are afraid of the idea of Voodoo for the same reason they're afraid of most things they don't understand. Because it grew up as a slave religion in Africa and the Caribbean, it got all twisted into superstition by foolish white folks who were scared of a slave uprisin'. The priests got denounced as witch doctors and the gods and spirits were condemned as evil. That's just dumb and wrong. It has all kinds of parallels with Christianity. Like Aida Wedo, the equivalent of the Virgin Mary. And Legba, the guardian gatekeeper, who's a spittin' image of St Peter. Then you got Oshun, the goddess of love and creation. Loco, god of the plants an' forests. It ain't a cult, or black magic, or devil worship. Voodooists don't sit around stickin' pins in little dolls and puttin' curses on folks. Just like Christians, they believe there's a hidden world where we go after we die, and meet up again with our loved ones who passed before us. Like Buddhists and Hindus they believe in reincarnation and karma. If you lived your life doin' good and bein' kind to others, you'll be reborn in human form and get to start a new life cycle. But if you're bad and wicked, you might come back as a Diab, a demon whose only pleasure is to cause pain and sufferin' on the innocent.'

'Lot of Diabs goin' around these days, Tyler said.

According to Keisha, Sallie Mambo kept herself isolated from the sinful hubbub of modern civilisation. She lived in the forest, gathered herbs to eat and to prepare as medicine, communed with Loco and the other benign spirits and existed in a state of harmony with nature. As a high priestess, she was protected by a band of devoted followers who formed a tight ring around her and were picky about allowing visitors. A whole community had sprung up in the remote area she called home, whose job it was to keep her safe.

'Will they see us?' Ben asked. Privately he was wondering whether any of this was worth the effort. But if there was a chance that Sallie Mambo could shed light on the mystery of Peggy Iron Bar, it couldn't hurt to give it a try.

'I hope so,' Keisha said.

After an hour's journey along one winding backroad after another, Keisha went quiet as she watched for landmarks. 'You sure you remember the route?' Tyler said. 'It's been a while.'

'Trust me,' she said. Then a while later, 'Here. Turn off here.'

Tyler shrugged and pulled the truck off the narrow road onto a rough track. Now Ben could understand why they hadn't used Keisha's Mazda, as the Jeep bounced and lurched over ruts and rocks, shaking them all around inside. There was a lot of squeaking of suspension and something was clattering ominously from under the floor pan.

'Is this ol' beater of yours gonna hold together?' Keisha said to Tyler. 'It's an awful long walk back if it don't.'

'It'll hold together.'

141

Ben thought, *so much for the gift of prophecy*. The moment the doubt had come into his mind, he scolded himself for thinking negatively of his generous hosts. They were committing a felony and risking serious jail time by helping him like this. He knew he would soon have to part ways with them, if only for their own good.

The track led on and on, growing wilder and less passable with every mile. Tyler could handle the Jeep expertly, but even he seemed to balk at times when they had to negotiate massive knots of exposed tree roots that lay across their path, or had to squeeze under overhanging branches that raked the roof like giant claws trying to crush them. The forest was an eerie place, dark and forbidding. The trees were thick with creepers and drooping Spanish moss, some of their trunks so twisted and gnarled that it was easy to imagine them as looking like tortured spirits. The dense overhead canopy of foliage allowed only a shaft of sunlight through here and there, so that the bright afternoon turned into twilight.

Nobody spoke for a long time. Then Keisha announced, 'We should be gettin' close now.'

A prediction that came true minutes later when Tyler muttered, 'Uh-oh,' and brought the Jeep to a halt.

Ben had already spotted them: four dark figures that seemed to have materialised from the shadows of the forest as if out of nowhere. Just as suddenly, they were joined by four more. They stalked silently through the trees and encircled the Jeep.

'Y'all let me do the talkin', okay?' Keisha said.

The eight were all African-American. Tall, lean, gangly, men with gaunt features and intense eyes. Mama Mambo's personal guard of Voodoo devotees, though there was nothing particular about them to denote it. They weren't wearing weird robes or necklaces of shrunken heads, and hadn't chalked their faces to look like skulls to frighten away unwelcome visitors. Their means of intimidation was more direct and practical. Ben counted four twelve-gauge shotguns and four hunting rifles. The purposeful way they were clutching their weapons, they could have been a squad of irregular militia fighters. Ben found himself momentarily transported back to the jungle war zones of his past experience, and he felt a pang of vulnerability for not being armed.

The men surrounded the Jeep. Their weapons stayed pointed at the ground, but they were ready to be deployed if a threat should arise. One of the men stepped up to the driver's window. He took one hand off his rifle and made a circular motion for Tyler to wind it down, like a traffic cop who'd pulled someone over.

'Lost your way, folks?' the man said. He spoke in a rich bass voice. He wore a ragged baseball cap with the visor pulled low over his eyes and sleeveless vest that showed the glistening muscles of his arms and chest. The bolt-action Remington dangled loosely from his grip. He shot keen glances around the inside of the Jeep.

Keisha leaned across the centre console to talk to him through the open driver's window. 'We come to see Mama Mambo,' she said with a pleasant smile. 'On account of our friend here. He needs help.' She nodded in Ben's direction.

Eight pairs of suspicious eyes turned on Ben through the Jeep's dusty back windows. It was clear what they were all thinking.

'This cracka needs he'p, he go get it from his own people,' the man said in his rumbling bass. 'You folks done come to the wrong place. Now you gotta turn around and haul your asses back where you come from.'

'Please,' Keisha said. 'I'm askin'.'

The man shot another hostile look at Ben. 'What kinda he'p he lookin' for from Mama anyways?'

'He's in trouble.'

The man shook his head. 'We don't want no trouble here.'

'Come on, podnuh,' Tyler said. 'We come a long distance to see Mama Mambo. Don't be turnin' us away.'

The man shook his head again, more emphatically. 'Mama Mambo don't see nobody. 'Specially not no strangers.'

'I ain't no stranger,' Keisha insisted. 'I met her once. She spoke to me. Laid her hands on me. I was called Keisha Beverote then. I was just a girl, but I reckon she'd remember me.'

The man raised an eyebrow, as though he was not unimpressed, but remained suspicious and guarded. 'Mama don't see no one,' he repeated. 'She old.'

This was getting nowhere. Ben decided he might as well join the conversation. Carefully opening his door he stepped out of the Jeep. A couple of the armed men raised their weapons to point his way.

'Whoa,' he said, and raised his open palms to shoulder height to show he was no threat. He turned to address the leader. 'Listen to me. My friends here are putting themselves in harm's way by trying to help me. They're good people, and right now I'm in a situation where I can't do without good people. I came to ask Mama Mambo a question. Just one question, that's all. Then I'm out of here.'

'What you wanna ax her?'

'It's about Charlotte Landreneau,' Ben said. 'The woman who was murdered two days ago in Chitimacha. And about someone called Peggy Iron Bar. I need to know who she was, and why she died. They tell me Mama's the wisest of the wise. If she can't help me with the information, I don't know who else can.'

The man's hard gaze lingered on Ben for a protracted moment, then he chewed his lip and seemed to soften a little. At a wave of his hand the weapons pointing at Ben were lowered. He said, 'Wait here.'

With that, he and his seven companions retreated into the forest and disappeared as though they'd never existed.

Ben leaned against the side of the Jeep and lit a Gauloise. Tyler and Keisha opened their doors and got out. 'Protective, ain't they?' Tyler said. The sweat beading on his brow wasn't just from the intense heat and humidity. 'Holy guacamole, brother, you got some balls steppin' out of the vehicle. I thought they was gonna shoot.'

'You can't blame them for bein' cautious,' Keisha said. 'These are bad times we're livin' in.'

'It's not the first time I've had a gun pointed at me,' Ben said. 'And not the worst. They weren't going to shoot. Like he said, they don't want trouble. The weapons are just for show. Probably not even loaded.'

'I'll take your word for it. Now what?' Tyler said.

Ben replied, 'This might take a while. I'd understand if you want to get back to the kids.'

'And leave you here alone?'

'You've done more than enough for me already.'

'Nonsense,' Keisha said. 'We'll wait right here with you. Besides, this might be the last chance I get to meet Sallie again. I couldn't leave without speakin' to her.'

'If they let us in,' Tyler said dubiously. 'Ain't lookin' good, if y'all ask me.'

Thirty minutes went by. Then an hour. Ben was ready to give up and say to Tyler and Keisha, 'Okay, we tried, now let's go back' when he heard the soft crack of a twig in the shadows of the forest and turned around to see the men returning. The same eight, emerging from the trees like before and spreading out around Ben and his companions. Nothing seemed to have changed in their terse expressions.

The leader stepped closer. Ben tried to read his face but could see nothing in his eyes. Tyler was probably right in expecting bad news. Ben was already planning forwards, trying to think what his next move could be.

Then the man said, 'Mama Mambo will see you. Follow us.'

Chapter 23

They left the Jeep on the track and followed the men through the forest. The long drive and the time spent waiting had consumed much of the day; what little sun filtered through the trees was beginning to fade as twilight approached. Keisha and Tyler walked together, clutching hands. Keisha's nervousness was obvious, Tyler's slightly better concealed under a mask of confidence.

Ben quickened his step and drew level with the leader at the head of the group. 'Let's start over,' he said. 'My name's Ben.'

The leader gave him a sideways glance and after a moment's hesitation reluctantly grunted, 'Carl.' Still full of suspicion, but a connection had been made. Ben left it at that.

The beaten track wound on for some distance through the trees before they came to a circle of huts. No attempt had been made to create a clearing for the settlement, if that was what it was. The people who dwelt here lived in full contact with nature around them. The place reminded Ben of the tribal village he'd known in the depths of the Amazon jungle.

As they got closer he made out a hut that was larger and slightly at a distance from the others. A young African-American woman emerged from one of the smaller huts, darted a glance at the strangers and waved shyly at Carl. He nodded back and she went running to the big hut.

Ben had already guessed that was where they were all going, so it was no surprise when Carl ushered them inside. The dwelling was constructed like an ancient roundhouse or a primitive yurt, out of sticks and thatch. There was no door, just an open arch which Ben had to duck low to step through. The interior was dim and shadowy, and smelled of smoke from the fire that crackled in a circular hearth at its centre, beneath a stone chimney raised on blocks that went up through the middle of the roof. The other smell was harder to pinpoint and came from a bubbling cast-iron pot, like a small cauldron, that hung over the flames. The young woman Ben had seen outside hovered near the fireplace, stirring the pot.

Carl said, 'Mama, these are the visitors.' His whole demeanour had suddenly changed and he spoke in a soft tone, like a devoted grandson.

A crackly voice from the shadows replied, 'Let them be welcome here.' Blinking to accustom his eyes to the darkness, Ben followed the sound of the voice.

Sitting on a simple mat of rushes in the dull flicker of the firelight, swaddled in a shawl, was one of the oldest women he had ever seen.

Sallie Mambo's features were like a dark, wrinkled prune and her hair was pure white. She wore a simple dress made of some rough material that looked like sackcloth. Heavy bead bracelets and charm pendants adorned her wrists and neck. Stepping closer, Ben could see the flames dancing in her eyes as she watched him with an intensity that belied her wizened face.

She said, 'Come, children, don't be afraid. Sit close where I can see you.'

Ben and his companions knelt close to the old woman. A small, thin hand reached out, the bead bracelet rattling, to touch Keisha's cheek. Sallie nodded sagely and said, 'I know you, girl.'

The emotion was clear on Keisha's face. 'Yes, Mama. It was a long time ago, but I was hopin' you'd remember me.'

'Mama remember everythin',' the old woman chuckled.

'Mama, this is our friend Ben. He's the one that needs your help.'

The old woman's strangely penetrating gaze turned on Ben and seemed to drink every detail. 'I can see that. Trouble be followin' you, child. You got bad, bad juju. What is it you need from me?'

Ben began by thanking her for seeing him. She just nodded graciously. He went on, 'I need to know about a person who might have lived here in Clovis Parish a long time ago. Her name was Peggy Iron Bar. I think she might have been murdered, and it's important for me to understand why, and by whom. I can pay money for information. Not a lot, this is all I have.'

Sallie Mambo said, 'Child, you can keep your money. I have no need for it.'

'Will you help him, Mama?' Keisha asked, close to a whisper.

The old woman closed her eyes and fell into a deep silence, sitting slumped and so immobile that Ben was suddenly concerned she might have expired of old age at just the perfect moment. Then she reopened her eyes and fixed on him with a clarity and sharpness that were almost frightening.

'Peggy Iron Bar,' she said. 'How'd you suppose a person could get a name like Iron Bar?'

'I thought it was a nickname,' Ben said. 'Something to

do with her personal strength, or her spirit.' He added, with a smile, 'Or else maybe her father was a blacksmith.'

Sallie laughed, a sound like rustling paper. 'That's good. You're a smart boy. But you're missin' somethin'.'

'Tell me what I'm missing,' he said.

Sallie said, 'See, Peggy Iron Bar go back a long, *long* time. Back in them days a lot of the negro folks was still second or third generation African. They still had their old surnames. Problem was, the white folks didn't like to speak 'em. Like mebbe they'd get dirty sayin' it. Or else because they couldn't get their tongue around them strange words. Or mebbe they just liked controllin' the poor negroes just for the hell of it. They'd already done robbed'm of their freedom and their dignity. Why not take away their identity too?'

Ben was struck by the lucidity of her words. The logic was so obvious, he should have thought of it himself. 'You're saying Iron Bar is a corruption of her original African family name?'

'Eyumba,' Sallie said. 'Peggy Eyumba. That was her name.'

'Then you did know her,' he said. His heart was beginning to beat faster. This could be the key to unlock the whole mystery. He glanced at Keisha, whose glowing expression was screaming out *Didn't I tell you?*

Old Sallie Mambo shook her head. 'No, no, I never knew her,' she said, and Ben's heart fell.

'You didn't?'

'Hell, child, I ain't *that* old,' she said. She paused to click her fingers at the young woman, who came over to hand her the long wooden spoon she was using to stir the pot with. Sallie poked the spoon around in the boiling liquid, then brought it under her nose to sniff it before returning it to the mixture. Ben waited impatiently the long silence, sensing more was coming.

'Met her sister, though,' Sallie said at last. 'Mildred. They was twins.'

'Mildred Iron Bar?'

'She'd gotten herself married and was Mildred Brossette when I met her. That was 1935. The year she passed, I reckon. Yes, that's right. Long time ago. I was just sixteen. She was eighty-eight, a lot younger than I am now.' Sallie found this amusing and gave another papery chuckle. She added, 'Mildred was famous around these parts. Oh yes, real famous.'

Ben did a quick mental calculation. Eighty-eight years of age in 1935 would make the twin sisters' birth year 1847. He asked, 'What did Mildred do to become famous?' The thread of the conversation seemed to be wandering away from one sister to the other, and he could only hope this would lead to something.

Sallie shook her head. 'Didn't do nuthin'. She weren't famous for herself. For her twin sister Peggy. Peggy was a legend. Bin gone a long time by then, of course, on account of she'd passed so young. Back in the year 'seventy-three, I think it was. Most Southern white folks had quit talkin' about her by the time I met Mildred all them years later. Didn't take too kindly to what she done, I reckon. But black folks, they still talked about it. Sure did.'

'Talked about what, Mama?' Ben asked. 'Why was Peggy Eyumba such a legend, and why didn't the Southern white folks like her?'

The old woman shot him a disparaging look. 'Hell boy, don't you know nuthin' 'bout history? She helped win the war for the Yankees.'

'She what?'

If the twin sisters had been born in 1847, Peggy would have been just eighteen at the end of the Civil War in '65. Ben had an absurd vision of a young black girl on horseback, leading a mounted charge against a fleeing horde of Confederate troops, the US Cavalry following in her wake, banners waving, sabres flashing.

Sallie must have seen what was in Ben's mind, because she shook her head in amusement. 'No, child, she didn't fight in the war. She was just a poor slave girl workin' for a rich white plantation boss.'

'Then how could she have helped the Union?'

'Why, by spyin' for them of course,' Sallie replied. 'Don't look so surprised, boy. Weren't that unusual for African-Americans to act as intelligence agents for the North. It was called "the black dispatches". A lot of them was women, too. I guess mebbe 'cause women had a way of gettin' into places where they'd hear things. Harriet Tubman was the most famous of all, managed to wreak all kindsa damage against the Rebs. Then you had Mary Elizabeth Bowser, who worked in the Confederate White House up in Richmond and smuggled secrets to the Union right out from under the nose of Jeff Davis hisself.' She chuckled at the thought of such audacity, then went on, 'Mary Touvestre – she was the one who warned the Yankees that the Rebs was workin' a new ironclad warship, and started 'em building one of their own.'

Ben was impressed. At ninety-nine or a hundred years old, Sallie Mambo's recollection of historical detail was pin-sharp.

'Mama, how did Peggy die?' he asked her.

'Terrible thing,' the old woman said. 'Oh, a terrible thing. Yes, yes.' She took one of the charm pendants that hung from her neck and clutched it to her brow, squeezing her wrinkled eyes tight shut and muttering some inaudible prayer.

'Was she murdered?'

The old woman nodded, eyes still shut.

Ben asked, 'Out of revenge for what she'd done during the war?'

Sallie slowly looked up at him. 'The war never stopped, for some folks. I dare say there's a few who're still fightin' it even now.'

'Was she stabbed with a sabre?'

Another sad, solemn nod. 'Couldn't have been more'n twenty-six when they done it to her, the poor babe. Mildred couldn't talk 'bout her without goin' into floods of tears, even sixty or more years later. You know how close twins is.'

'Did they ever catch the killers?'

'Bless your heart, child. This was Louisiana in 1873. Year of the Colfax massacre, when a hundred and fifty poor blacks got slaughtered on Easter Sunday by white men in Grant Parish. Weren't nobody was gonna give a cuss about some freed slave girl gettin' butchered. They was still lynchin' negroes in 1950.'

Ben was conscious that he was firing questions at her, but he had to keep pressing. He said, 'But someone might have been suspected of her killing, at the time. There could have been rumours, gossip. Her sister Mildred must have had her own ideas about who did it.'

'I believe she did. They came real close to gettin' her, too. Story goes, intruders broke into her home one night, just a couple months after her sister died. One of 'em had a sword, and he'd'a used it, if her man friend hadn't seen 'em off with his scattergun. Then they was married and upped and run off to live in Arkansas where nobody'd recognise her. She never came back until many years later.'

'I don't suppose she shared her suspicions with you as to who tried to murder her?'

'No, I don't s'pose she did,' Sallie said. She paused and scrutinised Ben with a thoughtful frown that created a thousand new wrinkles. 'Tell me, child, why's this so important to you?'

'Because it's like you said, Mama. I have trouble following me. Bad, bad juju. And tracing back the links to who killed Lottie Landreneau is the only way I'm going to shake it off. Somehow, these murders are connected and I mean to find out how, and why.'

Sallie Mambo held him with her gaze. Whatever it was she was thinking, it was masked behind her inscrutable expression. Then she heaved a long, weary sigh and said, 'Son, I's gettin' real tired. All this talkin' is sorely taxin' for an old lady. And my memory ain't what it used to be, neither. Reckon I've told you all I can.'

Carl had kept in the background all this time, but now he stepped out of the shadows to take charge of things. His tough attitude was back, too. 'We's done,' he told Ben. 'You said, once you got yo' answers, you'd get out of here. You got'm. Now you be gone.'

There seemed to be nothing Ben could do to drag any more out of the old woman. He thanked her, and stood up. Keisha clasped Sallie's hand. 'It was so wonderful to see you again after all these years, Mama.'

'You come and visit me again, girl,' Sallie said, sounding quite spent and exhausted. 'Don't go leavin' it too long, else I won't be here no more.'

'Oh Mama, you shouldn't talk like that.'

'We'll meet again,' Sallie said. 'In this world or the next.'

Ben could feel the looks Carl was giving him, but he couldn't leave without giving it one last shot. He scribbled down the number of his burner phone on an old receipt slip using a stub of a pencil he'd found in his jacket pocket. He held out the slip to Sallie. 'If you remember anything more, would you give me a call on this number?'

Carl snatched it from his hand and scowled at him. 'Mama don't use no phone. She ain't no messenger, neither.'

And then the meeting was over. Carl and the other guards escorted the visitors back outside. Evening had fallen and they threaded their way back to the Jeep by torchlight. The three of them got in, Tyler fired up the engine and headlamps and got turned around on the narrow track.

As they drove away, Ben looked in the rear-view mirror and saw the bobbing torch beams recede into the darkness of the forest.

Chapter 24

Nobody spoke until they'd come off the track and were heading back along the dark, empty road. It was Tyler who finally broke the silence. 'Well, that wasn't so bad, was it?'

Ben replied from the back seat, 'Not so bad. Going to see Sallie was a good call, thanks to Keisha. I owe you, once again.'

He didn't want to let them see his frustration that they had, in fact, come away with relatively little. The meeting with Sallie Mambo had produced nothing more than a hearsay account of the death of an undercover Union spy, a long, long time ago, that seemed to bear a resemblance to the murder of Lottie Landreneau. There was still no hard link between the two killings, and absolutely no leads for Ben to follow from here. After a promising start his trail had hit a dead end.

Keisha was turned around in the front passenger seat with her chin resting on her arms, watching him. 'I know what you're thinkin', except you're too decent to say it. You think we wasted our time back there, 'cause Mama wasn't able to come up with the name of Peggy Iron Bar's killers. Right?'

Maybe Keisha really was psychic after all.

'That would have been useful information,' Ben admitted.

'Still, can't blame her if she couldn't say.'

'Couldn't say or wouldn't say?' Ben replied. 'Until then she seemed to have perfect recollection of all kinds of facts, names, dates, places, the works. Suddenly, nothing. Her mind seemed to go blank.'

'I guess that's what happens when you get old,' Keisha said, defensively standing up for Sallie. 'Same thing happened to my Aunt Georgia, and she was only ninety-seven.'

'So what next?' Tyler said.

'What happened back in the 1870s is one thing,' Ben said. 'If there's a connection, what happened two days ago means that there's someone out there who's been holding a serious grudge against the Landreneau family, for a hell of a long time, and for reasons unknown, except that their motives are somehow related to those behind Peggy's death and the attempt to do the same to her sister Mildred. But before I can get to that, I need to know there really *is* a connection. What ties these people together? That's the next step.'

Tyler said, 'I'm guessin' that if Lottie Landreneau's mother told her the secret when she was little, it's obviously somethin' that's been common knowledge in their family for years, even generations.'

'Which suggests that they're related by blood,' Ben said. 'The Landreneaus and the Eyumbas, or Iron Bars, or whatever they chose to call themselves back in the day. And that's what I need to verify. If they weren't, I'm dead in the water. Back to Square Zero. Out of options. Might as well give myself up to Sheriff Roque right now, or spend the rest of my life running.'

'And if they were?'

'Then it can only point to one thing,' Ben said. 'A vendetta that's been kept alive for at least a hundred and forty-five years. A torch of hatred that's been passed down through time. Going after the Eyumba sisters wasn't enough. They want to wipe out their descendants, too. Lottie's mother knew that. It's why she passed the secret to her daughter, to protect her, and warned her never, ever to tell a living soul.'

'Holy crap,' Tyler said. 'That's some unforgivin' shit.'

'And carried out to the letter. Lottie was the last of her line. No siblings or children.'

Tyler asked, 'But if they were gunnin' for her, why'd they wait this long?'

Ben replied, 'Same reason they never managed to catch up with her parents, or theirs before them. My guess is that whoever's behind this lost track of the family tree for over a hundred years and only recently reconnected the threads.'

'A gap?'

'As if the vendetta went dormant, like a volcano, then was brought back to life much later on. Presumably by someone else, since the original killers would be old enough now to make Sallie Mambo look like a spring chicken. So, we'd be looking at a new generation of killers, so to speak. Perhaps literally, in the sense that they could be related to the historical ones in the same way that the Landreneaus could have been related to the Eyumbas. Following in the family footsteps, right down to copying the same MO by using a sabre as a murder weapon. It makes me think that the sword must be some kind of heirloom. Maybe it's the same actual sabre that was used to murder Peggy, and in the attack on her sister. Maybe the reason Lottie's killers left it behind was to make some kind of twisted statement. With her death, the revenge quest was complete.'

Tyler pondered over it all for a while, gripping the steering wheel as he concentrated on the dark road. 'I guess that's how it'd have to work, logically.'

'If it works at all,' Ben said. 'And if my theory's right, I'd say that this new generation of killers picked up the trail again sometime in the last three years. I wish I could pin it down more closely.'

Tyler shook his head. 'Now you lost me again. How'd you figure three years?'

Ben replied, 'Because that's the length of time Lottie had just spent travelling around Europe, where nobody would have been able to find her. It was only when she returned to her home town of Chitimacha a few months ago that she became a visible target again. Question is, whose?'

Keisha, who had been listening in silence, seemed to have had an idea. 'Okay, so the first thing we need to do is verify that there's a blood relation between the families, right?'

'Wrong,' Ben said. 'It's the first thing *I* need to do. I can't ask for you to go on helping me like this.'

'We can argue about that later,' Keisha said. 'Now, if I recall, the State Archives are in Baton Rouge. They have everythin' from birth, death, marriage, land and legal records datin' back centuries. It shouldn't be too hard to dig up the family connection, if there is one. Maybe that would create a starting point for figurin' out the rest of it.'

'Then that's where I'm going,' Ben said.

But Tyler seemed doubtful about Keisha's proposition. 'I hate to rain on your parade, folks, but let me tell you three reasons why that's a real dumb notion. First, Baton Rouge is a hundred and eighty miles away, okay? The police will have every major highway blocked up tighter than a fish's asshole. They'd pick Ben up before he crossed the parish line.'

'We'll see about that,' Ben said.

'Fine, then how about reason number two: even if by

some miracle you could evade the roadblocks and a zillion cops lookin' to plug you full of lead, how's the currently most wanted man in Louisiana goin' to walk in the door of a heavily guarded government building and ask politely to spend hours siftin' through a mountain of old records in the hope you might actually find somethin'?'

'Nobody said anything about walking in the door,' Ben said. 'I'll break in through the roof if I have to.'

'Oh, I'll bet you would. But let me save you the trouble of gettin' yourself all shot to pieces for nothing. 'Cause, reason number three, I can promise that's what you'll come up with in there. A big fat zilch.'

'How can you be so sure of that?' Keisha demanded.

Tyler replied patiently, 'Because, honey, I used to be a lawyer, and in that capacity I have spent more hours than I care to count wearin' out the seat of my pants in the Erbon and Marie Wise Research Library in Baton Rouge while diggin' through said State Archives, and I can tell you that birth records weren't required by law in the state of Louisiana until 1918. Even supposin' they had been, and even supposin' that anybody actually gave a rat's ass about such requirements back in them days, especially a bunch of poor black country folks, those archives only hold data goin' back that far for Orleans Parish.'

'That's pathetic.'

'This is the Deep South, baby doll. It ain't New York.'

They all fell silent for several minutes. Tyler drove on into the night. The road was empty ahead, just miles and miles of wilderness flashing by in their headlights. Like a dark tunnel stretching to infinity, which was how Ben saw his future at this moment.

Then Keisha said, 'Well, now, there's another idea. We could talk to Professor Abellard.'

'Oh, please, darlin', let's leave Abellard out of it. The guy's a hopeless drunk.'

'I know he is,' Keisha retorted. 'Else I'd have mentioned him before. But maybe he's cleaned hisself up since then. Maybe we'll get lucky.'

Ben said, 'Who?'

Chapter 25

The Clovis Parish Sheriff's Department had had its hectic times over the years, but nobody could recall having ever witnessed a scene like the one outside the Villeneuve Courthouse off Ascension Square the next morning. An armada of police patrol cruisers and gleaming black SWAT vehicles deployed in from all over the state filled the car park and spilled out onto the street, while squads of heavily armed officers togged up like paramilitary warriors swarmed everywhere both inside and outside the building as though it had finally been announced that the Russians were invading. An argument had broken out earlier that morning when the SWAT commander had tried to park his tank on the courthouse lawn. There were more automatic weapons on display than there were citizens in Villeneuve. And judging by the cheesy grins on many of the officers' faces, it seemed they couldn't wait for the bullets to start flying.

The CP Criminal Investigations Division, hub of the command centre from which Waylon Roque had overseen his domain throughout these last decades, was a cluster of cluttered offices within the prefabricated khaki building adjoining the rear of the courthouse. Sheriff Roque himself had occupied the same small, humble office since being first elected. Same battered old desk, same creaky chair, same malfunctioning air con, same faded pictures on the walls, same framed portrait of his long-suffering wife Philomena frowning down at him from next to the dusty star-spangled banner. He was not a man of fancy tastes and cared little for comforts. He was a man of action and results, and damned if he was going to fail to get results in the Landreneau case.

At this time the sheriff was sitting in the creaky chair at the battered desk, sweltering in the 9 a.m. heat and sipping on an iced tea while continuing to fret over a situation that was, to say the least, challenging. The gruesome murder had sparked off the biggest manhunt in the history of Clovis Parish and he presided over his forces like General Patton.

This was the first short break he'd taken since the operation had flown into action. His every waking moment from then until now had been spent strutting up and down like a man possessed, barking commands into phones and radios, delegating duties, and humiliating slow-witted deputies or anyone else who failed to meet his expectations. As a result, every able officer he could muster, and some who probably weren't so able, had been pressed into service.

Meanwhile a small air force of helicopters had overflown every patch of farmland, forest, swamp and bayou for miles around. Every principal route leading in or out of Clovis Parish had been roadblocked since the crack of dawn on the morning of the crime and hundreds of vehicles had been stopped and searched, while he'd had all available troops scour every imaginable location in Chitimacha and the surrounding area.

Sheriff Roque hadn't had this much excitement since the shooting of that dangerous desperado, Ethan Brister.

And yet, all attempts to find the chief suspect – now universally referred to by Clovis Parish law enforcement as 'the fugitive' – had failed. It was as though this man Ben Hope had simply vanished into thin air. Which, since bureaucratic wheels far beyond the scope of Sheriff Roque's little world had begun to turn and shreds of information about Hope fed back through the system, was increasingly fitting the profile they were building on him. The UK Ministry of Defence, liaising with officials of the US State Department and the British Consulate in New Orleans, had at first been extremely resistant to releasing any details of the former serviceman. Under pressure and in the spirit of international cooperation, certain highly secret files had been made available to US law enforcement, on a strictly eyes-only basis.

The upshot of all this complex wrangling was that Waylon Roque now had a reasonably accurate, though only very partial, idea of Hope's background, military experience and skillset. It made for depressing reading, from the point of view of someone whose job it was to catch him.

As an SAS major this guy had led black ops missions in places Roque had never even heard of. He was a master sniper, an expert in surveillance and counter-surveillance, special weapons and tactics, demolition and forward air control. Counter-terror raids; daring combat missions both on land and at sea; behind-the-lines sabotage assaults; hostage rescue team extractions in the face of superior enemy force: Hope's list of accomplishments made the Delta Force boys look like the Eagle Scouts. And this was just the stuff that the British government were willing to disclose.

'Dang it all, why'd this have to land on me?' Roque muttered. Maybe he should have retired years ago, came the nagging thought. Quit while the going was good.

In his frustration he slipped the old Colt revolver from his holster rig, thumbed it to half-cock and flipped open the reloading gate and dumped out each big .45 shell in turn from the cylinder. The cartridges rolled about his desktop and he sat them up on end in a row, then wiped the weapon down with an oily rag before reloading it again. It was a needless operation he'd repeated maybe thirty times in the last hour, like an obsessive compulsion. But tinkering with his trusty sidearm helped to alleviate his sense of helplessness and make him forget that he was really just some hick sheriff totally out of his depth, past retirement age and ready to hang up his gunbelt and go tend to his flower garden.

There was a knock at the door and in walked Mason Redbone. The deputy was out of hospital and reassigned to duty, by sheriff's orders, as all hands were needed on deck.

'Holy crap, Mason, that face of yours'd frighten a buzzard off of a gut pile.'

Mason's features were a mass of bruising that radiated out from his nose and upper lip and was as floridly multi-hued as a mandrill's backside. He wore his injury as a badge of honour, as the first responder to the killing and the only cop to have heroically come up against Ben Hope in deadly combat, as reported in the lengthy statement he'd given from his hospital bed.

'Thanks, Sheriff,' Mason said in his nasal voice. 'Came to say, everyone's ready for you.'

'On my way,' Roque answered, downing the last of his tea and getting up. He was due to address his underlings in the War Room, which was a spare office brought into service for this special occasion. He swept out of the office, straightening his hat and tie. Mason had to trot down the hallway to keep up. 'I don't suppose y'all got anythin' new to update me on?'

'Wish I had, Sheriff. Still no hair nor hide of the sumbitch anywhere.'

'Damn it. Where'd he up and disappear to like this? You'd

think, if he was hidin' in someone's barn or outhouse, they'd've spotted him by now and called it in.'

Mason replied optimistically, 'Hell, he could be layin' dead in a ditch someplace, for all we know. Sure done lost a lot of blood at the scene.'

The fugitive's injury had been the subject of much discussion. The blood trail began just steps away from where the victim lay dead, led upstairs and across the roof of the guesthouse to the neighbouring property. Forensic examiners had found more blood on the branches of the tree Hope had used to make his escape from next door's rooftop. From there they'd tracked his route across gardens into the street, where it eventually petered out quarter of a mile away at the exact spot where a Mr Chuck Buhler had reported his truck stolen. No sign had been found of the missing vehicle either.

The one clear deduction was that the fugitive was badly hurt, even though nobody knew how. Deputy Redbone had been unable to shed any light on the matter. Nor had any of the cops who had pursued him through the house claimed to have wounded him. The current theory, which seemed good enough, was that Lottie Landreneau had put up a fight and managed to inflict some hurt on her killer before she succumbed.

Roque shook his head. 'I agree, he's gotta be layin' up someplace. But he ain't dead. This guy's a goddamn ninja warrior. Seems he don't kill too easy.'

'He ain't so tough,' Mason muttered, gingerly rubbing his aching face.

Roque grunted, 'Looks like you missed your chance, then, huh, Deputy?'

'Next time.'

Roque pushed through into the War Room, which was

crowded with bodies and filled with the hum of chatter. All eyes were on him as he strode up to a desk that served as his podium.

'All right, all right, quieten down now.' He waited for the buzz to diminish, then launched into his announcement that the manhunt was being widened to take in all four parishes that bordered theirs. Sheriff Roque would remain in overall command, with the cooperation of Sheriffs Gradley, Chatelain, Juneau and Wiltz, who were all present at the meeting and none too happy to be relegated to second fiddle.

Roque spent a few moments detailing the logistics of the operation, which were on an unprecedented scale for the local area. 'Questions?'

There were none.

Roque cast a hard, frigid gaze over the sea of faces all watching him with rapt attention. 'Good. Now listen, people. I want this murdering psychopath found and his hide nailed to the wall. And if it turns out somebody's harbourin' him, they're gonna be awful sorry. But remember,' he growled, raising a warning finger, 'this man isn't some local redneck junkie delinquent or gas station holdup artist. He's a stone cold professional killer and he ain't gonna come quietly. You see him, you shoot first and ask questions later, and order your officers to do the same.'

'We'll get this bastard, Waylon,' Sheriff Juneau said, possibly hoping they'd catch him on his turf so he'd get the credit.

'We damn well better,' Roque grated. 'Because there ain't a man or woman here who'll get rest, sleep or food until he's dead or behind bars. Let's get to work.'

Chapter 26

As Keisha had explained to Ben the night before, Professor Reuben Cantius Abellard was one of the private tutors brought in to help with young Caleb Hebert's home-schooling. Or had been, until his unreliability had compelled the Heberts to dispense with his services.

In former times, Abellard had done a twenty-five-year spell as a history professor at Louisiana State University. Finally booted off the LSU faculty after many warnings concerning his overfondness for sour mash whiskey, he had returned to the decaying grandeur of his old family seat in Clovis Parish with the sole intention of slowly – he was in no hurry – drinking himself to death on his front porch.

Abellard was, Keisha informed Ben, what was generally referred to in the South as 'old money', an aristocratic label dating back several generations to when the Abellards had owned substantial acreages of timber land and sugarcane across the parish and been one of the wealthiest dynasties in the state. The fortunes made by his venerable ancestors were long since squandered and most of the land sold off, with just enough left in the bank to keep the sole remaining Abellard in liquor until the inevitable day when he'd be found dead in his rocking chair.

'Real shame to see such a brilliant man go to waste like

that,' Keisha sighed. 'Fine teacher, too, when he ain't fallin' about and incapable of speech.'

She described how much Caleb had loved his lessons with the batty old professor, until his 'groggy spells' had just become too much. Thereafter it had been Tyler who'd taken over the role of tutoring his son in history, his knowledge of which was pretty decent though utterly eclipsed by Abellard's. 'That man has a brain like an encyclopaedia,' Keisha said.

'If he ain't reduced it to pickled cauliflower by now,' Tyler warned. 'It's been two years since we last saw him. Lord only knows what kind of a state he's in these days.'

It had been late in the evening by the time they'd got back from the trip to see Sallie Mambo. Tyler and Keisha had dropped their secret visitor off at the homestead before driving over to pick up the kids from their neighbours, the Tanners. Once again, they had to ask Vernon and Ivy if they wouldn't mind having Noah and Trinity for a while the following morning; once again, the retirees were happy to babysit.

Then it had been back home for a late dinner of Gumbo à la Hebert and rice, followed by bed. Ben hadn't slept a wink all night as he'd lain restlessly thinking about slipping away. He couldn't go on endangering the Heberts with his presence. And yet, if there was a chance that a boozy old historian could fill in the gaps left by Sallie Mambo, Ben knew he had no choice but to hang on just a little longer.

Next morning, after Noah and Trinity had been left in the care of the Tanners, they set off again, this time in Keisha's little Mazda. It had been her idea to bring Caleb along, in the hope that the sight of his former pupil might stir the professor and incite him to keep off the whiskey, at least for the duration of their visit.

Tyler frowned as he saw the teenager clamber into the back of the car clutching his compound bow and a quiverful of arrows. 'What in hell, son?'

'I figured, in case we run into the police or somethin',' Caleb replied. He said it *po-leece*.

'There's no need for that,' Ben said. But the kid wouldn't be persuaded.

'Stubborn,' Tyler said with a grin. 'Gets it from his old man.'

The Abellard House, as it was called, was only a dozen or so miles east of Kadohadacho Creek, which made it practically next door. But it was still a dangerous journey, in case they came upon a roadblock or got pulled over for the slightest reason. Ben felt deeply uncomfortable, and not only for his own sake if anything bad should happen.

Nothing bad happened, but it was just a matter of luck that Keisha hadn't needed to take any major roads to get there. Just before 10 a.m. they rounded a sharp bend in the country lane, entered a gateway, and the once grand old mansion came into view at the top of a long, weed-strewn drive. It was immediately obvious that the Abellard House had suffered from decades of neglect. The paint was flaking, the grounds were a jungle, and the place was generally in a sorry state. Ben could only hope that its owner was in better condition.

Keisha pulled up in front of the house and they all got out. 'There he is,' Caleb said, pointing up at the shambolic figure that had suddenly appeared in the open doorway.

Abellard was a wasted sixty-year-old who looked eighty. His hair and beard were long and grey, and the shirt he was wearing might have been used to scrub the floor with. In one hand he clutched a near-empty bottle, in the other a near-full glass. He was staring wild-eyed at his unexpected visitors and appeared to be having some trouble staying upright.

Ben thought, *wonderful.*

'Looks like someone got started early this mornin',' Tyler grumbled. 'If he even went to bed at all.'

'Shush,' Keisha said irritably, then put on a broad smile and waved cheerily. 'Hey there, Professor. Ain't it a beautiful mornin'? Brought you some eggs.'

Abellard stumbled out onto the dilapidated front porch to greet them, blinking in the sunshine as though he'd spent the last week in darkness. Three steps from his door he collapsed on his face, went straight through the rotten planking and disappeared, glass, bottle and all, into the porch foundations.

It took a few minutes for Ben and Tyler to drag him out, watched by a horrified Keisha and a highly amused Caleb. Abellard was quite unhurt, sharing the propensity of many chronic drunks to walk away unscathed from all kinds of accidents. If anything the fall had had the effect of sobering him up a little. He dusted himself off, picked bits of rotten splinter out of his hair and beard, and thanked them very graciously for coming to his aid.

'Hope you don't mind our landin' on you like this,' Keisha said.

'Not at all, not at all. I seldom receive visits from anyone and it's so nice to see you. Oh, what fine-looking eggs. Thank you. Please, please, come inside. Mind the, uh, hole there. My, Caleb, haven't you grown.'

Amid all the chatter, Abellard seemed unaware that the Heberts had brought a stranger along. Noticing at last, he squinted at Ben and said, 'I don't believe I've had the pleasure of meeting you before, Mister—?'

'West,' Ben said. 'Bruce West.'

'You're British.'

'Bruce's a friend of the family, visitin' from London, England,' Tyler said.

'Delighted,' Abellard replied, shaking Ben's hand. 'I must apologise for my appearance. I wasn't expecting company.' Any concern Ben might have had about being recognised from the TV was soon allayed. Professor Abellard was obviously not in the habit of keeping up to date with current affairs, local or otherwise.

They followed Abellard through the rambling old mansion to a disordered kitchen that seemed to be mainly used as a lair for at least a dozen pet cats. Boxes of empty whiskey bottles filled an entire corner and every horizontal surface was thick with dust and cat hair. There was a markedly peculiar smell about the place. Keisha insisted on making coffee. Ben thought that was a very good idea.

As she hunted through cupboards for the necessary items, Abellard invited the rest of them to sit at the long, dusty table. Ben pulled out a chair to find it already occupied by a large moggy, which hissed at him as he discreetly ejected it from his seat.

'So to what do I owe the pleasure of your visit?' Abellard asked.

'Bruce here's a writer,' Tyler explained, following the narrative Ben had decided on earlier.

'A writer!' Abellard's bloodshot eyes crinkled as he smiled.

'Historical non-fiction,' Ben said. 'Actually I'm just starting out.'

Tyler said, 'Your name sort of came up in conversation, and he's kind of hopin' you might be able to give him a couple of pointers for this book he's workin' on.'

Abellard replied, 'Why, certainly, if I can. Welcome to the

brotherhood, Mr West. I happen to have authored one or two modest tomes in that line myself.'

In fact it was more like twenty, and the modest tomes were weighty volumes that together could have sunk a boat. All of them were long since out of print, dating back to the glory days of Abellard's academic career. Tyler had shown Ben a couple of them he'd purchased second-hand from the junk shop in Villeneuve. One was a densely researched work on the French and Indian War of 1754–63, the other an incredibly dry, stuffy thousand-page study of the battles of Lexington and Concord during the American Revolution. The author bibliography on the inside cover page was not unimpressive, but Ben wondered how many of Reuben Abellard's books had ever been read outside of research libraries.

'And your reputation precedes you,' Ben said. 'It's an honour, Professor.'

If there was one thing that studying at Oxford University had taught Ben all those years ago, it was that all academic types had in common a love of flattery. By the time Keisha brought the steaming pot of strong black coffee to the table, Professor Abellard had a new best friend and was eager to please. 'How can I be of help, young man?'

Ben outlined his book project, whose subject was to be the activities of lesser-known African-American female intelligence agents during the Civil War.

'I mean, everyone's heard of the famous names like Harriet Tubman and Mary Elizabeth Bowser,' he said offhandedly, just like a real historian. 'I'm more interested in shining a light on some of the obscure players. Like Peggy Eyumba, for instance.'

As a trained military sniper and counter-sniper who had taken down targets at over a thousand metres, Ben knew all about long shots. But this casual reference to Peggy Eyumba, in the hope that it might yield up useful information, was one of the longest shots he'd taken in his life. If he drew a blank – if Abellard replied, 'Sorry, son, I never heard of a Peggy Eyumba in my life' – then it was over.

Ben would soon find out which way it would go.

There was silence at the table. Abellard's expression remained perfectly blank for so long that Ben, tensely waiting for a response, became convinced that his long shot had missed by a mile. Caleb sat gazing deferentially at his former tutor. Tyler and Keisha exchanged uncertain glances.

After what seemed like a full minute of silence, Abellard picked up his coffee mug with long, skinny fingers, brought it up to his nose to sniff it as though searching for the scent of whiskey, then took a sip.

Ben couldn't stand it any more. He said, 'Well, Professor?'

Abellard smacked his lips and put down his mug. 'Well, Mr West, it seems you've already come a long way with your research. It's rare to come across anyone these days who's familiar with the history of Peggy Iron Bar, and the role she played in the War Between the States.'

'Not as familiar as I'm hoping you are,' Ben said.

'It would be difficult for any keen historian to resist learning about such dramatic events that took place so close by. If you have some time, it's certainly a tale worth hearing. You see, Peggy might be virtually forgotten now, but if it hadn't been for her, the outcome of that war might have been very different.'

As ravaged by the decades of boozing as his body and soul might be, Professor Reuben C. Abellard's brain was still far from being pickled. Now he began to talk, Ben listened, and the amazing story unfolded.

Chapter 27

Abellard said, 'You see, Mr West, it's easy to forget that the breakaway Southern Confederacy started the war with a great many advantages over their enemies in the North. The young men and boys of the rebel army were mainly poor country folks, who knew the land, had learned to hunt and shoot from an early age for their very survival, and excelled as guerrilla troops. Meanwhile the quality of their leadership, generals like Stonewall Jackson, Nathan Bedford Forrest and Robert E. Lee, far surpassed the pedestrian likes of George McClelland, to whom President Lincoln at first foolishly entrusted the command of the Union army. The Confederacy scored so many initial successes, such as the stunning victory at the First Battle of Bull Run in July 1861, that throughout the early years of the war it often seemed as though the Union would be defeated.'

Abellard paused, furrowing his brow. 'It behoves us to remember that this was no ordinary war. As much as any other moment in our history, arguably even more than gaining independence from the British Empire, it defined and shaped what we were to become. Had the South succeeded in holding on to its sovereignty as an independent nation, modern-day America would have been a very different place. The land would have remained split into two opposing countries that may well have entered into war against one another repeatedly throughout the remainder of the nineteenth century and perhaps all through the twentieth, serving only to weaken both sides. America might never have become the leading world power that it did. The course of global politics and economics would have been radically altered.'

The professor slurped his coffee. 'But I digress. In the event, as we know, the superior numbers and industrialised power of the Union began to prevail against those early Confederate successes. By early 1864, the tide had very much turned against the South. The Union had gained a formidable new commander-in-chief in General Ulysses S. Grant, in whom they had great confidence that he would lead them to victory. Our forces were demoralised and in disarray, underequipped, underfed and ripe for defeat. The South's long-held hopes of aid from their allies in France were bitterly dashed and they now found themselves alone in a desperate situation, as their cities burned, their citizens starved and the dead lay heaped by the tens of thousands in the cornfields. Clearly, something had to be done. And it was felt, in certain circles, that desperate times called for desperate measures.

'Many covert plots and conspiracies were hatched during the war,' Abellard went on. 'The assassination of Abraham Lincoln, for example, was on the cards long before it actually happened. But of all the schemes dreamed up to reverse the tide of defeat in the South's favour, none was as nefarious as that conceived in secret by a small group of Confederate commanders and a prominent Louisiana landowner, a Texan by the name of Dr Leonidas Wilbanks Garrett, whose vast plantation estate just so happened to be right here in Clovis Parish.'

The instant Ben heard the name Garrett, he was certain he'd heard it before, and recently. Unable to recall, he went on listening.

'Now Dr Garrett was an interesting character, by all accounts,' Abellard said. 'His ambition and flair as a businessman had amassed him a fortune that in today's money would be equivalent to hundreds of millions of dollars, perhaps even billions. But it was his expertise in science and medicine that led him to become the architect of this conspiracy, which, had it been successful in its objective, could have inflicted untold damage to the Union. Needless to say, this was not a military strategy of which the Confederate high command would have officially approved, however dire their predicament. In those days of warfare, before gentlemanly codes of conduct became extinct, the ends were not always taken to justify the means.'

The professor's coffee mug was empty and he was twirling it on the tabletop as he spoke. He coughed. 'Excuse me. I haven't done this much talking in years and my throat's parched drier than sawdust sauce.'

'You want me to fetch you a glass of water, Professor?' Keisha asked sweetly.

Abellard pulled a face as if she'd offered him poison. 'Bless your heart, but what I need is in that cupboard over there.' He pointed.

Keisha stood and went over to it. To nobody's surprise it was crammed with full whiskey bottles. Abellard held out his mug, and kept it held out until she'd reluctantly filled it up with liquor. 'Helps keep me focused,' he explained, taking his first gulp. 'Ahhh. That's better. Now where was I?'

'A conspiracy that could have done untold damage to the Union,' Ben reminded him. He was sure the professor's narrative was leading somewhere. Where exactly, and how long it would take him to get there, was anyone's guess. Especially now that the crazy old coot was back on the whiskey.

Abellard nodded. 'Mr West, how much do you know about the history of biological warfare?'

Ben stared at him. 'Are you serious?'

'Oh, yes. And so were Garrett and his co-conspirators. This was total war, in their way of seeing things. The time for fair and decent tactics had been and gone. Now, this form of warfare was by no means a new invention, even in 1864. As far back as antiquity, armies would drive hordes of infected sick onto enemy lands with the desire of causing epidemics. The water supplies of besieged cities were often spiked with hellebore and other toxic plant substances. During the Middle Ages it was not uncommon practice to use catapults to hurl the corpses and excrement of plague victims over the walls of enemy castles, for the same unpleasant reason. More recently, and perhaps more pertinently for Leonidas Garrett, it had been widely suspected that British military leaders in pre-revolutionary colonial North America deliberately supplied blankets infected with smallpox to Native American tribes. As one English lord by the name of Baron Jeffery Amherst, British Commander-in-Chief and one-time Governor General of the Province of Quebec, put it in a letter to a subordinate charged with the task, their intention was very openly to "extirpate this execrable race". The resulting outbreak of the disease was the first of several that would ultimately claim the lives of some half a million or so Native American Indians.'

'But that's genocide,' Keisha said, aghast.

'You're rightly shocked, Ma'am,' Abellard replied. 'Dr Garrett, however, took such heinous crimes as his inspiration. Through a medical contact who had been working to alleviate a terrible cholera outbreak in Bermuda, he arranged to collect a large quantity of infected clothing of the dead and have it sealed in specially-made airtight casks. These casks were then to be shipped to the Port of Galveston, in Garrett's native state of Texas, aboard a Confederate blockade runner. Such vessels often stopped in Bermuda to stock up on arms and ammunition for the war effort, and were adept at slipping by the Union fleet that patrolled Southern waters. Once in his possession, the casks would have been separately smuggled north to New York, Boston, Chicago and Washington D.C., where they would be opened and the contaminants released into the public water supplies of those cities.'

Chapter 28

Abellard paused for effect, and a long, thirsty gulp of whiskey. 'Now, I'm sure you can imagine the ravages of such a deadly disease breaking out simultaneously across the major population centres of the North. Cholera was a major killer in those times, and could spread like wildfire. The effect of Garrett's manufactured pandemic might easily have been several times greater than the damage the British had managed to inflict on the Indian tribal population in the previous century. It could have utterly devastated those Union strongholds, perhaps even struck at the heart of the government itself. Potentially weakening the Union war effort enough for the South to rally round and regain the upper hand, thereby changing the entire course of US history. That, we will never know.'

The enormity of what Abellard was describing had both Tyler and Keisha shaking their heads. Even Caleb looked horrified. Ben had got the picture and wanted to move on.

'Where does Peggy Iron Bar come into all of this?' he asked.

'I was just coming to that. She was an ordinary slave girl who had worked on Garrett's cotton plantation estate, Athenian Oaks, since the age of nine. It's thought that her mother had died of diphtheria, her father of tetanus. Life expectancy was short for plantation slaves, who were forced to live in appalling conditions. Peggy's only surviving relative was her sister.'

'Mildred,' Ben said. 'Her twin.'

Abellard nodded. 'Multiple birth was highly unusual among the slave population, as malnutrition was so rife, but yes. When the girls reached the age of fifteen or sixteen, Mildred remained on the plantation while Peggy was promoted to performing duties within the mansion itself. Cooking, cleaning, maid chores, serving at table, and whatnot. There's no indication that Garrett had any ulterior motives in employing her, although again that is something we cannot know for sure. From what little historians can glean she appears to have been a smart and capable girl, diligent, reliable and obedient as all masters liked their slaves to be. Unbeknownst to Garrett, however, young Peggy also happened to possess the rare ability to memorise entire conversations and repeat them verbatim later on. In modern neuroscience this form of exceptional recall is called mnemonic memory. A gift that came into its own when, purely by chance in the course of her duties, she was privy to the secretive discussions between Garrett and his would-be partners in crime. It's hard for us to imagine now, but such was the arrogance of many of the slave-owning class that they barely regarded these people as sentient human beings. Still less would Garrett and his ilk have imagined that this silent young girl going about her servant tasks in the background was in fact recording every detail of their plans.'

Abellard gently pushed aside a cat that had hopped up onto the table, and refilled his mug. The level in the whiskey bottle was dropping fast. He went on:

'This gifted young lady was also admirably brave. Realising the terrible import of what she had overheard, she knew she must somehow find a way to pass this information to those who could act upon it before it was too late. It's still unclear exactly how, but in the weeks that followed she was able to make contact with undercover agents of the legendary Pinkerton detective firm, who at the behest of Abraham Lincoln had infiltrated the entire South in their attempts to uncover such intelligence information. Espionage was endemic to the Civil War, as to all wars. The South had their own spies, like the infamous Belle Boyd, and the North had invested heavily in forming intelligence networks for the Union.

'Anyhow, things moved swiftly after that. Even as Garrett's blockade runner vessel lay at anchor off the Bermuda coast and the tainted caskets were loaded aboard, the Pinkertons' news reached the elephantine ears of President Lincoln who, duly alarmed, immediately despatched a squadron of Union navy frigates with orders to find, sink or burn her. Garrett's ship was intercepted before it reached the Bahamas, and destroyed. Meanwhile, under cover of the Union army's Red River Campaign which carved deep into Louisiana during late May 1864, a large detachment of crack troops was deployed to Garrett's estate in Clovis Parish to quietly assassinate the good doctor, since no Union court martial could condemn a Confederate citizen. The same afternoon that the town of Villeneuve was torched by Yankee soldiers, the special unit descended on the Athenian Oaks estate and began bombarding the mansion with artillery fire. Several of Garrett's staff and foremen were killed in the attack. But when the troops entered the smoking ruins of the house they discovered that Garrett himself had managed to escape. As reprisal for his evil plot they now carried out their orders to raze every inch of his estate and plantation to the ground.'

'I've seen the place,' Tyler said. 'Or what's left of it, which ain't much except a big ol' patch of wasteland, even now.'

'What about Peggy?' Ben asked.

Abellard replied, 'The story goes that Lincoln himself had expressly wanted her to be taken away to the safety of the North and recompensed for her bravery, but that she refused and remained in Clovis Parish with her sister. A noble decision, but one she would soon come to regret. As for Leonidas Garrett, he had gone into hiding after the attack, crippled by a Yankee shell that had brought down a ceiling of his home and almost crushed him to death.

'Immediately upon the cessation of hostilities and the establishment of the new government, his remaining assets were seized by the authorities and his business empire was scattered to the winds. Even the most loyal Southerners held him in disgrace upon hearing of the vileness of his scheme to murder countless innocent civilians. A broken man, Garrett disappeared. It was thought that he holed up in the Kisatchie Hills wilderness, where he later married and had a son. There were rumours that he had surrounded himself with a gang of disenfranchised former rebels, violent cutthroats and marauders, and that he had sworn an oath on the Dixie flag to take revenge against the negro bitch' – Abellard glanced at Keisha – 'excuse my language, Ma'am, no offence meant.'

'None taken,' Keisha replied graciously.

'– against the negro bitch who caused his downfall, and all her line.'

'All her line?' Ben said. Everything was falling into place now, or almost.

'This was a villainous rogue who had lost everything except the burning desire for retribution,' Abellard answered. 'It's easy to imagine that such a man wouldn't rest until vengeance was his.'

'Peggy was murdered in 1873,' Ben said. 'With a sabre.'

'The sword was thought to have been a gift from one of his accomplices. If indeed Garrett was responsible for the crime. No charges were ever brought, despite all her widower's attempts to pin blame on him and his gang.'

'Peggy had married?'

'To a freed slave, like herself, a man named Frederick Miller. They had two children.'

'What happened to them?'

'Who knows?' Abellard replied. 'If Frederick and the children went on to suffer a similar fate, it's not recorded by history. Likewise, the story of Leonidas Garrett fades into obscurity at this point. Nobody ever saw him again.'

The professor, too, was beginning to fade. The bottle was nearly finished. His voice was thickening and his eyelids were beginning to droop. As Ben and the others sat in silence, still stunned by what they'd heard, Abellard poured the last dregs from the bottle and down his throat. He hiccupped.

'At least,' he slurred, 'that's the legend. What do I know? I'm just a burned-out old fart.' And with those words, he rested his head on the table and went to sleep.

Chapter 29

'Well, there you have it,' Tyler grunted. 'Interestin' times we live in.'

'Is he still alive?' Caleb asked, poking the professor's arm with a finger and getting no response.

Keisha frowned sadly down at the comatose heap on the table. 'Won't be for much longer, if he keeps this up. Ben? What're you thinkin'?'

Ben leaned back in his chair and said, 'I'm thinking that the name Garrett is ringing a bell. Someone mentioned it to me, here in Louisiana, before all this mess began. But I'm damned if I can remember who or why.'

'Could've been anyone in Clovis Parish,' Tyler said. 'Everybody knows that name. Garretts are bad news around here. Always were, always will be.'

'Are we talking about the same family? Descendants of Leonidas Garrett?'

'This is the Deep South, Ben. Most everyone's related to each other, if you go back just a little ways. Why'd you suppose all the Cajun women have them gerbil front teeth?'

'They do not,' Keisha said. 'That's a disgraceful thing to say.'

'It's a fact that our gene pool ain't exactly diverse,' Tyler said. 'Diseases and mutations tend to run in the same certain blood lines. Craziness and what they call nowadays "learnin' difficulties" run in others. In the case of the Garrett clan, the genetic trait each and every one of those worthless dirt-bags shares in common is a propensity for lawlessness and psychopathic violence. Yup, goin' by what the good professor here just told us, I'd say that ol' sabre-totin' Leonidas came from the same illustrious stock as our dear present-day Garrett brothers. And I'd also say that another piece of your puzzle just popped right into place, my friend.'

Ben leaned forward in his chair and looked hard at Tyler. 'I think you'd better tell me more about the Garrett brothers.'

'There's three of 'em,' Tyler said. 'The worst goof I ever made in my lawyer days was to get hooked up as defence attorney for the youngest of the bunch, Logan. That was some years ago. He'd be about thirty now, but I don't suppose he'll ever learn the lesson of his ways. Logan's what you'd call a deeply unpleasant character. Gets his kicks settin' dogs on fire. You get the picture. He was arrested by Sheriff Roque's boys for possession of half an ounce of metham-phetamine with intent to sell. That's a Class B felony that carries a sentence of one to nine years in jail. The more I found out about what the Garretts were into, the more I regretted takin' the case. If the cops had landed on Logan just the day before, they'd have found a heap more than half an ounce of meth on him. That was just his personal reserve, all he had left over after the deal he'd done that mornin'. Fact was, they were movin' truckloads of it, and no doubt still are. But by the time I discovered all this, it was too late to back out. His elder brother Seth pretty much told me they'd blow my brains out if I didn't get Logan off scot-free. So that's exactly what I did, by squeezin' the little skunk through the door of unlawful search and seizure. That's another reason Sheriff Roque loves me so much.'

'I'm glad you ain't a lawyer no more,' Keisha said.

'Me too, honey. Two weeks after he walked away from that one a free man, he tried to rape an eighty-year-old lady in Shreveport. Sentenced to eight years in the state penitentiary, which then got reduced to five, on account of the Garretts produced some doctor who could testify Logan was mentally ill. Makes me sick to think about it, even now.'

Ben had a sudden flash of memory. 'I've just remembered where I heard the name Garrett before today. It was the night of the holdup at Elmo's Liquor Locker in Villeneuve. Sheriff Roque was talking about Billy Bob Lafleur and all the unsavoury company he keeps.'

Tyler said, 'That'd make sense. Unsavoury characters are drawn to the Garrett boys like flies to a turd.'

'Except he didn't mention the Garrett boys, per se,' Ben said, casting his mind back to the scene. So much had happened since then. 'He talked about an island. Garrett Island. I'm sure of it.'

Tyler looked blank. 'I never heard of any Garrett Island, and I've lived here all my life.'

'Nor me,' Keisha said.

Ben was silent for a while, thinking. 'You said there were three brothers. Logan and Seth and who else?'

'You don't want to know, trust me.'

'Who else, Tyler?'

With reluctance Tyler replied, 'Jayce Garrett. The eldest, by a few years. The smartest, because he's the only one of the bunch who's never been arrested. And the worst, because he makes Logan and Seth look like Buddhists. Seth told me that Jayce worked for a spell as a hitter for the mob in New Orleans. Killed a whole bunch of people, never pulled so much as a parkin' ticket. He's also reputed to have associated with the Dixie Mafia and a variety of neo-Nazi white suprem-acist terror groups in Tennessee and Mississippi. The swastika tattoo on his hand, that ain't just to look cool.'

'Sounds like a real charmer,' Ben said.

'After that, he switched careers and got into the meth business. Along with illegal gamblin', burglary, auto theft, money launderin', extortion and bootleggin'. Which, in case you thought it went out with the end of prohibition back in the thirties, is still very much alive and kickin'. I'm told the Garretts produce some of the cheapest tax-free moon-shine in the South. Made some folks go blind, but that don't seem to affect their business none. Those good ol' boys are rakin' in the money like it's goin' out of style.'

'You knew all this, but you never reported it?'

Tyler shrugged. 'There's such a thing as lawyer–client privilege, Ben. There's also such a thing as protectin' your family. Nobody in their right mind would speak out against the Garretts, or any of their associates, of whom there are quite a few, believe me. The whole parish is terrified of 'em. They got ears and eyes everywhere.' Tyler paused, then added knowingly, 'And connections in all kindsa places. Ones we might not have been able to figure out before, but make a lot of sense in hindsight.'

Ben knew that Tyler was thinking about the same person he was: Deputy Sheriff Mason Redbone. Sometime soon, Ben was going to have to catch up with him, too.

'Then it sounds like someone needs to put a stop to the Garrett brothers,' he said.

Tyler shook his head. 'We talked about this, remember? Goin' up against these kinds of people ain't good for your health.'

'I have a fairly robust constitution,' Ben said.

'These guys are ruthless. As I think you've already noticed.'

'Tyler, they don't know the meaning of the word.'

'It ain't what I'd do,' Tyler said. 'Then again, I'm not you. And if you catch 'em, then what?'

'Kill 'em dead,' Caleb said. His eyes were glowing as though this were the coolest conversation he'd ever heard.

'Caleb! Enough!' Keisha exclaimed.

'I don't think that'd be such a good idea,' Ben said. 'I'm already wanted for one murder I didn't commit. Adding another three that I did commit to my account won't help my situation much. The Garretts will have to face justice. Which they can do the easy way, by coming quietly. Or the hard way, if they choose to be awkward. That's their call.'

'And you expect them to confess to their crimes, just like that?'

'Not just like that,' Ben said. 'But there are ways.'

Tyler said, 'What ways?'

Ben replied, 'My ways.'

Tyler gave a little whistle. 'Then I wouldn't want to be in the Garrett boys' shoes. I reckon they're about to find themselves in a whole lot more trouble than you're in.'

Caleb said, 'Awesome.'

Ben stood. He put out his hand. Tyler looked at the hand and then grasped it in a firm, dry grip. Ben said, 'I want to thank you for all you've done for me.' He turned to Keisha. 'Same goes for you. I owe you a very great deal and I'll never forget your kindness.'

Keisha rose to her feet and hugged him tightly. 'This is you sayin' goodbye, isn't it?'

Ben nodded. 'It's time for me to go it alone. This is what I do best.'

Caleb got up and offered a hand to Ben, and they shook. There was a lot of power in the teenager's grip. He'd soon be a big, strong man like his father, with all the Hebert virtues of toughness and generosity that he would one day pass on to his own children. Ben felt a pang of sadness knowing this was the last time they'd see each other.

Caleb said, 'Thanks again for savin' my life, Mister Hope. There's somethin' I want to give you in return.'

Chapter 30

Professor Reuben Cantius Abellard was still quietly snoozing off the effects of his late morning liquid breakfast when his visitors went their separate ways. After swapping phone numbers and promising to keep in touch, Ben stood outside in the hot sun and watched the Heberts drive off. Caleb waved goodbye from the rear window.

Ben waved back, and then they were gone.

The grounds of the Abellard House were a sprawling acreage of oaks and sycamore woodland, as old and untended as the mansion they swallowed up in their midst, and thick with creepers and Spanish moss. He took a moment to get his bearings and turned and began cutting due west through the trees. West was the direction of his next port of call. Come what may, he was ready.

The pain of his wound hardly bothered him any longer. Over his right shoulder hung his green bag; over his left Caleb's parting gift to him: the hunting bow with which Ben had saved the boy's life.

Caleb's gesture had touched Ben. He hadn't refused the offer. A silent, powerful weapon might well come in useful again, before this was over.

It was a while before he reached the barbed wire fence that marked the boundary of Abellard's land and emerged from the trees at the edge of a narrow country road. The sun was hotter and the air more humid than ever. Ben took off his jacket and rolled the bow and quiver up inside it.

He followed the road, always alert to the sound of approaching vehicles and ready to slip out of sight among the thick greenery that lined the verges. Two freight trucks and seven cars came by in the next hour, four of which were a convoy of marked Clovis Parish police cruisers and a black state police SWAT vehicle going somewhere in a hurry with sirens and lights. No doubt racing off to apprehend the dangerous fugitive that some eager-beaver citizen had reported spotting on their property, Ben thought.

It was another hour of walking before he came upon a low-slung, tin-roofed roadside bar that from a distance he'd thought was a ruined shack. The rusted sign said JEBS TONK and Ben could hear country music blaring from inside. As much as he'd have appreciated a cold beer at that moment, he didn't think the locals would offer much of a welcome.

There were three pickup trucks parked outside the bar. The two on the left and right were the kind of rusted heaps that looked as though they belonged to some poor farmer or country dweller who had owned it for years simply because they couldn't afford to replace it. The one in the middle was a shiny late-model Dodge Ram crew cab with oversized tyres, not a speck of mud on its vast area of metallic silver paintwork and all the fashionable accessories like a winch and spotlights across the roof.

Risking a peek in through the barroom window, Ben identified its owner as an affluent-looking dude in a Stetson hat who was sitting with his two designer cowboy cronies, all rhinestones and alligator boots and lurid grins, quaffing pitchers of beer while trying to pester the barmaid, who obviously wasn't too receptive to their noisy advances.

A car thief with a conscience found it much easier to liberate the property of such individuals, and three minutes later Ben was blazing down the road. The Dodge had a full tank of fuel, probably enough to take him halfway to Canada if he'd been that way inclined. One of the cowboys had left his hat on the back seat, a black felt affair with a silver band, like something Tom Mix might have worn. He put it on and tilted the brim down low. Ben Hope, master of disguise.

The other useful item on board was a combined GPS and digital radio scanner mounted to the truck's dashboard. The rhinestone cowboys probably just used it for yakking with their buddies on Citizen's Band, but Ben was easily able to retune it to the local police radio frequency and eavesdrop on the busy chatter of the Clovis Parish Sheriff's Department as they raced here and there trying to find him. Meanwhile he used the GPS to plot a zigzag course to his next destination that avoided major roads. That destination being Pointe Blanche, where he had a date with his old friend Dwayne Skinner. Poor Dwayne just didn't know it yet.

Chitimacha was a hive of police activity, as if somehow the cops expected the fugitive to still be hanging around the scene of the crime. The irony wasn't lost on Ben. He kept his speed down and the hat brim low over his face, just another Louisianan going about his business. There was nothing on the police radio about the stolen Dodge. The rhinestone cowboys must still be gulping beer and catcalling the barmaid back at Jeb's Tonk.

West of Chitimacha, the police presence thinned out and Ben relaxed a little more. Arriving in Pointe Blanche he soon found the street he was looking for, and parked the Dodge a few blocks down from Dumpy's Rods.

He kept the hat on as he walked down the street. The bow was a little conspicuous wrapped up in his jacket, but the couple of people he passed by didn't seem to notice. Then he reached the chain-link fence of Dumpy's Rods and walked in through the open gate.

Dwayne Skinner was alone in the garage workshop, bent over the engine bay of a big, aggressive-looking muscle car. Custom flame paint, dark-tinted windows, glittering chrome sidepipes and mag wheels. A Pontiac Firebird or a Chevy Camaro from the late seventies. Ben knew a police detective in Oxford who liked these kinds of overblown, barge-sized Yank tanks. Personally, he'd rather stick with his BMW Alpina.

He walked up behind Dwayne, who still had his head and shoulders under the raised bonnet of the car, tweaking something with a large wrench. 'That oughtta do it,' Dwayne muttered to himself, and was just about to step away from the car when Ben sent him sprawling headlong into the engine compartment and slammed the bonnet lid down on him.

Dwayne let out a strangled cry of shock and pain. Ben raised the bonnet and slammed it down a couple more times for good measure, then grabbed him by the belt and dragged him out and dumped him hard on the cement floor of the workshop, wrench and all.

It took a few moments for Dwayne to get over the initial shock, but a worse one was to come. Lying sprawled on his back he stared up at Ben and his jaw dropped open. All he could manage to gasp was, 'Oh, shit.'

Ben leaned against the car and folded his arms. He said, 'Thought I'd drop in and say hello. You and I have a little unfinished business to take care of.'

Dwayne half scrambled to his feet, slipped and fell, then struggled upright and snatched the fallen wrench off the floor with a look of hatred. He staggered towards Ben with the tool raised like a club. Ben saw the clumsy blow coming before the spark of the idea had even been kindled inside Dwayne's tiny mind. By the time it arrived, he'd already mentally rehearsed a couple of times how he was going to block it. With his left hand he parried Dwayne's right arm, knocking the weapon out of his fist. With his left, he hammered a sharp web strike to Dwayne's throat.

Dwayne went straight down on his back, choking and gurgling. Ben placed a foot across Dwayne's neck and said, 'Now, don't be silly, Dwayne. You won't solve anything by use of force. That's my department.'

'W-what do you want, man?' Dwayne gasped, clutching his right arm as if Ben had broken it. 'You got some nerve comin' here. The cops are everywhere lookin' for you.'

Ben pointed at the muscle car. 'Is that yours?'

'It's Dumpy's. My boss. Jesus fuckin' Christ, man, you busted my fuckin' elbow.'

So there really was a Dumpy. Ben wondered if that was the name on his birth certificate. What a curse to lay on a baby boy.

'Your elbow's fine, so stop whingeing. And where is Dumpy now?'

'Florida, on vacation. Told me to fix it for'm while he's away. I asked you what you want, man.'

'I want you to take me for a drive,' Ben said, and pointed again at the car.

Dwayne stared at him. 'Uh-uh. No fuckin' way. Dumpy'd murder me if he found out I took his Firebird out, man.'

'And I'll murder you if you don't,' Ben said. 'Quite a quandary, isn't it? Now get in and let's go.'

Chapter 31

Ben grabbed Dwayne by the neck, frogmarched him to the car and bundled him in behind the wheel. Then he walked around to the passenger side, opened it up, tilted the front seat forward and tossed his stuff into the rear and climbed in next to it. He drew one of Caleb's hunting arrows from his roll and pressed its needle-point steel tip against the back of Dwayne's neck.

'Drive smoothly, Dwayne, and no sudden moves with the brakes. I'm not wearing a seat belt and it'd be so easy for this arrow to puncture all the way into your cerebellum. That's the part of your brain that makes you walk and talk normally.'

Dwayne fired up the Firebird's engine. Its throaty roar filled the workshop. Very carefully indeed, sitting as stiff as a board behind the wheel with the arrow pricking the base of his neck, he engaged drive and rumbled out of the yard and into the street.

Ben said, 'Take a right turn.' They passed the food market where he and Lottie had shopped for what turned out to be her last supper.

Dwayne croaked, 'I have no idea what you want from me, dude. Where are we goin'?'

'Here's the thing, Dwayne. I've been thinking back to our

conversation from last time we met. You do remember our last conversation, don't you?'

'What I said, I didn't mean nothin' by it.'

'You mean, like "don't feed the gorilla"? If you want to be a racist moron, Dwayne, that's your lookout. One day a gentleman of colour twice your size will stamp your scrawny little arse into the ground and leave you where he found you. I'm not here for that.'

'Then what then?' Dwayne pleaded, close to tears as he drove.

'It's about your pal Billy Bob Lafleur,' Ben said. 'I recall that when his name came up, it seemed that you were pretty well acquainted with him. Birds of a feather, and all that. Plus, I'm reliably informed that everybody knows everybody else around here.'

Dwayne tried to shrug, and winced at the jab in the back of the neck that it caused him. 'Sure, I know Billy Bob. We hung out together a couple times. Done business once or twice. He's a real A-hole.'

'I can't disagree with you there,' Ben said. 'Business, as in, drug business?'

'Guns, man. Sawed-off twelve-gauges. Pumps, semis, doubles, whatever we could buy in cheap. Cut'm down an' sold'm off.'

'Bank Robbers R Us. Very enterprising of you.'

'That was a long time ago. I told you, he's a real asshole. That what this is about? You wanna buy a gun?'

'No, I have all kinds of ways of killing people without making the slightest bit of noise. Remember that, Dwayne. Don't stop thinking about it for one moment.'

'I'm thinkin' about it,' Dwayne said, and Ben believed him. His hands were trembling on the steering wheel as they headed for the edge of town.

Ben said, 'Seeing as you move in such exalted circles, Dwayne, I'm guessing that you and Billy Bob must have a lot of seedy little mutual friends and acquaintances in the Clovis Parish crime scene. Am I right?'

After a long hesitation, Dwayne replied, 'I know a few people, yeah.'

'Like the Garrett brothers?' Ben said. He was watching Dwayne's eyes in the rear-view mirror. They were already brimming with anxiety, but the flash of fear that came into them at the mention of that name was unmistakable.

'I-I dunno who you mean. The what brothers?'

'Come on, Dwayne. Who do you think, Moe, Larry and Curly? I'm sure every aspiring tough guy in the state wants to be part of the Garrett boys' gang. And you're an aspiring tough guy, aren't you? Especially when you're showing off in front of your buddies. You really had me scared that day.'

'I-I don't know them, man. I mean, I know them but I don't *know* them.'

'Then you wouldn't know where they hang out, or anything like that?'

Dwayne was sweating like a pig. He took a hand off the wheel to wipe his face. 'No idea, man. Honest to God.'

'That's a real shame,' Ben said. 'I was so sure you would. But never mind. Seeing as you're no use to me after all, I'll just get you to pull over somewhere nice and quiet once we're out of town. Then I'll break your ankles, knees, elbows and wrists and all your fingers and leave you in the ditch while I take your boss's car for a nice long joyride, before I set fire to it outside the Villeneuve Sheriff's Office. How does that sound?'

Dwayne was suddenly sweating even more profusely. He shrank away. 'You're fuckin' crazy, man.'

'Oh, I'm a total raving psychopath,' Ben said. 'But you

must already know the things I'm capable of, if you follow the news.'

'I-I know this chick who's got a girlfriend who works for Logan Garrett,' Dwayne stammered.

'Progress at last. What is she, his administrative assistant?'

'She's a hooker, man. Name's Layla. Logan runs a string of hookers 'cross the parish.'

'You're a real font of knowledge once you get going, Dwayne. Now, I'm thinking that this Layla could point me in the direction of wherever Logan hangs out. Where would I find her?'

'I don't know, man! Ow!'

Ben jabbed the arrow harder. 'Wrong answer.'

'Okay, okay. They work at the Big Q. It's a motel.' Dwayne blurted out the name of the highway it was on, and Ben eased off the pressure with the arrowhead.

'How far from here?'

'Thirty miles, give or take. I ain't never been there.'

'Oh, I'm sure you haven't. Then today is your lucky day, because that's where we're going.'

'The cops are everywhere lookin' for you. They'll stop us for sure.'

'And if that happens, I assure you that you'll miss all the fun. Because you'll be the first to get it right in the neck.'

Neither of them spoke another word for the next half hour as Dwayne tooled west and then southwards down the highway. Ben stayed low down in the back seat, well concealed from outside thanks to the dark tint of the windows. He took out a cigarette one-handed while keeping Dwayne pinned with the arrow, lit it and savoured the smoke.

It was a gamble that they wouldn't come upon a police roadblock. But Ben had gambled before, and there was little sense worrying about it until it happened. He could leave the worrying to his feckless hostage. Dwayne was doing a lot of that.

Some thirty miles the other side of Pointe Blanche, they finally reached the Big Q Motel unscathed. It was the generic type of grubby fleapit Ben had passed a hundred of on his travels through the state, set off the highway with room doors on two floors, a weed-strewn parking area in front and a reception office with dirty glass doors and signs for No Smoking and No Concealed Handguns. What on earth was happening to America?

Dwayne swung the Firebird into the forecourt. The eyes darted in the mirror. 'Now what?'

Ben pulled the arrow away from Dwayne's neck and pointed with it. A tiny drop of blood oozed from the little hole the steel tip had bored in his prisoner's flesh.

'Pull up over there, where we can see the doorways. Then we wait, and watch, and you keep your mouth shut and pray that I don't start getting all impatient and irritable.'

In his time Ben had spent many hundreds, if not thousands, of patient hours on stakeouts, OPs and sniper duty. Even before the SAS had sharpened his skills to razor edge he'd had the ability to remain utterly still and absolutely focused on his target for extended periods of time, in anything from frigid mountain cold to melting jungle heat and humidity. A talent that his hostage lacked, but Dwayne was showing good sense in neither complaining nor trying to bolt for freedom. If anyone inside the office wondered what a flame-painted muscle car with black windows was doing just sitting outside their place of business, they didn't care enough to come and check it out.

It soon became apparent why the management paid little attention to the activities that took place at the Big Q Motel. Every so often, with metronomic regularity, a car pulled in off the highway and parked in a bay outside the room doors. Then the driver, invariably a solitary male, would get out, glance a little nervously around him as though checking that he wasn't being followed, then climb the steps and make his way to any one of three adjacent rooms on the upper floor, numbered twelve, thirteen, and fourteen. It was the same routine, every time. The guy would knock, the door would open, and a scantily-clad female would appear and welcome him in with a smile. The women in rooms twelve and fourteen each had the kind of teased blond hair Ben had thought had gone out after the eighties. Lucky number thirteen's occupant was dark, a little plump, and the least smiling of the three.

'That's Layla,' Dwayne said when she first appeared.

Ben said nothing.

At intervals of around twenty minutes, the routine would run in reverse: the door would open again, the punter would return to his car looking a little more relaxed, and drive off, soon to be replaced by another. All the coming and going added up to quite a busy little enterprise going on up there.

An hour went by. Then another. The Firebird was turning into an oven. After two and a half hours Ben was losing patience and ready to escort Dwayne up to pay an unscheduled visit to room thirteen. He definitely didn't want to walk in there while she was still occupied with her current client, and so waited for the guy to leave.

Just as Ben was about to make his move, a boxy black SUV the size of a small cottage with a Cadillac badge on its grille came tearing onto the motel forecourt and screeched to a halt in a parking bay. Once again, the solitary male driver jumped out and began marching towards the stairs. He was lean, about thirty years of age, and walked with the cocky swagger of a man suffering from overconfidence issues.

Spiky reddish hair, mirror-tinted dark glasses, blue jeans, fancy boots. He could have been just another client rolling up, but Ben instantly knew there was something different about this one.

And Dwayne instantly knew it, too. He said, 'Christ. That's Logan Garrett.'

Chapter 32

It wasn't hard to figure out the reason for Logan Garrett's visit to this motel room cottage industry. Ben thought it improbable that he was here to collect on the same kinds of services as the punters. More likely, if Layla and the two blondes were his girls, and if he was their pimp, he was here to pick up the nice little wads of cash they'd been busily earning for him.

Ben watched Logan trot up the stairway, stride up to the door of room thirteen and knock. Layla took a moment to answer the door. She didn't look especially happy to see him. He pushed past her into the room, and the door closed behind them.

It was going to take Logan a couple of minutes to pick up his money. Ben told Dwayne to drive around the side of the building. Dwayne shrugged, fired up the engine and did as he was told. At the rear was a scrubby area of parched grass and a row of dumpsters filled with broken chairs, old mattresses and carpet offcuts. Once the Firebird was out of sight of room thirteen's windows, Ben said, 'That's far enough. Now get out of the car. Leave it running.'

Dwayne halted the car, put the transmission in park and got out. Ben rocked the driver's seat forward and stepped out after him. 'Now open the boot.'

Dwayne frowned down at his feet. 'The what?'

'The trunk,' Ben corrected himself. 'Open it up.'

Again, Dwayne did what he was told. Then Ben glanced upwards and said, 'Is that a police chopper?' Dwayne craned his neck to scan the perfectly empty sky. And Ben hit him with a right uppercut to the side of the chin that spun his head around and knocked him out cold.

He caught Dwayne as he fell, propped his limp form against the back of the car and quickly went through his pockets. Dwayne was carrying about two hundred dollars in cash, a BlackBerry, some guitar picks and a Leatherman multi-tool. Ben didn't play the guitar but the rest of the stuff was useful spoils of war. He tipped Dwayne into the open boot. He'd briefly considered putting him in one of the dumpsters, but hostages were always a useful accessory to fugitives from justice.

'You're an idiot, Dwayne,' Ben said to the slumped shape in the boot, and then closed the lid. As an afterthought he took out the Leatherman, folded out some blades until he found a stubby Phillips screwdriver among them, and used it to punch a few holes in the boot lid. Dwayne might cook in there, but at least he wouldn't run out of air.

Ben quickly got behind the wheel, threw the transmission back into drive and pulled a tight turn back around the front of the motel, just in time to see Logan Garrett returning to his Cadillac. There was a bulge in each of Logan's trouser pockets the size of a roll of banknotes. Ben wondered what percentage of his ill-gotten gains the girls got to keep. Probably not much. What a life; but things were set to improve for them, because they soon wouldn't have a pimp any more.

Logan fired up the Cadillac and burned rubber out of the motel forecourt. Ben waited until he'd rejoined the highway and then followed. Logan was tearing along at over eighty miles an hour, which displeased Ben as the last thing he needed was to get pulled over for speeding. He kept pace with the Cadillac but hung well back for the sake of discretion, since a flame-painted muscle car with a huge fiery phoenix emblazoned across the bonnet perhaps wasn't the most anonymous surveillance vehicle. Then again, discretion might well be wasted on Logan Garrett, who didn't strike Ben as the most perceptive sort.

Logan headed north. Eighteen miles later he turned off the highway and struck eastwards along a country road that was almost devoid of traffic but twisty enough to enable Ben to stay back out of sight. It was just after five in the afternoon when Logan finally left the metalled road for a dirt one that snaked and wound upward into densely wooded hill country.

With no other vehicles to space between him and his quarry it was becoming harder for Ben to remain unnoticed. Forced to hang back two hundred yards and more, he got only the occasional fleeting glimpse of the Cadillac's tail ahead.

He wondered where Logan was leading him. Perhaps to the mysterious Garrett Island that Sheriff Roque had mentioned, but of which neither of the Heberts seemed to have ever heard?

One thing was for sure. Life was about to get more interesting.

For another forty minutes Ben carefully tailed Logan Garrett deeper and higher into the hills. As Ben reached a ridge the tree cover thinned out and the ground sloped away on his right to offer a broad view over a valley.

Two hundred yards further on, the dirt track had veered sharply around to the right and he could see the distant

Cadillac making its way down the slope towards a small cluster of rustic-looking buildings that stood alone in the middle of the vast empty wilderness. At this range it was hard to make out what the buildings were. A farm, maybe. Definitely not any kind of island. There was no water in sight. But whatever the place was, Logan appeared to be making right for it.

Ben rolled the Firebird to a halt, turned off the engine and got out, bringing his bag out with him. Inside was the compact but powerful pair of binoculars that he carried everywhere, just for times like these.

The edge of the slope was just a few yards from the track, strewn with rubble and wild grass. Ben made his way over to it, keeping low, then lay on his stomach with his elbows planted in the dirt and the binoculars to his eyes. He focused and panned and picked up the moving Cadillac as it progressed the rest of the way down the winding dirt road towards Logan Garrett's mysterious destination, trailing a dust plume in its wake.

Panning further to the right, Ben saw that the buildings were enclosed all around by a high security fence topped with concertina razor wire. The enclosed area consisted of maybe a quarter of an acre, nowhere near large enough for even the most diminutive rural smallholding.

Ben scanned the buildings to examine them in as much detail as he could, at this range. The whole place was crudely constructed out of planking and corrugated-iron sheets, most of which were weathered various shades of rusty brown. There was a larger structure in the centre, surrounded by a number of what were clearly storage sheds. Two of the sheds were of open-fronted lean-to design, and inside them Ben could make out rows and stacks of blue cylindrical objects that he at first thought were large propane bottles but then realised were container drums. There must be scores, even hundreds of them, arranged four or five high on wooden pallets. More loose drums lay untidily around the beaten-earth yard.

Another open-fronted barn was heaped ten feet high with sacks of something like grain or corn, some of which had split open and spilled their contents all over the ground. Yet another shed was stacked to the roof with firewood logs. A dismembered tree trunk lay on a saw horse in front of it, waiting to be chainsawed into segments and then split by axe on a chopping block. A lone worker in cap and dungarees was busily engaged in adding to the wood pile. He was a huge man, and from the way he moved it was clear there was something not quite right about him.

As Ben watched, the giant grabbed a sawed section of log the size of an armchair, placed it on the block and swung a large axe at it, splitting it apart with ease. He lumbered lopsidedly over to the scattered pieces, gathered them up in his monstrous arms and hurled them on the pile, then went lumbering back for more. Genetics.

The building in the middle was about the size of a hay barn, with side walls made out of warped planks and a rusty metal roof that sloped in four directions from a tall, jutting iron chimney with a ragged top that made it resemble the stack on Stephenson's *Rocket*. It was belching out a thin cloud of smoke that dissipated on the wind. The gentle hill breeze was blowing Ben's way, and even at this distance he could detect a whiff of a malty brewery smell coming from the building.

Ben smiled. Logan had just led him to the Garrett brothers' illegal moonshine distilling plant. Maybe one of several. If there were others, they would undoubtedly be in similarly remote locations to lessen the chances of discovery by local law officers or federal officers of the ATF. Judging by the messy state of the place, it had clearly been in operation for years. And the number of drums stacked up in the lean-to sheds made it easy to see that the Garretts' annual output of tax-free liquor was enough to intoxicate half of the Southern states. Business acumen obviously ran in the family.

Logan's Cadillac had reached the gateway into the enclosure, which was as tall as the fence and chained shut. As Ben watched, a bearded man in a cap and a red check shirt emerged from a tin guard hut and loped casually up to the gate to undo the padlock. He had a short-barrelled shotgun hanging off his shoulder. Maybe a product of the Garretts' other little line, supplying firearms to crooks. The chain fell loose and the bearded guy opened the gate for Logan to drive though. They exchanged a few brief words, then the bearded guy closed the gate behind him and redid the chain and lock before disappearing back into the tin hut.

Ben tracked the Cadillac as it drove across the yard, passed the main building and turned into an area between two large sheds where a row of other vehicles was parked. It made sense to keep the vehicles a good distance from the hub of the plant. Illegal stills were known to go up spectacularly in flames when things went wrong, usually when some drunken operator spilled a pot of pure methanol onto an open fire or lit a cigarette in the presence of highly explosive vapours. In pre-SAS days his army unit had once been deployed to the site of a suspected terrorist bomb factory in Northern Ireland that had exploded, only to find the smoking remnants of an illicit poteen distillery and a pile of charred body parts, all that remained of the culprits.

He watched now as Logan slotted himself into a parking space between a flatbed truck, so ancient that it could have dated back to the original prohibition days, and a couple of pickups. But those weren't the vehicles that drew Ben's eye and made his blood race in his veins as he twiddled the focusing ring for a sharper view through his binoculars. It was the sight of the dirt-streaked vehicle parked at the far end of the row.

A black Mustang. One that Ben recognised instantly as the same car that Lottie's killers had been driving that night.

They were here.

Chapter 33

Ben put away the binocs and returned to the car to get his jacket and Caleb's bow, arrows and quiver. Dwayne must have regained consciousness a while ago. Now very much awake, he was thumping on the inside of the boot lid and demanding in a muffled voice to be let out. He'd just have to resign himself to his fate and get comfortable in there. He had plenty of space. It wasn't a Fiat 500.

Ben grabbed his things and slipped over the edge of the slope. He zigzagged his way down the incline, moving from tree to bush to tree to conceal his approach. The Garretts believed they were safe up here, deep in the middle of nowhere. They were about to discover that nowhere was safe for them any longer.

Even so, Ben knew what he was coming up against. If there was one armed guard inside the fenced compound there were sure to be more. Not counting the monster with the axe and the Garrett brothers themselves. From what Tyler had told him, Ben could be certain that Jayce Garrett, the eldest, posed the biggest threat of the three.

At the bottom of the slope the ground rose up again in a steep bank of verdant ferns that grew thick and wild all the way to the base of the perimeter fence. Ben moved as slowly and cautiously as a hunting leopard. It took him a full ten minutes to stalk through the foliage towards the wire. Lying flat among the ferns he had a view of the compound yard, the vehicles and the main building. The only movement he could see was the slow plume of smoke drifting from the chimney stack. The axe-wielding giant was nowhere to be seen. The bearded guy with the shotgun hadn't re-emerged from his hut.

Ben took the multi-tool from his pocket and folded out the handles to reveal the combined pliers and wire cutters, then went to work snipping out a hole in the mesh large enough to crawl through. A passing guard might notice his entry route and raise the alarm – but odds were they'd know he was here before that happened.

Ben pushed his kit through the hole and then slipped inside the compound. He moved quickly towards the nearest shed and took cover against its rusty side, listening intently and hearing nothing but the rasp of a diesel generator coming from somewhere. He stalked across to the row of parked vehicles. Squatted on his haunches next to the black Mustang. Found the sharp little knife blade of the multi-tool, pressed its tip against the sidewall of the Mustang's right rear wheel, and gave the hilt a sharp blow with the flat of his other hand to punch the blade through the steel belting of the tyre.

The sudden escape of air hissed like a wounded snake. The tyre began to deflate and flatten and the rear corner of the car sank slowly towards the ground. He did the same thing to the other three tyres and then moved on, working his way along the line until he could be certain that none of the Garretts or their associates would be leaving here in a hurry.

Ben slipped away from the immobilised vehicles and headed towards the guard hut.

The hut was a crude wooden shed that doubled as a workshop, littered with tools and junk. The grimy window pane overlooked the compound's gates. The bearded guy was sitting slumped in a raggedy armchair in the corner. His shotgun hung by its sling from a nail in the wall. On the workbench next to him lay a walkie-talkie. But he made no attempt to reach for either as Ben stepped inside the hut, because he was asleep. Little wonder, judging by the reek of moonshine on his breath and the half-empty bottle at his elbow.

Ben needed to make sure the guy wouldn't wake up again too soon. He did that with the heavy rubber-headed mallet that was among the mess of tools on the workbench. One solid blow to the side of the head, and the guy was off to dreamland for a good long while. Ben proned him on his fat belly and crouched over him to hogtie his wrists and ankles together with some electrical wire. Then he stood and looked around him. Most of the workbench's surface was taken up with a large section of copper cylinder the size of a hot water tank. Various lengths of copper piping lay on the worktop next to it.

If Ben needed any final evidence of what the Garretts were up to, the dismantled still was it. Sometime before the bearded guy had drunk himself into a stupor he'd been working on repairing the thing – binding up sections of the piping with gaffer tape, and using drops of molten metal solder to fill little pinholes in the thin copper cylinder where potentially flammable liquids or explosive fumes could leak out. The soldering iron lay cold on the bench, next to a big roll of steel wool that the guy had been using to keep the tip of the iron clean and buff up the copper. Very industrious, Ben thought.

That wasn't all he was thinking. He was one man against an unknown quantity of opponents, all of them presumably armed, dangerous and very pissed off once they became aware of an intruder in their place of business. Even with the shotgun, Ben was going to be at a major disadvantage. And a bow wasn't much of a weapon against the kind of hardware he expected Jayce Garrett to be packing. Then again, there were ways to make a bow a lot more effective. Especially in a place like this.

Ben had to work fast. He picked up the walkie-talkie handset and saw from the readout that it had a full charge. He removed the battery compartment cover. Inside was a single nine-volt battery, the standard rectangular type with the two terminals attached to a snap connector at one end. He disconnected the battery and set it down. Then he drew an arrow from the quiverful Caleb had given him, and clasped it between his knees with the hunting tip pointing upwards. He tore off a generous wad of steel wool from the roll and bound it securely to the business end of the arrow with a length of gaffer tape. Once that was done, he picked up the bow and set about taping the nine-volt battery to its handle, so that the terminals were just below the arrow rest.

Watching him work, most people might have thought he was crazy. But that was because most people were unskilled in the art and science of causing maximum mayhem. Ben was a master at it, as the Garretts were soon to find out.

He replaced the doctored arrow in the quiver, then grabbed the bearded guy's shotgun from the nail where it hung and checked it. An old Remington 870 pump, five-round capacity, loaded with buckshot. Ben slung the gun over his shoulder. Checking the coast was clear, he slipped out of the guard hut. Still no sign of the monstrous woodcutter.

Ben made his way towards the main building. Ahead was an open doorway. He slipped through it and found himself in a crude, dank plywood ante-room at the end of a narrow passage, full of more junk and piled sacks of cane sugar and cracked corn and barrels of water loaded on a hand truck. The malty brewery smell was much stronger here, telling him that somewhere at the far end of the passage was a more open area where the business of distilling was taking place.

He stood very still. Listening hard and hearing faint voices. He closed his eyes and focused on the sound. Three men were talking. Their accents were local. The conversation they were having sounded more like an argument, but Ben couldn't make out the exact words.

He opened his eyes. Drew the modified arrow from the quiver. Fitted its nock to the bowstring and laid the shaft on the arrow rest. Silently, slowly, he moved along the passage in the direction the voices were coming from.

And moments later, Ben had found what he'd come looking for.

Chapter 34

Ben now found himself standing at the entrance to a cavernous, barn-sized space that was a full-scale distillery operation in full swing. The floor was smooth concrete painted industrial red. Much of its area, and the interior walls, was hidden behind a mass of sacks and water drums and firewood. Closer to the centre stood a dozen or more large cylindrical moonshine stills, over eight feet tall and four feet wide, set in a broad circle like the ring of Stonehenge, gleaming copper just like the one Ben had seen dismantled for repair in the guard hut. Pipes ran across and down from the top of each cylinder to a separate water drum and then to a collector vessel into which the distilled alcohol steadily dripped. Each still sat atop its own lit wood burner, and the combined smoke from the fires was channelled towards the centre chimney by a massive corrugated-iron hood.

The heat in the room was almost overpowering and the smell of cooking mash was chokingly thick, mixed with the stench of diesel fumes from a generator that rattled and rasped in the background, powering pumps and gauges and equipment whose purpose Ben could only guess at.

At the centre of the bizarre circle, dwarfed by the height of the copper cylinders, stood all three Garrett brothers.

The argument was over money. Logan appeared to be doing most of the talking. He'd taken off the mirror shades and his eyes were defensive and anxious as he fronted his two elder siblings. He was gesticulating and saying, 'Chill, guys, you know Biquaisse's totally good for it. If he says he'll pay in two weeks, he'll pay in two weeks. Ain't like he's ever let us down before.'

'Biquaisse my ass. This is ten fuckin' Gs, Logan. You gone pussy on this fucker, or what?'

'Come on, Seth.'

'You go back and tell this lyin' prick we want the money in two days or he's gator meat.'

Ben paid little attention to their dispute. He was just watching, very still and barely breathing. His heart rate was low and calm and his blood felt cold despite the over-powering heat.

Because this was it. The final shred of proof, if Ben even needed it. Logan Garrett's elder brothers were the same two men he had last seen escaping the scene of the murder that night. The one with the tied-back hair and the nasty scowl on his face, had been the driver of the Mustang. That would be Seth, Ben now knew. He was maybe thirty-five and wiry, with a few thousand dollars' worth of tattoos covering his arms and neck and a pearl-handled Beretta sticking out of the waistband of his jeans. To his right stood the eldest brother, Jayce, whom Ben now recognised without a shadow of a doubt as the man he'd watched running from the guesthouse as Lottie lay dying in the hallway.

Jayce Garrett had murdered her. Jayce Garrett had person-ally planted the sword through her body and nailed her to the floor.

Jayce was wearing a plain white T-shirt that hung loose over black combat trousers. He was the eldest by maybe three years, perhaps four, but he was in much more athletic shape. He had no visible tattoos except for the faded blue swastika on his right hand that Tyler had mentioned. His reddish hair, the same tint as his brothers, was freshly buzzed almost to the scalp, military-style. He didn't look angry, like Seth, or agitated, like Logan. His voice was soft and smooth as he addressed his youngest sibling, but the softness carried its own kind of menace.

'How many times I gotta tell you, Bro, you don't let nobody bullshit you?'

'Yeah, Bro,' Seth weighed in, 'it ain't the principle. It's the motherfuckin' *money*.'

Logan's shoulders slumped in defeat. The cocky pimp with the swagger in his stride now looked like a berated child. 'Okay, okay, I'll make sure he pays.'

Seth began, 'Sure, if he ain't halfway to fuckin' Nebraska by n—' Then he broke off mid-sentence. Both Logan and Jayce looked at him in surprise, then turned their eyes in the same direction Seth was suddenly staring.

Because Ben had just stepped out from between two copper cylinders to confront them.

Before any of them had time to speak, Ben drew the bow about three-quarters of the way. The last time he'd drawn it he was ready to collapse from exhaustion and pain. Now he felt strong and ready for whatever might happen next. He held the weapon steady with the first of his modified arrows pointing at the three brothers.

He watched their faces. Logan had turned purple with rage and seemed about to start blustering. Seth was staring at him with a look midway between alarm and aggression. Jayce's reaction was the most telling. His face was completely blank, as though nothing could possibly faze him. It was the look of a remorseless, psychopathic killer. Ben knew he'd been wearing the same empty, impassive expression when he'd slaughtered Lottie.

But even if all three Garretts responded differently to the sudden intrusion, none of them, not even Logan, was foolish enough to impulsively go for his pistol.

Ben took a step closer.

'Who the fuck are you?' Logan yelled, pointing.

'You know who I am,' Ben replied. 'I'm the guy you set up. Or tried to. Surprised to see me?'

Jayce Garrett spoke next, his voice still as calm and smooth as before. 'You're a real smart guy, findin' us here, that's a fact.'

'Talk to your little brother,' Ben said. 'He's the one who led me here. I don't think he's the brains of the family. That'd be you, Jayce.'

Jayce made a slow, cold smile. 'You're right about that.'

'But you're not as clever as you think you are. Killing Lottie Landreneau was a very stupid thing to do. Picking me to frame for it was even more stupid. You have no idea what you've got yourselves into.'

Seth Garrett laughed out loud. 'Says the dumbass who just walked in here with a goddamned bow and arrow. You got one shot. We're three guys packin' forty, fifty rounds between us, without havin' to reload. Let that arrow fly, you know what's gonna happen next.'

'Try me,' Ben said. 'Do you want to be the first to die?' He swivelled the arrow Seth's way.

Seth stopped laughing and said nothing.

'You know, I could ask you all kinds of questions about why you did what you did,' Ben said. 'About why it was so important to you to carry out some vendetta that's centuries old, and what you thought you were going to achieve by murdering an innocent woman, and how you found her after all this time. But truthfully, I don't care. You can save that story for the police.'

Logan sneered, 'So that's why you're here, to take us in? Like a citizen's arrest, right?'

'That's how it has to be,' Ben said. 'If it wasn't, all three of you would have been dead before you even knew I was here.'

'That a fact?' Logan shot back.

'Yes,' Ben replied. 'That's a fact.'

'Looks like he forgot to bring his army with him, boys,' said Seth.

'Just me,' Ben said. 'You think I need help to take down a bunch of yokel wannabe outlaws? Get serious. I'm only sorry there aren't nine of you. It might have evened the odds a little.'

'You got one helluva mouth on you,' Logan spat.

Jayce Garrett was silent. His eyes totally inscrutable. Body relaxed, hands hanging loose by his sides.

'So here's the deal, folks,' Ben said. 'You're each going to slip out your pistols, nice and easy, finger and thumb, no sudden moves. You're going to lay them down on the floor at your feet and slide them over to me. Then I'm going to have to ask you to strip to your underwear, so I can see you're not trying to hide any concealed weapons. Then we're all going to sit tight and wait for the police to show up. My pal Sheriff Roque will put you in a nice cell where you can confess your crimes and beg for mercy. I hear the state of Louisiana hasn't executed anyone in years because they ran out of lethal injections. That means you'll get to sit on death row for a long, long time, thinking about what it feels like to burn in hell.'

'Sounds like a shit deal to me,' Seth said.

'Best one you're going to get,' Ben replied.

Jayce spoke again. 'What if my brothers and I, we don't feel like signin' up for it?'

'Then we have a problem,' Ben said. 'Because if you decide to fight this, you're all going to die. And if you die, you can't confess, and I can't clear my name. Then I might as well go down fighting, too. In short, you have about five seconds to throw down your weapons or I'm going to blow this place up with all of us inside.'

Chapter 35

All three of the Garretts laughed. Jayce shook his head. 'Don't you just love this guy.'

'Got some balls, that's for sure,' Seth said. 'Still gotta smoke his ass, though.'

Logan's eyes glinted. 'Leave some for me, fellas.'

Ben said, 'Last warning.'

In case they didn't think he meant it, he pulled the bow to full draw. As the arrow slid all the way back on its rest, the wad of steel wool taped to the shaft brushed against the exposed terminals of the nine-volt battery he'd attached to the bow handle. The steel wool instantly began to glow red, then burst into a bright, hot flame. The faster the arrow flew, the hotter it would burn. Greek fire, revisited.

Ben raised the angle of the bow by a few degrees, to aim for the upper half of the copper still directly behind where the Garrett brothers were standing. The arrow's tip would punch through soft copper as easily as a bullet and instantly ignite a large quantity of ethanol vapour as volatile as gasoline fumes. The erupting fireball would blast the cylinder apart like a bombshell, engulf everything within its range, set off the rest of the stills and turn the whole building into a raging conflagration in moments. Nobody would escape alive and nothing would remain but a scorched hole in the ground.

And all three Garretts knew that very well.

'Told you it was a bad idea picking on me,' Ben said. 'Now we can all go to hell together, if that's how you want to call it.'

'Don't shoot,' Logan yelled. 'Here, there's my gun. Take it. Fuckin' take it!' He pulled out the concealed Glock he'd been wearing under his shirt and lobbed it at Ben's feet.

'Mine too.' Seth gingerly drew the pearl-handed Beretta that had been sticking out of his back pocket and laid it down, then skimmed it across the floor with his foot.

Jayce Garrett didn't move. A tiny glimmer of a smile played at the corners of his mouth. Ben could see the outline of a large handgun in a belt holster under the loose hem of Jayce's T-shirt. If Jayce went for it, it wouldn't be to surrender it.

'Don't bluff me,' Ben said.

'No?'

At that moment, Ben sensed a rushing movement coming up fast at his rear. He broke his aim and whirled around to see a flesh mountain looming towards him. It was the giant woodcutter he'd spotted from afar earlier on. Up close, the man was even more enormous. He was over seven feet tall, all lumpy and misshapen like a mutant, with rat-tail hair and bulging eyes that looked in two directions at once. His huge arms were raised overhead and his fists clenched the log-splitting axe that had just reached the top of its swing and was now falling like a guillotine blade towards Ben's head.

Ben sidestepped and ducked, and the blade missed him by an inch and crashed against the concrete floor with a shower of sparks. With a roar of rage the giant hefted the axe up again to take another lunge at this puny little man who dared threaten his masters.

Ben let the bow and the burning arrow fall from his hands, reached behind him and unslung the shotgun. But before he could bring the gun into action the axe was whooshing towards him again, a fearsome swing that could cut him in two if it landed. Even if he blew the monster's head off at this moment the heavy wedge-shaped blade would keep coming by its sheer momentum.

A gun had other uses. Ben raised the weapon protectively to parry the blow. The crushing force of the impact almost smashed the shotgun from his grip. The barrel crumpled like a length of cardboard tubing.

Ben fell back a step with the ruined weapon in his hands. The giant lumbered towards him, snorting something unintelligible and baring a set of jagged black teeth that looked as if he'd been chewing raw sugarcane all his life.

'Meet our good friend Rufus,' said Jayce Garrett. 'Rufus don't take kindly to folks bustin' in on our place of business. Now he's gonna chop your ass up into little pieces, and we're gonna watch'm do it.'

Rufus' little piggy eyes glittered to hear his boss's praise. He gathered his massive strength and swung the axe once again at Ben, in a horizontal arc right to left that would have separated neck from shoulders if Ben hadn't ducked. The sideways momentum of the blade carried it onwards, rotating Rufus' mass with it. Which opened up a gap in his defences, and Ben wasn't about to miss the opportunity. The giant might be inhumanly strong, but he was also ox-slow. Ben wasn't. He was playing to a hostile audience and needed to finish this job very quickly.

In days of yore when men were men and recoil-absorbing rubber buttpads were strictly for wimps, the old model 870 shotgun came with a hard rubber plate attached to the shoulder end of its wooden stock. Ideal for protecting a fine piece of American black walnut in the great outdoors. Also handy for smashing someone's face in, when circumstances required. Rufus let out a high-pitched squeal of pain and shock as the shotgun butt rammed him brutally in the mouth, crunching whatever was left of his teeth. He dropped the axe and teetered off balance.

Ben moved in hard and fast and hit him again, this time full in the throat. It was a savage blow both designed and intended to kill. One that Ben knew was very capable of that job. Seven pounds of wood and steel driven by a further 175 pounds of bodyweight all focused on Rufus' windpipe and crushed it flat. He went down like a felled oak tree, clawing at his throat and gasping for air that would never come, because Rufus had breathed his last.

The crack of a gunshot rang out, loud and harsh under the tin roof. Logan Garrett had managed to recover his fallen pistol and snatched it up to fire at Ben in such a scrabbling rush that he'd missed by a couple of feet.

His eldest brother would make no such mistake. Jayce was drawing a big stainless-steel automatic from his belt holster, smooth and fluid and practised.

Ben had about a second to get himself out of it, or else he was a dead man.

Chapter 36

Seth Garrett's Beretta was still on the floor, but it was too far away for Ben to make a grab for. The fallen bow was nearer, and it still had a couple of arrows left in its inbuilt quiver. He threw himself towards the cover of the nearest moonshine still and snatched up the bow mid-roll just as Jayce Garrett let off a booming shot that struck exactly where Ben's head was.

Or had been, a quarter second earlier. The bullet punched a 9mm hole into the still's copper cylinder as Ben disappeared behind it. A stream of pure alcohol jetted out, spattering to the floor.

Jayce Garrett clutched his pistol in both hands and ran bent-kneed around the side of the perforated still, ready to send a volley of bullets Ben's way. Ben had already retreated behind the next one in the row while loading another arrow to the bow.

As Jayce came into view, Ben drew and fired all in one movement. The arrow flew straight and true towards Jayce's head. Jayce saw it coming a split second before he could fire his pistol. He tried to flinch out of its path, but his fast reflexes weren't quite fast enough and he screamed as the arrow's hunting tip skewered his right ear and tore away a big piece of its lobe before embedding itself in the shiny copper cylinder behind him.

Another fountain of moonshine came spurting from the arrow hole and pattered to the floor. There was a growing lake of the stuff pooling all over the concrete. The fumes were dizzying.

Ben went to pluck another arrow from the quiver. As he fitted it to the bowstring he realised that Seth's gun was no longer on the floor, because its owner had retrieved it and was now sneaking between the stills to come up on his left flank. Which could have been a problem for Ben, if Logan had decided to stalk around on his right, catching him in a pincer movement.

But Logan had other things on his mind at that instant. He let out a yowl of alarm as he saw the river of moonshine rapidly spreading across the floor towards Ben's modified arrow that had fallen there, the steel wool wadding still burning away brightly. Logan bounded over to kick the arrow away before the entire lake of near-pure alcohol went up in flames, but he slipped on the wet floor and went down with a grunt and a splash.

The next thing, Logan Garrett was on fire. The superstrength moonshine blazed with a blueish, almost invisible but intensely hot flame as it engulfed his legs, then set light to his shirt and spread all up his body. Logan screamed and thrashed on the floor, desperately trying to beat out the flames, but his clothes were soaked with moonshine and there was nothing he could do to prevent himself from turning into a human torch.

As he rolled wildly he spread the flames to the second pool that was leaking from the other perforated still. A curtain of shimmering blue fire whooshed up across the floor.

Seth Garrett had been just about to shoot at Ben but now had to leap back to save himself. In his haste he stumbled and fell, and his gun clattered from his hand. Ben saw his chance and pounced to snatch it up, then had to retreat quickly to avoid getting burned himself.

Now the flames were leaping up everywhere, spreading with lethal eagerness through the whole distillery. Once the other stills began to catch alight, the entire place would erupt like a volcano – and that was just seconds away. Logan's body was now totally consumed by fire and he wasn't moving any more, just an indistinct black shape curled on the floor at the heart of the roiling blaze.

Ben raced back the way he'd come, heading for the passage, Caleb's bow in one hand, Seth Garrett's Beretta in the other. He paused for an instant to glance across the sea of fire and spotted Seth and the wounded Jayce smash through a window at the far side of the blazing building, making their own escape. There was no way he could follow them, but he had an idea where they'd be headed.

As Ben reached the passage another copper still blew, filling the air with an incendiary blast that shook the whole building. He could feel the scorching breath of the fire on his back as he raced down the narrow corridor towards the storeroom and the exit beyond. Any second now, thousands of gallons of moonshine were going to ignite simultaneously and bring the whole place down. He ran faster.

But then the way ahead was suddenly barred as three more Garrett accomplices appeared at the foot of the passage. One clutched a handgun, one a shotgun and the other a rifle, and all three looked utterly terrified. Ben could tell from the looks on their faces that these were not combat-hardened men, but just a bunch of local hicks brought in to work and guard the moonshine distillery and were only putting themselves in harm's way because they were even more afraid of their bosses. But three hopeless stooges could still get lucky against a single determined opponent. Especially the guy with the shotgun, who wouldn't even have to aim.

So Ben singled him out and shot him first, firing one-handed on the run. The guy spun and fell. The one with the rifle panicked, dropped his weapon and bolted. The plucky soul with the handgun bent into a combat crouch and got off a rushed shot that punched through the tin wall at Ben's elbow.

And then the moonshine distillery exploded.

Ben was hurled off his feet by the force of the blast. Perhaps if the other guy had been closer to the epicentre of the explosion, he might have been more fortunate. Because then he wouldn't have remained standing, and a jagged crescent-shaped fragment of copper shrapnel from one of the shattered stills wouldn't have taken the top of his head off in the fraction of a second before the roof collapsed on both of them.

Chapter 37

Ben fought his way out from under the wreckage of twisted corrugated-iron sheets and bits of timber. He was bleeding and scorched and bruised. But he was still alive. And he also still had a pretty good idea of where Jayce and Seth Garrett had made off to: straight for their Mustang, only to discover it and all the other possible escape vehicles were out of commission. *No getting away so easily this time, boys.*

Ben staggered to his feet, looking around him for his weapons. The storeroom and corridor were completely flattened. Behind him, the scorched remains of the moonshine distillery looked as if they'd taken a direct hit from a military air strike. The few structural timbers left intact were furiously ablaze and threatening to give way at any second. Barely visible among the belching smoke, the tall chimney was still standing but would not be for much longer.

There was no sign of the rifleman who'd bolted and run for safety. Ben picked up his discarded weapon, an old lever-action Marlin deer carbine. No wonder the guy had run away in fear. He'd racked the lever in such a hurry that he'd short-stroked the action and jammed it up solid. Marlins were known to do that. It was a gunsmith job to fix.

Ben tossed the useless gun down. That was when he noticed the limp, bloody arm protruding from under the debris. He paused to feel for a pulse. He wouldn't let a man suffer the fate of being buried alive, even an enemy who had just tried to kill him.

But it was already too late for this one. Ben snatched up the bow and pistol and went in pursuit of Seth and Jayce.

The sky was dark from the smoke and dust that were blocking out the sunlight. As Ben sprinted between what was left of the buildings, heading in the direction of the parked vehicles, the remnants of the distillery structure gave way and crashed into the flames. Then the chimney itself began to topple, slowly at first, with a groaning and buckling and rendering of metal.

Ben looked up and saw that it was on course to come down right on top of him. He could skid to a halt in the dirt as it blocked his path, or he could pick up his step and try to race past and pray he didn't get crushed to death.

He lengthened his stride. The chimney began to topple faster. He kept his eyes to the front and ran hard. The falling stack came down ten feet behind him, destroying what little remained of the Garretts' factory and flattening the store sheds adjacent to it.

Now the lean-to containing all the stacked moonshine drums was ablaze, too, threatening to set a thousand more gallons of high-octane alcohol off like a fuel refinery disaster. Ben pressed on through the mayhem, hurdling fallen wreckage and shielding his face from the intense heat of the many smaller fires that had broken out everywhere. A few yards further, the parking area came into view, near the perimeter fence. Ben stopped and scanned the row of vehicles. The Mustang was still there, along with the two pickups and the ancient flatbed truck and Logan's Cadillac, all sitting low to the ground on their deflated tyres and covered with dust from the explosion.

But there was no sign of the surviving Garretts themselves. Ben's eyes narrowed and he tightened his grip on the pistol, anticipating their appearance any second. Where were they?

Just then, he heard the roar of a motorcycle engine and spun round to see two dirt bikes come bursting out from another storage shed, just about the only one still intact. Jayce and Seth Garrett were making their escape, riding like wild men through the flaming debris. Jayce's neck and shoulder and the whole right side of his T-shirt were red with blood from his torn ear. He rode one-handed, clutching a sawn-off shotgun like a huge double-barrelled pistol in his left fist. He saw Ben standing there and levelled the gun over the handlebars to fire at him.

The shotgun boomed and spouted flame as Ben ducked behind part of a wrecked shed and the blast peppered buckshot holes in the corrugated-iron sheet just inches over his head. The bikes roared by, kicking up dust and dirt in their wake with their knobbly off-road tyres.

Ben stepped out behind them and let off three fast snapping shots with the pistol. A spurt of blood flew from Seth's upper left arm. His machine wobbled and kept going. Ben sprinted after them, firing as he went, but it was a moving target and hard to nail down in his sights.

The bikes raced straight towards the collapsed chimney stack that blocked their path. For a moment it looked as though both machines were going to smash straight into the obstacle. Then Jayce veered left, aiming for a section of the store shed the chimney had crushed flat. Part of its collapsed roof was jutting up at an angle like a ramp. Jayce's machine hit it with a thud and the bike engine yowled as he rocketed upwards into the air, clearing the fallen chimney like a stunt rider.

Seth followed right in his wake. The bikes landed on the

other side and kept going, with nothing now between them and escape but a locked gate. Ben scrambled up the ramp and jumped down the other side. His pistol was empty. He threw it away and kept running.

Jayce Garrett still had one barrel of his shotgun. He fired straight ahead of him at the padlock and chain that fastened the gates. The buckled lock fell and the chain parted. The gates swung open as the two bikes flashed through the opening without slowing down. Then they were off, accelerating noisily away up the dirt road and shrinking fast into the distance.

Ben chased them on foot as far as the open gates before he was forced to accept that they'd got away from him. He swore, knowing he'd underestimated his enemy. He might have struck the Garretts a serious blow and taken one of them permanently out of the picture, but he'd failed in his main objective.

Where to pick up their trail again, now that his one lead was gone? He had no idea, but he'd have to worry about that later.

For now, he had to focus on getting away from here before the unmissable black smoke skyscraper rising from the wreck of the distillery drew someone's attention and the police came swarming all over this place like ants.

It was a long run back to the car. Late afternoon was slowly morphing to early evening. As he scrambled up the slope Ben heard the faint thud of a helicopter far away in the distance. He looked up and scanned three hundred degrees of the horizon before he saw a tiny dark dot tracking above the forested hills, some miles off. His well-trained eye identified it as being most likely a Bell 430, a type favoured by a lot of law enforcement and military units. From this range he couldn't make out the tell-tale blue livery and gold stripes that would have marked it as a state police chopper. Nor would it be able to observe him from so far away. But the smoke rising and drifting from the site of the Garretts' moonshine distillery was too conspicuous to miss. If the occupants of the aircraft hadn't spotted it yet, they soon would.

He made it the rest of the way up the slope to the car, then slid in behind the wheel and fired it up and pulled a tight U-turn to go bouncing and lurching back down the track the way he'd come.

Ten miles later, he pulled sharply in at the side of a country road and got out. He walked around to the boot, opened the lid and said, 'How are you doing in there, still breathing?'

'It ain't human, keepin' me locked up like this for hours on end,' Dwayne Skinner protested.

'You're right, Dwayne. I've seen the error of my ways and decided to let you go.'

Dwayne's face lit up, then grew suspicious. 'Seriously? Y'all ain't gonna bust my arms and legs like you said?'

'Unless you try to rat on me, in which case I'll know where to find you again and you'll spend the next six months in plaster from head to toe, sucking baby food through a straw. Now get out.'

Dwayne clambered stiffly out of the boot and looked around him at the expanse of wilderness. 'Aw, hell, man. This is the goddamned middle of nowhere.'

'It's only forty miles or so back to Pointe Blanche. The exercise will do you good. Get moving and don't ever let me see your ugly face again. Understood?'

Dwayne was left standing by the roadside in a cloud of dust as Ben roared away.

His next move was an unknown quantity. He only knew that he wouldn't go back to the Heberts. Motels and trailer parks were unsafe refuges. The roads were even more dangerous. If there was an avenue not closed to him, he couldn't begin to think what it might be.

The more Ben thought about it, the faster he drove. The Firebird roared happily along at eighty, ninety, a hundred miles an hour. Trees and farms and bayous and open fields flashed by him. It was a big country and he needed to lose himself in it and remain a step ahead of his pursuers while he figured out his plan.

That was when he went speeding around a bend and almost piled straight into the police checkpoint.

Chapter 38

It was the co-pilot of the Louisiana State Police Air Support Unit Bell 430, an officer named Claude Daigle, who reported the sighting back to base after a couple of passes of the still-burning wreckage they'd spotted in the remoteness of the Declouette Hills, forty-five miles north-west of Pointe Blanche and close to the Elysium Parish line. His orders to land and investigate were duly carried out by him and his colleague, Officer Jerome Guidry.

The impression the policemen had got from the air was quickly confirmed once they were on site: that whatever incident they were dealing with here was still very fresh indeed. Much of the wreckage of the buildings was still burning fiercely. Elsewhere among the devastation they found discarded weapons that were still warm to the touch, a quantity of spent cartridge cases, and one dead body buried under a ton of debris. If there were more bodies, it would be a while before anyone could get close enough to dig them out.

Officers Daigle and Guidry also discovered a very agitated, smoke-blackened gentleman trying to free his friend who had received a nasty blow to the head and been hogtied with electrical wire inside a hut. The hut further contained items of evidence suggesting that the burning buildings had served as a remote illegal distilling operation that had until now escaped police notice. The officers' first assessment of the situation was that some rival gang of outlaw moonshiners must have attacked and destroyed it as a way of eliminating the competition.

The two apprehended suspects were immediately cuffed and read their rights. The bearded one with the swelling lump on his head had little to say, apart from give his name which was Willie Deeb. His friend Randy Prator, on the other hand, was so willing to talk that they couldn't shut him up. And the things that came out in Prator's babbling stream were enough for Daigle and Guidry to look at each other and agree, 'Sheriff Roque needs to hear this right away.'

Within minutes, Waylon Roque was hustling aboard a second State Police Bell 430 and being whisked rapidly to view the scene and hear the witness's statement for himself. The chopper landed next to the other on the approach track to the ruined distillery and Roque, bending low and clamping his campaign hat to prevent it from being blown away by the rotors' downdraught, hurried through the gates with his deputies Mason Redbone and Eli Fontaine at his heels. The sheriff cast his steely eye across the scene of carnage. Looked like one bunch of morons killing another bunch of morons, in his estimation. Done a pretty damn good job of it, too. There hadn't been a shoot-em-up war zone like this in Clovis Parish since the days of Bonnie and Clyde.

'This better be good,' the sheriff growled at Officers Daigle and Guidry as he stepped inside the hut where the suspects were being held, one hand on the butt of his Colt. 'I'm busy as a one-legged cat in a sandbox with this damn manhunt and I got better things to do than clear up some gang-related bullshit. So what've we got?'

'This went down just this afternoon, Sheriff,' Guidry said. 'Found a bunch of guns an' shell casings in the dirt. Reckon there're at least three crispies back there for the coroner to dig out of the wreckage. But it don't look like a gang thing.'

Roque looked sharply at Officers Guidry and Daigle. 'Then what the hell is it?'

Daigle nudged Randy Prator, who was sitting glumly cuffed on the hut floor next to his pal Willie. 'Come on, peckerwood, tell the sheriff what you told us.'

'Weren't no gang,' Randy Prator said. 'It was just one guy. Same fella who knocked Willie here on the head and damn near cracked his brains out.'

'One guy?' the sheriff said, his face tightening hard. 'Speak, son. Talk to me.'

'Tore this place apart like a goddamned one-man army,' Randy Prator babbled on. 'I saw'm shoot Landon, standin' right next to me.'

'Never mind Landon, tell me about the guy,' the sheriff grated.

'Some foreigner, English or somethin'. All I know is, Landon told me that he's the crazy-ass sumbitch broke Billy Bob Lafleur's neck and cut up that black girl in Chitimacha. Name's—'

'Hope,' Roque finished for him. 'Ben Hope, goddamnit.' He shook his head in bewilderment as he tried to make sense of this bizarre turn of events. 'I should have known that maniac would be behind this. Well, this proves he's still alive, anyhow. But what the hell's he doin'?'

'Beats me, Sheriff,' Daigle said, rubbing his chin. 'All I know is, these boys work for the Garrett brothers. This is their operation. Or was. Ain't much left of it now.'

'I don't know about that,' Deputy Redbone put in. 'The Garretts? Reckon not. Don't look that way to me at all.'

Roque looked at him. 'No? Just how does it look to you, Mason?'

Daigle nudged Prator again. 'Go on. Tell'm the rest of it.'

Prator bit his lip. 'I wanna lawyer before I say another goddamn thing. And I'm only talkin' if I get a deal. Y'all put me on the federal witness protection program or I ain't playin'.'

'You'll get your lawyer,' Roquè snapped, eyeing him with contempt and wishing he could just pistol-whip this clown like in the good old days. 'And a champagne and steak dinner down at the jailhouse, just as soon as you talk to me. So talk.'

Randy Prator was willing to spill whatever beans could help to get him off the hook. 'Damn right this was the Garretts' operation,' he blurted. 'Hell, Jayce Garrett himself was here in person earlier,' he added, with almost a note of pride, as if he'd rubbed shoulders with royalty. 'Seems like this Hope guy, he was fixin' to kill 'em all. Jayce and Seth rode off like two bats outta hell. Logan, I reckon he's all burnt up in that wreck back there, with Landon and Rufus.'

'That'd be Landon J. Lamarr,' Officer Guidry said. 'Ford pickup back there's registered in his name. OMV came back with nothin' on the other vehicles we checked out. Cadillac Escalade and a 1970 Mustang, both stolen out of state. Got zilch on this Rufus character either.'

Sheriff Roque listened, then motioned to his officers to follow him outside where they could confer. Mason Redbone was staying very quiet. 'What you make of it, Sheriff?' Daigle asked.

Roque took off his hat and scratched the grey stubble on his head. 'I busted Landon Lamarr, must be twelve, fifteen years ago, for assault and possession. Always figured he was in with the Garretts, never could prove it though. But I just don't get it. What business on God's earth does Ben Hope have goin' after these people?'

'It ain't no secret them boys have been runnin' illegal firearms for years,' Daigle said. 'You think mebbe Hope came up here to get gunned up?'

'Or mebbe he was part of their gang and they had themselves a dispute,' Guidry suggested.

Waylon Roque's craggy, iron-hard face showed no expression as he chewed those hypotheses over. 'Nah,' he said at length. 'I ain't buyin' that. My gut tells me somethin' else is goin' on here. But I'm damned if I can make head or tail of it. This whole thing has been a burr under my saddle from the beginnin'.'

It was then that the sheriff's radio began to fizz and splutter. He grabbed it impatiently. 'This is Roque. Whassup?'

'Sheriff,' came the excited voice on the other end. 'It's him. It's Hope! We got'm!'

Chapter 39

The cops had set rows of traffic cones across the road and had a marked Ford Explorer Interceptor blocking one lane and a pair of Dodge Charger pursuit vehicles either side. A yellow metal sign warned POLICE CHECKPOINT, for any half-asleep Louisianan motorist who'd failed to notice. Officers armed with pump-action shotguns loitered about the vicinity, smoking cigarettes and looking bored and demoralised after two days of fruitless stop-and-searching for a fugitive who had apparently vanished into thin air.

All that was about to change.

The instant Ben saw them he knew he'd have to take evasive measures. He let the Firebird slow to under fifty and then threw it into a violent handbrake turn, spinning the car around 180 degrees. The tyres howled and smoked as he stamped hard on the gas to accelerate away.

The cops were galvanised into a frenzy of action, tossing away their cigarettes and grabbing their weapons and yelling into radios and all but crashing into one another as they leaped into the two Chargers while the Explorer stayed behind to man the checkpoint. The patrol cars roared into life and skidded off the verge in pursuit of the fleeing Pontiac Firebird. Sirens were activated and lights flashed.

Ben saw their headlights flaring in his mirror and put his

foot down harder. The Firebird was fast, but he'd put enough souped-up specialist vehicles through their paces during his high speed pursuit and defensive driving courses back in the day to know that the police interceptors were good for at least a hundred and fifty miles an hour, with uprated brakes and handling to match. The needles on his dashboard soared and the V8 under the Firebird's bonnet howled as the road flashed towards him like a flicking black ribbon. The blazing lights in the mirror fell back, but soon started coming on again.

He was going to have his hands full getting shot of these guys. Not a great way to keep a low profile. The one advantage of getting chased by the police, as opposed to regular bad guys, was that the police couldn't just open fire on you unless threatened.

At any rate, that was the theory. On the other hand, regular bad guys weren't so well organised at doing things like radioing ahead for backup and air support, sealing off the area from other traffic and laying barriers and tyre spikes across the road to bring your wild antics to a very rapid halt indeed. And if you tried to resist arrest, *that* was when you'd likely get shot to pieces by a couple dozen officers with fully-automatic carbines.

Ben knew it was just a matter of time before he encountered a whole fleet of police coming the opposite way to block him off. But they weren't going to stop him, not if he could help it. He'd helped it plenty of times in the past.

He was a long way from the hills and forests where the Garretts had managed to hide their distilling operation for so long. The landscape rolled out flat and wide either side of him, endless expanses of wetlands and rice fields that looked like lakes in places and attracted huge flocks of geese and ducks and herons and cranes; here and there a flat-bottomed boat dawdling lazily through the open channels. Nice for some folks, living easy-going rural lives, who didn't have to worry about having two high-powered pursuit vehicles filled with armed men intent on incarcerating you for a crime you didn't commit and clawing steadily, determinedly closer to your tail as you wrung every last drop of performance from a forty-year-old motor whose fancy paintwork and chromed engine parts couldn't quite hide its age. At a hundred and twenty miles an hour the Firebird was beginning to run a little hot and bothered. Ben had a nasty feeling that the guys chasing him could keep this up a lot longer than he could.

Now the rice fields were disappearing behind him and the wetlands were dissolving into open water on both sides of the road as the abutment pillar supports of a long, stretched-out metal bridge loomed up ahead. The blacktop climbed and levelled out, and then the car was speeding high over the broad, mud-brown bayou.

Ben was halfway across the bridge when the inevitable sight greeted him from the far side. It looked like an ocean of black and white and flashing blue lights waiting for him over there. The exit from the bridge was completely blocked. Cops were spilling from their vehicles and taking up shooting positions from behind the open doors. *Subject is armed and extremely dangerous.*

Oh, well, Ben thought. If you want to play it that way.

Dumpy wasn't going to like this.

A hundred and ten miles an hour. Ben reached for the seat belt, pulled it across him and clicked it into place. He felt quite calm, but maybe that was how all stupid people felt when they were just about to do something completely nuts.

He slammed his foot down all the way to the floor, twisted the wheel sharply to the right and sent the Firebird crashing headlong through the side railing of the bridge.

The impact slammed him forwards in his seat. If the car had possessed anything as modern as airbags they'd have punched him in the face. Bits of aluminium spar and rail smashed against the windscreen and clattered violently over the roof.

And then the Firebird took to the air like its mythological phoenix namesake. The muddy waters came hurtling up towards him. Next, there came a second jolting impact as the car knifed into the still surface of the bayou with a huge murky splash and the rest of the world disappeared.

Chapter 40

The first rule of being trapped inside a submerged car: don't try to fight the water pressure, because it's a lot stronger than you are.

Ben unclipped his seat belt and then quickly wound the driver's window all the way down, to allow the murky brown water to flood the cabin. The car would sink faster as a result, which was exactly what he wanted it to do. Because what was coming next needed to happen out of sight of the onlookers gathering on the bridge.

The weight distribution of the car dragged it downwards nose-first as the cabin quickly filled up. Ben didn't have much time. He used it to loop his bag straps over his shoulders and make sure his bow was to hand. It was the only weapon he had, and he intended to hang on to it.

He sat there calmly waiting until the water reached his chin, then took a deep breath. Some free divers could hold their breath for up to ten minutes. After years of practice, Ben was good for about four and a half. That was all the time window he was going to get, and every moment would count.

When the cabin was completely full of water the car began to sink much faster. Only ripples and a few remaining bubbles would be visible on the surface now. As the water pressure equalised inside and out, Ben opened the driver's door. Visibility through the brown murk was about two yards. He grabbed his bow, slipped out of the open door and pushed away from the sinking car. Rescuing the bow meant swimming one-handed, but that was little hindrance to someone who'd been through the things he had. His old regiment might have been called the 'Special Air Service', but SAS men could perform every bit as well in water as their Navy counterparts in Jeff Dekker's old SBS could cut the mustard out of it. When the merciless Special Forces training instructors who made you swim kilometre after kilometre in full kit, often grappling two hundred pounds of wounded comrade along with you, said, 'You'll thank me for this one day,' they were speaking from experience.

Ben swam hard and fast, letting as few bubbles escape his lips as possible so as not to leave a trail on the surface. Far away over the roar of the water that filled his ears he could hear the screeching *whoop-whoop* of the police sirens on the bridge. He could picture the vehicles all converged in the middle and all the cops hanging over the edge where he'd smashed through, all eyes on the water, guns at the ready lest the dangerous fugitive come bursting from the surface intent on murdering them all.

Behind him the car touched down against the bayou bottom, disturbing the mud and turning the murky water even more impenetrable. Only the faint glimmer of light from above kept Ben orientated towards the surface. He'd been holding his breath for nearly two minutes now and he could feel the lactic acid building up in his muscles as his body became starved of oxygen. Underwater swimmers who were conditioned to make it past the 'struggle phase', when most people panicked, found their heart rate decreasing and their whole metabolism slowing as the body concentrated the flow of oxygenated blood to the brain and vital organs.

Two minutes and thirty seconds under. The sound of sirens seemed further away now as Ben kept ploughing doggedly ahead. Time seemed to have slowed right down, along with his biorhythms and normal perceptions. The dim shapes of fish flitted away at his approach. As long as he didn't meet one of those big things bristling with teeth, he'd be fine.

Three minutes under. Ben was just about reaching his limit. His lungs were on fire, his movements becoming sluggish. As the urge to kick for the surface became almost unbearable, the fingers of his outstretched hand brushed against something reedy, then something solid, and he knew he'd reached the bank. It took immense self-control to keep from bursting head and shoulders out of the water, gasping noisily for air. He paddled gently in the shallows, turned his face upwards and pushed his mouth and nose clear of the surface and sucked in the blessed oxygen until he felt his body start to return to normal.

He had swum about two hundred yards from the bridge. The bayou shoreline was thick with rotting vegetation and scummy algae that clung to his hair and skin and wet clothes. He made no attempt to brush them off, knowing that they offered excellent camouflage. Not that anyone was looking this way. Just as he'd pictured it, the distant uniformed figures crowded along the bridge railing were all still fixed on the spot where the car had sunk. But they wouldn't stand there gawping for ever. Pretty soon the police helicopters would be thudding overhead and diver patrols would be deployed to investigate the submerged vehicle in search of one drowned fugitive.

Ben intended to be far, far away from here by the time they failed to locate his body.

He paddled through the nasty green scum until he'd

rounded the shoreline past a big clump of mossy vegetation that hid him from view as he tossed his bow up onto the bank and pulled himself from the water. Half man, half slime creature, as if wearing a sniper's ghillie suit, he climbed up the bank trailing stinking strands and filaments of algae behind him, and slipped into the bushes.

Just as he'd predicted, the cops soon realised that the sunken car was empty and scrambled their air support unit to widen the search. By that time Ben had progressed a good distance downriver, cutting an unseen path through the thick verdant vegetation that overhung its banks. Hearing the first approaching helicopter long before it came into view, he slipped back into the water and hid among the floating green algae and reeds and cattails at its edge. As the chopper appeared over the tree line he sucked in another deep breath and ducked under the surface. Modern-day air cops were equipped with more than just binoculars for hunting their fugitive quarry. The best camouflage in the world couldn't hide your presence from the all-seeing eye of a thermal imaging camera, but the reflective water surface would bounce the infrared right back at them and cloak his heat signature.

Ben held his breath for a full minute, until he was certain the chopper had passed over, before he resurfaced.

His only real fear was that the police might back up their air surveillance with K9 ground search units. No manmade technology yet devised could match the skill of well-trained Belgian Malinois or German shepherds at tracking a fleeing suspect over any kind of terrain. His best chance of escape was the water, avoiding leaving a scent trail on land.

He remembered seeing boats back there among the wetlands. The Clovis Parish waterways were full of river folks looking for crawfish or catfish or gumbofish or whatever it was that inhabited these waters. If he clung to the shoreline, sooner or later he'd find an unattended boat. Nobody, least of all the cops, would pay much attention to just another hick dawdling downriver, going about his business.

No dawdling. Keep moving. The dreaded sound of baying dogs never materialised but Ben nonetheless stuck to his plan to keep to the waterways. The tree canopy was so thick in places that the creeks and bayous couldn't even be seen from the air, especially now that evening was falling. The sunset light filtered red and purple through the leaves and gradually darkened until he had to use his torch, keeping his hand cupped over the beam to give himself just enough light to see by.

The night creatures were awakening. Things crawled and slithered in the shadows and large fluttery moths were drawn to the dimmed torchlight. The sky was empty of helicopters but more immediate dangers existed on the ground, like the risk of stepping on a hidden snake among the waterside vegetation.

A long time passed before Ben saw the lights of the cabin through the trees. He killed the torch and stalked closer.

Chapter 41

As Ben crept up to within a few yards he saw it was little more than a shanty, built a short distance from the edge of the bayou and almost swallowed up by rampant ivy and weeds. Chinks of lantern-glow peeped through cracks in its shuttered windows.

Ben sniffed the air, smelling a putrid odour about the place, like rotting meat. He moved silently away from the cabin and followed the smell to a tall wooden A-frame structure erected a few yards from the entrance. It was the kind of thing hunters built to hang, gut and skin deer carcasses. Except the two animal corpses that hung from this one were large alligators, one partially skinned. There was an air line and compressor and all kinds of knives and hatchets and a bucket or two of offal, and other things Ben didn't hang around to enjoy identifying.

A short dirt path led from the gator hunter's home to a wooden jetty at the water's edge. The planking creaked softly as Ben cautiously picked his way past old lobster creels and barrels and coils of rope. At any second he half-expected to hear the bark of an alerted dog or an angry voice yelling out, 'Who's there?', maybe followed by the boom of a shotgun.

There was enough moonlight shining off the water to

make out the shapes of two boats tethered to the end of the jetty, bobbing almost imperceptibly on the gentle swell. Ben knelt down to inspect them. One was a fibreglass-hulled motorboat, the other a traditional wooden canoe. Firing up an outboard motor in the dead of night was just an invitation to get blasted by the gator hunter's gun. The canoe, by contrast, was ideal. Ben peeled two wet hundred-dollar bills from his dripping wallet and left them wedged in a crack in the jetty's weathered planking, in the hope that the owner would consider it a fair trade. Then he wedged his things into the canoe, climbed aboard and cast silently off.

He paddled on deep into the night as a perfect full moon climbed over the bayou, visible here and there through the gaps in the overhanging tree canopy where its light shone over the water. All that could be heard was the gentle rhythmic *sloosh* of his paddle and the music of crickets and frogs and night birds. He could navigate these waterways for days, maybe weeks, before he'd ever reach the end of this huge wilderness. A person could easily get lost here and never be seen again. No doubt, some did.

The bayou narrowed, then broadened out, then narrowed again. The air was fetid and jungly and smelled nearly as bad as the gator hunter's yard. In some places the green slime on the water's surface was so thick that clumps of spiky swamp plants were growing on it and Ben had to chop with the blade of the paddle to break it up. In other places he had to steer a zigzag line to navigate between the bald cypress trees that jutted from the depths of the bayou: eerie, dark sentinels of the swamp, bearded like strange old men with feathery Spanish moss that brushed Ben's face and shoulders as he passed through. The bottom of the canoe was constantly bumping and scraping over part-submerged tree roots.

There were other things in the water, too. Ben could hear all kinds of strange grunts and splashes around him. He shone his light and glimpsed the swirling movement of something black and glistening suddenly disappearing into the water. At first he thought it must have been a snake, or maybe a turtle. He cast his torchlight more broadly around him. Red lights glowed back at him from all over the water, like Chinese lanterns, floating among the algae and lilies. As he watched, one would abruptly vanish, to be replaced by another nearby. There were scores of them. No, hundreds.

Ben realised what he was seeing. They were eyes, watching him. The eyes of alligators that had emerged from their lairs after their long day's rest away from the heat of the sun. This was their time to hunt, and feed.

And it would soon be Ben's, too. He was hungry, just like they were. The reptiles weren't the only predators that lurked in the darkness.

A couple of miles further downriver he pulled into the side and dragged the canoe onto dry land, looking for a place to build his camp for the night. He stowed his things at the foot of a tree, then grabbed his bow and arrows and went looking for something to eat, marking his route so he'd find his way back. It was close on another hour before he came upon the wild hog, a young one, clearly visible in the shafts of moonlight shining through the trees. He stalked up as near to it as he could, keeping himself upwind to lessen the chance of its smelling him. The hog paused among the shadows, munching and rooting and unsuspecting.

Ben silently drew the bow, took aim, and released his arrow. A thud, a squeal, a brief rustling in the bushes, and the kill was done. He went to claim his quarry.

By midnight he was sitting in the flickering glow of a wood fire eating hunks of spit-roasted pig. He was stripped almost naked and had his clothes hung over the fire to dry, along with his wallet, money and phones. As he ate, he reflected on his situation. He was safe for now, but for how long, he couldn't say. And all the while the two remaining Garretts were out there somewhere, far out of his reach.

Just after 1 a.m., as Ben sat meditatively still, gazing into the flames of the dying fire, his dark, brooding thoughts were suddenly interrupted by the ringtone of his burner phone. He'd never heard it ring until now. Its sound, so incongruous and alien out here in the wilderness, surprised him as much as the fact that it was still working at all after getting so wet.

Ben picked up, hit reply and said, 'Who is this?'

The voice on the other end was deep and male and sounded familiar. 'Yo, Cracka.'

Ben said, 'Hello, Carl. To what do I owe this pleasure?'

'Mama wanna talk wichoo.'

Ben said, 'Why?'

'Because she knows shit you don't.'

Ben said, 'Okay. Put her on.'

'Uh-uh. Like I already told you, man, Mama don't use no phone. She wanna meet wichoo face to face.'

Ben was silent for a minute. He said, 'All right, let's meet. Where do I find you?'

'Listen real carefully.'

Chapter 42

People express grief in different ways. Some people internalise their mourning, or become depressed, or cry a lot. Others simply get drunk to cloud the pain.

Jayce Garrett's way of coping with the death of his youngest brother was to take it out on a suitable victim. That night, three Garrett accomplices had driven to the home of Louis Biquaisse in the small town of Fortune, Elysium Parish, forcibly abducted him with strict orders not to break too many bones, and brought him to the island to face punishment for his crimes.

Hooded, bound and gagged, he was dragged from the back of the van to where Jayce and Seth Garrett stood grimly waiting on the floodlit patio outside what they called the clubhouse, adjoining the main house, and dumped on the ground at their feet.

Seth's upper arm was bandaged where the bullet had nicked his tricep. Jayce wore a thick cotton dressing taped to his damaged ear. If they couldn't vent their rage against the man who'd killed Logan, they were happy to make do in the meantime.

When the hood and gag were removed and Louis Biquaisse's worst fears as to who had kidnapped him were confirmed, he wet his pants and started screaming even more loudly. The screams were cut short by a vicious kick from one of the Garretts' men. Biquaisse wept. He pleaded. He grovelled, kneeling before his captors and bowing his head to the ground in the faint and fading hope that they might offer him mercy if he acted pathetic enough. Through his bubbling tears and snot he swore to them that he'd never intended to hold back the ten Gs he owed. That it was all a big mix-up, and that he absolutely promised to get the cash tomorrow, if they'd only let him go. That he'd been just about to call Logan that evening to tell him he had it and—

'Logan's dead,' Jayce said, cutting him off. 'Your deal was with him. Now that's dead too. You got me to reckon with now, podnuh. And that's real, *real* bad news for you.'

Louis Biquaisse's jaw dropped. 'Shit, oh shit, oh shit, I swear I had nothin' to do with whatever happened to Logan.'

'We know that, asshole,' Seth said.

'Why, you think you could've killed our brother?' Jayce said.

'No, no!'

'You sayin' our brother was a pussy?'

'No! I swear! Listen, I'll get the money tonight! Right now! Just let me go, okay?'

'This guy is really startin' to annoy me,' Seth said. He rubbed his sore arm, and winced. 'Dang, that hurts.'

'Know what, Louis?' Jayce said. 'We don't even care about the money. It's too late for that now. We're gonna make an example of you.' He turned to one of the men. 'Floyd, that camera locked'n'loaded?'

Floyd held up the Panasonic camcorder. 'Good to go, boss. Hyuk hyuk.'

'Louis, your ass is about to go viral,' Seth said. 'Wait till your skank bitch momma sees her boy gettin' famous at last. She's gonna be so proud.'

Everyone piled into a pair of all-terrain quad bikes they used for roving about the island, and set off towards the area of its western shore where tonight's entertainment would take place. Jayce and Seth's daddy had built a pontoon there in the seventies, overhanging the water right around the far side of the island near the old boathouse, where it couldn't be seen from the land side. The old man used it for fishing and mooring his boat; mostly he used it for getting comatose on rye whiskey.

The brothers had adapted the pontoon for other purposes.

At the end of the track they dismounted from the quad bikes and dragged their screaming, struggling prisoner down the slope to the pontoon, where they already had everything set up. A heavy-duty extendable boom rig of the kind used for marlin fishing overhung the water, with a large steel hook and strong cable attached to a geared crank mechanism. The Garretts were well practised in its use. While Floyd Babbitt rolled the camera and his fellow associate Bubba Beane manned the crank, Jayce kicked and shoved Louis into position beneath the boom arm, and Seth attached the hook to the prisoner's belt. Once he was securely hooked up, Bubba took up the slack in the cable. A few more turns of the crank and Louis was hauled up into the air, spinning and flailing on the end of the cable like a big worm about to be offered to a waiting fish.

Except it wasn't fish that Louis was to be used as bait for.

The boom arm was extended right out over the water. It was easily able to hold Louis' weight. Next, Seth grabbed a bucket, from which protruded the handle of a large ladle. Floyd zoomed in for a close-up on the bucket's contents, which were in fact the remains of a Labrador retriever Logan had killed a few days earlier, now just a mess of blood and guts. Floyd said, 'Yugh, gross. Hyuk hyuk.'

Seth tossed a ladleful of gore out over the water, then another. 'Come and get it, bitches!' The blood spattered and spread out in an oily slick, glistening in the floodlights.

'Feedin' time at the zoo, boys,' Jayce said as he stood watching Louis slowly descend towards the water. Bubba Beane was grinning all over his scarred face as he worked the crank handle. Scars that had been put there by Jayce himself, a few years back, to keep him in line.

Right on cue, the alligators appeared, drawn by the scent of blood and the prospect of more. The ring of water that surrounded the Garrett stronghold like some historic castle moat was heavily populated with the creatures. The Garrett clan had been actively encouraging them for decades and always ensured they were well fed. The pets were about to receive another tasty snack.

Louis was screaming so frantically that his voice was breaking up. Bubba gave another turn of the crank and the prisoner's thrashing legs splashed down into the dark, bloody water. Instantly, an explosion of foam burst from the surface as a dark shape rocketed up from below, huge jaws distended and snapping.

'That's gotta be ol' Cyrus,' Seth said. Cyrus was reputed to be over sixty years old, and measured nearly fifteen feet from nose to tail. He was often the first to turn up at these events.

Cyrus' jaws closed around Louis Biquaisse and dragged him under. Louis' screams dissolved into a shrill bubbling gurgle. More swirling black shapes closed in and the water churned red. Bubba waited a few seconds, then brought up the cable. The hook was bare. All that remained of Louis were a few tatters of shredded flesh floating on the water. They would soon be gone, too.

'Show's over, ladies,' Seth said. 'You get it all, Floyd?'

'Sure thing. Hyuk.'

Faces would be blurred and names bleeped out before the video was uploaded to the web. People loved this kind of stuff, but those who knew the Garretts would take it as yet another dire warning not to mess with them.

Bubba and Floyd jumped back aboard their quad bike to go play billiards in the clubhouse. Jayce stood gazing at the ripples on the water. Seth joined him, and the two brothers shared a quiet moment of remembrance.

'Damn it, Logan,' Jayce said. 'Why'd you have to go and fuckin' die on us?'

'I miss that stupid sumbitch,' Seth said.

'He was dumber'n a box of rocks. Lettin' himself be followed like he did.'

'But he was our brother,' Seth said. 'Blood's thicker'n water. We know all about that, right?'

Jayce nodded. 'Reckon we do. And Garrett blood's the thickest.'

Chapter 43

The brothers rode back to the house. All three of them had shared the place since they were kids, and it seemed depressingly empty now without Logan.

It was the only brick building on the island, built in 1868 by Leonidas Garrett with a little help from the few remaining cronies who supported him following his downfall during the Civil War. To this day it remained the clan's headquarters and command centre, hidden away in their secret enclave where few dared set foot. The remote island itself, some fifteen acres of mostly impenetrable woodland, stood encircled and protected like a fortress by the muddy, gator-infested waters of the Bayou Sanglante – literally 'the bloody river' – with a heavily guarded wooden bridge the only way on or off.

Garrett Island had been home to its namesakes for so long that only the older Cajun folks, who'd heard it from their parents and grandparents, remembered what it used to be called before the Garretts came along: Voodoo Island, a tribute to its even darker history and the practices of the Creole people and Indians who once dwelled there. In some parts of the region there still echoed terrible tales of human blood sacrifice and satanic rituals said to have been practised on the island, long ago, and maybe still today.

Returning indoors, the brothers went into their small,

stone-walled living room. A TV in one corner and a fridge in another, a couple of armchairs and a crowded gun rack, were all the furniture they really needed. Seth yanked a half-finished litre of vodka from the chiller and poured himself a mugful, while Jayce helped himself to a bottle of Swamp Pop. Jayce didn't touch alcohol, especially not the kind of un-American shit that Seth favoured.

Seth was complaining about his sore arm. Jayce just sipped his Ponchatoula Pop Rouge and stood gazing at the family pictures over the old stone fireplace. There was a framed blow-up of their daddy, Willard 'Killer' Garrett, a violent tyrant who had been the only man Jayce had ever feared and happily drunk himself to death aged sixty-six. Next to that hung the sole surviving portrait of their ancestor, Jayce's great-great-grandfather, Leonidas Garrett. The oil painting had been among the few items rescued from the ruins of his plantation estate, Athenian Oaks, after the damn Yankees razed it to the ground. The stately mansion was shown in the background, white columns gleaming majestically under the blue sky.

Jayce Garrett had never been able to look at the painting without the same old bitter feelings boiling up inside him. He'd been brought up listening to stories of the billion-dollar fortune that would have been, should have been, the rightful inheritance of the family, passed down from father to son, all the way down the line. He and his brothers could have been the richest men in the state, had it not been for the actions of one filthy subhuman who'd dashed their prospects for ever with her treachery. It was entirely thanks to the despicable Peggy Iron Bar, may she burn screaming in hell for all eternity, that the brilliant patriotic genius Leonidas, hero of the South, had died a reclusive pauper in exile on his island.

Likewise, it was thanks to her that successive generations of Garretts had had to bust their nuts making their own way, surviving the Great Depression, Prohibition, two world wars and the determined efforts of a zillion lawmen to stop them from making a dishonest living. As proud as he was of his achievements, seldom had a day of Jayce's adult existence gone by that he hadn't reflected with simmering anger over the life of privilege and luxury that had been stolen from him, just as surely as it had been from his ancestor.

Beneath the picture was the empty space where Leonidas' cavalry sabre used to hang. The same weapon with which, legend held, he'd personally executed the traitorous slave bitch who had sold him out to the Yankees. The same one with which Jayce, all these years later, had rid the world of the last of Peggy Iron Bar's line.

How proud old Leo would have been of him.

And how poignant it was – or so it seemed to Jayce – that the fulfilment of their ancestor's oath had been possible thanks only to the dear, departed Logan. For all his soft tendencies and occasional lapses of judgement, he'd been the one to thank for tracking down Lottie Landreneau.

It had all started when Logan was serving his drug conviction sentence in the Louisiana State Penitentiary, known as Angola. Angola was a notoriously violent prison that housed all manner of murderers, rapists and psychopaths. Logan could handle himself okay, but there were inmates there who most certainly could not. Such was one Eric Schwegmann, a balding, bespectacled forty-year-old former genealogist serving four years for vehicular homicide after drunkenly mowing down a line of kids queuing for their school bus. When Logan had first begun sharing a cell with Schwegmann he'd neither known nor cared what a genealogist was. But as cellmates with nothing much else to do during those long lockdown hours, their conversation had turned to the subject of their past lives and Logan, who'd grown up hearing those same stories of betrayal and retribution as his brothers, had begun to see an opportunity that would enable him to rise up in the esteem of his elder siblings.

Eric Schwegmann was hopelessly out of his depth in Angola. In his first year there he'd been brutally beaten and sodomised multiple times, and he knew he could not survive the remainder of his sentence. He was depressed, suicidal, falling apart mentally and physically. And so Logan made him a golden offer: for the next three years, or until one of them was released, whichever came first, he would look out for the weaker man and protect him from bullies, rapists, crooked guards and other habitual hazards of life in Angola. In return, Schwegmann would use his expertise to find out the names of any and all living descendants of the person who had betrayed Logan's ancestor and robbed the Garrett clan of their rightful inheritance.

Naturally, Schwegmann leaped at the chance.

Like any prison, Angola was awash with contraband goods, and it hadn't been too hard for Logan to bribe a corrupt guard into supplying a laptop computer with illicit web access. Getting down to business, Schwegmann was able to upload a professional genealogy software package that allowed him to tap into a nationwide pool of data from adoption, cemetery, church, census, military, court, prison and land records, to obituaries, newspaper articles, probate and tax filings. It was all Greek to Logan, who watched idly as his new buddy set about honouring his side of the deal.

It turned out that Eric Schwegmann was one highly talented individual. He actually made it look easy to piece the puzzle together. Within a week, the picture was complete and it went like this:

In 1873, following the death of her sister, the recently-married Mildred Brossette, née Eyumba, relocated to Arkansas with her husband Samuel, where they purchased a modest property in Pulaski County. Three years later they produced a son, Avery. In 1899 Avery met and married Fannie Jones in Little Rock, and from this union was born a baby boy, Milton Brossette. The adult Milton didn't marry until 1936, the year after his grandmother's death, at which point the family line had veered back down south to its Louisianan roots. In 1938, now living in Baton Rouge, Milton and his wife Joyce celebrated the birth of their first daughter Marion, only to lose her to pneumonia at the age of three. The Brossettes' second daughter, Betty, born 1941, fared better and eventually tied the knot with a certain Elijah Landreneau in 1966, moving to Chitimacha, Clovis Parish, soon afterwards. Eli and Betty Landreneau had both died relatively young but their one child, Charlotte, born in 1971, was still very much extant. She had gone by the married name Dupré for a good many years; the divorce records showed that she'd more recently reverted back to her maiden name.

The line of Peggy Iron Bar, it thus appeared, was not yet ended. Hence, there was more work to be done in order for Leonidas Garrett's oath to be fulfilled – and for his descendants to feel a little more vindicated, even if nothing could bring back the money.

If Logan had been aiming to impress his brothers this way, it worked. Even Jayce had been all fired up at the news. After the initial burst of excitement came disappointment when Charlotte, or Lottie, Landreneau seemed to have disappeared. By the time she returned from her lengthy European travels and reappeared on the Garretts' radar, Logan had been out of jail for over two years. As for poor Eric

Schwegmann, Logan had stopped looking after him the moment he'd got the information. Schwegmann was dead within a fortnight, shanked in the prison showers by a fellow inmate called Posie.

The long-awaited plan to kill Lottie Landreneau had come easy. It became even easier when the chance appearance of a stooge named Ben Hope, who'd by chance gotten himself spotlighted in the local news by beating up on a one-time Garrett associate, Billy Bob Lafleur, provided the perfect fall guy for them. They had all found this sequence of events highly amusing. Oh, how they'd laughed.

Just like they were going to laugh when they watched the very same Ben Hope being fed to the gators. There would be no merciful quick dunking for this guy. The Garretts were experts at drawing things out. They'd lower Hope down an inch at a time and let the gators have a foot, maybe take off a leg below the knee, then they'd haul him back up and let him hang a while, and scream a while, before the party went on. It would be a night to remember. They could even sell tickets. Lay on beers and barbecued burgers, music and dancing girls.

As an old vendetta came to a close, a new one had just begun. And they intended to waste no time seeing it through.

Chapter 44

Four hours and forty-eight minutes after receiving the mysterious phone call, Ben was sitting in a borrowed sedan within sight of an abandoned gas station on a minor road some twenty miles south of Chitimacha, at the GPS location that his caller had given him.

The first glimmers of dawn were breaking in the east. It had taken Ben all night to get here. Now all he could do was wait and see whether the journey had been worth his trouble and risk.

His new temporary ride, a suitably nondescript beige-coloured Ford Taurus, belonged to a rat-arsed drunk gentleman Ben had found staggering along the road in the middle of the night with a set of car keys in his hand. The guy was too inebriated to say much, but appeared to have been returning home from an extremely late session with some friends when, quite sensibly, he'd decided to abandon his car and walk the rest of the way. Ben gave him a hundred bucks for the loan of the Ford and said his name was Frankie Prendergast. He doubted whether the guy would remember anything about anything when he eventually sobered up.

The rendezvous had been set for 6 a.m. Ben had purposely arrived early and found himself a useful vantage point where a narrow track wound up a bushy hillside above the old gas station. From here he could observe and detect any kind of a trap. Trust was something he was feeling a little short of, under the circumstances, though he could think of no logical reason to suspect Sallie Mambo of foul play.

The stretch of road Ben could see from his hillside was deserted and obviously very little used, hence the choice of location. He waited, and smoked, and watched. Right on schedule, a solitary vehicle that from a distance looked like a long black station wagon appeared at the head of a tail of dust. It came tooling down the road, then slowed at the approach to the gas station and pulled to a halt by the disused pumps. The driver's door opened and a lone occupant got out.

Ben picked up his binoculars for a better look. As expected, the driver was Carl, Sallie's minder-in-chief. But not as expected, Carl was alone. And very oddly dressed, in a dark suit, white shirt, black tie and black peaked cap.

The reason for Carl's attire, though not the entire reason, became clearer as Ben saw that the vehicle he'd turned up in wasn't a station wagon at all. It was a hearse, something long and wide and quintessentially American like a Plymouth or Lincoln. Old with a lot of miles on it, but its midnight black paintwork gleamed in the rays of the dawn. A hearse seemed like just a slightly strange choice of vehicle. Especially as the casket compartment in the rear wasn't empty.

Ben fired up the Taurus and rolled down the hillside to park up next to the hearse. Carl watched impassively as he got out of the car. The prices on the old gas pumps must have been from about 1982. A rusted Pennzoil sign dangled lopsidedly overhead.

'I thought I was meeting with Sallie,' Ben said. 'Imagine my surprise, you turning up alone like this.'

'I'm s'posed to take you to her.' Carl motioned at the hearse.

'Unusual mode of transportation you have there. So is that what you do for a living, drive dead people around?'

Carl shook his head. 'Ain't mine. Belongs to my cousin Antoine. He's a funeral director.'

'Who's your passenger?' Ben asked, pointing at the coffin in the back.

'Box is for you, Cracka.'

Ben stared at it, then at him. 'It's a little early in the morning for jokes.'

'The cops're turnin' the parish inside out huntin' for you, my friend. Figure even they won't go liftin' no coffin lid to see what's inside, though.'

Ben shook his head. 'Carl, when my day comes to be put into one of those, I won't complain. But that day hasn't come yet.'

Carl shrugged his shoulders, as if he really didn't give much of a damn one way or the other. 'How it's gotta be. Only way you gonna see Mama Mambo and find out what it is you need to know. You want I go back with an empty box, that's fine by me.'

Ben turned a slow three-sixty, scanning the horizon. The road was still deserted as far as the eye could see, not a soul for miles around. No witnesses to the peculiar sight of a man climbing into his own coffin.

He thought about it a moment longer and then nodded. Carl opened up the back of the hearse and released a catch that allowed the coffin to slide out smoothly on a platform like a drawer on rollers. He lifted the lid. Ben gazed inside at the creamy white satin lining. Still dubious, he said, 'Uh, I realise that ability to breathe inside one of these things isn't normally an issue, but—'

'It ain't airtight till it's sealed,' Carl said.

'I'm going to trust you, Carl. But if it turns out I'm wrong about that, you'll be the one they carry off in a box. Understand?'

Carl offered the merest of smiles. 'We cool, man. Just get in and think dead thoughts. We gotta get movin'. Mama ain't gonna wait for ever.'

Ben thought, fuck it, climbed up and lowered himself inside the coffin. Travelling feet first, just like a real corpse. He lay back as Carl shut the lid. Cocooned inside the cushy interior with no small measure of claustrophobia, he felt the coffin slide back into the compartment on its rails, followed by the slam of the rear hatch. A muted rumble as the engine started up, and they moved off.

It wasn't everyone who got a preview of what it would feel like to be transported to your own funeral. The coffin wasn't uncomfortable, and the air-conditioned hearse was pleasantly cool inside. After a while Ben began to relax, deciding that with nothing else to do he might as well use the time to catch up on lost sleep. He closed his eyes. And crossed his hands over his chest, just in case God decided this was a good time to pluck him from this mortal coil.

Some time later, he was awoken by the realisation that they'd stopped. He felt the coffin slide backwards from the tailgate of the hearse. Then the morning light made him blink as the lid opened.

'Best lookin' dead man I ever did see,' chuckled the crackly voice of Sallie Mambo.

Chapter 45

Ben sat up. They were inside an old cemetery. The early morning dampness in the air was yet to be burned off by the sun, and a low-drifting mist shrouded the uneven rows of gravestones. It looked like a forgotten place, belonging to another time.

Sallie Mambo wore a colourful dress that hung baggily to her hobnail boots. Several shawls draped her shoulders and a broad-brimmed hat covered her mane of snow-white hair, shading her face from what little sunlight poked through the mist. She was accompanied by two more of her devotees, or disciples, or whatever they considered themselves to be. The van in which they'd brought her was parked in the withered grass under a dead tree. They hovered close to the old woman, ready to catch her if she needed support, but she seemed determined to stand on her own, clutching tightly to a knotty walking staff that was as tall as she was.

Ben climbed out of the coffin and jumped down, grateful to be free once more. He said, 'Hello, Mama.'

'How's it feel to be born again, child?' she asked with a wrinkly smile. She looked even older in daylight. Beneath the brim of the hat her skin looked as thin and delicate as parchment. But the fire still burned in her eyes.

'Like I've been given a second chance,' he replied.

She shuffled closer, waved back her helpers and held her hand out to him. 'Come, walk with me. You be a gennelman now, and take an old lady's arm. I ain't ninety no more.'

'I think you're doing fine,' Ben said.

Carl stayed close to the hearse and the other two hung back by the van, all three pairs of eyes watching every move as Ben gently took the old woman's arm. It felt very thin. She probably weighed under eighty pounds, but she was wiry and still strong.

Ben was burning up with impatience to hear what she had to tell him, though he knew better than to press her. He looked around him at the cemetery as they walked slowly over the unkempt grass. Many of the gravestones were thick with moss and crumbled with age. Judging by the inscriptions that were still visible, nobody had been buried here in the last century or longer.

'Lot of history in this place,' he commented. 'I'm not surprised you chose it to meet up.'

'Oh, I visit here often, child,' Sallie said. She shook her head wistfully, adding, 'The dead, they gets lonely and appreciate someone takin' the time to come talk to them.'

'Just like I appreciate you taking the time to talk to me,' Ben replied. 'Last time we spoke, I had a feeling you were holding out on me. Is that what this meeting is about?'

She frowned and nodded slowly, gazing down at her feet as she walked. 'Been doin' a lot of thinkin' since then.'

'Me too,' he said. 'I think you know more than you wanted to tell me before about the connection between Peggy Eyumba's murder and Lottie Landreneau's. I think it was bothering you then, and it's still bothering you now. You're afraid of the Garretts, aren't you? You know they're behind this, just like back in 1873.'

'Child, you should be afraid, too. The Garretts are

possessed by evil spirits. Bad juju been in their blood for hundreds of years and always will be.'

Ben smiled. 'I don't believe in evil spirits. Just bad people.'

Sallie shook her head. 'You got no idea. Mama knows, because Mama understand magic. What you know about magic?'

'Voodoo magic? Only what Keisha Hebert told me.'

Sallie said, 'Keisha is a sweet girl. Got the gift, but she ain't got the experience. She don't see the things Mama can see. All she's known is the white magic. Natural magic, the ways of the plants and animals, the trees and the earth, rootwork and healin', like things I do with my herbs and powders and special things. Hoodoo is what they call it. In Hoodoo everythin' that you do is the plan of God. The power of good. That ain't the dark side.'

'The dark side?'

Sallie gave a low, crackling chuckle and squeezed Ben's hand. 'You don't want to go there, child. Lord, no. The dark side be the work of the devil. It feedin' on light. Suckin' the goodness out of your soul. Ruinin' lives and bringin' death and pain wherever it spread. Like a sickness it takes folks over. And once they're taken over they become its servants, instruments of the deepest, darkest evil that comes straight from hell. Folks like the Garretts.'

'I really think you mean it,' Ben said.

Sallie halted her slow stride and looked up at Ben with utter sincerity in her eyes. 'They is demons in human form, child. That's how come they have so much power over folks and nobody will dare stand up to 'em. They been carryin' on their wicked works since the days when ol' Leonidas Garrett used to torture, rape and murder his slaves right here in Clovis Parish. God have pity on their poor souls.'

Walking slowly on, still clutching tightly to Ben's arm,

she said, 'So now you know why I was too scared to tell you before. I be just a poor ol' lady. I ain't afraid of dyin', 'cause I know my Lord will take care of me when my time comes. Amen to that. But I want to go peaceful. I ain't lived all these years to be ripped apart by the hand of no demon.' A tremor shuddered through her body at the thought. 'The Garretts have a long, long arm, child. They know when someone's talkin' about them. Powerful, powerful magic.'

Ben said, 'Listen to me, Sallie. I've stood face to face with Jayce Garrett and I can tell you he's no more a demon than I am. He and his brother Seth are as mortal as you or I, and Logan's already dead to prove it. They're nothing but very twisted men who've done too many bad things and hurt too many innocent people. Now they've got to stand up and account for the harm they've caused. And I intend to see to it that they do.'

'I knows that, child.' Sallie slipped her arm out of Ben's and pressed a fingertip below one eye, pulling the lid down. 'Mama *knows*. Mama *sees*. You been sent to wash away the evil of the Garretts and cleanse this place from their curse. That's what I been thinkin', and so that's why I brought you here to this place. So the dead will know that deliverance has come.'

'I'm just a man, Sallie. I'm nothing special. Nobody sent me. I came to Louisiana to hear a jazz band. No other reason. It was pure chance that put me in this situation. Bad luck for me, and bad luck for the Garretts too.'

But Sallie was having none of it. She tapped his shoulder with the head of her walking staff, like a teacher scolding a pupil. 'That's where you be wrong, child. Nothin' happens by chance. Not ever. Jazz band,' she added with a derisive snort. 'You bein' here, that's fate. Now it be time for you to meet yours, and for the Garretts to meet theirs. And now it be time for me to play my part in this, 'cause I knows where they's at.'

Ben looked at her. 'What are you saying? You know where Garrett Island is?'

'That's what folks call it now,' she replied darkly. 'Weren't always known by that name.'

'Tell me how to get there.'

Sallie reached a thin, bony hand into the folds of her dress and pulled out a crumpled, stained piece of paper. She offered it to Ben, and he took it and uncrumpled it.

'Ain't hard to find, once you knows how,' she said.

The rumpled map Ben found himself holding in his hands wasn't the sort of crude hand-drawn affair he might have expected of someone of Sallie's generation. It was a printout of a Google Maps satellite image, zoomed tight down onto what looked like an area of Amazonian rainforest. When he looked more closely he could see that little notes and arrows had been penned in by hand to provide further directions, including GPS coordinates.

'Nice job,' he said. 'I didn't have you down as the techno type, Sallie.'

She brushed the air dismissively with her free hand and replied, 'I got a nephew who's good with all that kind of newfangled tomfoolery. Computers is the work of the devil, but I guess we can make an exception now and then.' The wonders of modern technology didn't seem to appeal much to Mama Mambo after all.

'These directions are pretty precise. Have you been to Garrett Island yourself?'

Sallie's face contorted into a mass of wrinkles. 'It was 1933, but I remember it like yesterday. We was just kids, actin' on a dare to see if all them terrible stories we'd heard was true. Four of us young fools crossed over the bridge, that's the only way you can get on the island, and crept through the woods near enough to see the house. I ain't never bin so scared in all my life. Then this big man in a long black beard come out yellin', wavin' a shootin' iron at us. It was ol' Elmore Garrett, Willard's father. They done fried his ass for murder later on, 'forty-eight I think it was. Anyhow, we ran for our very souls. Lord knows how we got away. Since then I knowed a few folks who crossed over that bridge and never come back. Not even the sheriff will set foot in that cursed place.'

'I don't believe in curses either,' Ben said.

'Don't believe in much, do ya?' Sallie said. She laughed mirthlessly, showing her bare gums. 'You will, child, you will. Here, I got somethin' else.' Reaching again into whatever deep pocket was hidden in the folds of her baggy clothing, she came out this time with a small flannel bag tied at the neck with a leather thong. 'Take it.'

Ben took it. 'What is it?' he asked.

She patted his arm. 'That be a gris-gris. A mojo bag. A talisman. You call it what you want, child. Got things inside that'll bring you luck and protection. I laid my tricks on it. But don't you open it, now. Won't work if you look inside. Wear it around yo' neck and don't never take it off. The demons can't hurt you then.'

She paused, eyeing him in a way that made it clear she expected him to put the charm around his neck right away. To please her, he slipped the leather thong over his head, then tucked the mojo bag under his shirt next to his skin. Sallie gave a broad, gummy smile. 'There. You safe now.'

'I appreciate you looking out for me, Sallie. Thank you.'

'Don't thank me, child. I's just doin' God's work. Now it's time for me to go. I gots to get back to my people.'

Ben accompanied Sallie back the way they'd come, where

273

her helpers were waiting to fuss over her and help her aboard the van. Carl gave Ben a surly nod and said, 'I'll take you back to your car.'

'Goodbye, Sallie,' Ben said, leaning on the van door.

'I be prayin' for you, Mister Ben Hope.'

Chapter 46

Waylon Roque was up early that morning after a fitful three-hour night's rest, overseeing the renewed search for this fugitive who seemed once again to have slipped maddeningly through his fingers. He was beginning to think this Hope was some kind of damn ghost or something.

Roque was watching the salvage crew hoist a battered Pontiac Firebird from the muddy bottom of Bayou Robicheaux when he received the urgent radio call summoning him back to base. 'You'd best step on it, Sheriff,' said the desk sergeant. 'These people are real nervous and edgy. I don't know how long I can keep them here.'

'What people?' Roque snapped back, irritated at being dragged away from more pressing matters.

'Vernon and Ivy Tanner. Retired couple.'

'I know 'em. Or of 'em, leastways,' replied Roque, who had long made it his business to know most things about most folks in his parish. 'Live up along the north end of Kadohadacho Creek. What of it?'

'Can't say for sure, Sheriff. They won't tell me much, but it seems real important. I reckon you need to get over here to talk to them in person. Somethin' tells me you won't regret it.'

Roque trudged back to his patrol car, and forty-seven

minutes later hurried inside the Sheriff's Office building to be informed by the desk sergeant that the Tanners were still there waiting for him. He found the couple sitting in a little interview room, sipping paper cups of iced tea and looking every bit as nervous and edgy as he'd been told.

Roque shook their hands and greeted them with a 'Now, Mr and Mrs Tanner, what can I do for y'all?'

'Fact is we didn't know what else to do, Sheriff,' Ivy Tanner said, wringing her hands in agitation. 'Bin talkin' about it for two whole days, and we just couldn't decide what was right. I still ain't sure about it.'

Roque pulled up a chair and perched opposite them. 'Talkin' about what, exactly?'

Vernon Tanner's face was blotchy and beads of sweat were breaking out all over his brow. 'We're God-fearin' people, Sheriff,' he blurted anxiously. 'We'd never betray a friend. But, well, this is somethin' else.'

Roque was beginning to realise that whatever this was, he would have to coax it out of them. He could only hope it was worth his while. Smiling his most patient smile he said, 'All right, folks, why don't we just take this nice and slow, relax and tell me in your own time what this is all about, okay?'

Vernon took a few deep breaths to compose himself. 'Well, you see, Sheriff, it's about the Heberts. Our neighbours.'

Roque pursed his lips and thought for a moment. 'Heberts. Heberts. Now that'd be Tyler Hebert, the lawyer fella? Married a coloured girl, if memory serves me right. Let me see now . . . Kate?'

'Keisha,' Ivy Tanner said. She spelled it out for him. Roque nodded sagely, hiding his impatience. Ivy added, 'They got two kids, Noah and little Trinity, plus there's Caleb from Tyler's first marriage.'

'I do seem to recall somethin' about him bein' married before,' Roque said. 'So what's the problem? Just that I have kind of a busy slate, folks.'

'We dearly love the children,' Vernon said. 'Never had any of our own, see. Especially the little girl, Trinity. The Heberts sometimes ask us to take care of 'em for a few hours if they have to take care of things elsewhere, and we're only too happy to oblige. Lately they been askin' us to take care of the kids more than usual—'

'Which ain't a problem—' Ivy said.

'Just unusual is all—' Vernon said.

His wife nodded. 'And you see, couple days ago we were havin' dinner with the kids when the little girl said somethin' strange—'

'Strange?' Roque asked, interrupting the Tanner tag team and resisting the urge to pull out his revolver.

Ivy nodded harder. 'Yes, Sheriff. Very strange.'

'So what did the little girl say?'

'Well, she said there was a man in their house.'

Roque frowned and leaned closer. 'A man? What kind of man?'

'Like a visitor. Said he talks funny, like he's foreign. From England or someplace.'

Vernon said, 'And when the girl come out with that, her big brother Caleb told her, "Quiet, Trinity, we ain't supposed to talk about him."'

Ivy said, 'Then Trinity replied how it was true, though, and how this English visitor had saved Caleb from the snake and all. They was fishin' in the creek when—'

'Never mind the snake,' Roque said, now fully engaged and anxious to know all they could give him. 'Tell me about the stranger. Did the kids say anythin' more, like a name or a description? How long's he been stayin' there with them?'

'Can't recall if they mentioned the fella's name,' Vernon said, scratching his head. 'Don't know for sure if he's there no more, neither. All we know is, the Heberts were actin' real peculiar for a few days. Dumpin' their kids with us at a moment's notice, not that we minded of course, and goin' off places without wantin' to say where. First time, they was away hours and came home real late at night, and even the kids didn't know where they went.'

'And this stranger, he went along with them on these trips?'

'Can't say for certain, Sheriff. But somethin' ain't been quite normal over at the Hebert place, that's for sure. Then we saw on the TV how the police was huntin' this fugitive and all—'

'And we thought you oughtta know,' Ivy said. 'Just in case. Can't be too careful these days, what with all the troubles in the world, foreigners and Russians and whatnot.'

'I do declare, this country's goin' to hell in a hand basket.' Vernon clasped his wife's hand. 'So, Sheriff, the TV said this fugitive feller was an English soldier. You reckon it could be the same man? Only thing is, how in God's name could the Heberts have got mixed up with someone like that? I'd sure hate for those folks to get into any trouble.'

Roque stood up so fast that his chair toppled backwards. 'We'll certainly look into it. I'm most obliged to you good folks for comin' to me. I just wish you'd told me this sooner.'

'We're sorry, Sheriff. We didn't know what was best.'

'You done the right thing. Now, if you'll excuse me, I have to make a call. One of the officers will show you out.'

The sheriff virtually sprinted from the room and down the corridor to his office. Within sixty seconds he was putting out a Code 35 suspicious person radio alert to all patrols in the vicinity of Kadohadacho Creek.

Deputy Mason Redbone's voice came back, 'Copy that, Sheriff, I'm on the road just twenty minutes out from the Hebert place. Gettin' right on it.'

'Watch yourself, Mason. Best wait for backup in case he's still there.'

'Don't you worry about that, Sheriff. I won't be takin' any chances this time.'

Chapter 47

Things had been somewhat quiet around the Hebert homestead since the departure of their house guest, but it was hard to pretend that life had gone back to normal. Keisha had managed to get a few days off work, and she and Tyler had uncharacteristically spent a lot of time glued to the TV. The latest dramatic local network reports on the flight of Louisiana's most wanted man from the clutches of the law had left them in fits of anxiety.

That morning KLAX news had shown a clip of the stolen car used by the fugitive to make his spectacular flying escape off the side of the Robicheaux Bridge being winched out of the water. Earlier speculation that the wreck might contain a drowned body had, to the Heberts' immense relief, turned out to be unfounded.

Once again, the whereabouts of the suspected murderer were unknown. The state governor was calling it an outrage and threatening to call in the National Guard. Sheriff Roque announced to a yabbering cluster of reporters gathered outside the Clovis Parish courthouse that it was just a question of time before they caught their man. No further comment, folks. At which point Tyler had turned off the TV in disgust, unable to look at Roque's face a moment longer.

'Where's this gonna end, baby?' Keisha kept asking her husband.

'I fear for him, I truly do. He can't go on like this.'

Now, as the sweltering mid-morning heat approached its peak of the day, Tyler had driven into Chitimacha to visit the hardware store for some tool or other he needed to fix the barn roof. Caleb was occupied with a homework assignment at the kitchen table while Trinity sat happily drawing with her crayons. Noah had been helping his mother feed the pigs, clean out the henhouse and collect their daily eggs, which he proudly carried in a basket, feeling all grown up and responsible.

Keisha and the boy were walking back towards the house when the police cruiser rolled up, lights flashing, tyres crunching on the dirt. She frowned uneasily at the sight of the approaching car. The sunlight reflecting brightly on the windscreen obscured the face of the solitary officer inside. She patted Noah on the head and said, 'You go on inside, now. Put them eggs away nice and safe and check on your sister. Momma will be there in just a minute.'

The boy ran towards the house, clutching the basket. Keisha stood in the yard with her arms folded and watched as the officer stepped out of the patrol car. What was this about? She was glad Tyler wasn't at home. Tyler struggled to hide his intense dislike of the police, all police, after what had happened in his past.

Mason Redbone was all smiles as he walked towards her. 'Mornin', Mrs Hebert. Sure is a beautiful day, ain't it?'

In as steady a voice as she could manage, Keisha replied, 'Mornin', Officer. What a nice surprise.' She kept her arms folded and mustered up the effort to keep her expression totally blank as her thoughts whirled and panic flooded through her. An unannounced police visit could only be about one thing. Someone must have reported Tyler and her for harbouring a fugitive. Was she about to be arrested? What would happen to the kids?

'Oh, I'm just stoppin' by for a social call,' Mason said, still smiling pleasantly. 'Is Mr Hebert at home?'

'He went into town,' she replied. She had visions of squads of police descending on Chitimacha to arrest her husband. Lord, what if he resisted and they shot him?

'So you're all on your lonesome, you and the kids, huh?' Mason said. 'Dearie me, ain't that a shame.' He stepped closer, to within a couple of feet of her. Which she felt was way too close. There was a weird vibe about him. She didn't like the way he was looking at her, or the way his right hand rested casually on the butt of his pistol. Or the fact that the weapon retaining strap on his duty holster was unsnapped. Or the big, florid bruise that discoloured the whole middle of his face and meant, as she now remembered with a shock, that this was the same sheriff's deputy who'd tried to kill Ben the night of the murder. She'd overheard him and Tyler talking about it.

Keisha moved back a step. Tyler's absence suddenly didn't seem like such a good thing after all. She swallowed. There could be no more hiding the fear and guilt that were etched all over her face. She wanted to turn and run, but where to?

'I see,' she quavered. 'And how may I help you?'

Mason Redbone's smile soured to an ugly leer. He quickly drew the pistol out of its holster and thrust it right into her face. She gasped.

'Here's how,' he said. 'Call your kids out here, right now. We're goin' for a ride. All of us together, ain't that cosy?'

'You can't arrest me like this. What have I done?'

Mason laughed. 'You hear me readin' you your Mirandas? I ain't arrestin' you, you dumbass boot-lipped bitch whore.'

Keisha thought she was about to faint. 'Where are we goin'?'

'To see some friends. They're just dyin' to make your acquaintance. Gonna have ourselves a party.'

She yelled, 'Take me, but leave my children out of it, you hear?'

'Don't work that way, nigguh. Now call them fuckin' kids or I swear I'll go in there and start shootin'.'

She wanted to scream, 'Babies, run! Get away, and keep on runnin'!' But he'd only go after them and hurt them. She was powerless to resist him in any way, and the realisation floored her. Tears streamed down her cheeks as she called their names. Caleb emerged first from the house and his eyes widened at the sight of the cop threatening his stepmother. Terrified he was about to defend her and get himself killed, she called out, 'It's okay, sweetheart. We're gonna be okay. Come over here. Noah, Trinity, you too.'

'Get in the car,' Mason said, waving the pistol. 'Them two filthy half-breed niglets piss on my seats, I'm gonna make you lick it up.'

The back of the police cruiser was like a prison van. The rear bench seat was low down and uncomfortably hard, and a steel mesh cage separated it from the front and covered the side windows. There was no way to unlock the doors from inside. It was a tight squeeze for all four of them. Keisha hugged the two crying young ones to her sides, trying to stem her own tears and be strong for her babies. Caleb was pale and shaking with impotent rage and kept shouting, 'Jerk! Asshole! Leave us alone!'

'Shut it, boy, or I'll hit you so hard your ass'll pop out your throat.' Mason fired up the car and took off at speed. His police radio was off.

They were quarter of a mile down the old Kadohadacho

Creek road when they flashed past Tyler's battered Jeep Cherokee heading towards home. The kids began screaming, 'Poppa! Poppa!'

Keisha pressed her hand to the barred window and caught a momentary glimpse of her husband's face turning to stare as he passed by them, his eyes flaring wide with horror. Twisting around to see out of the back, she saw the Jeep swerve to a skidding halt in the middle of the road. Tyler U-turned so fast he almost rolled the car, then came barrelling after them. Keisha moaned, 'No, baby, no!' She knew that the cop would kill him if he tried anything.

Mason saw the Jeep in his mirror, threw a leer back at his passengers and just put his foot down harder. The acceleration pressed Keisha back in her seat.

Tyler tried, and tried hard, to catch them. But the police car was too fast for him to follow, and Keisha soon lost sight of him. She clasped Noah and little Trinity even more tightly.

Would any of them ever see Tyler again?

She closed her eyes and sobbed.

Chapter 48

After another coffin ride, Carl dropped Ben off at the abandoned gas station and was about to drive off when Ben tapped on his window. Carl rolled it down and gave him a curt nod. 'Yo, whassup?'

'Before you go, I have a question for you.'

'Whassat?'

'Do you and your friends in the woods actually possess any ammunition for those old guns of yours, or are they just a bunch of wall hangers you bring out to keep unwanted visitors away?'

Carl looked at him as though weighing up whether to reply truthfully or not, then shook his head and said, 'Nah, man, they's just for show. Got no bullets or nothin'. I ain't never shot a gun in my life.'

'That's what I thought. See you around, Carl.'

The hearse departed. Ben watched it go, then walked over to where he'd left the Ford Taurus. It was oven-hot under the baking sun. He drove a mile and pulled up off the road, in the shade of some fragrant magnolia trees. He rolled open all the windows, lit up a Gauloise and sat for a long time studying the map that Sallie Mambo had given him.

The satellite image was zoomed in like an aerial view from about two thousand feet. Not close enough to make out individual details like the house or the bridge that Sallie had described, but the shape of the island was clearly visible. The piece of land, maybe a dozen or fifteen acres judging by the scale, was really just a prominence jutting from a sharp bend in the bayou shoreline. Over time the waters must have eroded away any land bridge connecting it to the shore, so that it stood isolated like its own little natural fortress surrounded by a mud-brown moat containing God-knew-what kinds of lurking reptilian dangers.

Now it be time to meet your fate. The old woman's voice echoed in his ears as he pensively fingered the mojo bag talisman she'd given him to hang around his neck.

Fate or not, there was no turning back now from what he had to do. He didn't doubt that Jayce and Seth Garrett, along with whatever force of men they had at their disposal, would be looking to find him and get their revenge for Logan and the destruction of their moonshine plant. But he had no intention of letting them come to him. He was going to meet them instead on their own ground, where he could be sure of getting both brothers where he wanted them. And this time, he intended to make sure they didn't get away.

To storm an island crawling with armed men under the command of the likes of Jayce Garrett, single-handed and unsupported: it didn't seem like Ben's idea of a tactically sound plan. Going up against challenging odds, sometimes even crazy ones, was something he had plenty experience of. But walking into a certain death trap was something else again, and definitely not an option he was inclined to choose. They had all the firepower, he had none. His element of surprise was blown, and a superior enemy force was stirred up like a hornets' nest. And he still had to take the Garretts down without killing them – a strategy that, so far, hadn't quite gone to plan.

In short, Ben was heavily outgunned and facing a serious disadvantage. The more he thought about it, the more he realised he had no choice other than to call on outside help.

The only question was, whose? He might have been able to muster up a few men from Sallie Mambo's little troop of guardians. But Carl's admission about their lack of experience and equipment had only confirmed Ben's suspicions. Camping out in the woods protecting an old woman nobody had any reason to harm in the first place wasn't quite in the same league as declaring war on a band of ruthless killers. Even assuming that he could persuade Carl's guys to help him, and that he could somehow magically procure an arsenal of decent weaponry to arm them with, he had no desire to lead a band of good, decent and woefully unprepared men to their deaths. The Garretts would wipe them out like swatting flies.

Who else was there? Ben reflected on the idea of calling Jeff Dekker. The two of them had been through many scrapes together and Ben knew that his old friend and business partner wouldn't hesitate for a single second to jump on a plane and come out to join him. But Ben also knew that the powers of international law enforcement would be watching Jeff, and their base in France, like hawks for just that very reason. The instant Jeff set foot on US soil, alarm bells would be sounding, the game would step up to the next level and it would be virtually impossible for Ben to hook up with him without the pair of them getting caught, this time not by local hick cops but by federal agents.

Ben was still mulling over his very limited options when his phone rang.

He took it out. It had to be Carl, calling back. Maybe he'd remembered that his cousin the funeral director also had a friend in the Navy SEALs or US Army Rangers who happened to have a personal pick against Jayce and Seth Garrett and would be happy to offer assistance with a truck-load of battle-hardened tough guys and automatic weapons.

Ben answered. But it wasn't Carl.

He recognised the voice right away as Tyler Hebert's. And right away, knew something was wrong. Very, very wrong.

'Tyler, calm down. Talk slowly. What's happened?'

Tyler managed to control his flurry of words enough for Ben to understand what he was trying to say. 'They snatched them, Ben. They got my family!'

Something took an icy two-handed grip on Ben's guts and twisted hard.

'Who got them, Tyler? What happened?'

'This mornin' . . . I hadda go into town . . . I was on my way home when I passed this police patrol car goin' the other way, and I looked, and there's Keisha and the kids in the back. Jesus, they looked so scared. I turned right around and tried to follow, but my old truck just couldn't keep up. I lost 'em.'

'I don't understand,' Ben said. 'The cops have nothing to connect you with any of this. Why would they have arrested Keisha?'

'This wasn't an arrest, Ben,' Tyler said breathlessly. 'This is a kidnap.'

'Hang on, Tyler. How can you know that?'

'It was Mason Redbone drivin' the patrol car. He was all by himself, too. Came to the house and kidnapped my family.' Tyler sounded as if he was going berserk with anxiety.

The instant Ben heard the deputy's name he thought, *shit.* 'Try to stay calm, Tyler. That still doesn't prove anything. It looks bad but we don't know for sure whether—'

'Oh, we know for sure, all right,' Tyler interrupted him. ''Bout an hour later I got a call from Jayce Garrett.'

Now Ben's blood was turning very cold and his grip on the phone was making the plastic casing creak with strain.

'What did he say, Tyler?'

'He said they had Keisha and the kids, where nobody'd ever find 'em and nobody could save 'em. Then he told me what he and his brother and their guys were gonna do to 'em if—' Tyler's voice cracked up and his frantic flow of words dissolved into sobbing.

'If what? Tyler, talk to me. If what?'

It was as though Tyler couldn't bring himself to answer. In a tortured moan he said, 'They're gonna rape my wife in front of my kids. Then they're gonna make her watch while they feed the kids alive to the alligators. Trinity, then Noah, then Caleb. Then he said they're gonna do the same to Keisha . . . and I believed every word he told me, Ben. I'm sorry.'

Ben said more firmly, 'If what, Tyler? What does Jayce want?' He already knew what was coming.

'He wants you, Ben. He wants to trade. My family for you.' Tyler's voice sounded ghastly. 'Gave me a rendezvous location. The Big Q Motel. It's—'

'I know where it is,' Ben said.

'They'll have their men waitin' there for you. Said if you ain't there by nightfall . . .' Tyler started weeping. 'I'm sorry, I'm sorry,' he repeated through his tears. 'I don't know what to say.'

Ben felt a strange calm come over him. His grip relaxed on the phone and the coldness in his body began to dissipate. He almost smiled. He said, 'Listen to me, Tyler. Tyler. Listen.'

'I'm listenin' . . .'

'Do not worry about this. I will make this all right. Do you understand? Your family are going to be fine.'

'But—'

'But nothing. Jayce Garrett wants me, he can have me.

We'll trade. Me for them, just like he said. You'll get Keisha and the kids back safe, I promise.'

'What do I need to do?'

'Sit tight and wait. Are you at home?'

'I can't go back there. Whole place is crawlin' with cops. I'm scared they're gonna arrest me. They must know somethin', right?'

Ben agreed. He was picturing the whole thing in his head. Somehow, someone must have found out that the Heberts were helping him, and reported it to the police. Most likely just by chance, the Garretts' inside man Mason Redbone must have got to the scene first, abducted Keisha and the children and snatched them from the scene before the rest of the police got there. Sheriff Roque must be wondering where the hell his deputy had disappeared to.

Ben was silent for a long moment. His mind felt as focused as a laser as he understood exactly what it was he had to do next.

Tyler's hoarse voice said, 'Ben? You still there, buddy?'

'I'm still here,' Ben said. 'Okay, here's what I want you to do. I want you to go back to your place right now and let the cops arrest you.'

'Are you crazy? How's that gonna help my family?'

Ben said, 'Do you trust me?'

'You know I do.'

'Good. Now listen and do exactly as I say.'

And Ben told Tyler the plan that had formed in his mind.

Chapter 49

Ben had worked solo as a private hostage rescue operator for many years. He'd fallen into it soon after quitting the army, putting the skills that the SAS had honed to a razor's edge in him to good use. Instead of fighting other people's wars and serving hidden, usually duplicitous and often shady agendas in the name of Queen and Country, he'd become a protector and saviour of innocent people and a ruthless pursuer of those who exploited them for gain.

K&R was the name of the business. It sounded like a shipping line, but in fact the kidnap and ransom racket was one of the fastest-growing and most lucrative criminal enterprises on the planet. Easy money, if your moral compass was screwed enough. There was no shortage of crooks willing to get into the game, and certainly no shortage of potential victims just waiting to be plucked like sweet, ripe fruit off the money tree.

During that phase in Ben's career he'd called himself a *crisis response consultant*, because no worse crisis could befall any family than for one of their loved ones to be taken by pitiless men demanding large sums of cash in exchange for their lives. Sometimes in these situations, the kidnappers were true to their word and released the hostages more or less unharmed once they got paid off. In most cases, however, release was never the intention, and kidnap victims were doomed to a bad end whether the ransom was paid or not. Which was where Ben came in. No negotiations. No money. Just a swift intervention that generally ended the same way for the kidnappers as they'd intended for their victims.

Ben had been extremely successful at what he did. One of the reasons he'd been so effective in his role was that he went by certain rules. One of which was that he worked strictly alone, allowing him to move fast, strike explosively and get the hostages out unscathed and away to safety before the kidnappers knew what had hit them. Another of his golden rules was to do all he could to avoid letting the police get involved in a rescue mission. Too many times, he'd seen things turn ugly when the swinging dicks of law enforcement came rolling up on the scene, tried to muscle in and ended up getting everybody killed. Ben could trace his uncomfortable relationship with police officers everywhere – one or two notable exceptions notwithstanding – to those bad and often tragic experiences.

But his years with Special Forces had also taught him flexibility. There were occasions when you had to throw out the rule book, adapt to ever-changing situations in the field, accept that you couldn't be in full control all of the time, and learn to compromise.

This was one of those occasions.

By the time Ben had finished telling Tyler his plan, he was already speeding towards his destination: the Heberts' homestead. His instructions to Tyler had been clear. The former lawyer was to give himself up peacefully and voluntarily and offer no resistance as the police slapped on the handcuffs. He was to say nothing about Keisha and the kids being kidnapped. Instead, he was to tell the cops all about how the fugitive had threatened the family to coerce them into giving him shelter. That Hope had been using their remote farm as a base all along, against their will. And that he was due to return there that afternoon.

The pieces would soon fall into place. The cops would encircle the homestead with a dozen snipers and scores of hidden officers ready to pounce when the fugitive made his appearance. They'd drop their air support units, partly as they no longer needed eyes in the sky to locate their man, and partly because even the police would realise that the presence of hovering helicopters might just give away the ambush. Likewise the K9 units, for the same reason. Meanwhile, Waylon Roque would have to be crazy to miss the opportunity to lead the operation and personally apprehend the most wanted desperado of his whole career as sheriff of Clovis Parish. He could retire tomorrow and live as a hero for the rest of his days.

And all of that was exactly what Ben wanted. But it wasn't going to happen the way Roque and his troops were expecting.

It was early afternoon by the time Ben was entering the vicinity of the Heberts' place. The closer he got, the more intently he kept watch for any sign of police activity. The fact that he saw none almost certainly meant that the cops had already laid their trap for him and wanted the coast to look clear.

When he'd got as near as he dared approach he abandoned the Taurus for the last time on a narrow deserted backroad shaded by overhanging trees. He didn't bother to wipe the car down for prints. The next stage of his plan didn't require anonymity. He gathered his bag, bow and remaining arrows and stood for a moment, listening to the emptiness and silence broken only by the cawing of birds.

If his calculations were correct, about three-quarters of a mile of woods separated him from the Heberts' homestead almost exactly due west. That put him just a little over thirteen hundred yards from his target. Well outside of the police cordon, which would form a circle not much over one hundred yards in radius because of the close tree cover surrounding the homestead and limited visibility for the snipers. By that reckoning, then, Ben was some twelve hundred yards from the outer circle and first contact with the enemy.

It was time.

Ben headed west. The woodlands croaked and chittered and hummed with their constant living chorus. The fierceness of the sunlight was broken and dappled by the dense green canopy overhead, which trapped the moisture in the air. If the humidity had been any higher, he'd have been swimming. Sweat dripped from his hair and eyebrows as he moved silently over the mossy, wet terrain, watching every shadow for hidden threats, skirting cautiously around patches of bog and swamp and clambering over rotting tree trunks that lay in his path.

Ben's estimations had been dead right. Twelve hundred yards deep into the woods, he stopped in his tracks and sniffed the air. If the tell-tale aroma of cigarette smoke was something they warned against in the Louisiana state police SWAT school, someone hadn't been paying attention in class. It was coming from nearby, right up ahead.

Ben moved on a few silent steps and caught a glimpse of the Hebert house peeking through the trees a hundred yards or so away. But that didn't draw his eye for long.

What did, though, was the shape of the man hunkered down prone nearby in the moss and dirt, clad in green camo with a black rifle resting on a bipod in front of him. Smoking a cigarette.

First contact.

Ben thought, *Got you.*

Chapter 50

The police marksman had his rifle set up over the top of a fallen tree, and was using bush cover to hide him from the front, making the assumption that his target would come into play from that direction and not sneak up from the rear.

Assumptions like that were never a good thing in a tactical situation. Nor was setting up your sniper's nest with no more than a thirty-degree view of your possible field of fire and every chance of hitting one of your own people in the heat of the action. And as for taking off your tactical helmet and resting your weapon on its butt while sneaking a quick smoke on duty . . .

Ben shook his head. Amateurs.

He stalked closer.

The guy didn't sense the presence behind him until it was too late. Ben grabbed his collar and cracked his head against the hard shell of his helmet to stun him, then pinned him in a choke hold from which he had no possibility of escaping. Eight seconds, the guy's frontal cortex was beginning to shut down. Nine, and he was fully unconscious. While he was out for the count, Ben tore off two strips from his camouflage jacket. He balled up the first and stuffed it in the guy's mouth, then wrapped the second around his face as a gag. He removed the guy's duty belt, kept the extending baton for himself and unsnapped the handcuffs from their pouch.

Twenty seconds later, as the unconscious sniper was beginning to wake up, he found himself trussed by the wrists and ankles with his own belt and cuffs, and going nowhere fast. The guy's eyes bugged out and veins bulged purple in his forehead as he helplessly watched Ben pick up his rifle. It was the latest model of RSASS, short for Remington Semi-Automatic Sniper System. Based on the AR15, with a twenty-round magazine, unavailable to civilians. Ben dropped the mag, thumbed out the rounds and tossed them into the bushes. Then, risking a little noise, he swung the rifle hard against the nearest tree so that the barrel was reshaped like a banana.

'Now you can shoot around corners with it,' he said softly to the sniper, who could only grunt furiously in reply.

Ben left him lying there struggling and rolling in the dirt, and moved on. Using the Heberts' house as the centre of a circle with an area of about thirty-one thousand square yards and a radius of a hundred, he tracked around an imaginary circumference line clockwise through the trees and bushes. He reckoned on three or four snipers being set up around the perimeter of the field of fire, positioned with enough strategic common sense to at least not catch one another in a crossfire.

Like before, his estimate was correct. If the first sniper position was at zero degrees, Ben came across the second at sixty degrees and the third at a hundred and fifty. Neither of them were smoking cigarettes and they were fully intent on their job, but that didn't save each one in turn from suffering the same fate as his predecessor. Ben stalked up from the rear and used the extending baton on them, then followed up the stunning blow with the exact same choke and trussing-up technique as he'd used on the first guy.

Ben almost felt sorry for them. There would be a lot of red faces later. Maybe they would learn something from the experience, he thought. Probably not.

He checked out the rest of the circle, as far as the edge of the Heberts' driveway track, before he was satisfied that he'd got them all. Three for three.

He doubled back on his tracks to the point where he'd left the third sniper bundled up in the weeds. The last RSASS Ben had left loaded and undamaged. Proning himself in the dirt he scanned the Heberts' house and yard through its scope. The only sign of movement he could make out was the strutting and scratching of chickens in their enclosure. He wondered how many troops Sheriff Roque had brought to play with.

Time to find out.

Ben laid down the rifle while he quickly unstrapped his bag and made a few last-minute preparations. Then he picked the weapon up again. He had no intention of shooting anyone. He hadn't come here to do battle. He pointed the rifle's muzzle straight up in the air, at a patch of clear blue sky far above the tree canopy. Flipped off the safety catch. *Now let the fun begin*, he thought, and pressed the trigger.

The deafening blast of the high-velocity rifle shattered the silence. As fast as he could flick his right index finger, Ben emptied the entire twenty-round magazine into the sky. All at once the quiet, peaceful setting of Kadohadacho Creek sounded like a war zone. Birds erupted from the treetops. The Heberts' chickens scattered, flapping and squawking.

And the police officers lurking out of sight about the homestead, waiting in readiness to spring their trap on the fugitive, were flushed panic-stricken from their hiding places. A couple came sprinting from the big hay barn. Three more jumped out from behind the shed where Tyler kept his truck. Two more pairs emerged from both ends of the house. Pistols and shotguns were waving in all directions and there was a lot of discoordinated yelling going on. Louisiana's finest, springing into action like the well-oiled machine they were.

At the same moment two marked state police Dodge Chargers came roaring down the track into the Heberts' yard with their sirens whooping and blue lights flashing. Behind them came a black paramilitary vehicle with six huge knobbled tyres, a massive ramming bar and winch on the front and SHERIFF emblazoned on its armoured flanks. The monster truck skidded to a halt in the middle of the yard with the police cars either side of it.

Ben had already thrown down the empty sniper rifle and snatched up the bow. His last three arrows were fitted to its quiver. His last-minute preparations had been to doctor each one with a taped-on wad of steel wool. What had worked for the Garretts' moonshine plant would work just fine here, too.

As the police vehicles roared into the yard, he quickly loaded an arrow and tugged the bowstring back to full draw. The steel wool wadding touched the battery terminals and burst into flame. He aimed at the rear quarter of a police Dodge and let fly, and watched as his fire arrow streaked straight and true towards its mark. The hunting tip lanced through the car's flimsy bodyshell. He was disappointed by his accuracy. He'd been aiming for the fuel tank lid. He was maybe two inches off.

But close enough. In a matter of instants the back of the patrol car erupted in a dirty fireball as the gas tank caught light. The two officers inside flung open their doors and dived out to the left and right of the blazing vehicle, scrambling for safety. SWAT troops in military garb spilled from the armoured truck, weapons shouldered and searching for a target. They seemed marginally more in control than their regular cop colleagues, who now started shooting wildly in all directions as if a full-scale attack had been launched on them. A couple of bullets whizzed over Ben's head and a third smacked into a tree six feet to his left, but if they got him it would be by accident. Nobody seemed to have any idea where the arrow had come from.

Ben loaded another. Drew it back to full draw, let it catch fire, then let go. It soared towards the yard, went knifing through the pall of black smoke that poured from the burning car, and thunked into the back of the second Dodge. Same result, even more impressive this time as the fuel tank ruptured like a volcano and spewed flame all over the SWAT truck. The troopers scattered for cover and the driver leaped from his cab. They all disappeared from view behind the roiling smoke and heat ripples that distorted the air. Ben could see running figures flitting back and forth. The burp and splutter of radios and hoarse yelling of frightened men could be heard over the crackle of the flames.

It was total pandemonium, utter confusion. Zero casualties, maximum chaos. They were probably all wishing they'd brought their dogs and helicopters after all.

Ben smiled to himself at the spectacle. He still had one arrow left, but any more damage would be overkill. He set down Caleb's bow, gave it a grateful goodbye pat and then snatched up his bag and began skirting through the trees towards the house.

Chapter 51

Sheriff Roque was alone in the Heberts' kitchen, his temporary command centre, watching in slack-jawed stupefaction from the window as fire and explosions turned his carefully-planned sting operation into a chaotic nightmare. His men were in disarray, his radio was frantic, and he had no idea what to do to contain the situation. He was absolutely certain that this Ben Hope must have called in an entire unit of Special Forces crazies to back him up. It was unbelievable.

'Holy shit,' he muttered to himself. 'Holy shit.'

He was so distracted by the awful scene unfolding before his eyes that he never sensed the presence behind him until he felt his revolver slip out of its holster. He whirled round in sudden alarm. His hand instinctively went to his gunbelt and clapped against empty leather.

'You,' was all he could croak as he saw the fugitive standing there pointing his own Colt .45 at him.

'Thought I'd find you in here, Sheriff. Leading from the rear, like a real commander.'

Ben leaned back against the kitchen worktop. Just days ago he'd sat in this same cosy room while Caleb diligently did his algebra homework at the table and Tyler cooked up his trademark Gumbo à la Hebert. Now Caleb was a prisoner of the Garrett brothers along with his stepmother

300

and half-brother and -sister, and Tyler was sitting in a jail cell.

Reflecting on those facts didn't make Ben very happy. He thumb-cocked the hammer of the ancient Colt and levelled it at the sheriff's midriff. The gun felt solid and heavy and balanced in his hand. Old-fashioned blued steel and walnut were a far cry from space-age polymer and fancy alloys.

Ben said, 'I'd heard that some of you old timers were still using cowboy guns. I had to see it to believe it. Not ready to enter the twentieth century yet, Sheriff?'

'You're outta your goddamn mind, pointin' a gun at me,' Roque blustered.

'And yet here we are,' Ben said. 'Live with it.'

'I'll be damned if this ain't your handiwork,' Roque said, motioning at the window. Outside, some cops were still running around in a panic, firing into the trees while others cringed behind whatever cover they could find, waiting for the attack to be over.

'In my line of work we call it a diversion,' Ben replied. 'Would you like me to spell that for you?'

'What the hell do you mean, a diversion? Diversion for what?'

'I felt it was appropriate for the two of us to have a private chat,' Ben said. 'You see, Sheriff, I'm getting tired of being on the run. I decided it was time for a change, so I'm here to turn myself in.'

Roque gaped at him and shook his head. 'All I can say is, Hope, you got a helluva way of doing it.'

'I wanted to surrender to you personally because I know you're a reasonable man and you wouldn't do anything like gun down an innocent civilian. That is, if you had a gun.'

Roque almost laughed. 'So you're innocent now?'

'I think you know it, deep down. You've got nothing on

me, except for a couple of scorched police cars and a few bruised officers, and they brought that on themselves by getting in my way. I didn't murder Lottie Landreneau. She was my friend. And I'm not in the habit of killing my friends. But I know who did.'

Roque said nothing.

'Think about it, Sheriff. You saw what happened to the Garretts' little moonshine setup.'

Roque wet his lips with the tip of his tongue. His eyes were narrowed into slits like cracks in a granite cliff face and watching Ben guardedly, but thoughtfully. 'That was you, wasn't it? I figured as much.'

'And you must have asked yourself why I'd go and do a thing like that,' Ben said. 'Doesn't make sense, does it, unless I had some reason to strike at the three Garrett brothers. Now reduced to two, but that wasn't strictly my doing. I'd be happy if it had been.'

'The Garretts killed the Landreneau woman. That what you're sayin'?'

'Wow. No wonder they elected you sheriff. That's right. That's what I'm saying. And it strikes me that you don't appear too surprised. You know what they're capable of. They've been getting away with it for years, and you lot were too chicken to do anything about it. That's about to change.'

'That a fact?'

'Yes, Sheriff, it is. And there's more. You won't like it.'

'Try me.'

'Your deputy, Mason Redbone. He's in with the Garretts.'

Roque grimaced. 'That's insane.'

Ben used his free hand to pull up his shirt and show Roque his wound. Roque's frown deepened when he saw it.

Ben said, 'That's what caused the blood trail you fellows

must have been able to follow from Lottie's house that night. Your pal Mason stuck a stiletto boot knife in me. That's after he tried to shoot me, using a handgun with the serial numbers filed off. I did ask myself why he would do that. Any thoughts, Sheriff?'

Roque made no reply. The wild scene outside the window was beginning to settle down, as if the cops had finally realised they were no longer under attack.

'The answer is that Jayce and Seth Garrett own Deputy Redbone,' Ben said. 'I was set up to be the stool pigeon for killing Lottie Landreneau, and your guy's job was to make sure I couldn't speak out in my defence. Case closed. Except it didn't quite work out so neatly. Now the Garretts have given Mason another job to do. In case you wondered why Keisha Hebert and the kids aren't here, it's because Mason kidnapped them earlier today and delivered them to the Garretts. They're hostages.'

Roque had just turned a shade paler. 'Hold on a darned minute. I got Tyler Hebert in the parish jail and he never said a thing about—'

'Because I told him not to,' Ben cut in. 'Better you heard it from me. This situation needs to be dealt with properly.'

'But—'

'Don't waste time with questions, Sheriff. The clock's ticking. It's not money the Garretts want in exchange for Keisha and the kids. They want me, because they blame me for what happened to Logan. They're going to kill them if I don't stop it. But for that I need your help.'

'You need my help.'

'If I could tackle the Garretts and all the people alone and unarmed with no backup, we wouldn't be having this conversation. You'd never even have seen me. Just the smoke rising from their island and the two brothers lying hogtied in the street outside your office, with a signed confession stapled to their foreheads.'

The sheriff stared at Ben as though he was an alien in a space suit. He shook his head. 'I can't believe a word of what you're tellin' me.'

'Then don't take my word for it. Let's hear it from Deputy Redbone. Where is he now?'

Roque frowned again. 'That's the funny thing. He ought-ta've been the first to get here, after the Tanners reported to us about you and the Heberts.'

Ben sighed. So it had been the Tanners. 'But he never called in to say he'd got here.'

Roque shook his head, frowning even harder. 'Fact is, I ain't too sure where he is now.'

'Three guesses. He's been on the island, drinking beer with his cronies and having a laugh at your expense.'

'I just don't know, Hope. I just don't know. This whole business sounds as crazy as a soup sandwich.'

Ben looked at his watch. 'Sheriff, the Garretts are arranging for me to be picked up outside the Big Q Motel at nightfall. That's about five hours from now. I don't have time to stand around listening to your droll Southern colloquialisms.'

Roque gave the helpless shrug of a man overloaded with confusion. 'So what'm I supposed to do?'

Ben uncocked the revolver, flipped it around butt-for-wards and offered it back to the sheriff. Roque hesitated, then took the gun. But he didn't point it at Ben. A thousand conflicting thoughts seemed to be churning around behind his eyes.

Ben held out his arms, offering both wrists. He said, 'Here's what you do, Sheriff. I'm all yours. Take me back to Villeneuve. The heroic law officer captures the dangerous armed fugitive, single-handed. The crowning moment of your career.'

'Then what?'

'Then you put out a call to Deputy Redbone. Make it sound like everything's okay. Then we sit tight and wait for him to return to base.'

'Okay, and what next after that? Say for one moment that you're right about this. He's gonna confess to kidnap, accessory to murder and colludin' with criminals, just like pretty please with cherries on top?'

'He'll talk,' Ben said. 'Leave that part to me.'

Chapter 52

By mid-afternoon the police convoy was racing back towards Villeneuve amid a chorus of wailing sirens. Waylon Roque's car led the column as they rolled into town like a victory parade and crammed Ascension Square with noise and activity. Word spread rapidly that the manhunt, having kept the local media buzzing virtually nonstop since the night of the murder, was finally over. The good folks of Clovis Parish could now sleep easy in their beds knowing that the savage killer was about to be put behind bars. Photographers snapped eagerly and spectators thronged up against the police cordon outside the courthouse as the sheriff personally escorted the cuffed prisoner from the back of his patrol car and inside the building. A heavy guard of armed cops crowded the doorway, ready to gun the desperado down should he try to make a last-ditch bid for escape.

Away from the public hubbub, it was a very different story. Nobody, not even Roque's deputies, knew that the prisoner was yet to be formally charged or read his rights, because they assumed that the sheriff had already done so when he'd single-handedly managed to overpower and apprehend the desperate criminal. But they could all tell from the sheriff's odd behaviour that this was a far from conventional arrest. Rather than march the prisoner downstairs to the basement holding facility to be booked, logged into the system, finger-printed, photographed and then stuck in a cell pending transportation to the Clovis Parish jail, Roque led him through the building and down the corridor to his own office, ushered him inside and closed the door, just the two of them alone together.

Roque was well known for not always following exact book procedure, but this was unprecedented and just plain bizarre. In the corridor outside the closed office door the bemused Deputy Eli Fontaine said, 'What's up with that?' To which another, Bob Trahan, shook his head and replied, 'Damned if I have any clue what's goin' on, buddy.'

A minute later, the sheriff poked his head out of the door to say, 'Eli, I want you to get hold of Mason Redbone for me. Tell him I got a special new assignment I need him to take care of personally, and I want to see him in my office asap.'

'I'll get right on it, Sheriff.' Fontaine hesitated. Trying to peek through the gap in the door, he added, 'Uh, everythin' okay in there?'

'We're fine, Eli. Jump to it, will you?'

Roque closed the door. He turned to Ben, who had taken a seat on the sofa by the window. It sagged in the middle and looked as though it had been slept on many times in its life.

Ben said, 'Nice work, Waylon. That should do the trick. Unless Mason's decided to switch tracks entirely and quit his job without notice.'

'I'm takin' a hell of a chance on you,' Roque said. 'And don't call me Waylon.'

'You don't have much choice, Waylon. If I'm right, which I am, this trumped-up manhunt was the biggest and most corrupt abuse of police powers in this parish since you shot

307

Grace Hebert to death. Remember her? You'd best treat me nicely, or I might just decide to tell the world how rotten to the core your department really is.'

'You threatenin' to sue?'

'Not my style,' Ben said. 'But Tyler might. And he's a pretty good lawyer.'

Roque pulled a sour face. 'I get the idea, Hope. But if you're wrong—'

'Then feel free to book me for auto theft, assaulting officers and damaging police property,' Ben said. 'I don't think wrecking an illegal moonshine plant is against the law, is it? Apart from that, you don't have a single shred of evidence against me.'

'We'll see,' Roque said. 'I wouldn't get too cocky, if I was you.'

'You can start making reparations by taking these off,' Ben said, and held out his cuffed wrists. 'Don't worry, I won't hit you.'

Roque gave a surly grunt, then pulled a ring of keys from his desk drawer and undid the locks on the cuffs.

'Thank you, Waylon.'

'Asshole.'

Ben leaned back on the sofa. Roque sat at his desk. He took the Colt out of its holster and laid it in front of him, next to an old-fashioned desk intercom system that looked like an instrument panel from the Millennium Falcon. He turned the gun so its barrel was pointing at Ben.

'You still don't trust me, do you?' Ben said.

'We'll see,' Roque said again.

Ben closed his eyes and settled in to wait for Mason Redbone. Outwardly he was calm and peaceful, but every tick of the wall clock was like a ball peen hammer tapping a raw nerve inside his brain. He couldn't stop thinking about

Keisha, Caleb, Noah and Trinity. Tyler must be going out of his mind with worry.

Forty-seven painful, silent minutes had ground by when the intercom beeped. Roque reached out and pressed a button. A voice from the speaker said, 'Mason Redbone to see you, Sheriff.'

'Sure, send'm right in.'

'Might want to frisk him for concealed weapons,' Ben said. 'He's apt to be tricksy.'

'I know how to handle my own men,' Roque snapped.

'Do you?'

There was a knock. The door opened and Deputy Redbone stepped through it, full of confidence. 'You wanted to see me, Sheriff?' With the angle of the open door, he couldn't see Ben.

'Close the door, Mason,' Roque said.

Mason closed the door. Then saw Ben sitting there, and the part of his face that wasn't already mottled purple and blue turned the colour of raw liver. He started backing towards the doorway as if he was about to bolt. His mouth opened and closed soundlessly a few times before he managed to gibber, 'I don't . . . I don't get it. What in hell's *he* doin' here?'

Ben stood.

Roque rose from his chair, walked around the desk and held out an open palm. 'Mind if I see your service weapon, Deputy?'

Mason's face turned from blood red to snow white. He began to protest loudly, but the expression in Roque's eyes quickly shut him up. He reluctantly drew the Glock from his holster. For an instant, Ben thought he was about to start shooting. Mason swallowed hard, then handed the gun over.

Roque laid it on the desk. 'You wouldn't be packin' any

more hardware I should know about, Mason? Like a concealed firearm or a boot knife? You know that's not permitted, right?'

'What in hell's name is this about, Sheriff?' Mason protested angrily. Guilt was written all over his face. The Academy Awards would have to wait for another year. 'I was told you had an assignment for me.'

'What happened to you today?' Roque asked. His voice was soft, but menacing. 'We sorta lost track of your whereabouts for a while there.'

'Nothin'. I—'

Roque took a step closer. 'Did you pay a visit to Keisha Hebert?'

'What?'

'Did you take her and the kids away in your car?'

Mason let out a strangled laugh. 'Oh, come on now, Sheriff, where'd you go gettin' ideas like that?'

'Did you see Jayce and Seth Garrett today?'

Mason's jaw dropped open. He glanced nervously at Ben, then back at Roque, who was advancing towards him like a glacier.

'I truly do not want to believe what this man is allegin' against you,' Roque said. 'But somethin' about this whole story is beginnin' to smell bad enough to gag a maggot. I want answers, Mason. Right now, you heah?'

Mason shuffled back a step, then another, retreating in a little semi-circle that took him nearer the desk.

Roque's face had turned harder than gunmetal. 'Why so nervous, Deputy? You're sweatin' like a sinner in church. You got somethin' to say you best start talkin', son.'

Mason's eyes flashed with sudden, intense hatred. He was caught, and he knew it. 'Think you're pretty smart, don't you, y'old coot? Well kiss my ass!' His arm whipped towards the desktop and his fingers closed on the butt of his pistol. He snatched the weapon off the desk and aimed it at Roque's head.

And then Mason was being lifted off his feet and letting out a garbled squawk of terror as Ben pinned him against the wall, one hand around his throat and the other twisting the pistol out of his grip with enough force to dislocate his trigger finger.

'Talk,' Ben said.

'You kiss my ass too!' Mason screamed.

Still holding him tight against the wall, Ben leaned close to Mason and whispered in his ear. Mason's eyes bulged out like a throttled pug's.

Ben let go.

Mason slid down the wall, all the way down to the floor. His uniform trousers were suddenly wet with urine and a pool of it was soaking into the carpet.

Roque stared in astonishment, first down at his deputy and then at Ben. 'Holy crap, what did you just say to him?'

'Over to you, Sheriff,' Ben said. 'He's ready to confess everything.'

Chapter 53

And Mason Redbone did confess. It all came out, right there in Roque's office in front of Ben, Roque himself, and four more officers brought in as witnesses. Every word was recorded as, weeping and snivelling, Mason admitted that he'd been involved with the Garrett brothers' crooked enterprises for over three years.

He needed the extra money, he bawled, what with a mortgage and two kids and another on the way. In return for their backhanders he protected the Garretts by threatening potential snitches, concealing evidence of a multitude of crimes, and even helping to sell their merchandise for an extra cut. He'd never meant to let it go so far, but the Garretts had just sucked him deeper and deeper into the quicksand, until he was in over his head.

Yes, he'd been complicit in the Garretts' plan to frame Ben Hope for the murder of Lottie Landreneau. Yes, he had tried to kill him that night, so nobody would ever question the narrative or suspect Jayce and Seth. And yes, he had personally kidnapped Keisha Hebert, her two young children and her stepson, and delivered them to the Garretts earlier that day.

'It's not like I wanted to do it,' he groaned in misery. 'Them poor kids. Lil' girl reminds me of my own daughter Sarah. I told Jayce over and over, this ain't right. After this,

I'm done. Next time you boys need my help, you can include me out.'

What a performance, Ben thought.

Roque stopped the recording, looking at his deputy as though he were something unsavoury he'd stepped in. 'Mighty honourable of you, Mason. Funny, didn't seem that way just now when you were fixin' to blow my head off. If this man you tried to frame for murder hadn't stepped in quicker'n green grass through a goose, I'd be dead. He shoulda killed you that night.'

'I'm sorry, Sheriff!' Mason sobbed. 'I don't know what I was thinkin'.' His head fell and the tears dripped from his chin. 'Oh, God, I'm so ashamed.'

'Believe me, Mason, you ain't a quarter as ashamed of yourself as I am of you,' Roque said. 'You're a dismal piece of shit, and you're goin' to prison for a long, long time. Know what they do to cops in Angola, don't you?'

Roque turned to the other cops, who had listened grimly to every word of the confession and were staring at Mason Redbone as if they were seriously considering shooting him. Roque said, 'Eli, Bob, Jacob, Carter, please get this no-good dirtbag out of my sight. Take'm downstairs and book'm for . . . hell, what *ain't* we bookin' him for?'

'You want me to get'm a dry pair of pants, Sheriff?' Eli said.

'No, let'm sit in his pissy ones awhile.'

The officers were more than happy to carry out the order. Mason was frogmarched away in handcuffs, shamefaced and crying like a child and nursing his dislocated finger.

Alone once more, Roque turned to Ben. 'All right, Mister Hope, looks like I owe you an apology. I was wrong about you.'

'I don't want your apology,' Ben said.

'Then what do you want?'

'First off, I want you to let Tyler Hebert out of his jail cell.'

'Consider it done,' Roque said. 'He's a free man. And so are you, I reckon. All charges dropped. Under the circumstances, it's the least we can do. Don't go burnin' any more patrol cars, and we'll call it even.'

'Do I get that in writing?'

'I'm a man of my word.'

Ben nodded. He stepped over to the window and parted the blinds with two fingers so he could peek through the gap. 'In that case, you need to go outside and say a few words to the crowd of reporters who are all waiting to hear the latest on my arrest and conviction for murder.'

Roque shrugged. 'What you want me to tell 'em?'

'Only half the truth. That I'm being released without charge in the light of new evidence, but that the murder hunt is ongoing and you have no other suspects at this time.'

'Why would I say that?'

Ben turned away from the window and replied, 'Because the Garretts will be watching the TV, and worrying that their prisoner exchange scheme has fallen apart with me going to jail. This puts things back on track. But you need to do it quickly. The sand's running out of the hourglass.' He pointed at the office wall clock. 5.06 p.m.

'You really think the Garretts'll kill a bunch of kids?'

'No, I think they'll rape, torture and mutilate them first, and make their mother watch it happen before it's her turn. And I'm sure they're looking forward to it. If they haven't already begun. This whole thing is hanging by a thread.'

'Jesus Christ.' Roque gave a weary sigh. 'Okay. I'll go tell the reporters like you said. It's a smart play. Then the Garretts'll be expectin' you to show up at the Big Q after all. Come nightfall, there'll be a SWAT unit on the motel ready to pounce on them sumbitches so hard and fast it'll make their heads spin. Believe me, by the time I'm done with 'em they'll be more'n ready to let those kids go.'

'Worst thing you could do,' Ben said. 'Jayce and Seth won't be there in person. They'll be sending a few of their thugs to collect me and take me back to the island. The moment they realise something's up, it's game over for Keisha and the children.'

'Fair enough. So how do you plan to go about this?'

'By striking where they least expect it,' Ben said. 'A surprise tactical assault right on their home ground. Garrett Island itself.'

'You lost your mind?'

'It's got to happen while Jayce and Seth's men are en route to the Big Q to pick me up. That's when they'll be at their weakest in terms of manpower and most off their guard, because they'll be too busy thinking about how they're going to chop me up in pieces and feed me to the alligators. The raid team will move in fast and hard, take out their defences and snap them up before they even know what's happening.'

Roque suddenly looked ten years older and infinitely wearier. 'I'm a year off retirement. I bought a fishin' boat. I got grandkids. I'm too old to go gettin' myself into a gunfight with a bunch of lunatics.'

'It's only the psychos like Jayce Garrett who aren't afraid,' Ben said. 'The rest of us are human. I'm scared, too. And I'm becoming more scared the more I watch that clock ticking, because every minute that passes is a minute gone for the Hebert family. Are you going to help me, or not?'

Roque clenched his jaw and seemed to collect himself. 'All right, goddamn it. Let's do this. But let me tell you, that place is like a fortress. Surrounded by water, terrain thick

315

as a damn jungle. If we're gonna hit it, we need to hit it like it's Iwo Jima. I'd have to muster every trooper in the state, with air support and SWAT tanks, the whole kit and caboodle.'

Ben shook his head. This was exactly the reason he hated bringing the police into this. They all thought the same way, like a hive mind.

He asked Roque, 'How long have you been sheriff of Clovis Parish? Around forty years?'

'Watch it, son. I ain't *that* long in the tooth. Twenty-eight years next month.'

'And how many hostage rescue missions have you led in that time? Let me take a wild guess. Around none?'

Roque shrugged uncomfortably. 'Well, I gotta confess, there ain't been much call for that kind of thing in my job.'

'That's what I thought you'd say,' Ben said. 'I've led scores of them. It's what I used to do, and I'm good at it. But it has to be done right. No helicopters. No fanfare. You let the keystone cops go roaring in willy nilly with guns blazing all over the place, the way they did today, you might as well execute the hostages yourself.'

Roque wasn't liking it much, but he bit his tongue and listened, frowning.

Ben went on, 'I've seen too many kidnap rescue missions go bad because local hick law enforcement dropped the ball. And you know as well as I do that your lot are about as hick as it gets.'

'All right, all right. You're sayin' you want to be on the team. I get it. There might be some way I can bring you in as an observer, or somethin'.'

Ben shook his head. 'I'm not interested in playing second fiddle to an inexperienced commander. If I'm in, I'm all the way in.'

'Now hold on a goddamned minute, Hope. Surely you don't mean—?'

'That's exactly what I mean,' Ben said. 'I want to be able to do whatever is necessary to save those hostages and take down Jayce and Seth Garrett. For the Heberts to stand any chance of surviving, this will need to be done my way. *Completely* my way. Not only that, but I expect to be immune from any kind of comeback from what happens out there.'

Roque exploded. 'You've gotta be three pickles shy of a quart if you think I'd agree to such a—'

'You're the chief of police, aren't you?'

'So what if I am? Not even the governor could grant you that authority!'

'Then do it without his authority,' Ben said. 'Under the table. A gentlemen's agreement between us that nobody else needs to know about. As far as anyone on the outside is concerned, I can be brought on board as a special adviser or tactical consultant, whatever you want to call it. I have more than enough credentials to make that stick. You remain in nominal command of the mission, but you answer to me. My call. No questions. Do we have a deal?'

Roque said nothing.

'Come on, Sheriff. Make a decision. Do the right thing. And save your own skin into the bargain.'

Roque looked sharply at him. 'How'd you figure that?'

'Because if you do nothing, and the Garretts harm Keisha Hebert and the children as a result, that blood will be on your hands. And if that happens, I know what Tyler Hebert will do. Never mind a lawsuit. He'll gun you down without a care for the consequences. The only reason he didn't come looking for you after Grace stopped one of your bullets with her head was that he still had Caleb to think of. Take away his family, he'll have nothing left to lose.'

Roque stared at Ben for the longest time. In a softer tone he said, 'You know, what happened to Grace Hebert – I mean, I think about it sometimes. I never meant for that poor woman to get hurt. It damn near broke my spirit at the time.'

'I think Tyler would have appreciated knowing that. The general impression was that nobody gave a damn for some stupid woman who happened to get in the way.'

'I want to make things right,' Roque said. 'I truly do.'

'Then here's your golden opportunity,' Ben said. 'Just don't take all day to mull it over. Murdering kidnappers aren't known for their powers of self-restraint.'

Roque fell silent. Ben could see the wheels spinning so fast in the sheriff's mind that he expected smoke to come out of his ears. Finally Roque relented. His shoulders sagged. He shook his head. 'Holy jumpin' Jesus, but you drive a hard bargain. All right. We do this your way. Your call. No questions.'

'"The way of a fool is right in his own eyes, but he who hearkeneth unto counsel is wise." Book of Proverbs. I knew you'd see sense.'

'Whatever you say, Commander. Or do I got to call you "sir" now?'

'No need for that,' Ben said. 'I never liked it much anyway. Now go and tell the world that Ben Hope is a free man. Then we've got work to do.'

Chapter 54

Things could still move fast in the Deep South. Within minutes of breaking the news of the prisoner's unexpected release to the reporters outside the building, Sheriff Roque had finished hastily scribbling his sworn affidavit, detailing the witnessed and recorded confession of Mason Redbone and requesting an arrest warrant for Jayce and Seth Garrett on charges of murder, attempted murder and kidnap. The document was then quickly whisked off by a runner to the Clovis Parish courtroom for the urgent attention of District Judge Aloysius E. Claybrook, the man on whose signature the entire plan depended.

Meanwhile, Ben was laying out the details of the hostage rescue raid for Roque and writing up a shopping list of required items. It was a tense moment waiting for the judge's decision. They needn't have worried. Deputy Redbone's confession was evidence far beyond reasonable doubt, and plenty enough to convince Justice Claybrook. Precisely eight minutes after the affidavit was submitted, the requested warrants were duly faxed to Roque's desk bearing the judge's signature, and the operation was formally greenlit.

While Roque got busy marshalling his troops, Ben had two reunions to take care of. One with his possessions that the police had taken from him when he was arrested, and the other with a newly released, very confused and deeply distraught Tyler Hebert. Tyler's face was ashen and his eyes looked smudged with coal. Ben held him tightly and patted him on the back.

'What's happenin', Ben?' Tyler asked, his voice barely above a whisper. 'How come they let you go? Where's my family? Nobody's tellin' me jack shit.'

'It's complicated,' Ben said. 'All that matters is that your family will be okay. I'm working with the Sheriff's Department to make sure we bring them back safe, Tyler. I promise.'

Tyler shook his head. 'I don't know what kind of deal you cut with them, Ben, but you can't trust Waylon Roque. I told you what kind of man he is, didn't I?'

'He wants to do the right thing,' Ben said. 'I think he means it.'

'Well, that's just a little hard for me to swallow right now.'

'I know. I'm not asking you to forgive him. But when a man wants to atone for his past sins, you have to cut him enough slack to let him at least try.'

Tyler heaved a deep sigh. His face twisted and he seemed ready to burst into tears. He gripped Ben's arms in his big fists. 'You'll be there, right? You'll make sure nothin' bad happens to my family.'

'I'll be there,' Ben said. 'Roque's not in charge of this. I am.'

'What are you gonna do?'

'Get them back,' Ben said. 'It's as simple as that.'

Too bewildered to make sense of it all, Tyler muttered, 'You saved my kid before. I have to believe you'll do it again.'

Ben gently pulled his arms free of the big man's grip, then clasped Tyler's hands in his. 'Go home, Tyler. Sit tight and I'll call the moment it's over.' And don't worry about the burnt-out cop cars sitting in your yard, he might have added.

'I can't bear to go home right now, without them.'

'Then wait here. You'll see them again soon.'

Ben left Tyler standing alone, and made his way to the War Room where Roque had said he would assemble his team. Ben had instructed the sheriff to gather eighteen of his most dependable and capable officers. Whatever that translated to. He could only hope his team wouldn't consist half of wet-behind-the-ears youngsters straight from police academy, and the other half of grey-haired fatbellies who couldn't run twenty yards without getting a coronary.

But Roque had done his job. As Ben walked into the War Room he was pleased by what he saw. The sixteen male and two female officers were lined up like soldiers, keyed up and ready to be briefed on whatever this was all about. The two women were trim and fit, one white, the other black, with hair scraped back from their faces and serious eyes and assertive body language that left no doubt as to their capability. The white one looked especially tough. Her face was lean and her hands looked hard and strong. No rings.

Judging by the looks Ben got in return, a few of the assembly were less pleased to see him. Others were plainly baffled by his unexpected appearance in the War Room. A ginger-haired cop who looked like he spent eight hours a day pumping iron grumbled in a loud voice, 'Didn't we just arrest this guy?'

The cop standing next to him, Officer Trahan, one of the men Roque had summoned to his office earlier, nudged him with his elbow and said, 'He's off the hook, Charlie. Mason Redbone confessed to the whole damn thing.'

'Mason? You're shittin' me.'

'Nope. I was right there, heard it with my own two earballs. We was after the wrong man all along.'

'Holy cow.'

'Who'd have thunk it, huh?'

The buzz of general astonishment died down to a quiet hum as Roque stepped up to address the team.

'Listen up, people. Now, you don't need me to tell you there's been some mighty strange developments goin' on around here, and I can't go into it all right now. The upshot is, we have a serious hostage situation takin' place at the location some of you may know as Garrett Island. Judge Claybrook just signed warrants for Jayce and Seth Garrett, and I mean to serve and enforce 'em just as quick as I can. Innocent lives are dependin' on it.'

Roque briefly laid out the details of the kidnapping to his stunned audience. He managed to make it sound as though the suspects had abducted the victims in person, and studiously avoided any mention of their disgraced accomplice who was at that moment cooling his heels in a holding cell downstairs.

Another officer, who sported a droopy Wyatt Earp moustache, put up his hand. 'Pardon me, Sheriff. Did you say we're actually mountin' a raid on *Garrett Island*?'

This was unheard of. Generations of Clovis Parish law enforcement officers had made a point of staying away from the place, like a corner of the garden so infested with weeds that they preferred to forget its existence and leave it to its own devices.

'You heard me right, Trey,' Roque replied. There were a lot of murmurs and shaking heads. The sheriff hushed the chatter down with a gesture.

'Now listen up, people. I know each and every man and woman in this room, and I have faith in your ability as the best law enforcement officers it's ever been my honour to work with. I'm askin' you to volunteer for a special task force to go in there and get these people out. It ain't gonna be easy. The Garretts are hardcore crooks, as everyone in Clovis Parish knows all too well. They've been a blight on our community for as long as we all can remember. It's about time we got shot of 'em, once and for all.'

Roque motioned an arm towards Ben. 'Now, this fella here, I don't need to introduce. Y'all know a bit about him already.'

'We sure do,' Wyatt Earp said dryly, and got a few laughs.

Someone else said, 'What's he doin' here, Sheriff?'

'Mister Hope is comin' on board this operation as a special adviser,' Roque explained. 'Now I know this is all a mite irregular, but you're just gonna have to bear with it for now. We ain't never dealt with a delicate hostage situation of this nature before, and I'm pleased to have him along for the ride. Yes, Officer Fruge?'

The ginger-haired muscleman had a question. 'Okay, but I don't get why it's gotta fall on us? The FBI have their special hostage rescue team all set up to handle stuff like this.'

'This man trains HRT agencies from all over the world,' Roque said, pointing at Ben. 'He's as expert as anyone at this kind of job. Plus we have a serious time element to consider. Our parish is a helluva long way from Quantico, Virginia, and there just ain't enough clock goin' spare to sit around waitin' for the fibbies to copter in and take charge of our lil' problem for us. It's my belief we can resolve this ourselves. Are y'all with me?'

'We're with you, Sheriff,' the white female officer said.

'Yowzah,' said another.

Ben stepped forward, wanting to wrap up the briefing as fast as possible. 'Gentlemen and ladies, this is a stealth raid. Our objective is to infiltrate Garrett Island undetected shortly before nightfall tonight, then launch a surprise attack while at the same time locating and extracting the hostages. I've proposed organising our force into four units of five men each, designated Teams A, B, C and D. Sheriff Roque will head up B Team. I'll be with A team.'

'Adviser,' the white female cop muttered out of the corner of her mouth, a little too loudly. 'Adviser my fuckin' ass.'

Roque snapped, 'That's enough talk, Officer Hogan.'

'The island is accessible only from a single point,' Ben went on. 'We don't have time to float rigid inflatables down the Bayou Sanglante and we can't afford to make a helicopter drop for reasons of noise, so we'll be going in that way. Once we gain access to the island, we'll split up into our respective teams and move into position.'

'And the Garretts're just gonna let us waltz in there easy as pie?' said a tall African-American officer who stood behind Hogan.

'I'll be very surprised if they do,' Ben said. 'Which is why I've prepared this equipment inventory.' He picked up the sheet of paper from the desk. 'Every raid team member will be issued with a semi-automatic carbine and two full magazines, sixty rounds of ammunition. I've also included night-vision equipment, and ballistic vests for every team member as well as extra for the hostages, rated to stop a 7.62 NATO rifle bullet at the minimum. For transportation, we'll proceed to the target in five unmarked Ford Explorer interceptors, backed up by an armoured SWAT vehicle into which we'll load the hostages, once recovered, to protect them from any gunfire we might encounter during exfiltration.'

Wyatt Earp said, 'I thought you said this was a stealth raid. Sounds more like we're fixin' to start World War Three.'

'Fine by me,' said Officer Hogan. She was getting all worked up and looked game for a major battle. Ben made a mental note to pick her for his A Team so that he could keep an eye on her. The big ginger-haired one, too. But the tall African-American officer looked more level-headed.

'I expect resistance,' Ben said. 'But if we do this right, I'm confident the operation can be pulled off successfully without the need for undue force and no casualties suffered on either side. Okay? Any more questions?' He scanned the room. A few shaking heads, a lot of fierce excitement. Any trepidation over the idea of setting foot on Garrett Island seemed to have left them. Nobody had anything to ask.

Ben said, 'Now, time is of the essence, folks. We need to be ready to roll in short order.' Turning to Roque he asked, 'Sheriff, how quickly do you think you can get all this gear together?'

'We're emptyin' out the armoury, even as we speak,' Roque said. 'Everythin' but a tactical nuke.'

Ben said, 'Fine. Then let's get to it.'

Chapter 55

Jayce had been indoors, stuck to the television, ever since the news broke earlier about Ben Hope's arrest. He was raging, because now it turned out that his plan to incriminate Hope for the murder of the Landreneau woman had worked so damn well it was coming back to screw things up.

As he watched, his mind was busily working through the ways they could still get to Hope even behind bars. Jayce had plenty of contacts in prison. One call, and he could muster up a gang of good ole boys who'd be only too happy to take care of business for him. Dip dip dip, pop pop pop, they'd stab him so full of shiv holes you could use him as a colander, and that would be it for the Limey sonofabitch. Job done.

But such an outcome would deprive Jayce of the pleasure of doing it himself, and it was irking him.

Then all of that suddenly changed when KLAX interrupted their schedule with the latest news update.

Jayce perched on the edge of his armchair and watched as the TV cut to a clip of reporters clamouring outside the Villeneuve courthouse. There stood the sheriff, surrounded by microphones and looking edgy and sour as he made the unexpected announcement that the suspect had been released without charge. Yes, we are still pursuing this murder investigation. No, we have no other suspects at this time. No further comment.

Jayce permitted himself a small smile of satisfaction at this turn of events. Things might just work out, after all.

He blipped off the TV, got up and went to the fridge and grabbed himself a Swamp Pop. Filé Root Beer, his favourite. He tipped the neck of the bottle in a silent toast to his improved fortunes, and took a long celebratory swig. He'd glugged down half the bottle when his phone began to burr in the back pocket of his Wranglers. He fished it out and checked the caller ID before answering.

'Yo. Talk to me, bitch.'

The caller's voice yakked agitatedly in his ear. Jayce listened calmly, said nothing more, and when he'd heard everything he needed to hear he turned off the phone and slipped it back into his pocket.

Jayce left the room, walked out of the house into the late afternoon heat and headed over to the clubhouse. Bubba Beane was alone in there, sitting on the edge of the pool table where he had all the components of his MAC-10 submachine gun laid out on the green baize. He was using an oily rag to clean the parts before putting it all back together, a ritual he observed several times daily whether he fired the weapon or not. Machine gun fishing was a popular pastime on the island.

'Seen Seth?' Jayce asked, standing in the doorway.

Bubba looked up from his task and replied, 'Uh-huh. He's down at the pontoon with that nigger woman and them niglets. The other kid, too. I do feel sorry for that poor white boy, bein' raised with porch monkeys.' Bubba shook his head with a sigh, lamenting the state of modern America.

Jayce said, 'What's he doin' down there?'

'Guess he thought they needed a little exercise,' Bubba said with a shrug as he wiped some excess oil off his bolt mechanism.

'Hm.' You didn't waste words on a man you had once disfigured with a Bowie knife. Jayce turned and left the clubhouse. He crossed the compound to where the communal quad bikes were parked, and saw that two of them were gone, along with the small cage trailer. He climbed on the Kawasaki that was left, fired up the motor and went speeding off eastwards down the rough track that led through the woods and sloped down to the waterside.

Before he even got close, he could hear the screaming.

Sure enough, Seth was down on the pontoon. Floyd was with him. As Jayce had already sussed out from all the noise, the pair were in the process of merrily tormenting the prisoners. They'd rigged up a rope harness around the little girl and hooked her up to the cable, dangling her over the water from the end of the boom arm. Seth and a manically cackling Floyd were flinging chunks of meat hacked from a fresh deer carcass into the bayou. The surface of the water was being churned pink by at least nine or ten gators thrashing about in a feeding frenzy just a couple of metres below the dangling child. A lot of the shrill screaming was coming from her, as she gyrated round and round and wriggled in terror on the end of the taut cable.

Seth and Floyd had tied the girl's mother and the two boys to a tree close to the water's edge, so they could watch the fun. Noah's face was a mass of tears. Caleb was yelling wild obscenities at the men. Keisha was beyond hysterical and virtually in a faint, hanging limply from the rope that bound her to the tree.

Jayce dismounted from the Kawasaki and ambled over. Seth turned and greeted his brother with a wide grin. He'd invented a new way of assuaging his terrible grief over Logan's death, and it seemed to be working. He'd even forgotten all about his sore arm.

Jayce said, 'Goddamn it, Seth, I told you nothin' was to happen to them until afterwards.'

'Chill, Bro, we're just havin' some fun, is all.'

'Got us a lil' black-ass piece of gator bait. Hyuk, hyuk.' Floyd was obviously having a good time, too.

'Shame ol' Cyrus ain't showed up to join the party,' Seth giggled. 'He must be downriver someplace, makin' baby gators.'

Jayce eyed the empty Dixie beer cans that littered the bank. 'Reckon you've had enough amusement for one afternoon, boys. Floyd, how about you take the guests back to their accommodation so's Seth and I can have a private conversation?'

'Oh, sure thing, Boss. Hyuk.' Floyd could see the serious look in Jayce's eye and obeyed without hesitation. He swung the boom back over the pontoon and cranked the little girl down to the weathered planking. Trinity Hebert was rigid with shock, trembling and whimpering. Floyd unhooked the cable, picked her up and laid her inside the galvanised steel cage trailer they'd used to cart the prisoners out here. Then he drew a Ka-Bar from his belt sheath, slashed the ropes holding the rest of the family to the tree and bundled them into the trailer one by one. Keisha was too weak from emotion to put up any kind of fight. Caleb was a different matter, but a couple of hard slaps quietened him.

Floyd hopped onto the quad bike and sped off with the trailer rattling and bumping behind him.

Jayce looked at his brother. 'Shit, Seth. What'd I say?'

'Quit buggin' me. Ain't like we was doin' no harm.'

'Yeah, well, while you were havin' your entertainment,

I've been takin' care of business. They just announced on the TV that Hope walked free from jail this afternoon.'

'What, they just let him go?'

'Free as a bird. Sheriff told the reporters they don't have a clue who else to go lookin' for. No other suspects at this time. His very words.'

Seth snorted, 'What a bunch of asshats. So we're back on with the plan, huh?'

'Yup.'

'Then I reckon the boys oughtta be hittin' the road about now. They got a long drive to the Big Q.'

Jayce looked at his brother. 'Nuh-uh. They'll be hittin' the road, but they won't be goin' to the Big Q.'

Seth pulled a frown and said, 'Bro, what the hell are you talkin' about? I thought the whole plan was, Hope gives himself up to us at the Big Q or else we carve up the woman and kids. Then Hope went and got himself arrested and there wasn't no plan. But now it's happenin' again, just like before. Right?'

'Wrong,' Jayce said. 'That was never the real plan.'

Bemused, Seth replied, 'It wasn't?'

Jayce shook his head. 'That other shit was just the shit we told that double-dealin' prick lawyer to tell Hope. Make'm think we're a buncha hick dumbasses who'd actually come up with a bullshit plan like that.'

'Okay,' Seth said, thoroughly lost. 'So then what's the real plan?'

Jayce smiled and put a hand on his shoulder. 'It's real simple. Let me explain. Bubba and Floyd and the boys don't need to go to the Big Q, because Hope ain't gonna show up there. Never was. He's way too smart to let himself be taken like that. He's fixin' to double-deal us.'

'How do you know that?'

'Because it's what I'd do,' Jayce said. 'Because I'm smart. 'Cept I'm smarter.'

'Double-deal us like how?'

'Like by hittin' us right here on the island, where we ain't expectin' to get hit. He'll wait until he thinks our guys are on their way to collect him, then he'll make his move, bettin' on how fewer of us makes an easier target.'

'It ain't no big deal anyhow,' Seth said. 'He's one guy. Okay, he burned up our moonshine operation and he done for Logan, but that was a sneak attack. This time we'll be ready. What've we got to be afraid of?'

'Oh, I ain't afraid,' Jayce says. 'But he won't be one guy. He'll bring a whole bunch of cops with him.'

'But the cops are done with him. Just because they let him walk, it don't mean they're on his side. Does it?'

''Fraid it does, Bro. Ain't you gonna ask how I know?'

'Hell, Jayce, you know everything.'

'Matter of fact I don't. But that's what we have informants for. A certain friend of ours just called with a heads-up. Lettin' us know that Hope and Waylon Roque are all buddy-buddy now. They're gettin' together a task force to pay us an unannounced visit and haul our asses in for murder, kidnap, you name it. Seems that our friend Mason up and went turncoat on us.'

'Shit, you can't hardly trust nobody these days. What's the world comin' to? So that was all a lie about "no more suspects at this time".'

'My, you're catchin' on fast, Seth.'

Seth kicked reflectively at the dirt. 'This is bad, Jayce.'

Jayce nodded. 'It's bad, all right. Bad for them. Come with me. I want to show you somethin'.'

Chapter 56

They rode back towards the compound on their quad bikes. Just before the clubhouse, Jayce veered left. He rode down the beaten earth track past the underground hole where the prisoners were being kept.

It was the Garretts' own take on a dungeon of old, though it dated back to previous generations of their clan, when imprisonment, starvation and torture of enemies, business rivals, snitches and other expendables had already been commonplace on the island. In earlier times it had just been a hole in the ground, bottle-shaped to make escape impossible, and covered with an iron grid. The present-day brothers had excavated it deeper and wider, lowered in a shipping container and backfilled the hole to bury the container completely except for a small access trapdoor from which a retractable ladder led down to the dark, dank bowels of the underground prison. There was a ventilation pipe, too, so that those incarcerated inside could get a little air, and the shaft was wide enough to drop a little food and water down there from time to time. The Garretts weren't all nasty, at heart.

By the time Jayce and Seth rode by, Floyd had finished putting the hostages back inside the dungeon, pulled up the ladder and padlocked the hatch. The brothers didn't even glance at it. A little way further on down the track, Jayce pulled up next to a prefabricated steel building where they kept various trucks and cars, many of them stolen.

Behind a roll-up shutter door to the side of the main building was Jayce's private lockup, to which he had the only key. The brothers shared most things, including women, but Jayce had always been secretive about what he kept inside the lockup. For about the last year he'd been working on some enigmatic 'project' that often led him to shut himself away in there for hours, sometimes whole days. During these absences, strange bangings and the screech of power tools could be heard from within, but he'd never wanted to talk about what he was working on.

It seemed that Seth was about to find out.

Jayce unlocked the shutter and hauled it up with a rattle and a screech. The lockup was long and deep, so that the light of the sinking sun only flooded the first few yards nearest the entrance. Seth peered through the doorway and blinked at the sight of what was inside.

The olive-green wooden boxes that lined the side walls of the lockup were stacked six feet high in places. Their sides were letter-stencilled in white paint and said things like 12 GRENADES, RECON MK1 FRAG W/FUSE M204A2 and AMMUNITION FOR CANNON WITH EXPLOSIVE PROJECTILES, with all kinds of lot numbers and designations that Seth couldn't understand. All he knew was, this was fairly awesome. Once he started grinning from ear to ear, he couldn't stop.

'Holy moly, Bro, where'd you get this stuff?'

'From them white power boys in Tennessee,' Jayce replied. 'But that ain't what I wanted to show you.'

Jayce walked deeper into the shadows of the lockup and flipped on a light switch. A naked bulb dangling from the ceiling and hooked up to the generator circuit illuminated the depths of the space. There were workbenches and tool racks on both sides. Jayce had some heavy-duty hardware including a welding torch, oxy-acetylene cutter, bench lathe, angle grinder and pillar drill all messy with metal swarf. He'd been busy, all right.

Squeezed into the aisle between the workbenches with inches to spare either side was the fruit of his labours, except Seth couldn't see what sat hidden beneath the big tarpaulin draped over it. The object was nearly two metres tall and five metres long. Seth said, 'What you got there? A big ol' heap of guns?'

Jayce replied, 'Check this out.' He walked up to it, grasped the edges of the tarp and dragged it away to reveal something that made Seth's eyes pop.

'We got plenty of guns,' Jayce said. 'Hell, this island's 'bout ready to sink under the weight of 'em all. But this is what I call my *piece de resistance.*'

At first Seth thought he was just looking at a truck, albeit the most impressive f-you beast of a truck he'd ever laid eyes on. The ex-military Humvee pickup had been heavily modified. It sat high off the ground on raised suspension and enormous knobbly tyres. The roof, windows and screen had been removed. So much thick armour plating had been welded over its bodywork that it must have weighed an extra ton. A further piece of plate was attached lengthwise across the middle of the open cab to separate the driver from the gigantic device mounted where the front passenger seat would have been.

It took Seth a moment to realise that he was staring at the biggest gun he'd ever laid eyes on. He could only gape at it, speechless. The thing looked like a cathedral pipe organ rolled up into a cylinder, welded to a rotating mount made of riveted steel.

'M61 Vulcan rotary cannon,' Jayce said. 'Like you see in all them war movies, Bro, except this ain't no movie. She come off of a Starfighter jet that got used in 'Nam, that's where my buddy who sold it to me brought it back from. These six barrels spew out a thousand rounds a minute each. Bro, you are lookin' at a gun that can level a fuckin' mountain in about as much time as it takes to use up the four thousand rounds of belt-feed twenty-mil cannon ammo I got stored in the back there. I got tracer, high explosive incendiary, armour piercin', and somethin' called "penetrator with enhanced lateral effect".' Jayce shrugged. 'Gotta say, I don't even know what that's for. I ain't never fired her. But she's ready to rock. Ain't she a beauty?'

Seth had to agree that the monstrous weapon was the loveliest thing he'd ever beheld. He was almost weeping at the sight. He'd seldom ever seen his elder brother so entranced, either. It was like when they were little kids messing in the woods with their very first Uzi, stolen from their father's collection while the old man was drunk as a skunk one day.

Jayce clambered up onto the truck and caressed the silky-smooth, lovingly oiled metal of his pride and joy. 'You heard of the Gatlin' gun, right? First ever real machine gun, only back in them days you had to crank it with a handle. The Yankees used 'em against us in the war. Dude who invented it wanted to make a weapon that'd scare people so bad it'd make 'em stop fightin' and give up havin' armies. Like that's ever gonna happen. Well, that's what this is, a modern Gatlin' gun. I call it the Garrett gun. You could blow up a fuckin' main battle tank or sink a battleship with this baby.'

'Oh, man, this is one righteous work of art,' Seth breathed, finding words at last. 'So this is what you been workin' on all this time. How come you never told me?'

'Wanted it to be a surprise,' Jayce said. 'Only finished puttin' on the final touches a couple weeks back. Just in time for the battle of Garrett Island.'

'Oh, man,' Seth murmured. Then an idea struck him and he looked at his brother as if he'd just had a vision of God. 'You know what this feels like, Jayce? Feels like the goddamn hand of fate.'

'Couldn't have put it better myself,' Jayce agreed. 'They can send all the cops they want. This baby fits right in with my plan.'

'Tell me about it.' Seth loved nothing more than a good plan.

'Got three phases to it,' Jayce said. 'Phase one, when Hope and his asshole sheriff buddy get here, we're gonna let'm eyeball the boys drivin' off, and then they'll walk right in. We won't twitch a finger to stop 'em. Phase two, couple miles down the road the boys pull a U-turn and come right back to block off the bridge so's they can't escape. Just one way onto this island, and no way off.'

'I love it.'

'You ain't heard the best part,' Jayce said. 'Phase three, once Hope and the cops are good and trapped just where we want 'em, that's when we give the fuckers a good ol' taste of the Garrett gun.'

'They won't know what's hit 'em,' Seth said, almost drooling with relish.

'We're gonna tear'm apart, Bro. Mow the fuckers down like crabgrass. None of them cops is leavin' this island alive.'

'What about Hope?'

'Don't you worry. That part of the plan still sticks, just

like before. Hope goes last. He's gonna suffer like nobody ever suffered in the history of pain.'

Seth's eyes were all aglow with excitement. He was grinning so hard that his cheeks were cramping. But then his eyes suddenly dulled and the grin faltered as another thought came to his mind.

'Hold on a minute, though, Jayce. We kill a buncha cops here on the island, you know what's gonna happen, right? The feds will be all over us.'

Jayce sneered at him. 'You ain't gonna turn chicken on me, are you?'

'They'll send in the freakin' army, Bro. They got bigger guns than this, plus fuckin' assault helicopters, Black Hawks and shit. They'll napalm the crap out of us so hard, it'll make Waco and Ruby Ridge look like a possum shoot.'

'You're right,' Jayce said. 'That's exactly what they'll do. Just like the Yankee forces of tyranny descendin' on our ancestral home. They'll raze it to the ground. You're the one talked about fate, right? If that's the fate of this island, so be it. But we'll already be gone.'

'Gone where?'

'Take a look around you, Seth. This is a big territory, and nobody knows it like we do. Ain't it already time we moved on anyhow? We'll do what our great-granddaddy did when them blue scumbellies came for him. Hole up and lie low, rebuild someplace new, start afresh. Maybe find us a couple of nice bitches and get to makin' some baby Garretts. They never caught ol' Leonidas, and they'll never catch us.'

'You sure?'

'Don't you never forget who we are, Seth. We got the brains and the money to do whatever the hell we like and there ain't a man born who's gonna stop us.'

Seth seemed to be coming around to the idea. Then he

frowned and jerked his thumb back over his shoulder in the direction of the dungeon. 'What about the Hebert woman and her kids?'

Jayce smiled. 'I got my plans, Bro. Just like we talked about, remember?'

Chapter 57

Dusk was gathering as the raid team made their approach towards Garrett Island. After a long, hot day the evening was muggy and almost unbearably humid. Rainclouds were slowly gathering in the west as the full moon rose in the east. Everyone could feel the storm coming.

The satellite image had revealed what turned out to be a tree-camouflaged deer trail on solid ground among the semi-tropical swamp and marshy terrain about a third of a mile west of their target. They left the SUVs and SWAT truck hidden there out of sight, with drivers on radio standby to move in fast at a moment's notice, while the twenty-strong team made the rest of their way on foot, marching through the thick, tangled and wild countryside.

They were heavily laden with all the weaponry, ammunition and equipment they could carry. Ben had selected an M4 carbine from the police armoury, the military A1 version capable of fully-automatic fire. He was wearing a ballistic vest under a black jacket with STATE POLICE in white across his back, and a navy LSP baseball cap worn backwards over which was attached the head harness for his night-vision goggles, plus radio earpiece and throat mic. Some of the team had opted for tactical helmets, including Officer Hogan, who, Ben suspected, wanted to look as much like a soldier as she could.

Sheriff Roque had stubbornly rejected any paramilitary apparel and insisted on sticking with his regular uniform and campaign hat, as well as his trusty Colt and a Winchester lever-action shotgun that was a century old, like a relic from the days of the American west. The beast was loaded with a fistful of ten-gauge buckshot shells that made regular shotgun cartridges look smaller than wine corks, each one loaded with twelve solid lead balls. Enough to knock a brick wall down with.

'You can keep your newfangled plastic contraptions,' Roque had said back at headquarters. 'If you can't get the job done with six rounds of ten-gauge you might as well be dead anyway.'

The first objective was to position themselves at a useful vantage point where they could observe the sole access point on and off the island. Ben led the way with Roque behind him and the rest of the column following in single file, some of them now and then stumbling on the rough ground and softly cursing at having to be weighed down with so much gear. Not Hogan, though. Behind the look of ferocious determination it was obvious she was having the time of her life.

Stalking through the thicket at the head of the heavily armed assault team took Ben straight back to a hundred SAS operations he'd led, back in the day, each of them still fresh in his mind. Fear of imminent violent death had a way of branding those experiences permanently onto the memory. The difference was, back then he'd been working with the cream of seasoned operatives, men he could rely on one thousand per cent and who couldn't have contrasted more starkly with the motley crew he was heading up now. Still, he told himself, they were what he had. And they were the best chance Tyler Hebert had of ever seeing his wife and kids alive again.

Ben spied the glimmer of dull moonlight on water ahead through the trees, and knew they were approaching the bank of the Bayou Sanglante. He signalled for the column to halt, and moved forward on his own to scout the OP.

Fifteen yards from the black water the tree line gave way to a thicket of waist-high vegetation that dripped with humidity. Ben crept as close to the edge as he dared, and took his binoculars from the bag around his shoulder.

It was a good vantage point. The island rose up hump-backed and ominous from the water, cut off from the shoreline like a river fortress. Its rounded top was too thickly wooded to make out any signs of habitation. Panning slowly down the island's contour towards the bayou that surrounded it, Ben saw that he'd been right to decide against approaching the Garretts' stronghold by boat. The banks, or at any rate what he could see of them, fell so steeply to the water's edge that a marine assault force would have had a difficult time climbing up them. If things had gone badly and their approach been detected, the island's defenders would have been able to pick them off from the higher ground like shooting crabs off a rock.

At the point where the island lay closest to the shoreline, separated by maybe sixty or seventy yards of open water, was the old wooden bridge. Ben scanned it slowly from end to end. The Garretts' sole access to their secluded home might have been erected more than a century and a half ago, but the builders had carried off a fairly impressive feat of rural engineering. Parallel rows of wooden posts as thick and gnarled as cypress trunks supported its length from shore to shore. It had been built wide enough for a wagon and two horses back in the day, and strong enough to with-stand the transport of building materials, lumber and whatever other cargoes, illicit or otherwise, the island's inhabitants had ferried back and forth through the generations since. All of which meant it would have no problem accommodating the weight and width of even a large truck such as the SWAT vehicle Ben intended to use to bring out the hostages.

So far, things were looking promising enough. Then again, they were yet to set foot on the island. *One step at a time*, Ben told himself. But he kept thinking about Keisha and the kids, and the more he thought about them the more restless he became.

He sensed someone coming up behind him, and turned. It was Roque, clutching his Winchester. Ben passed him the binocs, and Roque took them without a word. The sheriff crouched in the moist vegetation, laid down his shotgun and scanned the target much as Ben had done. He passed the binocs back to Ben, nodding as if he was coming to the same conclusions as he had.

The sweat was shining on Roque's brow and the muscles in his jaw were twitching. Ben noticed that the casing of the binoculars was slick with perspiration from the sheriff's hands. He said softly, 'Nervous?'

Roque grunted. 'I gotta admit, I'm wound up tighter than a three-day clock.'

'Let the nerves work for you,' Ben said. 'Stay sharp and focused and you'll stay alive. Let them get the better of you, and you're done. I won't be able to watch your back, if things kick off.'

'That's damned reassuring,' Roque muttered.

Ben fell silent and went back to watching the bridge through the binoculars. Nightfall was coming, precipitated by the dark and heavy storm clouds that were rolling across the sky and encroaching on the risen moon.

Ben expected something to happen soon.

And soon, something did.

The bright headlamps of a vehicle appeared at the island end of the bridge. He tracked it as it crossed over. There was still enough light to make out the details of the bulky Rhino GX SUV with tinted back windows, jacked-up suspension and auxiliary light bar bolted across the roof sporting an array of big green spotlamps. For night-time hog hunting or some such activity, Ben supposed.

He could plainly see the figures of a pair of men sitting up front, both wearing baseball caps. Right on cue, this had to be the Garretts' thugs being sent out to the Big Q to pick him up. He could be pretty certain there'd be at least a couple more of Jayce and Seth's henchmen sitting in the back, because there was no way they'd send out just two guys to deal with such an important task. Four altogether, at a conservative guess. Add that to the losses the gang's numbers had already incurred, and it meant that their force remaining on the island was now significantly reduced. Just as Ben had been counting on. Another step of his plan had come together perfectly.

The vehicle rumbled across the bridge, accelerated as it reached the dirt road on the other side, and disappeared off into the distance.

'There they go,' Roque said, grimly satisfied. 'I reckon on ninety minutes to get to the Big Q. Another ten or fifteen before they realise you stood them up, then another ninety comin' back.'

That timeframe sounded about right to Ben. The team would have amply long enough to get into position and mount the attack before Jayce and Seth got the call telling them that he hadn't shown up at the motel. That would be the moment of maximum danger for Keisha and the kids, but it could all be over by then. While the freed hostages were being whisked back to Villeneuve a police rearguard would stay in place to wait for the thugs returning empty-handed from their Big Q rendezvous, arrest them and haul them back to jail to join their friends. Then the confessions would begin.

Roque slipped out his Colt, clicked the cylinder around to check the chambers. Then twirled the gun back into his holster and racked the lever of his Winchester and lowered the hammer to half cock, ready for action. 'Let's go and get this over with,' he said, getting up.

'Wait.'

'For what?'

'Fools rush in where angels fear to tread, Sheriff.'

Ben went on watching the bridge as the shadows deepened over the island and the water. No more vehicles emerged from the Garretts' enclave. No sign of the Rhino doubling back, someone having forgotten their phone or gun or wanting to visit the bathroom. Moronic murderers were known to do things like that.

Five more minutes of zero activity on the bridge was long enough to persuade Ben that the coast was clear. He slung the binocs around his neck. In doing so he felt the Voodoo talisman that Sallie Mambo had given him, still tucked under his shirt. *Don't never take it off,* she'd said. *The demons can't hurt you then.*

How much truth there was in that, Ben supposed he was about to find out.

'Okay, *now* let's go,' he said to Roque.

Chapter 58

The raiding party tracked along the shore to the mouth of the old bridge. Ben was the first one to set foot on it. The planks were warped with age, but tempered harder than iron and thicker than railway sleepers. The massive supports that jutted from the water were rimed with shiny algae.

In single file and total silence they crossed the span of the Bayou Sanglante towards their target. The water each side of them was almost black and seemed mirror-still, blotted here and there with floating patches of green that gave off a stench of rotted vegetation and dead fish. Ben felt too exposed on the bridge and was glad when they reached the far side.

There, they were met by a set of sturdy wooden gates, ten feet tall, faced with riveted iron sheeting and topped with curly coils of razor wire. A crude spray-painted sign across the front of the gates proclaimed PRIVATE PROPERTY – TRESPASSERS WILL BE SHOT. A bravado warning that graced a million property entrances across America, but in the Garretts' case Ben was perfectly willing to take the threat at its word.

The gates had been left open when the Rhino came through. If they hadn't, they would have been tough to get past without heavy-duty cutting tools. The raid team had just breached their first potential major obstacle. So far, so good.

'This is it,' Roque said in a low mutter, more to himself than anyone else. 'Point of no return, I guess.'

'You could always wait it out, Sheriff,' Ben replied, sotto voce so the others wouldn't catch his words. 'Go back to your fishing boat and let us handle things from here.'

Roque said nothing more. Ben led the team through the open gates. A driveway of crushed oyster shell wound through the thicket of overhanging foliage like a road through a jungle. Shadow was everywhere, deep and menacing, as though hidden monsters lurked in the darkness.

Before going any further Ben paused to examine the tyre tracks on the makeshift road. The driveway clearly saw a good deal of traffic. Heavy truck wheels had compacted the crumbly oyster shell deep into the dirt. Narrower, lighter tread impressions had been made by cars and motorcycles. As a way of trying to determine how many men might be living on the island, it didn't tell him much.

Ben motioned for the party to split into their prearranged four-man units. As per his instructions, they fell into formation on opposite sides of the road, keeping to the verge so as to leave no tracks on the oyster shell. Ben's A Team moved along the right edge. Roque's B Team kept pace on the opposite side. The sheriff clutched his old shotgun in the low-ready position and walked like an infantryman expecting screaming enemy hordes with fixed bayonets to charge at him from the bushes at any moment. Maybe he was right, Ben thought. Team C moved behind Team A and was mirrored by Team D on the left side. They kept well spaced apart, the way he'd instructed them to.

The tension was palpable, and it wasn't all just coming

from the sheriff. There were a lot of anxious faces and nervous eyes glinted in the dappled moonlight. Ben could feel it pouring in waves from Officer Hogan, the frustrated US Marine, who stalked behind him with her rifle poised for action. He understood very well how they felt, remembering the nerve-shredding experience of his own first-ever military raid operation as a young soldier.

The truth was, you never got used to it. And in fact, you shouldn't. Because the day you did might well be the day you'd drop your guard, get blasé, fail to notice the threat coming at you out of nowhere, and end up being flown home in a flag-draped coffin.

Ben slackened his pace a touch, allowing Hogan to draw level with him. She looked at him in surprise as he moved closer. He whispered, 'You'll be fine. Stay near to me, okay?'

Hogan whispered back, 'You worry about your own ass, buddy.'

So much for sympathy.

On they went. The winding road snaked ever deeper towards the heart of the island. The tree canopy became thicker, blotting out the moonlight until it became so dark that Ben flipped down his night-vision goggles and turned them on. The world suddenly turned to that familiar eerie shade of green through which enemy tracer fire looked like science-fiction-movie laser bolts.

But no gunfire erupted from the trees. No murderous gangs of rednecks came at them with axes or machetes. The raid team must be close to the centre of the island by now, Ben thought, and they were yet to encounter a living soul, let alone meet any kind of resistance.

But it was just a question of time before things happened. And you never could tell what that would be. As military tacticians had been wisely observing for centuries, war was the realm of chance, and the best-laid strategic plans could fall into total disarray at the drop of a hat. Ben had seen it happen enough times to understand how old sayings got repeated so often they became clichés, bandied about by every army training instructor he'd ever known. But they were no less true for being unoriginal.

Some minutes later, a glimmer of light through the trees up ahead sparkled bright green in Ben's NV goggles. He held up a closed fist to signal the others to halt. The way he'd done before, he left them hovering uncertainly to his rear and moved on ahead a couple dozen yards to scout the way, moving like a shadow.

The oyster-shell driveway curved around sharply to the right. Cutting the corner, Ben stalked closer to the source of the light and saw that it was coming from a house, some thirty yards away through the dense vegetation. Very slowly, very quietly, he approached alone for a better look.

It was a small, simple, stone-built house, little more than a cottage. Rough in its lines, not quite square or true. Ben guessed it had stood here since Leonidas Garrett first staked his claim and settled on the island, just after the Civil War, more than a hundred and fifty years ago.

The ground around the little house had been levelled and hard-packed with stone and oyster shell to form an unfenced compound that comprised a variety of other buildings. The nearest was a modern prefab that looked like a barracks hut, long and low. Other metal sheds were clustered in the background, the moonlight shining dully off rusty sheet roofs. All the buildings were in darkness except for the house, from whose narrow windows the glow of light sparkled like green magnesium flares in Ben's goggles. No movement from the windows. If someone was at home, they were keeping well out of sight.

Ben remembered Sallie Mambo's account of how she and

her friends had managed to sneak onto the island all those years ago in 1933 and got close enough to see the house, before the sudden appearance of a wild-looking man with a gun had made them run for their very souls, as she'd put it. Elmore Garrett. By Ben's reckoning it was his grandsons who now lived here.

But nobody was bursting outside to confront the intruders this evening. There was no sign of movement and not a breath of sound from anywhere. No night birds sang on the island. Even the insects seemed to have abandoned it.

Quiet. Too quiet. To Ben's ears, the silence was deafening. The deathly stillness of the place, bathed in that eerie green light, made him think of the evil spirits that Sallie believed to dwell here and possess the souls of the wicked. And for a moment, he could almost have believed it too. He was suddenly oddly aware of the little mojo bag she'd given him, still hanging around his neck.

Waylon Roque's hoarse whisper rasped in Ben's radio earpiece. 'What's happenin'? Over.'

Ben replied softly into his mic, 'Come and see for yourself. Over.'

A few moments later he heard the rustles and snapping twigs as Roque and the troops gathered behind him. He turned to face them, putting a finger to his lips. A herd of foraging wild hogs would have made less commotion.

Roque had finally given in to the need for night vision. His campaign hat was awkwardly jammed on over the headgear of his goggles, making him look like some kind of weird space cowboy. The sheriff stalked up to where Ben was crouched among the bushes. The shotgun was clenched tightly in his fists.

Roque surveyed the buildings and nodded authoritatively, as if he was still fully in charge of this mission. 'We got 'em,' he whispered fiercely. 'Like rats in a trap. All we gotta do now is surround the house and move in.'

Ben looked again at the compound. Those darkened buildings. The light pouring from the empty windows. The total stillness. He didn't like what he was seeing. His sixth sense was telling him that something wasn't quite right.

His mind suddenly began to race. He thought again about the open gates, and how easy it had been to just walk onto the island. How even a group of harmless children couldn't venture into the Garretts' sanctuary without being challenged.

It was bugging him. It was wrong, somehow.

And that was when three things happened.

The first was that Ben looked up. He would never know why he did, at that particular moment. A sudden rush of paranoia, maybe, as his mind became gripped by uncertainty. Looking around him for inspiration. Psychic intuition. Or just pure chance.

But what he saw sent an ice-cold spike through his heart and momentarily drained the breath from his lungs. The trees above him were rigged with wireless miniature cameras and motion sensors. Dozens of them, all around, everywhere. He'd been so focused on the light coming from the house that he'd passed right under them, oblivious of a security monitoring system that could have been triggered by a spider crawling in the dirt anywhere near the compound.

Which meant the Garretts had been watching the raid party the whole time. They'd probably been following their progress from the very moment they'd stepped onto the island. And that the light from the house had been a deliberate distraction to lure them in.

And that Ben and the entire raid team had just blundered right into a trap.

Then the second thing happened.

The words 'Fall back!' were still forming on Ben's lips when the darkness of the woods behind them suddenly came alive in a sweeping burst of green light that detailed the bark on the trees and threw a confusion of giant shadows everywhere. With a throaty growl the big Rhino SUV came tearing up the driveway from the direction of the bridge.

Ben could suddenly see the enemy's game plan unfolding. Jayce and Seth Garrett hadn't despatched their men to the Big Q Motel after all. Anticipating the raid with uncanny precision, they'd set the whole thing up as a feint to invite the police to walk straight into an ambush.

How could they have known?

Ben couldn't answer that question. But he could be certain that the gates to the island, left open deliberately to entice the intruders, would now be locked shut. And that he, Roque and the rest of the troops were now prisoners in the Garrett brothers' own private hell. The trap was well and truly sprung.

And the Hebert family . . . Ben couldn't even begin to imagine what would happen to them now.

The Rhino kept speeding up the driveway, big tyres crunching and pattering on the oyster-shell surface. The dazzling roof lamps lit the forest up so brightly that Ben's NVG bloomed out, the image turning solid green-white as the goggles became overwhelmed by all the photons pouring in. He ripped them off, blinked against the strong light and shouldered his rifle to take aim at the incoming vehicle. But just as he was expecting the Rhino to keep coming right at them, instead it suddenly veered off sharply in the other direction, lurching and bucking wildly over the rough ground.

It rolled to a halt, its doors burst open all at once, and

five men jumped out, all clutching guns. Ben held his fire. He couldn't shoot until they did. This was a police raid, not a war. But instead of opening fire, the five men scattered and took cover among the trees as though—

As though they knew something else was about to happen.

And something was. Something not even Ben could have anticipated.

Chapter 59

From behind the house came the thunderous engine note of a big, powerful V8 turbo-diesel, throatier and deeper than the sound of the Rhino. It was a sound that Ben had heard on battlefields in the Middle East, Africa and war-torn eastern Europe, and would have recognised anywhere. The unmistakable tank-like roar of what the American military mind had dubbed the High Mobility Multipurpose Wheeled Vehicle, HMMWV, and everybody else called a Humvee. A monster all-terrain truck that could climb vertical walls and carry enough armour to survive land mine explosions.

The dark hulk came racing out from its hiding place behind the buildings and sped across the compound, straight towards where the intruders were hiding in the bushes. Then blinding halogen spotlamps three times brighter than the Rhino's suddenly blazed into life, flooding the woods with a harsh white glare and turning night into day. Ben, Roque and the others were suddenly exposed right out in the open with nowhere to hide.

The light was too bright to make out the driver's face, but Ben instantly recognised the silhouetted outline of Jayce Garrett at the wheel of the open cockpit.

The cops were breaking into a panic. Amid the sudden

chaos, out of the corner of his eye Ben saw the big ginger-haired officer, Charlie Fruge, making a break for it towards a thicket of trees and throwing himself flat in the dirt. Roque brought up his ten-gauge, thumbing its hammer back to full cock. Hogan had followed Ben's lead and thrown away her NV goggles. She had her carbine shouldered and was swinging its muzzle wildly here and there, eyes pinned wide open in a look of grim determination as her law enforcement training melted away under the heat of self-preservation instinct and she searched for a target to start blasting away at.

But if Hogan had been betting on getting in the first shot, she was about to be beaten to the post. Because in the next split-second, all hell broke loose.

The night erupted into shattering noise and fire.

Ben had seen, driven and destroyed all manner of light combat vehicles like Jeeps and technicals equipped with everything from heavy machine guns to rocket launchers. But what he glimpsed now as he instinctively threw himself to the ground was like nothing he'd come across before. The weapon mounted on the roofless top of the Humvee lit up like a jet afterburner. Its screeching roar, so continuous that it was impossible to hear the individual shots being fired, was the nightmare of infantry divisions and tank regiments. It was a Vulcan rotary cannon from a fighter aircraft, transplanted onto a truck. It threw a shell weighing nearly quarter of a pound at three times the speed of sound. A hundred of them every second. Such a monster weapon was designed to destroy buildings, armoured fighting vehicles and other solid materiel targets from medium to long distances away. Turned on human beings at point-blank range, the effect of its firepower was pure carnage.

As the raid team were about to discover. The shockwave

of the weapon's power seemed to suck the air away. Tree trunks came crashing down as though a giant chainsaw had sliced through them. A storm of splintered wood and severed branches, bark and pulp and sap spattered over Ben as he lay pressed tightly down against the mossy wet ground.

Some of the cops had been too slow to do the same. Wyatt Earp of C Team had barely registered what was happening by the time he was sawed in half below the sternum. The upper and lower portions of his body hit the ground yards apart. Hogan's female colleague had been turning to flee in horror when the cannon fire blew away her right leg at the hip and she fell into the bushes, the sound of her scream drowned by the thunderous gunfire. Sheriff Roque let off a blast from his shotgun and then corkscrewed to the ground, blood flying in the glare of the spotlamps. As Ben watched, Deputy Fontaine and four more of the police officers were cut down as the woodland was razed to stumps around them. They had no chance. It was pure slaughter.

The Humvee came rolling forward, still firing continuously. Aircraft pilots could only let off short blasts from the dreaded Vulcan, for fear of the massive recoil stalling their planes. Jayce Garrett had no such concerns. The cannon went on and on, swivelling left and right on its mountings, churning up the ground, hammering ruined trees into matchwood, spattering dead bodies that were already diced into pieces.

Still clutching his rifle, Ben was pinned motionless behind a knot of tree roots that he knew was utterly useless cover. The cannon shells would rip through iron-hard wood as though it was playdough, pass out the other side virtually unscathed and convert him into mincemeat. He just had to stay hidden and pray.

If anyone up there was listening. A strafing volley sent

explosions of dirt showering over him as it passed much too close to where he lay. He felt a stunning impact all up his arm as a random shell struck the rifle in his hand. He jerked his hand back as if he'd been bitten, and rolled violently out of the weapon's trajectory expecting to feel a hellfire volley of shells tearing his body apart. But the withering fire of the cannon was already carving its swathe of destruction elsewhere.

Ben saw his chance. He rolled over another turn, and then another, until he reached a patch of shadow out of the glare of the Humvee's lights. Then he jumped to his feet and looked desperately around him for some way to make the killing stop. He saw none.

It was then that he spotted Hogan on the ground nearby. She was curled up on her side. She'd lost her helmet, and her hair had come loose and covered her face. At first he thought she was dead, but he could see no blood; then in the next moment he realised she was trembling as she lay there clutching her knees to try to make herself as small as possible, like a frightened child.

He ran over to her, snatched up her fallen M4 and opened fire on the Humvee. One long sustained rattle of full-auto, until the magazine was spent. Bullets sparked and zinged harmlessly off the armour-plated bodywork. He might as well have been shooting a kid's airgun at it.

Ben threw away the empty rifle and reached down to yank Hogan to her feet, yelling, 'Come on!'

Hogan's eyes gleamed in the light. She stared at Ben for an instant as though she wasn't sure if he was friend or enemy. Shock and terror could numb the mind that way. But then she focused, and took his hand. He hauled her upright and they ran. Just in time, because Jayce Garrett had seen the muzzle flash of the M4 and rotated the cannon back in their direction. A second later, there was a fresh crater of torn earth and ripped foliage where Hogan had been lying.

Ben and Hogan made their escape through the trees, darting from shadow to shadow. Ben felt his foot nudge a body on the ground, looked down and saw it was Waylon Roque.

The sheriff had managed to crawl some way from where he'd been shot. He was still alive, but badly injured. A shell had hit his right shoulder. It was a mess. Ben was no surgeon, but he could tell that there wasn't much holding Roque's arm on except a few torn ligaments.

'We have to move,' Ben said. He bent down, took the sheriff's good arm and crooked it around his neck. Roque's teeth were gritted and the veins were standing out all over his blood-spattered face, but he was too tough to cry out in pain as Ben lifted him to his feet. Roque doggedly clung on to his shotgun with his useable hand.

Ben felt a pang of admiration for the sheriff. He was a tough old bird. He'd faced up to his fears, done his duty, done all he could to atone for his past mistakes. If he didn't make it out of this alive, he would not have disgraced himself.

The cannon suddenly stopped firing. It seemed to have gone on for ever, but only about thirty-five or forty seconds had gone by. In that time, the woods this side of the compound had been reduced to a devastated wasteground. Very little was moving. Smoke drifted in the brightness of the lights. A couple of downed cops were groaning. Someone more badly hurt screamed in tortured agony.

The Humvee had rolled to a halt. There were raised voices and laughter from the Garretts' men, who now began to re-emerge from their hiding places.

Ben and Hogan, supporting the injured Roque, scrambled

away out of sight. Forty yards diagonally across from the stationary Humvee, a big thorn bush lay in a dark pool of shadow. Ben lowered Roque to the ground behind it. There was a lot of blood. Ben felt the sheriff's pulse. It was weak and fluttering. He seemed to be drifting in and out of consciousness.

'He's in a real bad way,' Hogan whispered anxiously.

'He's not the only one,' Ben replied.

He watched from the shadows of the bushes as the Garretts' men converged on the battlefield, sauntering casually among the devastation. The five from the Rhino were joined by half a dozen more.

Jayce Garrett clambered out of the Humvee's roofless cockpit and appeared to spend a few moments fiddling with the cannon. Maybe he'd run out of ammunition, Ben wondered, or perhaps something was wrong with it. As though he hadn't done enough damage, in any case.

After a few seconds Jayce seemed to give up on the weapon, and jumped down to the ground. As Ben went on watching, Seth Garrett appeared and came running over to join his brother, hooting with maniacal laughter. The pair were gazing around them as though even they couldn't believe how wonderfully destructive their little toy had proved to be. They slapped hands in a high-five.

Then both Seth and Jayce Garrett drew pistols from their belts and walked out among the shattered trees with their men.

Ben realised what was about to happen. They were searching for survivors. They were going to execute them.

The pistol shots sounded like tiny pops after the devastating noise of the cannon. But a tiny pop can be all it takes to end a human life. One by one, the Garretts stood over the bodies of the dying and shot them in the head.

And it was at that harrowing, gut-twisting moment that

Ben became certain, beyond any shadow of a doubt, that Keisha, Caleb, Noah and Trinity were already dead. They'd probably died that morning or early afternoon, soon after Mason Redbone had delivered them to his patrons.

This had been the Garretts' plan all along. They'd been a step ahead of him from the start. It had never been about a prisoner exchange. Their intention had been nothing more or less than cold bloody murder. The cops, the hostages, him, everyone.

Ben closed his eyes. His mind numbly replayed the image of himself sitting at the Hebert family dining table, what seemed like a thousand years ago. He remembered the little girl's sweet prayer of Grace. He remembered the look of loving pride on her parents' faces, and Keisha saying, 'That was beautiful, Trinity.'

Then his mind filled with the nightmare of the child's screams as he involuntarily pictured the Garretts butchering her under the eyes of her mother. Then Noah, then Caleb. Then Keisha too. The horror of it was too much for him to bear.

And it was he, Ben Hope, who had brought these good, kind, innocent people into this by turning up at their house. They wouldn't have been involved, except for him.

He might as well have murdered them himself.

When he reopened his eyes, they were wet with tears. He wiped them dry and felt the white, cold fury of resolve flooding his mind and body.

He jumped to his feet and snatched up Roque's Winchester. One round gone, four left in the tube, one up the spout. The sheriff wasn't going to be in a fit state to pull the trigger himself anytime soon.

'Where are you goin'?' Roque croaked.

Ben said, 'To finish what we came here to do.'

Chapter 60

In the shadows of the bushes Ben said to Hogan, 'What's your name, Officer?'

She looked at him. 'Officer Hogan.'

'I mean your real name.'

'Jessie.' She sounded coy, as though it made her blush to say it. Underneath that thorny exterior she was still just Jessie Hogan who'd grown up in Clovis Parish, Louisiana, attended the local school and would one day marry some local guy named Bo or Billy Ray whom she'd known since she was nine.

'Jessie, I need you to stay here and look after him. If I don't come back, do what you can to get yourselves out of here.'

Jessie Hogan pulled a big steel Kimber from her duty holster and nodded. As he began to turn away she said, 'Hope?'

He looked back at her. 'Call me Ben, Jessie.' It might be the last time anyone spoke his name to him again.

She said, 'Ben, you kick those fuckers' butts four ways to Sunday, okay?'

'Just watch me.'

'And Ben?'

'What?'

'Try to stay alive, okay?'

Ben left them and began working his way back towards the Humvee. He could hear the thump and rumble of the diesel motor still ticking over. With sickness in his heart he knew this wasn't a rescue mission any more. He'd never find Keisha and the kids now, anyway. His sole reason for being here was now revenge. And he wouldn't stop until he had it.

The Garretts' men were still going around searching for injured cops and shooting them, but they were running out of execution victims and the flat pistol reports were becoming fewer. While they were still distracted, Ben reached the Humvee and quickly, quietly, jumped aboard. His plan wasn't a complicated one. He just wanted to get behind the wheel of the monster truck and go charging in among them and run as many of the bastards down before they got him.

But plans were made to be changed.

As he clambered aboard the Humvee he noticed the coiled-up belt of unfired ammo still draped from the receiver of the rotary cannon. It hadn't run out, it had just stopped working.

Ben's soldier's mind was conditioned to instantly want to know why. A gun was just a machine. When they broke down, there was always a reason. Dud rounds happened, as could feed jams, and either could bring an automatic weapon to a grinding halt like a stalled engine. Except the M61 Vulcan rotary cannon had been designed to keep firing even if rounds misfired, thanks to its external electric power drive.

With that thought, Ben's mind flashed on the solution and he saw that one of the electrical leads connecting the big electric motor to a high-capacity marine battery in the rear of the Humvee had come loose, probably rattled free with the vibration. Jayce Garrett's home-made system was pretty crude. It was just a matter of reconnecting a crocodile clip, and the Gatling gun was back in business.

The pistol shots had stopped. The men were gathering in a bunch among the shattered trees, talking. There was more laughter. Someone lit a cigarette. Ben could see them clearly outlined in the glare of the spotlamps. He counted eleven figures. With a shock he realised that the Garrett brothers were no longer among them. Jayce and Seth had gone.

It couldn't be helped. Ben would have to deal with them later.

He scrambled into the rear of the Humvee, grabbed the loose end of the wire, opened the jaws of the crocodile clip and jammed them onto the naked battery terminal. It sparked. He had power.

With murder in his heart he jumped into the open cockpit. The big red fire button on the dashboard looked like an emergency stop button taken from some industrial appliance and rewired as a straight on-off switch. Jayce was a handy sort of guy. It was a shame he hadn't turned his practical skills to better use. Now his eleven cronies were about to pay the price.

Ben angled the gun and slammed the red button with his fist. And the world around him disintegrated into a cacophony of incredible noise as the weapon started up again, a whirling, howling tornado of destruction.

'Shoe's on the other foot now, boys,' he muttered, but even the loudest yell would have been drowned out by the noise. The eleven men were right in his sights. They scattered like flies as they heard the Gatling gun start up again. Too slow for seven of them, who were swiftly diced up in a pink mist under the blazing lights of the Humvee. A direct hit. Like throwing them into a liquidiser. With nowhere else to hide, the remaining four more dived behind the cover of the Rhino, obviously thinking a 20mm cannon couldn't touch them behind there. They were about to learn otherwise. Ben swivelled the gun.

The destruction of the vehicle was spectacular and brief. The cannon shells chewed up its bodywork and rugged chassis like papier mâché. It caught fire, then exploded. Ben kept pummelling it until there was nothing left but a heap of burning scrap metal spread out all over the ground. All that remained of the four men who'd taken cover behind it was something resembling chopped watermelon.

Now the Gatling gun really was out of ammo. The six barrels continued whirring, inaudible over the high-pitched tinnitus whine in Ben's ears. He grabbed Roque's Winchester and jumped down from the Humvee. Before he went looking for Jayce and Seth he wanted to make sure no more of their cronies were lurking among what was left of the woods.

As he scouted through the shadows his foot nudged a body that the Garrett thugs hadn't needed to finish off with a shot to the head. It was the sectioned remains of Wyatt Earp. His Glock pistol was lying half buried in the mud where the Gatling gun had chewed up wet furrows in the ground. Ben picked it up and started wiping off some of the caked dirt.

Then stopped. A movement had caught his eye. A figure among the trees, skirting the edge of the light in the direction of the bushes where Roque and Hogan were hiding.

Ben quickly slipped the Glock into his pocket and raised the shotgun to take aim at the figure.

Chapter 61

It was a cop, wearing the same kind of bulky jacket as the rest of his colleagues, now mostly dead, with POLICE emblazoned across his back. Ben lowered the gun and watched him. There was no mistaking the large, brawny shape of the ginger-haired officer named Charlie Fruge, last seen hurling himself into the undergrowth.

Ben hesitated, thought for a moment, then ran over to the bushes to rejoin them.

He found Charlie Fruge standing next to where Hogan crouched over the prone Sheriff Roque. Hogan looked up at Ben in bewilderment. 'What the hell just happened? Did you get them?'

'Not all of them,' Ben replied. Turning to Fruge he asked, 'Where did you pop up from?'

The big man appeared completely unscathed. Apart from a smear of dirt on one cheek and plastered on his knees and elbows from where he'd gone crawling in the wet undergrowth, he might have been on a weekend jaunt in the national park. But he was all keyed up and agitated, and seemed all the more so for Ben's sudden and unexpected appearance. He signalled towards the far side of the newly-formed clearing. 'I was hidin' over there. They never saw me. Shit, man, are we all that's left?'

'I need help to get Seth and Jayce Garrett,' Ben said. 'You with me?'

Fruge hesitated. 'I, er, I lost my gun.'

'Take this one,' Ben said, handing him the Glock from his pocket.

'I thought you were goin' alone,' Hogan said.

'Change of plan,' Ben replied. 'Now that Charlie's here.'

Hogan's eyes burned hotly. Ben could see she resented being left behind and overstepped by a male colleague. A female cop's lot in life.

Roque stirred and raised his head off the ground. His eyes were ringed with agony and the sweat gleamed on his face. 'You go with 'em, Jessie. I'll be okay.'

'You sure?'

'Go,' Roque repeated. 'That's an order, dammit.'

'Quickly,' Ben said.

They left the sheriff hidden among the bushes. Then the three of them made their way towards the compound. The lights were still on in the old stone house. It was the first building Ben wanted to check and clear. He waved Charlie Fruge in ahead of him. The big guy seemed jumpier than ever, and kept glancing at Ben.

The Garrett brothers' home was the kind of redneck bachelor pad that gave redneck bachelor pads a bad name. As he checked the living room, Ben noticed the portrait over the fireplace. An old oil painting was an incongruous sight in a home that was essentially a shrine to hunting trophies, guns, girls and TV. Knowing what he knew about Jayce Garrett's leanings, he wouldn't have been too surprised if the painting had been a portrait of Adolf Hitler. Instead, he found himself looking at a likeness of a gaunt, severe, grey-bearded man he had little doubt was the famous Leonidas Garrett, the mastermind of the failed biological warfare plot against the Union army. Great-grandfather of the brothers.

Minutes later, it was clear that the brothers themselves were nowhere in the house. Ben hadn't truly expected them to be.

'We're clear,' Hogan said tersely.

Ben said, 'Move on.'

They slipped back outside, spread out and headed towards the dark buildings behind the house. The gathering storm was crackling like static electricity in the air. It was going to be a big one.

All was silent, but somewhere behind the silence Ben was sure he could feel the presence of his quarry. The sick feeling had left him now. It would return later for sure, with a vengeance. But for the moment he felt nothing but predatory calm. His senses were focused to needlepoints. His heart rate settled, his breathing deep and slow. The Winchester shotgun felt solid in his hands.

A little way from the empty house Ben noticed a row of quad bikes parked under a lean-to. He moved on down an alley between the tin sheds, with Hogan's edgy, nervy presence to his left and the big, blocky shape of Charlie Fruge to his right. The dim moonlight picked out the ridges of corrugated sheets and threw black shadows in recesses and doorways on both sides.

Jayce and Seth Garrett, or any of their remaining men, could be lurking anywhere, ready to jump out or start shooting from within. Ben's finger was on the trigger.

He smelled them before he heard them, and heard them before he saw them. A whiff of sour body odour; the scraping shuffle of boot soles on hard-packed earth; then two dark figures appeared from the shadowy doorway of a building on the left, and became visible in the moonlight.

They weren't Jayce or Seth.

One of them wore an ugly scar that distorted his face from temple to chin, an obvious knife slash from long ago. His eyes went wide at the sight of Ben, Hogan and Charlie Fruge. He clawed for the .357 in his belt but Ben blew him down hard with the ten-gauge before he could get to it. The kick of the shotgun was ferocious, its impact on target even more so. They really knew how to kill folks in the old west.

As the other one simultaneously reached for his pistol, Charlie Fruge pointed Wyatt Earp's Glock at him in a two-handed combat stance and yelled, 'Drop it, Bubba! You're under arrest!'

The Garretts' guy ignored the warning and fired, but his bullet went wide. Hogan nailed him twice in the chest with her Kimber and he went down with an arc of blood sailing from his open mouth.

Ben said, 'Nice work.'

Hogan shrugged. 'They had it comin'.'

Fruge wiped his perspiring brow with the back of his hand and puffed his cheeks. 'That was a close one, huh? You reckon Jayce and Seth are still hangin' around?'

'I don't know,' Ben said, truthfully.

'Then what do we do now?' Fruge asked.

Ben said, 'Now you're going to take us to where they were keeping the hostages. If they're dead I need to see it for myself.'

The big cop glowered at Ben. His eyes gleamed in the moonlight. 'How the hell would I know where they wuz keepin' them?' he rasped. Defensive.

'Same reason you seem to know a lot of things,' Ben replied. 'Like you knew that guy's name was Bubba just now.' He pointed at Bubba's corpse.

'I already arrested him once before,' Fruge protested, but

not very convincingly. 'Bubba Beane. That other one you just shot, he's Floyd Babbitt.'

Ben shook his head. 'You'll have to try harder than that to persuade me, Charlie. Because earlier on, I saw you hit the deck *before* the shooting began. Just as if you knew what was about to happen. And I think you did.'

Fruge glanced at the silent Hogan, then back at Ben. 'What? You're freakin' crazy.'

'And you're a moron, Charlie. Only a complete idiot would get himself involved with the Garretts. They had more than one inside man in the local police department, didn't they? There was Mason Redbone, and then there was you. You were the one who tipped them off that we were coming here tonight. And you knew what we were walking into. The death of your fellow cops is on you. And a lot more besides.'

'This is nuts. Hogan, you gonna stand there and listen to this wacko bullshit?'

Hogan said nothing. She was watching her colleague carefully with her head cocked to one side. Now she was beginning to understand why Ben had wanted Fruge out here with him.

Ben continued, 'Then when you popped up out of hiding, I think you were planning on killing Jessie and Sheriff Roque, too. Got a knife tucked away somewhere, or were you going to use those brawny hands of yours? Nobody would ever have known it was you. Did you think Jayce would give you a nice big hug for helping him out? Or maybe a juicy cash bonus?'

Fruge backed away a step. A shaft of moonlight fell across his face. It had turned the same colour as Mason Redbone's in the Sheriff's Office.

'You're right,' he said. 'Nobody will ever know.'

And he levelled the Glock at Ben's head and fired.

The pistol flashed and boomed. Then came the cry of shock and pain. Fruge dropped the weapon and clutched at his mutilated right hand. The gun had burst and blown away half his fingers. He fell to his knees, whimpering as the blood began to pump.

'Dirt in the barrel,' Ben said. 'Plugged up solid when it got dropped in the mud. You should always inspect your weapon before use, Officer. That's lesson number one.'

Lesson number two was a hard and brutal blow to Fruge's face. Ben used the forend of the shotgun. Solid wood and steel. He liked the way it felt, so he hit him again. Fruge toppled sideways to the ground. His lips and nose were split wide open. He jammed his ruined hand between his legs and gibbered, 'Don't kill me dear Lord don't kill me please.'

Ben stood over him with the gun clenched in his fists. 'Give me one reason why I shouldn't just beat you to death, right here, right now.'

'I know where they put the woman and kids. I can lead you there.'

'Then do it,' Ben said.

Chapter 62

Fruge led the way, bent over in pain and clutching his mangled hand. The blood spots he left in his wake looked black in the moonlight as Ben and Hogan followed him.

Hogan was having a hard time believing that her fellow police officer could have betrayed them like that. 'Our own guys,' she kept muttering. 'You sack of shit, Charlie.' She kept her Kimber trained on Fruge's wide back. Ben sensed she was having a hard time resisting pulling the trigger, too.

They didn't have far to walk. The compound was a rambling lacework of little paths leading here and there, added to over the years as the Garretts had gradually extended their home base. Fruge seemed to know the layout pretty well. A regular visitor, obviously. Maybe he and Mason Redbone had often hung out here drinking with their buddies on the other side of the law. Cosy.

Fruge led them past the long, low building nearest the house, then turned left down another path. After a couple dozen paces, he stopped.

'This is it, right here. This is where they put 'em. It's kind of like a prison, a buried container. It's where they always put people before . . .' His voice trailed off miserably.

'Before they kill them,' Ben said.

'And other things,' Fruge said. 'See, they—'

Ben said, 'Shut up.'

Fruge shut up.

Ben looked and saw the circular manhole in the ground, black against the darkness. It had a short section of metal drum extending a few inches, to stop dirt and ground water trickling in. He could picture the kind of dank, squalid hellhole that lay below ground. The Garretts' answer to a medieval dungeon.

He walked over to it, and saw that the lid of the dungeon, a heavy iron drain cover, had been lifted away and dumped on the ground nearby. He peered into the black hole. The stink of dampness and human waste made his nose twitch. He'd seen kidnap victims kept in worse places, but he really couldn't remember when.

Ben needed more light to see by. He reached in his bag, found his mini-Maglite and shone it down the hole. The calmness of combat had deserted him now. His heart was thumping so powerfully that he was sure the others could hear it.

The rungs of an aluminium ladder glinted from inside the mouth of the hole. Ben rolled the light beam around. He saw no signs of recent violence. No blood. No bodies. Nothing at all. The dungeon was empty.

'They're not here,' he said. His throat was almost too tight to speak. 'If Jayce and Seth were going to kill them, where else would they have done it?'

Hogan said, 'Ben, maybe you don't want to know what happened to them. If they're dead, they're dead.'

That was when Charlie Fruge said, 'They ain't dead.'

Ben and Hogan both stared at the big man. Ben shone the Maglite in his face. His broken nose was a swollen mass of blood. His pupils shrank down to hard black pinpoints in the bright light.

371

Ben said, 'What did you just say?'

'They ain't dead,' Fruge repeated. 'I thought they might still be here. Looks like we wuz too late.'

Then Fruge was on the ground again, flattened on his back and pressing his good hand to his freshly-rebroken nose as Ben stood astride him with the shotgun muzzle jabbing hard under his chin.

'Talk to me. Three seconds, or I'll blow your brains all over this island.'

'I-I tried to tell you,' Fruge stammered through the blood and tears. His voice was choked and nasal-sounding. 'They don't always kill'm. They sell'm.'

Alarm pulsed through Ben's whole body. 'Who do they sell?'

'Women and girls, mostly. Black ones.'

'To who?'

'Klan,' Fruge said. 'Hammerskins. White Aryan Resistance. Over in Texas, up in Tennessee, Mississippi. I don't know 'em all. Jayce used to hang out with them boys. They pay money for slaves.'

'Jesus Christ,' Hogan said. 'Step out of the way, Ben. Let me shoot this sick sonofabitch.'

Fruge held up his bloody palms in supplication. The three missing fingers on his mangled, scorched right hand suddenly didn't seem to be bothering him as much. The prospect of imminent death could have that effect.

'No! I ain't got nothin' to do with that. But they're alive, see? The woman and the lil' girl, anyhow. They might've shot the half-breed boy and the older kid, unless Jayce kept'm alive for somethin'. I can't say. I'm bein' straight with you. Please! You can't kill me like this! It's murder!'

'We ain't gonna murder you, Charlie,' Hogan said through

clenched teeth, clutching her Kimber with a shaking hand. 'There's no word for what we'll do to you.'

'Where are they?' Ben said.

Fruge replied, 'I truly don't know. I swear, that's the truth!'

Ben said, 'You know what, Charlie? This time I actually believe you.'

And pulled the trigger.

Charlie Fruge's brains didn't splatter all over the island. But it was close. The loud BOOM rattled off the buildings and echoed above the roofs.

Ben stepped away from Fruge's body. He saw the look on Hogan's face.

She said, 'You asshole.'

'Why, because I shot an unarmed man in cold blood?'

'No, because you made it too quick and easy for the motherfucker.' Hogan was all about mushy sentimentality.

She shook her head. 'Oh man, this whole thing is FUBAR. Everybody's dead, we don't have the Garrett brothers and we don't know where the Hebert family are.'

A hard voice from the shadows said, 'Right here, bitch.'

Ben whirled around and instinctively raised the shotgun butt to his shoulder. Hogan dropped into a combat stance with her pistol sights lined up on the darkness where the voice had come from. But before either of them could get off a shot, there was a loud detonation and a tongue of white-orange flame and Hogan staggered, dropped her gun, and fell on her back.

Ben racked the Winchester. He was on the brink of delivering a lethal blast of buckshot straight back at the shooter when he suddenly froze.

'I wouldn't do that if I was you, buddy,' Jayce Garrett said as he stepped out of the shadows.

Jayce wasn't alone.

Chapter 63

Ben had been intent on finding the Garrett brothers, and now he had his wish. But he hadn't reckoned on catching up with them quite this way.

Jayce and Seth had the Heberts with them. The big stainless steel revolver Jayce had used to shoot Hogan was now jammed against the side of Keisha's head. Tears of terror were flooding down her cheeks. She was clutching little Trinity in her arms. Noah was clasping at his mother's legs, making a keening sound. Caleb was tightly in the grip of Seth Garrett. The knife held across the front of the boy's throat glittered in the moonlight.

Ben could see the swellings and mottled bruises all over Caleb's face. He guessed that the teenager had been pluckily trying to resist their captors and learned the hard way that they were a lot tougher than he was.

Jayce Garrett said, 'I figured you'd come lookin' for them, Hope. Been waitin' for you.'

'Take it real easy with that scattergun, now, fella,' Seth said with a mocking grin. 'This here merchandise is as valuable to you as it is to us, I reckon.'

On the ground at Ben's feet, Hogan wasn't moving.

Ben relaxed his finger on the shotgun's trigger, but he didn't lower the muzzle. The calculations churning through his mind were all about ballistics, speed, reaction time and odds. He was only fifteen paces away from the Garretts and their hostages. At such short range, the shot pattern of the ten-gauge wouldn't spread out much. All twelve heavy lead pellets would hit their mark more or less as one, striking the target with the equivalent brute force of a dozen 9mm hand-guns firing simultaneously. He was confident he could take Seth out without hurting Caleb. That part was easy enough. But the next part wouldn't be, because there was no way he could rack the Winchester, eject the fired shell and chamber another and turn the weapon on Jayce faster than Jayce could pull the trigger of his revolver and blow Keisha's brains out. No human being alive could make that shot.

And the converse was just as true. If Ben opted to save Keisha by shooting Jayce, Caleb would die with Seth's knife buried in his neck.

Only a miracle could save them both. Miracles were in short supply, as a rule. And at this moment, with Jessie Hogan lying inert at his feet, Ben felt very alone.

But he wasn't about to let the enemy see that.

'This is over,' he said to Jayce Garrett. 'Whichever way it goes down, you're done. Make it easy on yourself and let them go, right now. I'll see to it that you spend the rest of your lives in a nice, cosy cell. Who knows, it might be years before they give you the needle.'

Jayce smiled. 'That's rich, comin' from a cop killer.'

Seth nodded down towards the body of Charlie Fruge on the ground, and tutted. 'Shootin' officers of the law, now that's a death penalty rap, right there.'

'Looks like we're all in a spot of trouble, doesn't it,' Ben said.

'Looks that way,' Jayce said. 'Except some of us are gonna come out of it, and some aren't.'

Ben called out to Keisha, 'Are you okay? Have they hurt you?'

Keisha looked frail and ghostlike in the moonlight. In a hollow voice she called back, 'They beat Caleb.' She winced and went quiet as Jayce's gun muzzle pressed harder against her head.

'Kid's gotta serious attitude problem,' Seth said. 'Had to teach him a lesson or two.'

'I'm a businessman,' Jayce said. 'First rule, never damage the stock. They're in pristine condition. Just like you see.'

Seth giggled. 'In better shape than your cop buddies, that's for sure.'

His elder brother had no time for amusement. He kept his eyes fixed unblinkingly on Ben.

'Now, speakin' of business, you and we had kind of a deal. Looks to me like you went and broke it. But I'm a reasonable man. The offer's still on the table.'

'I give myself up to you, you let them go,' Ben said. 'Is that what you had in mind?'

'Not exactly. You got the first part right. You give yourself up to us. Then you face the punishment for what you done to Logan. The second part is, we let the Hebert boys go instead of skinnin' the little shits alive and feedin' 'em to the gators. They ain't no use to us. The bitch and the lil' girl, that's a different story. They're already spoken for.'

Keisha squeezed her wet eyes shut and hugged Trinity for all she was worth. Noah was howling in fear. Caleb struggled to get away from Seth, but was powerless against his iron grip and the knife against his throat. A thin dark trickle of blood ran down his neck.

'You wouldn't want to let down your business partners in Texas and Tennessee,' Ben said.

Jayce gave a pretend-nonchalant shrug, still keeping the big revolver hard up against Keisha's head. 'You see how it is. I got the orders already lined up. Gotta look after commerce.'

'Then we have an impasse,' Ben said. 'Because I don't much like your terms.'

'Like they say,' Jayce replied. 'Non-negotiable.'

'In other words, that's tough shit,' Seth spat out.

'You should know me by now,' Ben said. 'But you're still not getting it, are you?'

Jayce's eyes narrowed. 'What's that mean?'

'It means that if you knew me, you'd know that I'd rather kill these people myself than let them end up the way you've got planned for them. I still have three rounds left in this gun. One is all I need to destroy your precious merchandise. Guess where the other two will go.'

Jayce smiled. 'You're one hardcore mofo. I hate to say it, Hope, but I like the way you think.'

'You won't like it so much when your innards are spread out all over that wall behind you,' Ben said. 'This isn't going to end well for anyone. Especially you.'

'We'll see about that,' Jayce said. 'Seth, cut the kid's throat.'

Things happened very quickly after that.

Grinning like a man possessed, Seth gripped the teenage boy in a lock and jerked his head back to expose his throat. The knife's edge began to slide across the milky flesh of his neck. The blood began to trickle faster. Caleb screamed. Keisha screamed. Trinity and Noah were wild with horror as they watched their half-brother about to be murdered by the bad man.

And Ben blew the side of Seth Garrett's skull out with a blast of buckshot.

As he pulled the trigger and the explosion filled the night, he knew that he was killing Keisha, too, because in the next instant Jayce would shoot her in the head.

But then a miracle happened.

Chapter 64

The last thing that went through Seth Garrett's mind was an ounce and a quarter of cold swaged lead alloy buckshot. His legs were already cut off from his brain as they crumpled under him. His lifeless fingers released the knife and his other hand let go of Caleb, who scrambled away from him as he fell to the ground.

The average reaction time for a healthy, alert human to a visual stimulus is around 0.25 seconds, and 0.17 seconds for an audio stimulus. The sight and sound of his brother's brains getting blown out was a combination of both for Jayce Garrett, whose reactions were somewhat quicker than most people's. Factor in a few extra milliseconds for the order to flash down from his brain to his trigger finger and let off the revolver he had to Keisha Hebert's temple, and she would be dead pretty fast.

But somewhere in the middle of that extremely short time interval, before the neurotransmitter cells in Jayce's brain were able to relay their instruction message to his body, another loud shot boomed out from the darkness somewhere behind Ben. A bullet slammed into the shed wall right next to where Jayce was standing, close enough to make him flinch and let go of Keisha. She stumbled to the ground, crying out in confusion, thinking the gunshot had been Jayce's.

And in the next few milliseconds Ben cracked open the lever of the Winchester, slammed out the smoking spent shell that had emptied its contents into Seth's head, and closed the lever to chamber the next one that was intended for his brother. But before the eject/recock cycle was complete, Jayce's trigger finger received its delayed FIRE command and the revolver, now pointing straight at Ben's chest, went off.

The impact of a heavy slug travelling somewhere north of the speed of sound knocked Ben backwards off his feet as though he'd been kicked by a horse, still clutching the shotgun which fired harmlessly straight up into the air. In the midst of the turmoil of confusion that comes with being shot in the chest with a large-calibre weapon, he registered the fact that he wasn't dead, because the ballistic vest he was wearing under his jacket had stopped the bullet.

Then came the sensation of pain and the knowledge that he'd cracked an upper rib, around his heart area. Kevlar could prevent a high-powered projectile from penetrating your vital organs, but the energy still had to go somewhere.

Next, the hidden shooter in the darkness let off another round. This time, the bullet struck Jayce Garrett in the right hip. The impact made him spin and drop his gun, but he stayed upright. As he went to scoop up his fallen weapon, a third shot kicked up dust at his feet and forced him to stagger back. There was little question who the unseen gunman was shooting at. Jayce stood there swaying on his feet for maybe half a second, then his face twisted into a leer and he bolted away into the shadows, limping badly.

Ben stood up. He was dizzy and hurting, and had to blink a few times to shake off the shock and confusion still buzzing through his mind. He pointed the shotgun towards where Jayce Garrett had been standing a moment earlier, but Jayce was gone. His blood glistened on the ground. A thick trail of it, leading off.

Hogan still hadn't stirred. Ben wanted to reach out to her, but he had to attend to Keisha and the kids first. They were gathered around their mother and clamped tightly to her as she clutched them and sobbed loudly. She turned to Ben. 'Oh God, I thought you were dead. I thought we all were.'

'You're safe now,' Ben replied. 'It's over.'

'Where's Tyler?'

'He's fine. He's waiting for you.'

'Oh, Ben.' Keisha burst into a flood of tears and hugged him. Caleb hugged him too. There was blood on the kid's neck, but the knife had barely cut him. Another half a second, and it would have been a very different story.

Ben let go of them and crouched next to Hogan. At the same moment that he realised she still had a pulse, her eyes fluttered open. He put a hand under her and helped her to sit up. 'You had me worried there for a moment.'

'I feel like I got hit by a baseball bat,' she groaned, rubbing her torso where the bulletproof vest had taken the hit. 'Knocked the crap outta me.'

'I know the feeling,' Ben said.

'What happened?'

'A miracle,' Ben said.

He looked around as the mystery shooter came staggering out of the shadows towards them.

'Or maybe not,' Ben said.

Sheriff Roque looked as though he might collapse at any moment. His face was pale and cadaverous in the moonlight, his jacket was shiny with blood and his right arm was hanging limp.

'Thanks for the help,' Ben said.

'It's a damned good thing for you I can still point this thing with my south paw,' Roque muttered, holding up the Colt in his left hand. He glanced down at Seth Garrett's body, and at his brother's blood trail leading away into the darkness. 'Jayce?'

'Still out there, but he's hurt. I think your second shot broke his hip.'

'Good. The sumbitch deserves to suffer.'

Roque's own pain must have been tremendous but he was bearing it with amazing fortitude. He eyed the remains of Charlie Fruge, then looked at Ben, then looked at the ten-gauge in Ben's hand, and Ben could tell that the sheriff knew exactly what had happened to Fruge.

Roque pulled a pained but knowing smile and said, 'The Garretts sure made a mess of him, didn't they?'

'He was one of theirs, just like Mason.'

'Guess we'll never know now, will we?'

'No,' Ben said, 'I don't suppose we will.'

The sheriff turned to Keisha. 'Ma'am, I'm mighty relieved to see y'all in one piece.'

Keisha seemed as though she was about to hug him, too, then saw the blood and the dangling arm and frowned in concern. 'But you're hurt, Sheriff,' she said. 'You're hurt real bad. I'm a nurse. Let me take a look at it.'

Roque shook his head. 'Thank you kindly, Ma'am, but it'll have to wait. I got things to do. The first of which is to get you and these kids choppered offa this godforsaken island and back to Villeneuve. Officer Hogan, you did well tonight. I'm real proud of you.'

Hogan's face was ashen but she beamed with satisfaction.

Roque said to Ben, 'We'll soon have this island crawlin' with more state troopers and federal officers than you ever saw in your life. If Jayce Garrett's still alive, we'll find him. Unless, of course, someone else finds the dirtbag first.' He raised an eyebrow.

Ben said, 'Jayce is mine.'

'Thought you might feel that way. Then you'd best go get him, son. I don't suppose he'll have got too far, with a busted hip. Before you go, reach in my pocket and tell me what you find in there. I can't do it.'

Ben hesitated, then felt inside the sheriff's blood-soaked right breast pocket. His fingers closed on something hard and thin and angular. He pulled it out and examined it under what little moonlight remained as the rainclouds blocked out the night sky. It was a blue and gold metal star, all sticky with blood.

'You might have to clean it up a little,' Roque said. 'It's yours.'

Ben wiped it on his sleeve and looked at it more closely, straining to see in the fading light. The badge's centre bore a State of Louisiana eagle emblem with the words UNION; JUSTICE; CONFIDENCE. Below that it said CLOVIS PARISH, and above was a scroll displaying the title HONORARY DEPUTY SHERIFF.

'You've got to be joking,' Ben said.

'I am not. Consider yourself sworn in as a special officer of the law, Mister Hope,' Roque said. 'Now whatever you do, it's legal.'

'I still want him alive.'

'We can't always get what we want, son. Anyhow, I think we've got all the evidence we need, if that's what you're worried about.' Roque pointed at the Winchester in Ben's hand. 'How you doin' for ammo?'

'One round left,' Ben said.

'Maybe you oughtta take this old girl along, too,' Roque said, offering him the Colt .45. 'I don't think I'll be needin' her again tonight.'

Ben took the sixgun and checked the cylinder. The old timers carried their Peacemakers loaded with five and the hammer on an empty chamber, for safety. Two live rounds were left. He ejected the three spent cartridge cases and reloaded them with spare shells from Roque's gunbelt.

Roque said, 'Now, Deputee. Whatever it takes to finish off that evil piece of shit Jayce Garrett, you go and get it done.'

Chapter 65

Now it had come down to just the pair of them. Like duellists or gladiators of olden times, each man would stand alone and face the other in single combat.

Ben was ready. He'd been born ready. Jayce Garrett had the advantage of being on home ground, but he was badly hurt. That much was obvious from the thickness of the blood trail that Ben was able to track away from the buildings even as the black storm clouds rolled ominously over the face of the moon.

Jayce would be moving slowly. He might not be able to get very far. But he was still dangerous, like a wounded man-eater crouched in a jungle thicket as a hunter stalked nearby, unaware of the hungry eyes watching him. Jayce could be lurking in any of the shadows of trees or tin huts that Ben passed in his search. He could have rearmed himself and be lying in wait to shoot his enemy at any moment. Ben didn't dare to use his torch, for fear of making himself an obvious target in the darkness.

Now at last, the gathering storm that had been building up pressure all this time finally broke. The first fat raindrop splashed down on Ben's shoulder, as heavy as a pigeon dropping. Then another, and another, and within moments a deluge was lashing down with fierce intensity, bouncing off the tin roofs of the Garrett compound and running in rivulets across the ground. A flash of lightning violently split the night sky, followed immediately by a rumbling snarl of thunder.

As the crack of the thunder died away, Ben suddenly heard an engine starting up. Not a truck this time; it sounded more like a motorcycle. Remembering the quad bikes parked near the house, he turned and took off in that direction. For a few moments he was disorientated, confused by the maze of pathways that crisscrossed here and there throughout the compound. Then he heard the rev of the engine more clearly and knew he was close.

As Ben went sprinting around a corner he glimpsed the quad bike speeding away from him with the dark figure of a man bent low over the handlebars as though desperately wringing every drop of power out of the machine. Jayce Garrett was tearing off towards the woods on the other side of the compound. Ben wondered what was down there. Jayce was obviously planning his escape somehow, and a speedboat was the most obvious answer. He couldn't be allowed to get away.

Ben ran for the rest of the quads, praying that he'd find one with keys in the ignition. The rain was cascading and gushing from the roof of the lean-to under which the vehicles were parked. He ducked under the waterfall and quickly checked each one in turn.

No keys. That would delay him giving chase, but it wouldn't stop him. He fell into a crouch by the nearest machine and shone his light under the steering column, looking for the nest of ignition wiring he could use to hotwire the thing. Then he saw the ripped-out spark plug cables lying on the ground, and realised that Jayce had anticipated his move and sabotaged all the remaining vehicles.

No time. No choice. Ben's only option was to pursue him on foot. He swore and took off again, sprinting after the disappearing sound of the quad bike. Rivers of rainwater swirled under his feet and turned the hard-packed earth of the compound to slippery mud as he chased the tracks of the quad's tyres. They led along a beaten path that twisted through the woods, but the terrain was so awash with water that he could barely follow them.

The storm was raging even harder now. Another flickering, strobing glare of lightning danced across the sky. Another crash of thunder. Then another, as continuous as an artillery barrage. Ben couldn't hear the quad bike any more.

He slowed his pace and turned off his torch, suddenly anxious that Jayce might have pulled over and be waiting to ambush him. He stood there, dripping, straining his ears over the rolling thunder and willing his eyes to see into the impenetrable patches of shadow among the dense foliage, every muscle in his body tight with the knowledge that, at any moment, the hunter could become the hunted.

Then another flash of lightning sliced a brilliant white zigzag above the trees, and for an instant Ben was able to see the imprints of blocky all-terrain tyres, half washed away but still visible, telling him that Jayce had come this way and wasn't lying in wait for him.

Ben ran on, stumbling in the mud, blinking rainwater from his eyes, whipped across the face and body by unseen branches. The torrent was coming down with fury, soaking him right through his ballistic vest and plastering his hair across his brow. Still, no gunshot rang out from the darkness. His cracked rib was burning like a hot brand inside his chest, but he ignored the pain by focusing all his mental energy on what lay ahead.

He was beyond the apex of the island's humped curve and the ground was sloping downhill now, heading towards the eastern shore and the Bayou Sanglante beyond. As he emerged from the trees he could see the path winding down towards the water's edge. A dark shape at the end of the path made him squint to see it clearly; then another white flash of lightning illuminated the shoreline and he saw that it was the quad bike, abandoned and overturned on its side with a wheel still spinning. This was the end of the line for motor vehicles, and its rider must have braked to a halt in such a hurry that he'd skidded and rolled the machine.

Ben scrambled down the path to the quad. He could smell the sharp tang of leaking petrol. There was no sign of Jayce Garrett.

Then once more the sky frazzled with an arcing spasm of electricity that seared the horizon from north to south, and in its momentary strobe-light glare Ben made out the tracks in the long grass leading away from the overturned vehicle, all flattened out as if someone had dragged a wooden board over it. Jayce must have literally crawled away, determined to escape no matter how badly hurt.

But where had he gone?

In the lull before the next clap of thunder crashed and rolled overhead, Ben detected another sound. This time the motor he could hear firing up was the distinctive puttering chug of a marine outboard. His fears had been right. Jayce was going to try to escape by boat. Once he'd crossed the bayou he had a vast wilderness to lose himself in. Alive or dead, he might never be found or seen again.

Ben turned towards the sound, and through the curtain of lashing rain he saw the dark shape of a little boathouse down by the water's edge, next to a pontoon with a fishing boom rig and a narrow jetty nearby.

Ben raced through the long, wet grasses and reeds towards the boathouse, hoping that he could intercept Jayce before he got out onto the water.

But Ben was too late. Before he got there he saw the dark silhouette of the boat emerge and start tracking across the bayou. The motor was straining and whining and the propeller was churning up a white wake behind it. He could see the outline of the man slumped at the stern, working the rudder as he steered out into the open channel. Jayce Garrett was getting away.

Ben ran to the edge of the dark, murky water. He raised the shotgun to his shoulder and swivelled the barrel along the line of the boat's path. But the short-barrelled scattergun was no use at this range. Its spread might easily hit Jayce by mistake, and he still wanted to bring him in alive if he could.

Ben threw down the shotgun, yanked Roque's revolver from his belt, thumbed back the hammer and took careful aim at the escaping boat. Even if the stinging rain in his eyes hadn't made it hard to see the sights, the old gun was no target pistol. But he knew he had to disable the boat somehow, before it got too far away. That outboard motor was its Achilles' heel. One solid hit, and he could bring it to a halt. That was the plan, at any rate. It was the only one he had right now.

Five shots. *Make them count*, he thought. He squeezed the trigger, and the revolver's butt kicked sharply against his palm and the loud report of the .45 cracked out across the water.

No dice. The boat kept chugging along, apparently untouched.

Ben recocked the hammer, lined up the sights and fired again. His second shot was drowned out by a clap of thunder. Same result. This time he saw the plop of the bullet hit the water, about three feet from the boat's stern as it continued on its course, putting more distance between itself and the shore.

Third shot. Nowhere near close. The bullet splashed down a body's length ahead of the boat's prow, now more than sixty yards from shore and getting further away with every second.

Fourth shot. Ben saw splinters kick up from the boat's gunwale. He was definitely getting Jayce Garrett's attention, but nothing more.

'Get it together, you idiot,' Ben muttered to himself as he cocked the hammer for his fifth and last shot.

He took a deep breath, steadied his aim and fired.

Chapter 66

Ben's last bullet hit its mark. But the result wasn't what he'd expected. The outboard motor sputtered out and then burst into flame. He must have severed a fuel line. The fire was just a small flickering orange glow at this distance, but which suddenly grew bigger and brighter – and Ben realised that the flames must have touched off a spare gas can. Maybe Jayce had needed to refuel the boat and in his haste spilled some petrol or neglected to close the jerrycan lid.

Whatever the reason, he was in trouble.

Ben dropped the gun and watched as the silhouetted figure of Jayce Garrett hobbled upright in the swaying boat and scrambled away from the flames. The fire was spreading quickly along the length of its hull, unabated by the lashing rain. Jayce backed up all the way to the prow, seemed to freeze for a moment, then leaped into the water with a splash. He was going to try to swim for the opposite shore. But with a broken hip he was sure to drown.

Which Ben could stand here on the shore and watch happen, or else try to do something to prevent. And as much as Jayce Garrett deserved to die, right here, right now, Ben wanted to hear him confess to the murder of Lottie Landreneau. He wanted to fly home to France with the knowledge that the man who'd sent her to her grave was being carted off in chains to begin his terminal stay in the Louisiana State Prison.

So Ben now became the rescuer of the man who'd framed him for a crime he didn't commit, kidnapped his friends and tried to kill him.

The loose boards of the little wooden jetty clattered under Ben's feet as he sprinted along its length. He reached its end and launched himself into a dive, and went knifing headlong into the murky black bayou.

Stroke after powerful stroke, gritting his teeth against the pain in his chest, he narrowed the distance to the burning boat. Jayce Garrett was in even worse trouble now. As another writhing snake of lightning lit up the whole wide expanse of the bayou, Ben saw the bobbing shape churning up the water in his desperation to stay afloat.

Twenty more yards. Then ten, then five, and then Ben was on him. Jayce was choking and spluttering and beginning to sink as Ben wrapped an arm around his chest and hauled his head back above the surface.

Jayce spouted water and was coughing violently. But some people just didn't want to be rescued. He ripped free of Ben's hold. His eyes focused on his enemy with an intensity of hatred so demonic that Ben couldn't help but remember the things Sallie Mambo had told him about the devils of Garrett Island.

Devil or not, Jayce fought with inhuman force and energy as the two men locked together in the water. He tried to grab Ben by the throat. Ben rolled his hands away and slammed a punch into his face. Jayce clawed at Ben's eyes. Ben head-butted him in the teeth. Jayce lashed out with a knee aimed for the groin. Ben deflected the knee and drove his own hard into Jayce's broken hip.

The violent struggle seemed to go on for several minutes.

Ben was battling to keep his head above the surface with the weight of his furious opponent trying to drag him down. It was a fight to the death, maybe both their deaths. Punch after punch, kick after kick. Ben slammed Jayce Garrett so many times in the face and throat that he should have been half dead, but he kept coming back. He seemed to feel no pain. As he grappled with one hand he reached down to his ankle with the other and whipped out a concealed boot knife like the one Mason had stabbed Ben with. Ben saw the knife lunging up towards him, a vicious strike that would have plunged the blade right up through his jaw into his brain if he hadn't twisted aside at the last moment. He palmed the knife off course, gripped Jayce Garrett's wrist and in one hard, fast movement folded the joint inwards and sideways, all the way down, until he felt the snapping and crackling of the wrist breaking. Then he smashed his elbow into Jayce's eye socket. Then pummelled him with a hammer punch to the bridge of the nose and broke that, too.

Still Jayce wouldn't give in. With a wild roar he surged up and rammed the hard crown of his skull into Ben's cheekbone. A white flash that wasn't from the electrical storm raging overhead spangled Ben's vision. Stunned, he felt the surface slip over his head, tasted the brackish water filling his mouth. He was sinking. Jayce was pulling him down into the blackness like some kind of mythological aquatic evil spirit intent on dragging him to the bottom.

Ben hit him. And hit him again, with a savage strength born of desperation. Bubbles burst from Jayce's lips. His face was a ruin. Teeth gone, nose splattered sideways. At last, as Ben's energy was almost spent, Jayce Garrett started to go limp and his struggles subsided as his lungs filled with water.

Ben wrapped an arm around Jayce's body and kicked upwards towards the surface. He drew in a rasping breath and coughed as he treaded the water, keeping Jayce's head up.

It was a couple of moments before he could speak. 'Jayce Garrett, you're under arrest for the murder of Charlotte Landreneau.'

There was a load of stuff about rights to remain silent and have an attorney present during questioning, but Ben reckoned that could all wait until they reached the shore.

'Screw you,' Jayce spluttered in a mushy voice.

'Whatever you say, Jayce. You're going to jail. And consider yourself the luckiest man alive.'

Jayce said no more after that. Ben kept on towards the shore, now about forty yards away. The driving rain pocked the surface of the bayou and the thunder shook the sky.

And the black water suddenly churned white as a huge dark shape sliced towards them from the hidden depths and erupted from the surface. Glistening armoured scales caught the light of another flash. The enormous creature came at Ben with its jaws open wide.

He would never know it, but old Cyrus had just arrived on the scene.

Ben kicked out, and the alligator veered away from him. Its black-green tail, thick as a tree trunk, cut the water like a whip. Before Ben could swim another yard it had circled round for another pass, torpedo snout rising from the depths. This time it went for Jayce Garrett. Its huge jaws scissored wide and Ben saw the glint of one tiny reptilian eye and the uneven conical teeth with bits of rotting flesh stuck between them from its last meal. Then the teeth snapped shut around Jayce's torso and Ben felt the full force of the monster as it tore its prey from his grip.

Jayce screamed and thrashed and blood spouted from his mouth. The giant alligator shook him like a terrier shakes a rat to snap its spine. Then rose up from the water with the man still in its jaws, and bellyflopped down on the surface, sending up a spray of red and white foam that glittered like diamonds and rubies in the next flash of lightning.

For one brief moment the frenzied screaming rose to a terrible high-pitched wail, before it fell forever silent. The alligator crunched the dead body in its jaws and then sank below the surface, still clutching its prize. A swirl of foam and bubbles was all that remained to mark the spot of Jayce Garrett's passing.

Ben was suddenly alone in the darkness. He stared for a moment at the sudden stillness of the water around him, then began swimming for shore. He could sense the presence of the creature somewhere close by in the murk, but he knew that it wouldn't need to hunt again tonight. Now it would carry its catch back to some hidden swamp lair and leave the masticated meat to tenderise a while before it enjoyed its feast.

Ben reached the reeds of the bank and hauled himself up onto dry land. He stood and watched as the burning boat's remains finally slipped away beneath the surface and the orange glow of the flames was snuffed out. Bits of wreckage floated and gently bobbed on the bayou. Smoke drifted over the water and was dispersed by the rain. There was no more trace of Jayce Garrett, and there never would be.

Ben turned away. He retrieved his borrowed weapons and began the trek back across the island.

Chapter 67

Ben got back to the compound as the pilot of a State Police Bell 460 was skilfully bringing his helicopter down between the trees to land in the Garrett compound. There was a flight paramedic on board, who checked the released hostages and then attended to the sheriff. A fleet of ambulances was already en route. Ben didn't say it, but he hoped they'd packed a large supply of body bags.

He flew back with Keisha, the kids and Officer Hogan. The chopper took them directly to the Clovis Parish Medical Center near Villeneuve, where doctors and trauma nurses were waiting to examine the Heberts for physical injury and shock. The place was buzzing with grim energy as the staff prepared for the return of the first ambulances and Coroner's Office vehicles ferrying in the wounded and, mostly, the dead. Ben did his usual thing of trying to resist the attentions of the nurses, but to little avail as they herded him into an X-ray room and from there to a cubicle where they set about cleaning up his battered face. He had to admit, he looked a bit better after they were finished.

A horrified nurse failed to see the funny side when he asked for whisky in lieu of painkillers. No sensayuma. Then they let him go. He wandered the corridors, looking for Jessie Hogan. He didn't find her, but found someone else instead.

The medical personnel weren't the only ones waiting at the hospital to greet Keisha and the children. The moment word had reached the Sheriff's Office an obliging cop had driven Tyler Hebert over to be reunited with his family. Ben met him in a lounge area, where Tyler had spent the last anxious hour pacing the floor and chewing his fingernails to the quick. When Tyler saw Ben walk into the waiting room he ran over and squeezed him in a suffocating and painful bear hug.

'Careful,' Ben said, wincing. The X-ray had confirmed that he'd cracked a rib, and he was feeling a little tender.

'They're okay, ain't they?' Tyler asked in a fluster. He hadn't been allowed to see them yet. He was almost weeping from a mixture of relief and frustration.

'They're fine. A bit shaken up, and Caleb took a couple of knocks, but that's all.'

'You told me you'd get 'em out. And you did. How can I thank you, Ben?'

'One good turn deserves another,' Ben said. 'You did as much for me. More, even.'

'No way, buddy. You're a goddamned hero, is what you are.'

'Buy me a beer sometime.'

'You betcha I will.'

Minutes later, a male nurse appeared to say that they'd finished with Mrs Hebert and the children, and that Mr Hebert could see them now. Tyler couldn't get there fast enough.

Ben didn't hang around to see the moving reunion. The family needed their privacy. But he could imagine the scene well enough, and it made him smile.

One by one, the ambulances and coroner's vehicles came screeching into the hospital. Ben collared a doctor who, in a tearing rush, told him that Sheriff Roque was in the ER but would do okay.

Soon after he'd spoken with the doctor, Ben was approached by a pair of state troopers who'd come looking for him and said they were to drive him back over to the Sheriff's Office. Ben walked out with them to their patrol car, and twenty minutes later found himself seated across a desk from a very serious-looking, bald-headed, overweight plain-clothes man with a crooked tie, who introduced himself as Agent Donald F. Kassmeyer from the FBI office in Baton Rouge.

Kassmeyer appeared tired and harassed as he hunched over a pile of papers. One of them was the affidavit signed by Judge Claybrook authorising the arrest of Jayce and Seth Garrett. Another was Sheriff Roque's official statement, also rubber-stamped by the judge, dropping all prior charges against the original suspect in the case, one Benedict Hope. Another again was the sheriff's pre-operational report on the raid on Garrett Island.

Kassmeyer had a lot of questions for Ben about the dramatic and terrible events of that evening. Ben was calm and polite, but intended to say as little as possible.

'I don't know how much assistance I can be to you, Agent Kassmeyer. So much happened, so fast. In any case, as you know, my involvement was strictly in an advisory, observational capacity. I was very much on the edge of things. You'd really have to talk to the surviving officers themselves.'

'Which doesn't leave a lot of folks to talk to, does it?'

'Sadly not.'

Kassmeyer gave a weary sigh and spent a moment pinching the bridge of his nose with his eyes shut, as if he had a migraine coming on. 'It's a nightmare. Anyway, so happens we already spoke with Officer Hogan. She says that the Garrett brothers each confessed to the murder of Charlotte Landreneau before Seth Garrett was then shot to death by one of his own men, who also shot Officer Fruge before she shot him. While Jayce Garrett apparently managed to escape. Can you confirm that's what occurred?'

'If that's what Officer Hogan says happened, that's what happened,' Ben said. 'She was right in the thick of the action. As I told you, I was barely involved.'

'We have teams combing the area for Jayce Garrett. I don't suppose you'd have any idea, strictly in an advisory capacity that is, where the sonofabitch might've run off to?'

'None,' Ben said. 'I didn't see him.'

'Just one more matter I wanted to get straight, Mr Hope. I'm told you were formally sworn in as a deputy for this operation. Is that so? Strikes me as bein' a mite unconventional, under the circumstances.'

'I'm not fully conversant with your rules,' Ben said with a smile, 'being a foreigner and all. I think the sheriff was just indulging me. I'd told him I always had a thing about the wild west, growing up. You know, *The Tin Star*, with Henry Fonda? That was a favourite of mine.'

Kassmeyer grunted. Not a fan of old westerns, clearly. Then again, neither was Ben, particularly. Kassmeyer asked, 'You still got the badge? It's government property.'

It was in Ben's jacket pocket. 'Sorry to say, I lost it when I fell.'

'Fell?'

Ben pointed to his face. 'How do you think I picked up these bruises? Took a bit of a tumble in the dark. Must've tripped. Clumsy.'

'I thought you were supposed to be some kind of SAS hotshot superhero.'

'Oh, that was a long time ago, Agent Kassmeyer. 'Fraid I've gone off the boil a bit. Comes to us all, I suppose.'

Kassmeyer shuffled some more papers, looking a little bemused. His line of questioning now run out of steam, he heaved another deep sigh and got to his feet.

'Well, this whole affair seems pretty bizarre, but as far as we're concerned we have no reason to detain you any longer. I guess you're free to go, Mr Hope. Plannin' on remaining for any length of time in the US?'

'I'll be flying home to France just as soon as I can,' Ben replied.

Kassmeyer seemed pleased about that. He stuck out a square, blunt hand and said, 'You have a pleasant trip, now.'

Ben left the Sheriff's Office and walked out into the cool night. The air was sweet with the scent of tree blossoms and the constellations were sharp and clear in the night sky. As he lit a cigarette, a Clovis Parish police car came roaring up and squealed to a halt beside him. The driver's window whirred down and a familiar face smiled out at him. She'd changed into a crisp, clean uniform, washed her hair and didn't look remotely like someone who'd been engaged in deadly close-quarters combat just a few hours earlier.

'How are you feeling, Officer Hogan?'

'You can drop the officer shit. I'm okay. Takes more'n a forty-four magnum round to the chest to slow me down.'

'That's my girl.'

'Shucks. You're makin' me blush. Wanna come for a ride? Actually, I was sent to get you.'

Ben flicked away his cigarette and climbed into the car.

'Where are we going?'

'Back to the hospital. He wants to see you.'

Chapter 68

The sheriff was sitting up in bed in a private room, surrounded by monitors and tubes and things that bleeped. A drip on a stand was attached to one arm. The other was encased in plaster all the way to his shoulder and raised up on an elevated rest. The old implacable face was as sour as ever, but there was a twinkle in his eye as Ben and Hogan were shown inside the room.

'How're you doing, Sheriff?'

'I'm as pert as a ruttin' buck. Takes more'n a—'

'More than a twenty-millimetre cannon round that almost blew off your arm to slow you down. You Louisianans.'

'Bred tough,' Roque said. 'Not like you soft-ass Limeys. No wonder we kicked your butts back into the sea in 1781.'

'Did you summon me here just to insult my countrymen?'

'Matter of fact, no, I wanted to thank you for what you done. Hadn't been for you, this parish might never have gotten shot of the curse of the Garrett boys.'

'That's awfully sweet of you to say, Sheriff. But you didn't do too badly yourself.'

Roque shook his head wistfully. 'We sure paid a heavy price for it. Lost a lot of good people out there today.'

Ben nodded. 'Yes.'

'Guess you'll be fixin' to head home soon?'

Ben nodded again. 'First thing.'

'You oughtta stick around at least another day. They're buryin' the Landreneau woman tomorrow mornin'. Thought mebbe you'd want to attend. There's the other thing, too.'

Ben said, 'What other thing?'

'I guess you hadn't heard,' Roque said. 'I mean, what with all that's been happenin'. You had other matters on your mind.'

Ben said, 'Heard what?'

'If memory serves me right, I recollect you tellin' me you came here to Louisiana for a jazz concert?'

'Don't rub it in.'

'You're in luck, son. If you'd been followin' the news, you'd've known that ol' Woody McCoy called off the show at the last minute. Postponed for a couple of days, for health reasons. Which means you ain't missed nothin'.'

'You're kidding me.'

'I never kid,' Roque said. 'Turns out that the greedy sonofagun filled his face with so much of his hometown smoky Creole gumbo with hot sauce that he got a bad attack of dyspepsia and had to spend two days in bed. Show's been rescheduled for tomorrow night.'

'Then I suppose that puts paid to my travel plans,' Ben said. 'Looks like I'll be around a little longer.'

'So you're a jazz fan, huh?' Hogan said, smiling at him.

Ben smiled back. 'You?'

She shrugged. Non-committal. 'Even if I was, I'm on duty tomorrow night.'

'Not any more you're not,' Roque said. 'You're takin' the week off, effective immediately. That's an order, Officer Hogan.'

She beamed at the sheriff, then at Ben. 'Hear that? Looks like you got yourself a hot date, honey pie.'

'Got somewhere to stay the night?' Roque asked him.

Hogan shot Ben a sideways look and her cheeks turned pink.

402

Roque said, 'Easy there, Jessie.'

'Seems I'm homeless,' Ben admitted.

'Philomena and I have a vacation cabin over by Bourbeaux Lake,' the sheriff said. 'Got a spare set of keys in my desk drawer at the office. Jessie'd run by and get 'em for you, wouldn't you, Jessie?'

And so it was that Ben spent that night in the tranquil setting of Bourbeaux Lake, Clovis Parish, which he was unable to appreciate as he slept for nine straight hours and had to rush off early in order to attend Lottie Landreneau's funeral at the First Baptist Church on the edge of Villeneuve.

It was a sad, sombre occasion. A large crowd was in attendance, out of which Ben was one of the few white faces. He kept to the rear of the gathering, faintly worried that some uninformed folks might still think he was the murderer. Nobody tried to lynch him. The ceremony ended. The crowd began to disperse. Feeling a gentle tap on his shoulder, he turned suddenly.

'Sallie!'

The old lady had turned up with several of her entourage, including Carl, who at least hadn't brought a rifle along for the occasion. He wasn't driving the hearse, either.

'You done good, child,' Sallie said.

'All thanks to you, Mama.' He showed her the mojo bag, still hanging around his neck. 'Kept me safe from the demons, just like you said it would.'

She squeezed his hand and a tear rolled from her eye. 'Don't you never take it off.'

'I won't,' he promised her. He bent and kissed her softly on the cheek.

'Goodbye, Sallie. Look after yourself.'

'Be seein' you in Heaven, child.' The old lady turned and shuffled away towards a waiting car, accompanied by her people.

Evening came. Ben met Jessie Hogan at the Cajun Steakhouse for an early dinner of T-bone and fries washed down by a few Dixie beers that she drank from the bottle like a real Southern gal. Her hair was loose, her jeans were tight and she wore a red check shirt tied at the waist. She looked quite different with mascara and lipstick.

'So you're goin' home in the morning, huh,' she said.

'Unless something dramatic and unexpected happens in the meantime,' he replied.

'You got a wife waitin' for you there?'

'Probably not exactly waiting for me,' Ben said. 'And we're not married.'

She took another pensive swig of Dixie and said, 'But you got a girl, right?'

'I wouldn't call her a girl, either.'

'A female, then.'

'Definitely a female,' he said.

'Just my luck.'

'Have another beer,' Ben said.

Soon afterwards, it was time. They left the grillhouse and joined the throng of people heading for the Civic Center. Jessie Hogan took his hand. Not the tough cop any more. He didn't stop her.

The place was packed. Ben threaded his way to the front row. Jessie pressed herself to his side, even more excited than he was.

Then to a roar that almost lifted the roof off the building, Woody McCoy and his Quintet came out on stage.

Woody yelled, 'How are y'all doing?' The audience went wild.

Then the venerable jazzman raised his saxophone to his lips, and the music began.

Read on for an exclusive extract of the new
Ben Hope thriller by Scott Mariani

Valley of Death

Coming May 2019

Chapter 1

Haryana, India

Kabir removed his pilot's headset and began flipping switches on the Bell Ranger's instrument panels to shut down the rotors. He turned to grin broadly at Sai in the co-pilot seat, then at Manish sitting behind.

'Ready to make history, guys?' he said over the falling pitch of the turbine.

Kabir's two associates beamed back at him. Manish said, 'Let's rock and roll.'

As the helicopter's rotors slowed to a whistling *whip-whip-whip*, the three companions clambered out and jumped down to the rocky ground. It had taken less than an hour from the urban hubbub of their base in New Delhi to reach the remoteness of Hisar District, Haryana, out in the middle of nowhere several miles north-west of a once barely-heard-of village called Rakhigarhi.

Kabir stood for a moment and gazed around him at the arid, semi-desert terrain that stretched as far as the eye could see in all directions. Far away beyond the barren escarpment of rocky hills behind him to the north-east lay Punjab, the Land of the Five Rivers; in front of him lay the wide-open semi-desertified plains, arid and rocky with just a few desiccated shrubs and wizened trees scattered here and there and offering no shade. It was mid-September and the merciless heat of summer was past its worst, but the sun still beat fiercely down, baking the landscape.

Kabir was hardened to the heat, because of the outdoor demands of a job that often took him to difficult and inhospitable places all across the ancient Near East; unlike his elder brothers, one of whom spent all his time in air-conditioned big-city boardrooms, and the other who, for reasons best known to him, had chosen to live in chilly, rain-sodden Britain. Very strange. Though if it was the life he shared with his beautiful new wife that kept him tied to London, Kabir couldn't entirely blame the guy. She was something, all right. Maybe one day he too might be lucky enough to find a woman like her. For now, though, Kabir's sole devotion was to his work.

Kabir stepped back to the chopper, reached into a cool box behind the passenger seat and pulled out three cans of Coke; one for him and one each for Manish and Sai. His two bright, trusty graduate students were both in their early twenties, only a few years younger than Kabir who happened to be the youngest professor ever to teach at the Institute of Archaeology in New Delhi. With his warm personality and winning smile, he was widely held to be the most popular, too – though he was far too modest to admit it.

Sai rolled the cold can over his brow, then cracked the ring and look a long drink. 'That hit the spot. Thanks, boss.' Sai never called him 'Professor'.

'No littering, please,' Kabir said. 'This is a site of special archaeological interest, remember.'

'Doesn't bloody look like it,' Manish said.

Sai finished the can, crumpled it between his fingers and surveyed it with a thoughtful frown. 'Just think. If I chuck this away among the rocks, four thousand years into the future some guy like us will dig it up and prize it as an ancient relic of our culture, wondering what the hell it can teach him about the long-lost civilisation of the twenty-first century.'

Kabir smiled. 'That's history in action for you. Now let's go and see what we can figure out about the people who lived here four thousand years ago.'

'I don't think they drank Coke,' Manish said.

'Nah, something else killed them off,' Sai joked. 'Question is, what?'

It was one of the puzzles that Kabir had spent his whole career trying to answer, and it was no joke to him. He tossed his own empty Coke can back into the cooler, then took out his iPhone and quickly accessed the precious set of password-protected documents stored inside.

Those documents were the single most important thing in his life right now. The original from which they had been scanned was an old leather-bound journal dating back to the nineteenth century. Not particularly ancient, as archaeological finds went – and yet its chance discovery, only weeks earlier, had been the most significant he'd ever made. And he was hoping that it would lead to an even bigger one.

Outside of Manish and Sai, there were very few people whom Kabir trusted with his newfound secret. The precious journal itself was still back in New Delhi, securely locked up in a safe while its new custodian travelled out to this arid wilderness, full of excitement and determined to find out if the amazing revelations of its long-dead author were indeed true.

Only time would tell. Sooner rather than later, he hoped. His eagerness to know the truth sometimes bordered on desperation. Yes, it was an obsession. He knew that. But sometimes, he reminded himself, that's what it takes to get the job done.

Shielding his eyes from the sun's glare, Kabir slowly scanned the horizon. The chopper was parked on a rocky plateau from where the ground fell away into a rubble-strewn valley. Heat ripples disturbed the air like tendrils rising from the ground, but he was able to make out the curve of the ancient dry river bed that wound for miles into the far distance. Millennia ago, a mighty river had flowed through here, nourishing the land and raising lush vegetation all along its banks. Now it was so parched and dusty that even looking at it made Kabir thirsty for another cold drink.

He looked back at the iPhone and scrolled through the selection of documents until he came to the scan of the map from the old journal. The hundred and eighty-plus years it had lain undiscovered had done the book few favours: some pages were nibbled around the edges by mildew and rodents, others so badly faded and water-stained as to be barely legible. Kabir had used specialised computer software to enhance the details, and a UV camera to photograph the worst-affected pages. He'd been pleased with the results. The digitised map now looked as sharp and clear as the day the journal's author had drawn it in the pages of his book. Its key feature was the undulating, meandering curve of a river whose line, as Kabir stood there comparing the two, closely resembled that of the dry bed that stretched out in front of him.

That was when Kabir knew he was in the right place. A strange chill ran up and down his back.

'What do you reckon, boss?' Sai, at his shoulder, was gazing at the screen of the iPhone.

'I think we found it,' Kabir replied. His voice was calm, but his heart felt ready to leap out of his chest. He took a couple of deep breaths, then started leading the way down the rocky slope down towards the river valley. He ran ten miles every day, kept himself super-fit and was as nimble as a mountain goat over the rough terrain. Sai markedly less so, being overly partial to calorie-laden Delhi street food, and Manish was a city kid too used to level pavements. But they'd toughen up. Slipping and stumbling and causing little rock slides under their feet, they manfully followed their leader down the hillside. By the time they reached the bottom, Kabir was already tracking along the river bed, walking slowly and scanning left and right as though searching for clues.

It was hard to believe that such an arid and inhospitable

area could have once been a major centre of one of the largest and most advanced cultures of the ancient world. But that was exactly what it was.

To say that the lost Harappan, or Indus Valley Civilisation, was Kabir's overriding interest in life would have been a crashing understatement. Long, long ago, over a stretch of time spanning one and a half thousand years during the second and third millennia BCE, the culture had thrived throughout the north-western parts of South Asia. Their empire had been larger than that of Mesopotamia; greater even than that of ancient Egypt or China. It had covered a vast area comprising parts of what were today Afghanistan, Pakistan and north-west India. At its peak, it was thought to support a population of five million inhabitants, which by ancient standards was enormous.

And yet, virtually nothing was known about these people. Nobody even knew what they called themselves, let alone how they organised their society. Or what had finally caused their whole civilisation to crumble and disappear. Kabir had devoted most of his career as an archaeologist to uncovering those secrets, and expected to spend the rest of his life doing exactly the same thing.

For years, it had been widely assumed in the archaeology world that the main centres of the Indus Valley Civilisation had been the excavated cities at Harappa and Mohenjo-Daro, both in Pakistan. Which had been a major frustration for archaeologists from India, since tensions between the two nations made it hard for them to travel freely in their neighbouring country. More recently, important finds made at Rakhigarhi in India's Haryana region had radically changed that view. Many historians and archaeologists now believed that the sheer size of the site excavated at Rakhigarhi pointed to it being the capital of the entire civilisation. If that was true, as Kabir fervently hoped, then it might offer scholars the opportunity to finally start unravelling the mysteries that surrounded the ancient lost culture.

Exactly what he hoped to find here, twenty miles to the north of the Rakhigarhi site, Kabir couldn't say for certain. But if the journal's claims were even half true, he could be standing on a literal treasure. He'd already made some private, tentative enquiries among his contacts in the Indian government. They were unlikely to agree to fund a new excavation project, but as long as they agreed in principle, Kabir was more than willing to pay for it out of his own pocket. His very own private dig, fully under his own supervision. He calculated that to bring in sufficient manpower and equipment to get things rolling would cost him at least a hundred million rupees – about one and a half million American dollars.

Kabir didn't blink at those figures. The benefits of being born into wealth.

Manish and Sai caught up with him and the three of them walked on, following the river bed. Each man was silent, gazing at the rocky ground underfoot and imagining what wonders might be hidden below. It was a heady feeling. Finally, Manish said, 'Wow, Prof, you really think it's here somewhere?'

'I'm certain it's here,' Kabir replied. He held up the iPhone as though it were the old leather-bound journal itself. 'Masson believed it. That's good enough for me.'

Sai was about to say something when he suddenly froze. 'Hear that?'

'What?' Manish said.

Now Kabir heard it, too, and turned to look in the direction of the sound.

The approaching vehicle appeared on the ridge above the river valley, some eighty yards to the west. It looked as though it had come from where the helicopter was parked. Kabir instinctively didn't like the look of it. As he watched, it tipped over the edge of the slope and started bouncing and pattering its way down the hillside towards them, throwing up a dust plume in its wake. It was moving fast. Some kind of rugged four-wheel-drive, like the Nissan Jonga jeeps the Indian army used to use.

'Who are they, boss?' Sai asked apprehensively.

'No idea. But I think we're about to find out.'

The jeep reached the bottom of the hillside and kept coming straight towards them, lurching and dipping over the rubble. Then it stopped, still a long way off. The terrain on the approach to the river bed was too rough even for an off-roader. The doors opened. Two men climbed out of the front. Three more climbed out of the back. All of them were clutching automatic rifles, but they definitely weren't the Indian army.

'Daakus!' Manish yelped.

Sai's jaw dropped open. An expression of pure horror plastered his face. 'Oh, shit.'

Daakus were bandits, of which there were many gangs across north-west India. They were growing bolder each year, despite the increasingly militarised and notoriously brutal efforts of the police to round them all up. Kabir had read a few days earlier that an armed gang of them had robbed a bank in Haryana. Their sudden appearance was the last thing he'd have expected out here, in the middle of the wilderness. But all the same he now cursed himself for having left his Browning self-defence pistol at home in Delhi. His mouth went dry.

'They must have seen us landing,' Sai said in a hoarse, panicky whisper. 'What are we going to do, boss?' Both he and Manish were looking to their professor as though he could magically get them out of this.

The five men were striding purposefully towards them. Spreading out now. Raising their weapons. Taking aim. Looking like they meant it.

'Run,' Kabir said. 'Just run!'

And then the gunshots began to crack out across the valley.

Chapter 2

One month later

The walls of the single-storey house were several feet thick and extremely well insulated, solidly reinforced on the outside and clad on the inside with thick, sturdy plywood. The house featured several rooms and offered spacious facilities well suited to its purpose.

But it wasn't a dwelling in which anybody would have wanted to live. Not even the mice that inhabited the remote compound's various other sheds and outbuildings would have been tempted to make their nests in its walls. Not considering the activities that went on there.

Yet, the building wasn't empty that autumn afternoon. At the end of a narrow corridor was the main room; and in the middle of that room sat a woman on a wooden chair. She wasn't moving. Her wrists and ankles were lashed tight and her head hung towards her knees so that her straggly blonde hair covered her face. To her right, a kidnapper in torn jeans reclined on a tattered sofa with a shotgun cradled across his lap. To her left, another of the woman's captors stood in a corner.

Nobody spoke. As though waiting for something to happen.

The waiting didn't go on for long.

The stunning boom of an explosion shattered the silence and shook the building. Heavy footsteps pounded up the corridor towards the main room. Then its door crashed violently inwards and two men burst inside. One man was slightly taller than the other, but otherwise they were indistinguishable in appearance. They were dressed from head to foot in black, bulked out by their body armour and tactical vests, and their faces were hidden behind masks and goggles. Each carried a semiautomatic pistol, same make, model and calibre, both weapons drawn from their tactical holsters, loaded and ready for action.

The two-man assault team moved with blinding speed as they invaded the room. They ignored the hostage for the moment. Her safety was their priority, which meant dealing with her captors quickly and efficiently before either one could harm her. The taller man unhesitatingly thrust out his weapon to aim at the kidnapper in the corner and engaged him with a double-tap to the chest and a third bullet to the head, the three snapping gunshots coming so fast that they sounded like a burst from a machine gun. No human being alive could have responded, or even flinched, in time to avoid being fatally shot.

The other man in black moved across the room to engage the kidnapper on the sofa. Shouting, 'DROP THE WEAPON DROP THE WEAPON DROP THE WEAPON!'

The kidnapper made no move to toss the shotgun. The second assault shooter went to engage him. His finger was on the trigger. Then the room suddenly lit up with a blinding white flash and an explosion twice as loud as the munitions they'd used to breach the door blew the shooter off his feet. He sprawled on his back, unharmed, but momentarily stunned. His unfired pistol went sliding across the floor.

The room was full of acrid smoke. The kidnapper in the corner had slumped to the floor, but neither the bound hostage nor her captor on the sofa had moved at all. That was because they were the latest type of life-size, high-density foam 3D humanoid targets that were being used for live-fire hostage rescue and combat training simulations here at the

Le Val Tactical Training Centre in Normandy, France. The 'kidnappers' had already been shot more full of holes than Gruyère in the course of a hundred similar entry drills performed inside the killing house. So had the hostage, more than her fair share. But they'd survive to go through the whole experience another day, and many more.

The taller of the two assault shooters made his weapon safe and clipped it back into its holster, then pulled off his mask and goggles and brushed back the thick blond lock that fell across his brow. His haircut definitely wouldn't have passed muster, back in his SAS days. He walked over to his colleague, who was still trying to scramble to his feet.

Ben Hope held out a gloved hand to help him up. He said, 'Congratulations. You're dead, your team are dead, your hostage is dead. Let's review and start over.'

The second man's name was Yannick Ferreira and he was a counter-terror unit commander with the elite Groupe d'Intervention de la Gendarmerie Nationale or GIGN, here on a refresher course. He'd wanted to hone his skills with the best, and there were none better to train with than the guys at Le Val: Ben himself, his business partner Jeff Dekker, their associate Tuesday Fletcher and their hand-picked team of instructors, all ex-military, all top of their game. Ferreira was pretty good at his job too, but even skilled operators, like world-class athletes, could lose their edge now and then. It was Ben's job to keep them on their toes.

Ferreira said, 'What the hell just happened?'

Ben replied, 'That happened.' He pointed at the floor, where a length of thin wire lay limp across the rough boards where Ferreira had snagged it with his boot.

'A tripwire?'

'You must have missed it, in all the excitement,' Ben said.

The wire was connected to a hidden circuit behind the wall, which when broken activated the non-lethal explosive device right beneath Ferreira's feet. Seven million candle-power and 170 decibels of stunning noise wasn't quite the same as being blown apart by a Semtex booby trap, but it certainly got its message across.

'Devil's in the detail, Yannick,' Ben said. 'As we all know, our terrorist friends have no problem blowing themselves to smithereens in order to take us out with them. It can get just a little messy.'

Ferreira shook his head sourly. 'I can't believe you caught me out with a fucking flashbang. That was a dirty rotten trick, Ben.'

'Dirty rotten tricks are what you're paying us for,' Ben said. 'How about we stroll back to the house for a coffee, then we can come back and run through it again?'

Chapter 3

'Keep pouring,' Jeff said grimly, holding out his wineglass until Ben had filled it to the brim. Jeff downed half the glass in a gulp like a man on a mission, and smacked his lips.

'I think I'll get rat-arsed tonight,' he declared.

'Sounds like a brilliant plan,' Tuesday said dryly. 'Don't expect me to carry you back to your hole after you fall in a heap, though.'

Another busy work day had ended, evening had fallen and the three of them were gathered around the big oak table in the farmhouse kitchen, preparing to demolish the pot of beef and carrot stew that could have fed the French army, which was simmering on the stove. Ben was seated in his usual place by the window, feeling not much less morose than Jeff despite the glass of wine at his elbow, his loyal German shepherd dog Storm curled up at his feet and one of his favourite Gauloises cigarettes between his lips.

While he'd been working with Yannick Ferreira, Jeff and Tuesday had been putting two more of the GIGN guys through their paces on Le Val's firing ranges. Tuesday had been a top-class military sniper before he'd come to join the gang in Normandy. His idea of fun was popping rows of cherry tomatoes at six hundred yards with his custom Remington 700 rifle, which generally upstaged and occasionally cheesed off their clients. Especially the ones with a tough-guy attitude, who for some reason didn't expect a skinny Jamaican kid who was forever smiling and ebullient to be so deadly once he got behind a rifle.

Ben had warned Tuesday in the past about the showing off. 'We're here to teach them, not embarrass them.' Still, Ferreira's guys hadn't taken it too badly. After class the three trainees had driven off to the nearest town, Valognes, in search of beer and fast food to help soothe their wounded pride and prepare them for another day of humiliation ahead.

Even Tuesday's spirits were dampened by the gloomy atmosphere around the kitchen table. But the glumness of the three friends had nothing to do with the tribulations of their work. The theme of the dinnertime conversation had been women troubles. Tuesday, who appeared to enjoy a stress-free and uncomplicated love life largely because he was always between girlfriends, had nothing to complain about. For both Ben and Jeff, however, it was a different story.

Ben had recently returned from an unexpectedly adventuresome trip to the American Deep South. There, in-between dodging bullets and almost getting blown up and eaten by alligators, he'd met and befriended a female police officer called Jessie Hogan. They had dinner and went to a jazz gig together, and although Jessie made it pretty obvious that she liked Ben, nothing happened between them. Ben drove back to New Orleans and boarded his flight home without so much as a kiss being exchanged. But that wasn't the impression that Ben's French girlfriend, Sandrine, had formed.

Ben and Sandrine had been together for a few months. It wasn't love's young dream. Both of them had been hurt before, and it had been a somewhat cautious, reticent start to the relationship before they fell into a comfortable routine. She was a head surgeon at the hospital in Cherbourg, some kilometres away, whose punishing work schedule meant she didn't live at Le Val and only visited now and then.

It had been on one such visit, a couple of days ago, when the two of them had been hanging out in the prefabricated office building and Ben had needed to step outside for a few minutes to attend to a delivery of some items for the range complex. While his back was turned, as luck would have it, an email had landed on his screen: Jessie Hogan, saying what a great time she'd had with him and expressing a strong desire to see him again if he happened to swing by Clovis Parish, Louisiana, anytime in the future. She'd signed off with a lot of kisses.

Sandrine hadn't taken it too well. Ben had stepped back inside the office to be met with tears and anger. 'So this is what you get up to on your travels, is it?'

Calmly at first, Ben had protested his innocence. But nothing he said could persuade her, and after a bitter quarrel Sandrine had driven off in a rage. It was Jeff who'd stopped Ben from going after her. Jeff had been right: following a row with a car chase wasn't such a good idea.

Ben hadn't been able to get through to Sandrine on the phone since, and she wasn't responding to emails. He'd decided to give it a few days and drive up to Cherbourg. But it wasn't looking good, and her accusations of infidelity had shaken him to the core. It would never have occurred to him not to trust her, if the situation had been reversed. Maybe he was just naïve when it came to these matters.

'Women,' Jeff said with a snort. His glass was empty again. He motioned for the bottle. Ben slid it across the table, and Jeff grabbed it and topped himself up, clearly intent on polishing off the whole lot before uncorking another. Tuesday rolled his eyes.

'Come on, mate, it's not that bad.'

'Isn't it?'

Jeff's whirlwind love affair with a pretty young local primary school teacher called Chantal Mercier had come as a surprise to his friends at the time. The rugged, rough-around-the edges ex-Special Boat Service commando seemed like the last kind of guy a woman like Chantal would go for. To Ben's even greater amazement, not long afterwards Jeff had announced that he and Chantal were getting engaged.

It all seemed to be going full steam ahead. The wedding date was set for later in the year, at the nearby village church in Saint Acaire. Jeff had even been trying to learn French.

But while Ben was in America, a long-simmering dispute between Jeff and his fiancée had finally blown up. Chantal could live with her future husband's military past but couldn't tolerate that he made his living by teaching people how to, in her words, 'kill people'. After much soul-searching, she'd come to the conclusion that she couldn't reconcile his violent and morally corrupt profession with her calling as a teacher of innocent, vulnerable little children. Chantal would have no truck with Jeff's explanations that Le Val was a training facility devoted to teaching the good guys how to protect innocent people from the bad guys, and that all the firearms at the compound were kept strictly secure in an armoured vault, and that the place was about as morally corrupt as a Quaker convention. Adamant, she'd given him an ultimatum: if he wouldn't give up his position at Le Val and let his partner take over his share in the business, then he could wave goodbye to the future he and she had planned together.

Jeff had flatly refused to quit. Whereupon, true to her promise, Chantal had broken off the engagement. The dramatic collapse of their relationship had floored Jeff, and he was still extremely bitter about it. He talked about little else – and Ben got the feeling he was about to start talking about it again now.

'She knew what I did when we got together,' Jeff groaned, staring into his glass. 'What the fuck's wrong with her? Don't answer that, I already know.'

Tuesday looked at Jeff with wide eyes. 'You do?'

'Damn right I do. She's a do-gooder, that's what she is.' Jeff took another gulp of wine and tipped his glass towards Ben. 'Just like what's-her-name. That activist chick Jude runs around with.'

Jude was Ben's grown-up son from a long-ago relationship, now living in Chicago with his girlfriend. Ben would never have described her as a 'chick', but 'do-gooder' was admittedly apt.

'Actually,' Ben said, 'things aren't going too well there either. Jude called last night. Looks like they might be splitting, too.'

'There must be something going around,' Tuesday said.

Jeff grunted. 'He should never have hooked up with her in the first place. Let me guess, she finally realised Jude isn't enough of a liberal soy boy commie liberal for her tastes.' Jeff really wasn't in a good mood tonight.

Ben said, 'She's become a vegan.'

'Oh, please. Give me a break.'

'And apparently she expects Jude to follow suit.'

'What, like, and live on rice and egg noodles?'

'Can't have egg noodles,' Tuesday said.

'Why not?'

'Got egg in them,' Tuesday said. 'It's exploitation of chickens. Like honey is exploitation of bees.'

Jeff shook his head in disgust. 'Jesus H. Christ. What is it with these food fascists? It's like a disease. It's spreading everywhere.'

'Nah,' Tuesday said. 'It's not a disease, it's psychological. They're stuck in a developmental phase that Freud called the oral stage. The kid learns as a baby that it can manipulate its parents' behaviour by refusing to eat this or that. Basically, it grows up as a control freak, having learned at an early age how to get its own way and be the centre of attention all the time. From their teens they start attaching moral or ideological values to justify using food as a weapon.'

Jeff, whose idea of using food as a weapon was restricted to mess-room grub fights and custard-pie-in-the-face comedy routines, stared at the younger man. Tuesday had a way of coming out with things out of left field, whether it was some obscure quotation, a snippet of poetry or assorted little-known facts of knowledge.

'Where the hell do you get all this stuff from?' he asked,

not for the first time since they'd known each other. 'Fucking *Freud*?'

Tuesday shrugged. 'Brooke got me interested in it. We were talking about psychology last time she was here.'

The name Brooke was one no longer mentioned too often at the table, or for that matter anywhere around the compound at Le Val. It referred to Dr Brooke Marcel, formerly Ben's own fiancée, before things had gone bad there, too. Ben's friends knew that it was a sensitive topic to raise. Likewise, nobody would have dared to mention the fact that the situation with Ben and Sandrine was like history repeating itself. The bullet that had killed the relationship between Ben and Brooke had been the sudden reappearance of an old flame, Roberta Ryder. Nothing had happened there, either. Brooke hadn't seen it that way. Then again, maybe Ben's failure to turn up for their wedding had had something to do with it.

Tuesday regretted his slip the instant he'd blurted out Brooke's name. He gave Ben a rueful look. 'Sorry. It just came out. Jeff's fault.'

'How's it my fault?' Jeff demanded.

'You asked me. I answered.'

'How was I to know what you were going to come out with? How can anyone know what you'll say next?'

'It's okay,' Ben said, to quell the tensions before Jeff's foul mood made things escalate into a heated debate. 'Don't worry about it.'

All these names from the past, all these lost loves, all these bittersweet memories. Ben sometimes felt as though his whole life path was just a trail of destruction, sadness and remorse. It was little comfort to know he wasn't the only one. He wished that their conversation hadn't taken such a downward turn. Perhaps it was time to open another bottle of wine, or get out the whisky.

Before Ben could decide which, Storm the German shepherd suddenly uncoiled himself from the stone floor at his master's feet, planted himself bolt upright facing the window and began barking loudly. The lights of a vehicle swept the yard outside. There was the sound of a car door.

'Hello, the GIGN boys are back awfully early,' Jeff said, looking at his watch. It was shortly after seven, only just gone dark outside. Nobody had expected Ferreira's crew back until close to midnight, once they'd had their fill of junk food and cheap beer.

'I guess they were less than impressed with the night life in Valognes,' Tuesday said with a wry grin. 'Welcome to the sticks, fellas.'

The GIGN guys drove a monster truck with enough lights to fry a rabbit crossing the road. Ben turned to look out of the window. It looked like the headlamps of a regular car outside.

'It's not them.'

Jeff frowned. 'We expecting anyone else?'

Tuesday said, 'Not that I know of.'

Unannounced visitors at this or any time were a rarity at the remote farmhouse, not least because the only entrance to the fenced compound was a gatehouse manned twenty-four-seven by Le Val's security guys, who wouldn't let in any stranger without first radioing ahead to the house to check it was okay.

There was a soft, hesitant knock at the front door. Ben said, 'Let's go and find out who the mystery visitor is.' He stubbed out his Gauloise, rose from the table, walked out of the kitchen and down the oak-panelled hallway. He flipped a switch for the yard lights, then opened the door.

The mystery visitor standing on the doorstep was a woman. Medium height, slender in a sporty, toned kind of way. She was wearing a lightweight leather jacket and had a handbag on a strap around one shoulder. Her auburn hair ruffled in the cool, gentle October evening breeze. Her face was shaded under the brim of a denim baseball cap. Her body language was tense and self-conscious, as if she didn't really want to be here but felt she had to be.

Behind her, a taxicab was parked across the cobbled yard, its motor idling. The courtesy light was on inside and the taxi driver was settling down to read a paper.

But Ben wasn't looking at him. He stared at the woman. He was aware that his mouth had dropped open, but for a few speechless moments couldn't do anything about it.

At last, he was able to find the words. At any rate, one word.

Ben said, '*Brooke?*'

Valley of Death
Coming May 2019

DON'T LET THEM GET INSIDE YOUR MIND . . .

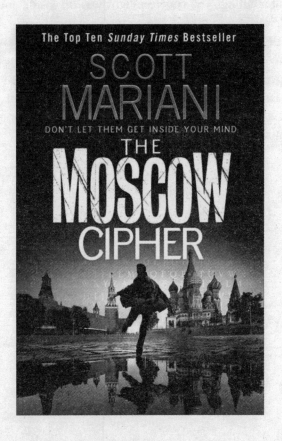

'If you like your conspiracies twisty, your action
bone-jarring, and your heroes impossibly dashing,
then look no farther.' MARK DAWSON